If you're
nothing goes according to plan.

Blood Apprentice

When a map to the mysterious fortune of notorious privateer Miguel Enríquez falls in the lap of Ben and Tenzin, only one of them is jumping at the opportunity. Tenzin can't wait to search for a secret cache of gold. Ben, on the other hand, couldn't be less excited.

All Ben knows about Puerto Rico is what he hears on the news and a few lingering memories of his human grandmother. Going back to his roots holds zero appeal for the carefully constructed man he's become.

But in the end, the lure of hidden gold can't be denied.

Ben and Tenzin head to Puerto Rico where the immortal world is ruled by *Los Tres*, a trio of powerful vampires commanding the wind, the waves, and the mountains that make up their small island in the Caribbean.

To find Enríquez's treasure, they'll have to walk a fine line between flattery and secrecy. To leave the island might mean a bigger fight than either one of them foresaw.

Blood Apprentice is the second novel in the Elemental Legacy, a paranormal mystery series by Elizabeth Hunter, author of the Irin Chronicles.

PRAISE FOR ELIZABETH HUNTER

Elizabeth Hunter's books are delicious and addicting, like the best kind of chocolate. She hooked me from the first page, and her stories just keep getting better and better. Paranormal romance fans won't want to miss this exciting author!

— THEA HARRISON, NYT BESTSELLING AUTHOR

Developing compelling and unforgettable characters is a real Hunter strength as she proves yet again with Kyra and Leo. Another amazing novel by a master storyteller!

— RT MAGAZINE

This book more than lived up to the expectations I had, in fact it blew them out of the water.

— THIS LITERARY LIFE

A towering work of romantic fantasy that will captivate the reader's mind and delight their heart. Elizabeth Hunter's ability to construct such a sumptuous narrative time and time again is nothing short of amazing.

— THE READER EATER

BLOOD APPRENTICE

AN ELEMENTAL LEGACY NOVEL

ELIZABETH HUNTER

Blood Apprentice
Copyright © 2018
Elizabeth Hunter
ISBN: 9781796554991

Cover: Damonza
Content Editor: Amy Cissell, Cissell Ink
Copy Editor: Anne Victory
Proofreader: Linda, Victory Editing

Recurve Press LLC
PO Box 4034
Visalia, California
USA
ElizabethHunterWrites.com

To the people of Puerto Rico
Your pride, your spirit
and your compassion
inspire me.
This book is dedicated to you.

1

B en Vecchio was a thief.

Tenzin swung the saber diagonally, but the thief blocked her with his own blade, a Japanese-forged katana she'd trained him on.

"You're insane," Ben shouted. "I didn't eat your cannoli."

"Then where is it, Ben?" She parried, forcing him to back up. "Did it just disappear? Did a mouse break into the refrigerator?"

A pink box that contained two cannoli and one cheese danish had occupied the refrigerator the night before. She'd risen from her meditation at nightfall. The danish had survived, but both cannoli were gone.

Ben growled as he blocked her relentless blows. "I am not responsible for your food, woman."

Tenzin wasn't a woman. She was a vampire. She didn't survive solely on blood, but she also didn't eat much.

She'd been waiting for the cannoli, and now it was gone.

He lunged right, tipping her off-balance and forcing her across the training mat. The first floor of their apartment contained a large training area, various weapons, and oddly enough, dance equipment for their new roommate.

"I'm telling you, I had one. I don't know what happened to the other one. Why don't you just eat the danish if you're hungry?"

Tenzin's eyes went wide. "The danish isn't mine. The danish is Chloe's. The cannoli was mine. Only one person loves cannoli more than me in this house." She spun around and slapped the back of his thighs with the flat of her sword. "You didn't even get rid of the evidence. You're worse than a thief. You're a *bad* thief."

Ben's eyes narrowed. "Take it back."

"No."

He attacked. The room filled with the furious clashing blades of two enemies ignited by righteous fury. She forced herself to stay on the ground. Just because she could fly didn't mean she would. Not when it would only draw complaints about the unfair advantages of being immortal.

Oh no. Tenzin wanted vengeance, and she didn't want to hear Ben whining about it.

Blood or no blood? She decided she didn't want to hear complaints from Chloe about cleaning up the training area, so she kept to slaps with the side of her blade.

"You're a bad thief." She taunted him with a slap to the bicep. "Slow."

"Shut up." He slapped back and her ass felt it. "I'm the fastest human you know."

He *was* the fastest human she knew, but Tenzin wasn't going to admit it. Ben was a human in an immortal world, and he did everything possible to even the playing field.

He practiced and trained relentlessly, carving his tall, lean body into a weapon as flexible and lethal as a rapier. He mastered martial arts from South America and Asia. He'd studied knife fighting with masters. He'd killed his first enemy at sixteen in defense of a friend, matched wits with emperors, and bargained with ancients.

"If you're so fast, maybe you should have run out and gotten another cannoli instead of stealing mine." She darted to the side, just escaping the blade that would have slapped the back of her knee.

Close.

Tenzin narrowed her eyes. That was the closest he'd ever gotten without her allowing it.

She jumped into the air and flew over his head, kneeing him in the right kidney and quickly punching her knuckle into the nerve above his elbow.

Ben grunted and fumbled his blade. "Cheater."

"Thief."

He dropped his shoulder and flipped her over. "It is the height of hypocrisy for you to be calling *me* a thief!"

Tenzin hit the ground and Ben was on her, straddling her hips with his knees and twisting her wrist until she loosened her grip on the weapon she carried.

Did she notice how broad his shoulders had become? Perhaps. Did she notice how lean his hips were and how penetrating his gaze was? Yes. She'd have to be blind not to see what an attractive man he'd become.

He still made her irrationally angry. "That was my cannoli."

"Enough." His normally affable expression was gone. It had been gone for months.

"Why would you buy me a treat and then take it for yourself?" she asked. "That makes no sense."

"Because I didn't." He rolled off her and lay flat on the mat. "Don't pick up that fucking sword again, or I'm gonna lose my last nerve. I swear it."

She'd been hoping a good fight would perk him up, but it seemed to have only annoyed him. And his lip was bleeding.

Oops.

"What is wrong with you?" He pinched the bridge of his nose. "Were you just bored? I was trying to wrap my brain around this fucking Bucharest job, and you're busting my balls about cannoli, for fuck's sake."

"Is it wrong that I kind of like it when your New Yorker comes out?"

"What the fuck are you talking about?"

Tenzin couldn't stop the smile.

Ben stood, reaching a hand out to help her up before he grabbed the katana and the dao they'd been fighting with, walked to the long racks at the edge of the training area, and put both weapons in their place. Then he grabbed a towel from the bench nearby.

Just one. Tenzin didn't sweat.

She crossed her arms over her chest. "The Bucharest job is vexing you because Radu hasn't given you all the information yet. You still don't know who his sire is, so you don't know if he has any siblings, so you don't know if anyone else has a claim on that icon. Until you find out if he's the only one with a claim, you're not going to feel comfortable bending the rules necessary for this job. Conscience, Ben. It's your greatest weakness."

"I'm so glad you think so," Ben muttered. "Radu's not going to tell me who his sire is."

"Then tell him you can't help him."

He wiped the towel across his forehead. "This would be our first job in Eastern Europe. And Radu knows every vampire between Prague and Tbilisi."

"Radu is a pain in the ass," Tenzin said. "Every vampire between Prague and Tbilisi knows Radu is a pain in the ass.

We're not going to lose face if we tell him we don't want the job."

"The finder's fee on this one is healthy. Giovanni encouraged me to say yes. He's not officially my boss..."

"But he's kind of your boss," Tenzin replied. The jobs that she and Ben took were closer to the art world than the historical-documents world that Ben's adopted uncle, Giovanni Vecchio, had worked in for centuries. But the concept was the same. If you were an immortal who'd lost something, they could help you find it. Ancient Tibetan scroll? Giovanni was your man. Medieval Russian icon? That was Ben and Tenzin's department. "And Gio probably considers a job for Radu character building. He's self-righteous like that."

"But is he right?"

"Maybe. Do you really need your character built more?"

"According to my uncle"—Ben raised a familiar eyebrow —"character is a construction of eternity, an endless striving of the self to be subsumed to the greater good."

Tenzin rolled her eyes, partly because Ben's imitation of her old friend was just that good. "Ancestors, save me from philosophers."

Ben almost cracked a smile. Almost. "Right now I'm more motivated by Radu's bank account."

"Neither of us needs the money." She eyed the new construction next to the training area. "But the money would be nice."

She could smell plaster dust in the air from the workmen who were finishing the bathroom attached to the new bedroom they'd added. Chloe had overseen the construction, just like she was now overseeing most human aspects of their business. She answered mail and ran errands. She kept track of various accounts and helped Ben move money when it was necessary.

Tenzin didn't need to move money from banks. She kept all her earnings in gold.

She liked gold. Radu was offering to pay in gold.

"He's been missing that icon for a hundred and fifty years," Tenzin said. "And bitching about it for at least a century. Send him something by courier and tell the courier to get lost. You can put him off for at least another year with that trick."

"Really?" Ben looked skeptical.

"Trust me. I've used it many times. Especially if my father summons me."

"Good to know."

She tilted her head back to look at him. "Did you eat that cannoli?"

Ben tapped her forehead. "Fucking one-track mind. No. I did not eat your cannoli. And I'm ending this conversation before it gets more ridiculous. I'm hungry. I'm going to make dinner."

"Fattoush?"

"I made that last night. Chloe is picking up some lamb. Figured I'd try making polo if you want."

"Well, if there's no cannoli..."

The edge of his mouth barely tilted up. "I'll make enough for three."

Tenzin followed Ben up the stairs. "You should put ice on that lip."

"Thanks for the tip." He peeled off his shirt, which was covered in sweat, and tossed it over his head, hitting her smack in the face.

Tenzin wrinkled her nose and held the shirt with two fingers. "But you should shower first. You stink."

"Yeah, I got ambushed before I could clean up. I wonder how that happened?"

"I consider cannoli theft between partners a serious

offense." They made it up the stairs, and Tenzin heard Chloe humming in the kitchen. "Hello, Chloe."

"Hey, guys!" The cheerful human—the only one in the house these days—waved at them. She must have just come from rehearsal because she was wearing leggings and a loose top. Her dark spirals of hair were pulled up into a giant ponytail, and her light brown skin glowed with health. She'd made vast progress since she'd left her abusive boyfriend and moved in with them.

Tenzin was definitely going to keep her.

"Ben, the lamb you wanted is in the fridge." Chloe looked up. "What did you do to your lip?"

Ben turned and glared at Tenzin. "Ask Tiny."

"Sparring?" Chloe turned to the fridge. "Oh! Tenzin, before I forget. I ate that cannoli Ben brought home yesterday because a chocolate craving hit hard before rehearsal, but I got you another one from Masseria."

"Thank you." Tenzin walked to the fridge. Excellent. A fresh cannoli was even better than a day-old one, though Masseria's cannoli crust always held up well, even overnight.

Ben's mouth was open. "That's it?"

Tenzin opened the refrigerator and removed the pastry from the box before she answered. "What?" She took a bite and sighed in happiness.

Ben walked across the kitchen, slammed the refrigerator door shut, and towered over her. "You ambush me, give me a bloody lip and a bruise in my fucking hamstring because you think I took your cannoli, and Chloe waltzes in, admits to stealing the thing, and all she gets is an 'okay, cool'?"

Tenzin held up the crusty pastry tube of deliciousness. "But she got me another one."

"Unbelievable." He stormed out of the kitchen and down

7

the stairs. A few minutes later, Tenzin heard the water in the shower switch on.

Chloe pursed her lips. "He's so tense right now."

"I know. I keep trying to think of ways for him to relax, but nothing is working."

Chloe cut her eyes toward Tenzin. "I can think of one thing."

"Wrestling?"

"I suppose some people might call it that."

"You're right. He hasn't had a good jiujitsu match in ages. We should research facilities in the neighborhood. There have to be some options."

"Jiujitsu." Chloe smiled. "Sure. That's exactly what I was thinking."

"Yes, you're very smart for a human."

"Well, I'm glad one of us is."

Tenzin bit her lip to keep from laughing. She wasn't as clueless about the tension between her and Ben as they all liked to think.

She just didn't know what she wanted to do about it yet.

HE LIVED MOST of his life at night. He slept when the sun was at its zenith and came to life with the stars. If workmen filled the house, he sometimes took refuge in the library, sleeping in a dark corner on the pallet Tenzin used for meditating. When he was tired, he slept, and it could be anywhere in the loft that had become home to the strange little family of human, vampire, and whatever hybrid Ben had become.

He was in the library that night, searching for more information on a medieval Russian icon. Though Chloe had gone to sleep, Ben remained awake. He was lithe and silent, his body trained to move in ways that avoided attention. Tenzin watched him from her perch in the sheltered loft he'd designed with her in mind. It was sun-safe, no matter the hour of the day. It was plain but spacious. Most importantly, only Tenzin had access to it.

Though Ben occasionally dragged a ladder over if he was feeling ornery.

He wasn't particularly tall for a modern human, though he was far larger than Tenzin. His features were a blend of the blood that had made him, half from the Old World and half from the New. His human father had been Puerto Rican. His mother, Lebanese. The blood of every continent flowed in his veins.

But his eyes—those dark, watchful eyes—came from the vampire who had made him the man he was.

Ben moved silently in the library, opening one reference book after another, jumping between his laptop computer and the books. He was following a trail of some kind, slowly narrowing his search area.

He had become a fine hunter.

It was an odd thing, Tenzin thought as she watched him, to see the slow transformation of a novice. Ben had never been a child to her. She'd met him when he was a teenager who looked no older than she did, but he had never been a child. Life had taught him early that fate was not kind to the young.

While he remained human, he would grow older every year. Unlike Tenzin, whose face hadn't changed in five millennia, Ben's features grew more rugged. His beard became thicker. His expression more solemn.

While he remained human...

"I don't want it, Tiny. You know I don't. I'm too familiar with vampire life to idealize immortality."

He knew nothing.

"Promise me."

Tenzin had made many promises over the years. She'd broken most of them.

She spotted the map he'd been avoiding for a year. It was sitting in a clear plastic sleeve on the edge of a bookshelf.

Tenzin cocked her head and thought about the map to the rumored treasure of the famed privateer Miguel Enríquez, about an island still ravaged by a hurricane and an old woman who carried Ben's last true link to the human world.

"I don't want it."

And yet....

Are you truly human anymore, my Benjamin?

Tenzin flew down to him, grabbing the map from the bookshelf before she sat next to him on the table.

Ben looked up from his computer and spotted what she was holding. "Not this again."

"It's been a year."

His expression was carefully neutral. "And we only got a letter back from the island a couple of months ago."

"We didn't need to wait for a letter. You know that."

"We did. Giovanni—"

"This isn't about protocol, Benjamin." She put the map in front of him and bent down. "This isn't about appeasing the current vampire in charge of—"

"Three, actually. There are three vampires in charge of Puerto Rico."

She kept talking and ignored the way the Spanish name rolled off his tongue. Ben was annoyingly attractive when he spoke Spanish. "This is about you avoiding your past. Avoiding a place that might still have some hold on you."

"You think so?" His eyes were heated. "Don't pretend this is about me. I've never been to Puerto Rico. It has no *hold* on me. I wanted nothing to do with this map. You want to hunt pirate treasure, Tenzin. You don't care what the island had been through or what conditions people are living in."

"Yes, I want to find the treasure. Other people are not my problem. And I was right to think we should have gone earlier. The chaos directly after the hurricane would have cloaked our movements. And there was almost no electricity. You know I love that."

Ben closed his eyes. "Could you at least pretend to care?"

"Why? I thought this wasn't about your family, Ben. Why would I care about strangers?"

He had no answer for that.

"You care," she said. "And that's fine. Your empathy doesn't bother me. Maybe when we go down, you can do more than send money anonymously to your grandmother. All I care about is following this map and finding treasure. You are delaying for personal reasons that don't have anything to do with business."

He opened his eyes and glared at her. "Fine. You want to hunt pirate treasure, we'll hunt. But we're doing this in a respectful way, and we're not charging down there without an introduction."

"Excellent." She sat up. "Then you'll be happy to know I made a date for you and Novia to have drinks tomorrow night."

Why was Spanish so effective? She even found it attractive when he was cursing.

2

_____

Ben was meeting Novia O'Brien at Gavin Wallace's new bar in the theater district, the Dancing Bear. The place had quickly attracted a local crowd of performers, artists, and theater regulars since it was open until four in the morning and had a rooftop bar where everyone looked the other way when it came to smoking.

Late hours were also very attractive to vampires, and since Gavin was one, that made the Dancing Bear his most common haunt. The fact that Chloe was rehearsing with a new dance group in the area might have been another motivation.

Ben exited the subway at the 50th Street station and walked over to 9th where he turned right and looked for the red door that led upstairs to Gavin's pub. He was early, but Chloe was working that night, which meant he'd be able to catch up since he'd fallen asleep at dawn, when she was first rising.

Though Chloe and Gavin were... dating? Involved? Dating seemed too human, and involved seemed too casual. Either way, Chloe had been firm about keeping to a relatively human schedule, which meant she was awake during the day. Luckily for Gavin, she was also a dancer, which meant she was used to late hours. She'd moved from Gavin's first pub in Manhattan to the new one in Hell's Kitchen when it opened. She didn't work as many hours, but the hours she did work, Gavin made it a point to be there.

Ben walked up the stairs, immediately hit by the smell of paint and chocolate. The paint he understood—the pub was still undergoing renovations—but the chocolate was curious. He poked his head into the party room and spotted the reason.

"Is that a fountain?" He raised an eyebrow. "Seems a little pedestrian for you, Gav."

Gavin Wallace, wind vampire and whiskey enthusiast, lifted his head from the buffet table where Chloe was arranging a three-tiered chocolate fountain that was already flowing.

"The ridiculous bride wants a chocolate fountain," he muttered, "the ridiculous bride gets a chocolate fountain."

"Bride?"

Chloe looked up with a chagrined smile. "Bachelorette party. They booked the party room almost as soon as we opened. I told them it would still smell like paint, but they insisted. They also insisted on a chocolate fountain."

Ben strolled over and grabbed a strawberry from beneath protective plastic wrap. He poked it on the end of a skewer and stuck the berry under the chocolate waterfall, then popped it in his mouth and nodded in appreciation. "It may not fit your vampire hipster aesthetic, my friend. But don't knock the chocolate fountain. That's delicious."

"What are you doing here?" Gavin asked.

"Didn't Chloe tell you?" he asked. "Work's a little slow right now, so I'm moonlighting as a stripper for bachelorette parties."

Chloe burst into laughter, and even Gavin had to crack a smile.

"Good God, Vecchio. Warn me before you start taking your clothes off. That's all I ask."

"It's the gig economy, man. Everyone has to have a side hustle."

"Oh?" Gavin looked at Chloe. "What's yours?"

"You." She stood on her toes and kissed his cheek. "Or more accurately, your bar." She walked toward the door. "The party starts in an hour. We'll have to catch up later, Ben."

Gavin said, "I thought I was your main hustle."

Chloe turned at the door and shook her head. "Delusions of grandeur," she said sadly. "I hear they often affect the elderly." She winked. "Tell Albert we're going to need more chairs from the back."

"I'll pay you back for the elderly comment later." Gavin turned to Ben. "Other than stripping, you taking a meeting with my sort?"

"Novia. She didn't call?"

The corner of Gavin's mouth lifted. "Novia O'Brien is the favored child of the most politically powerful vampire in New York. She doesn't have to check with me before she swings by. She always gets a table."

"I'm glad you added the 'political' label there."

"Everyone knows Tenzin is the most powerful immortal. Don't let her ego get the better of you too."

Ben smiled. "It's always refreshing to meet someone who isn't in awe of her."

Gavin walked behind the bar and took two glasses from the counter. "Awe? No. Fear? Yes. Healthy fear is a necessity when it comes to Tenzin. When it comes to anyone that old in our world."

"Your world."

Gavin rolled his eyes and poured two fingers of whiskey in each glass. "Get over your insolent humanity, will you? It's annoying at this point."

"I watched the sun come up this morning. It was delightful."

"So did I. The nature channel has a sunrise program. This morning I got to hear birdcalls in the Costa Rican rainforest." He sipped his drink. "Try this one. I'm considering sending a bottle to your uncle."

Ben sipped. "Peaty. Beatrice would like this one more than Gio."

"Yes, I thought so, but if I send it to her, she'll toss it in the trash. And I couldn't do that to a perfectly innocent bottle of scotch."

Beatrice and Gavin had a history that included Gavin handing Ben's aunt over to a mortal enemy at one point. It was an old story, but Gavin and Beatrice weren't on the best terms.

"Still," Gavin continued, "she no longer glares at me after I deeded that vacation house in Switzerland to them. Let that be a lesson to you, young Ben. Bribery works."

"I'll keep that in mind." He finished the whiskey and set the glass down.

"What are you and Novia meeting about?"

"Los Tres."

Gavin frowned. "Not following."

"The trio of vampires who run Puerto Rico. They're called Los Tres."

"How imaginative. You're going to Puerto Rico?"

"Maybe. And Los Tres has held power on the island for almost five hundred years, so it might not be the most imaginative name, but it works."

"Fair enough." Gavin raised his glass. "Novia isn't Puerto Rican, is she?"

"No, but she's familiar with the court. Her human family is Cuban. She still travels regularly through the Caribbean. I don't know much more than that, but she's the one who sent an introduction."

"Have you heard back?"

"A couple of months ago."

"Hmm." Gavin leaned on the bar. "Putting things off. That's not a Ben Vecchio trait normally."

Ben didn't feel like getting into it, especially not with Gavin. Chloe knew more about his childhood than most of his friends, but he still didn't like talking about it with anyone. At all.

"It's complicated." That was all Ben felt like sharing.

"Understood." Gavin might have been a friend, but he was also a vampire. And vampires didn't pry about the past. "You can take that corner booth in back. The place will start filling up around one, but that corner's the quietest. If you need something more discreet, the snug is yours."

"Tell me why." Novia leaned back, stretching both lean arms across the red velvet upholstery of the booth. She was dressed for clubbing, and the tips of her dark corkscrew curls had been recently dyed a vivid blood red. "I mean, I wrote the letter already. I did that because we're friends, Benny."

"Are we?"

She gave him a slow smile, both fangs showing. "Of course we are."

Were you supposed to find friends mildly frightening?

"I can't just tell you details." Ben leaned forward and gave Novia his most charming smile. "It's not really my job. Tenzin is point on this."

She raised an eyebrow. "Then you definitely need to tell me why."

He scooted closer and nudged Novia's arm until it was across his shoulders. "Darling."

Novia started to laugh, amused by his attempts to flirt, even if she saw right through them.

"Darling," he continued, "do you want to know out of curiosity? Or are you looking for a cut of whatever it is we're going after?"

"Oh?" She widened her eyes. "Are you going after something shiny?"

"I'm always after something shiny." He reached up and played with the heavy crystal dangling from her left ear. "Don't worry. It doesn't belong to anyone alive."

"None of my sort?"

"Nope. You look amazing tonight, by the way. What perfume are you wearing?"

"Aren't you cute? It's called Rosa." Novia made sure to roll the *r*.

"I haven't heard of that one." Ben reached for his drink.

"Neither had I until I fed from her this evening. She was delicious." Novia smiled and touched her tongue to the tip of her fang as Ben tried not to choke on his martini.

"I'll keep that in mind."

"You should. She likes boys too." Novia ran a hand down Ben's shoulder and arm, sliding her fingers across his thigh. "You're too smart to let all this get old and sad, Benny. We all know what's coming."

Ben gave her a tight smile but didn't try to move her hand. Novia liked to flirt. With men. With women. Vampires and mortals. She was an equal opportunity predator. "You know, every time a vampire assumes I'm going to turn, I put off thinking about it for a few more years."

"Contrary boy." She smiled. "But you *are* thinking about it."

"Are you done teasing?" he asked. "Can we talk business now?"

"Humans." She sighed. "Always in a hurry."

"Hurricane season is just around the corner."

"Isn't it always?" Not so much amusement now. "So you want to know about Los Tres?"

"Yes. And I promise to bring you back something shiny."

Novia's smile returned. "Fair enough. The thing to remember about Los Tres is that they don't really abide by any modern kind of rules. The island is run by a Taíno chief. *A cacique* named Macuya. And that old man has been running Puerto Rico long before anyone from Europe arrived. He's just pissed Columbus spoiled his food supply."

"He sounds delightful."

"He's an old asshole is what he is."

"I thought it was a trio in power."

Novia shrugged. "To the outside world maybe. He's taken two wives. One Spanish and one African. They were political marriages."

"Aren't most vampire marriages political? At least in the hierarchy?"

"Fair. I should have said they were... concessions. 'Look, new Spanish vampires, I have a Spanish wife. You can give me your loyalty. Look, former slaves, I have an African wife too. Don't rise up and kill us in our sleep.' He uses his wives to give the appearance of equal rule. It's not the reality."

"So he's not well liked."

"Nobody likes him. But they do fear him. He's old, which means he's strong as hell. He's an earth vampire, and he lives in the mountains around Lares. That's his stronghold. He doesn't care what the humans in San Juan are doing as long as they keep attracting nice, tasty tourists to the west side of the island."

"So he's not involved in human government?"

"Not at all. His sister deals with anything involving humans. Inés. You'll likely meet her first. And his *nitayno*."

"His what?" Ben felt like he should know this stuff—he was

half Puerto Rican, for God's sake—but he knew nothing about the island's indigenous history.

"His nitayno. Like a general, kind of. His general is Spanish. A water vampire by the name of Vasco." Novia smiled. "He's a bit friendlier than most of that group."

"Got it." Ben decided she didn't need to elaborate on that one. "So I'll probably meet this Inés first?"

"Probably. She's got a big fancy house on the beach in Mayagüez. Gorgeous place. And then there's the estate in the mountains. Try to meet her in the mountains. It's closer to Macuya."

"And she's a sister?"

"She's Taíno too. I don't know if they started out as blood relatives, but they had the same sire, though nobody knows who that was. Probably an ancient, judging from how powerful Macuya is."

Ben wanted to take notes, but he knew Novia wouldn't appreciate it. This was a friendly conversation. No records needed. He filed as much away as he could, hoping he remembered it all.

"What's my way in?" he asked. "If I want something—"

"Money." Novia sipped her cocktail. "No... maybe status? The old man likes flattery. He respects money, but he respects power more. Reputation. Favors. He's old school. He'll be impressed by Tenzin, but he'll be threatened too." Novia's mouth turned up in the corner. "He has a *thing* about powerful women."

"I'll keep that in mind." Not that she'd really answered the question. Ben still didn't know how he was going to wrangle permission to search the caves where the map said this treasure was buried. But there was no way he was going searching underground in Puerto Rico—in the territory of an earth vampire—without getting some kind of permission.

"And Benny? Macuya is smart, and he rewards immortals for loyalty. Remember that. People who are loyal to him are true believers. Trying to get any of his court to betray him will be difficult."

"I'll remember." He settled back into the booth, allowing the music and the energy from the crowd to fill him. "So what's new with you? Rosa, huh?"

Novia shrugged. "It's nothing serious. Maybe." She nodded at Chloe behind the bar. "I'd take a taste of that if Gavin wasn't so greedy."

"Chloe is not food, Novia. She's my friend and Tenzin's assistant. She's under my uncle's aegis."

"I know." She held up a hand. "I'm just sayin'."

"And besides all that, it would definitely not fly with Gavin."

"You know I don't poach." Novia watched Gavin cross the pub. "Hell, I'd play with both of them if they were into it."

Ben shook his head. "I am not even touching that one."

"What about you, huh?" She elbowed him a little harder than she'd probably intended. Ben was likely to have a bruise in the morning. "What have you been chasing lately?"

"Other than jobs?"

"Boring." She stuck her tongue out at him. "You're too young for all that shit. Have some fun in your life."

The last time he'd "had fun," he'd ended up falling for an innocent face and playing the fool in a rival's game. He'd learned that lesson well. "I like my work."

"And it lets you spend all your time with a certain vampire we won't mention, *he-ey*." Novia winked. "That's okay. I know the score between you two."

"I don't know what you're talking about."

He knew exactly what she was talking about.

"Chemistry, Benny. It's zinging all over the place." She

raised a hand. "I'm not asking. That way you don't have to lie. Just know that I love your little games and I want to *be* Tenzin when I grow up, so you have my complete admiration."

"Novia, I'm telling you—"

"Hush." She put a hand over his mouth and closed her eyes. "Don't deny it. What I see in my imagination is too hot to be ruined by your denial."

He nipped at her fingers and she let go. "Chemistry?"

"From you. From her. Ancient vampire and hot young thing?" She threw her head back. "'Bout time my idol *got some*. You know that girl has some pent-up aggression."

Ben didn't need to hear this. *Nobody* needed to hear this. "Do not say anything about this. To anyone."

Novia batted her eyelashes. "About what?"

"Exactly." Ben finished his drink and scooted to the edge of the booth. "I have to go."

"Why?"

He stopped and smiled slowly. "I have work to do."

"Boy, you're just trying to kill me now."

BEN LET himself into the loft and paused at the door, listening for the telltale signs of Tenzin. It was three hours before dawn. If she wasn't out flying, she'd probably be reading or weaving in her room.

He heard the quiet thud of a wooden fork against wool, so he dragged the tall ladder over from the library and climbed to Tenzin's loft. He pulled himself up, sat cross-legged, and watched her, her fingers flying over the half-made rug. She pulled and tied. Tightened and tamped. The process was hypnotic and often her preferred way to pass time, particularly when the weather was wet.

"Cara," he called out, "play 'Creation Chant.'"

The lonely echo of a flute filled the loft as Ben watched Tenzin work. She didn't turn or acknowledge him, though she knew he was there.

Ben crawled over and lay on the piled rugs and furs in the corner of the loft, drifting between wakefulness and sleep as the hours passed. Something about being in this corner of the loft, away from the library, away from the training mats, even away from his own spartan bedroom, allowed him find peace.

He drifted in and out of dreams, and the quiet thunk of Tenzin's weaving fork turned into the rhythm of a wood pestle hitting the bottom of a bowl. The smell of garlic and fried plantain.

SHE SAID it was called *mofongo*. Ben had never had anything called mofongo before, but it smelled pretty good. Like garlic and onion and something Ben didn't recognize. Sometimes Joe ate food that smelled like that, but he never gave any to Ben.

There were birds in the window, little green birds hopping around in a birdcage. Ben thought they were called lovebirds, because Mr. Ortega, who owned the bodega on the corner by Ben's mom's house, had birds like that, and he called them lovebirds. They had green bodies and orange faces instead of red, but they looked mostly the same. Ben loved watching the birds. Sometimes, Mr. Ortega let Ben feed them.

The old woman looked over her shoulder with a tentative smile, and Ben took another drink of the milk she'd put in a plastic cup. The wooden table in her kitchen was smaller than the one in his mother's apartment, and it was much prettier. Smooth golden wood unmarred by cigarette burns or white circles.

"You're staying for dinner," she said. "You're too thin."

Joe had told him the old lady was his mother. Did that make her Ben's grandmother? He wasn't sure about that, and he didn't know if he should trust her. His mom told Ben that Joe came "from a bunch of lazy beggars." But the old lady wasn't a beggar. Her house was pretty and smelled good. She had already given Ben a cookie and a glass of milk. The cookie was too sweet, but the milk felt good going down his throat.

His mom lied a lot about people. He probably shouldn't believe her about Joe's family.

Ben rested his chin on the edge of the table. "Is Joe coming for dinner?"

"You call your father Joe?"

Ben shrugged and didn't say anything. He didn't want to do anything wrong. If he stayed longer, maybe he would get more milk.

"That's okay." The old lady smiled. "You can call him Joe. Or José. That's his name. Did you know that?"

Ben shook his head.

"Hablas español, mi amor?"

"Just a little," Ben said quietly. He didn't want to tell her most of the Spanish he knew was bad words he heard from Mr. Ortega's store. The men who sat around outside said a lot of bad words, but they gave Ben quarters if he threw their beer bottles in the trash.

"That's okay." The lady brought the wooden bowl over to the table and began pounding the wooden stick up and down again. "You can call me *abuela* and I can speak Spanish with you, but I speak English too. I was the head secretary for a big factory before I retired. I spoke to all the bosses in the office every day. I even translated for them when they needed to talk to the workers. I'm very good with languages."

Ben watched her hit the bottom of the bowl over and over.

She was mixing something. Every now and then she'd get up, throw something else in the bowl, then start pounding it again. Watching her work made Ben a little dizzy. He hadn't eaten anything that day except the cookie and glass of milk. He drank a lot of water though. Water made you feel full.

He crossed his arms and rested his chin on them, watching the birds hop in their cage. "Does *abuela* mean grandma?"

She smiled. "You're smart, aren't you?"

Ben shrugged again. His mom said he was her smartest boy. But he was her only boy, so that didn't mean much. "Do you live here?"

"Sometimes. This is your aunt's house. Most of the time I live in Puerto Rico. Do you know where that is?"

"No."

"It's the most beautiful island in the world." Her face bloomed like a flower when she smiled. "It has palm trees and beautiful forests and lots and lots of flowers. There are beaches where the water is so warm. Not like here." She made a face. "The water is clean in Puerto Rico."

"Why did you leave?"

The old woman, his abuela, looked sad. "Someone told me that Joe had a little boy. I was pretty angry with him."

"Because he had a little boy?" Ben felt his heart race.

"No, no, no." She put her hand out. "Not because he had a little boy. Because my son had a son! And for six years he didn't tell me. I didn't even know you existed, Benjamin."

His heart was still racing. He looked at the old lady's hand. If he took it, would she grab it? Would her hand hurt? Was she happy her son had a little boy? Would she have given Ben a cookie if she was angry with him?

"Now that I know you're here, I can visit more." The lady withdrew her hand and started working again. "I can be your abuela. Do you have another grandmother? Does your mom have a mom?"

Ben shook his head. "Her whole family is dead. That's what she says, but she lies a lot." Ben felt sick. He shouldn't say bad things about his mom. "I mean, she lies sometimes."

A strange look came over his abuela's face. "That's okay. We all tell little lies sometimes. Sometimes we do it to make people feel better. I've done that before. Have you?"

Ben nodded, but he didn't say more. His mother didn't lie to make anyone feel better. But he knew what the lady was talking about.

Sometimes Mrs. Novak downstairs made him food. It didn't smell great; it smelled like cabbage and he didn't like cabbage. But he always said thank you and took it because cabbage filled you up. She asked him if it was his favorite, and Ben always said yes because it made Mrs. Novak smile and Mrs. Novak was nice.

The lady called abuela patted Ben's hand and stood. "You must be thirsty. Would you like more milk?"

"Yes, please." His mother always told him he would get more money if he used polite words. He knew lots of polite words, even in different languages. "Gracias," he said when she refilled his milk.

The old lady smiled, and it looked like flowers again.

BEN WOKE, realizing the weaving fork wasn't tapping anymore. The scent of garlic and onion drifted from his memory, and he blinked his eyes open. He could taste the milk on his tongue and feel the smooth, polished table under his chin.

That had been the first time he'd eaten mofongo, but it hadn't been the last.

Tenzin lay next to him, reading a book. Her fingers skimmed over the pages. It was an auction catalogue. Coins were on every page. Three more auction catalogues and a numismatics text were sitting on the floor next to her along with a Spanish-language biography of Miguel Enríquez.

She was a mad, obsessive little magpie, flying after shiny things with gleeful greed and a single-minded glint in her eye.

Ben absolutely adored her.

He rolled toward her and pressed his face into her shoulder. "Fine."

"Fine what?"

She smelled like wool and cinnamon. He wanted to do more than sniff her shoulder.

Not the time. Not the place. Not... possible.

"Fine," he said. "We'll go to Puerto Rico."

3

———

Chloe watched Ben stride through the loft, tossing phone chargers and batteries next to his backpack on the couch. "We'll be in pretty remote areas at times, so use the satellite phone if my mobile doesn't work. From what I've heard, nothing is reliable. Not power. Not cell signal. I'm bringing the solar chargers, so we should be fine with the satellite phone."

"But only for emergencies," Chloe said. "Tell Tenzin I'm not calling her to report on the flowers blooming."

"I'll let her know, but..."

"No! Enough. She's obsessing."

"That's what she does." Ben shrugged. "And you have to admit the garden does look really good."

Ben had relented and allowed Tenzin to plant a full garden on the roof, including fruit trees, a water feature, and a fire pit.

"Just tell her she has to trust that I will not kill all her plants. She's showed me what to do at least a dozen times. And you guys are going to Puerto Rico, not Kathmandu."

Ben squinted. "Do you know where Kathmandu is?"

"Do you?"

"Nepal."

Chloe threw a balled-up sock at him. "Fine. Still, it's like four hours from New York, not the ends of the earth. I'll survive without you two."

"If you need money—"

"I have access to Tenzin's account here."

Tenzin's mind-boggling account.

Chloe had no idea how much money Tenzin actually had, but the account Chloe used to pay bills and run Tenzin's financial life was... intimidating. Chloe could buy a modestly priced home in Queens with a check.

But most of the time with Ben and Tenzin, Chloe tried not to think about how much anything cost. She knew how much the remodel was—roughly—but Ben had instructed the builders to send all bills to him. Everything in New York City cost a fortune, even for someone accustomed to Los Angeles. So she gritted her teeth, let Ben pay for everything, and plotted how long it would take for her to get her own place.

Not that she didn't like living in the loft. She was ridiculously grateful, enjoyed working for Tenzin, and often felt like she had the entire place to herself. Tenzin had been unusually quiet the past six months, Ben was gone a lot, and Chloe was often the only one awake during daylight.

She was slowly making friends again. Arthur and she had grown close again, though the hilarious designer was somewhat obsessed with her employers. Gavin spent a lot of time with her, but he was more comfortable in the bar or at his place.

He'd once muttered something about "territories being a bit complicated."

Chloe had no idea what he meant. Chloe had no idea how a lot of stuff in the vampire world worked. She didn't want to know too much. She had her people—and her vampires—but she did not want to get deeper into the sticky politics of immortal life. She'd seen how that had affected Ben.

He was striding through the apartment, muttering about flight details, Jeep rentals, and contacts in San Juan. Muttering more about some place called Arecibo and various names she didn't recognize. The two she'd been listening for never came up.

Ana Lisa Rios.

Liza Ochoa Rios.

They were the only family members Ben had ever mentioned to her. Other than his vampire family, Ben didn't use names. He sometimes referred to his father or mother, but his grandmother, Ana Lisa Rios, and his cousin Liza were the only ones he ever mentioned by name, and that had mostly been since Hurricane Maria.

He'd been worried. He'd been *frantic.* Then he'd called his uncle, and a few days later everything had calmed down.

Chloe didn't know much because Ben was secretive. Sometimes she felt like the boy she knew was evolving into a man she didn't recognize.

She knew his family was still on the island. His cousin was a forest ranger in El Yunque. His grandmother had a little farm in the country. Chloe didn't know where. She thought they were closer to the east side of the island, but Ben had specifically said he and Tenzin were going west.

He was stressing about everything *but* the two people he was related to.

Chloe sat next to his backpack and started putting things in. "Are you going to see them?"

"See who?" Ben was staring at his laptop.

"You know who."

He looked up. "I don't know."

"Hmm."

He frowned. "You think I should see them?"

"Yes."

"I haven't seen them since I was ten years old."

"Then you really need to see them." She looked up. "I know you keep track of them. They probably have no idea they have a guardian angel in New York."

"Of course they don't."

"Who do they think sends them money every month?"

"I set up a fake settlement from one of my grandfather's old employers. He was injured on the job in 1953. The company no longer exists, but I was able to make it look legitimate by funneling it through a law firm."

"And that's it? You're going to send them money, but you're not going to see them?"

"What is there to say?" he asked. "Hey, Abuela. Sorry I've been gone for like fifteen years. Got adopted by a vampire. What have you been up to?"

"Just... try."

He slammed the laptop shut. "Try what?"

"Try seeing them. Can you imagine what your grandmother had to think? She lost contact with you when you were ten. She never saw you again. She's probably worried sick."

"How do you know she even looked?"

"How do you know she didn't?" Chloe stood and walked over to him, putting her arms around his waist and leaning into a back that felt hard as stone. He wasn't budging on this. "Just try. Stop by the house. Tell her you're from the law firm or something. Just making sure she's getting the money."

"That doesn't make sense. It's a direct deposit into her bank account."

"Then think of something! This is you. Try."

"She wouldn't recognize me, Chloe. I was a skinny little kid when I was ten. I was short for my age. Never had enough food."

Every time Ben let another fact about his childhood slip out,

Chloe's heart hurt. "Maybe she won't recognize you, and maybe she will. Either way, you could set her mind at ease. Maybe get to know your cousin."

He broke away and walked toward the stairs. "I'll think about it."

CHLOE CLOSED her eyes and leaned into Gavin's shoulder, letting the bubbling hot water soothe the muscles she'd worked that evening during rehearsal. "I'm worried about him."

"He'll be fine." Gavin rubbed her shoulders. "He's traveled in far more dangerous places than Puerto Rico. From what I've heard, most of the power has been restored—even in more remote parts—and the infrastructure is clawing back. Ben has excellent survival skills. Puerto Rico will not be a challenge."

"I'm not worried about him surviving. Tenzin will be with him once he gets to San Juan. Tenzin won't let anything happen to Ben. That's not what I'm worried about."

"Then what?"

Chloe struggled with how much to share with Gavin. "I'm worried about him... personally."

"Personally?" Gavin tilted her chin to the side so he could look at her face. "Does he have family there?"

Chloe sighed. "I can't say."

"I know he's part Puerto Rican. He's mentioned as much in passing. It didn't even occur to me that he might have living family." Gavin frowned. "I assumed Giovanni had adopted an orphan."

"I don't want to break confidence. Just know that most of Ben's childhood was awful."

"That much is evident." He stroked curly wisps of hair back from her forehead and kissed her temple. "There's a look a person comes to recognize after a hundred years or so. One can tell which humans have lived hard lives and which have not. Some vampires take advantage of that." His hand stopped moving. "I've taken advantage of that, I'm sorry to say. Or at least I did in the past."

"And now?"

He wrapped his arm around her waist. "It would make me a sad kind of thing to prey on the wounded, don't you think? That's what I realized. Humans only have a few years at the end of the day. It's not for me to make their lives more difficult when their own kind do that enough."

The sharp twist in her chest was familiar now, though no less painful.

"Only a few years."

He was right. Compared to Gavin, Chloe only had a few years. She would be a handful of fleeting moments in his very long life.

"Anyway ..." Gavin poured warm water over shoulders that had gone cold. "Ben has that look. I always assumed he'd had a hard childhood. He used to be much easier to read, you know. He's a bit foggy now."

"Foggy?"

"Give him a few years and he'll be as hard to read as his uncle. Of course, he'll likely be a vampire by then. Are you ready for that?"

Chloe's eyes went wide and she spun around. "Ready for what?"

Gavin frowned. "For Ben to be a vampire."

Her heart slowed down. "Oh. That."

His eyebrows went up. "Did you think—?"

"No, of course not."

"Because that's... that's a conversation."

"I didn't. I mean, I don't... That's not something we need to talk about."

"Ever?" Gavin stared at her, that deep, penetrating stare that asked Chloe for everything and offered more than she was ready to receive.

"Don't ask me yet," she whispered.

Gavin touched the tip of his finger to her chin, drew it up and around her lips, tracing the sensitive outline before he leaned in and took her mouth. His kiss spun her around and unraveled her. Every time. She could feel the iron control in his shoulders when she placed her hands there. Feel the desire he leashed for her.

The quick inhale at her neck. The tightening fist in her hair. He pulled her to straddle his waist, gripping her thigh just above the knee. His hand, like the rest of him, was just as controlled. Firm grip on heated flesh.

Chloe was the soft to his hard, melting into his chest and letting her muscles rest against his. Her breasts to his chest. Her mouth soft and yielding to his.

He pulled away. "You undo me."

She leaned forward and pressed her face into his neck, putting her lips against the place where his heart should beat. It only gave the occasional flutter, usually when he was aroused.

Why do you still wait? Haven't you gotten tired of me yet?

She didn't say those things—didn't even want to think them —but they were the voice in her head. The constant, nagging whisper that tried to convince her that she shouldn't get too attached, shouldn't let her guard down too much.

He ran his fingers up and down her spine, massaging the bare edge of her glute with such perfect pressure she wanted him to go farther down. Under the bathing suit. Bare skin to bare skin.

And then what?

Chloe took a deep breath and lay against his chest, allowing herself the pleasure of his touch for as long as he was willing to offer it.

Gavin was a dazzling predator, a powerful and rich immortal with connections she knew nothing about and influence she didn't stop to ponder. He didn't flaunt any of it. He wore power like one of his perfectly tailored suits.

He'll get bored with you eventually. Probably right after you agree to have sex with him.

He didn't push, and she hesitated. They were in stalemate, a pair of would-be lovers too cautious to make the first move after months and months of foreplay. She didn't know what kind of status she had in Gavin's world, other than she was under Ben's uncle's aegis, and vampires at the bar no longer flirted with her.

At all.

She knew they considered her Gavin's... something. She had no idea what that something was. No doubt they assumed she was his lover. That they slept together. That he fed from her.

A frisson over her skin.

Gavin's hands stopped and pressed in. "What are you thinking about right now?"

Oh God. He knows when you're turned on.

Sometimes living around vampires made Chloe seriously want to die. They smelled everything. They heard everything. The silent burp you manage to hide on your date? Not hidden if that date was a vampire. No bodily function was a mystery to them.

"What were you thinking about?" he whispered.

The mental image leaped to the front of her mind. Gavin's fangs, long in his mouth, breaking her skin.

Her body responded. His hands gripped tighter. "Chloe?"

"What do you think I was thinking about?"

"Sex."

She laughed. "I wasn't actually. But that's a good guess."

"So not sex. Now I'm even more curious." His fingers went to work again, stroking up and down her back, teasing the top of her ass, the small of her back, the curve of her neck—

"Hmmm." He trailed a hand down her arm. "Goose bumps again."

The hand went back to her neck. His lips followed. Gavin gripped the hair at her nape and tugged, pulling her head back and exposing her skin to the cold night air and his mouth.

Goose bumps. She felt them everywhere.

Gavin kissed across her collarbone. "Were you thinking about me biting you?"

Her heart took off at a gallop just as his lips reached her pulse point.

"I think you were," he murmured. "And I think you like the idea."

Yes, I love the idea, and I must be going crazy.

Chloe shut her eyes and said nothing.

"Just so you know," Gavin said. "When I bite you, I *will* enjoy a taste from your pretty neck." He nipped her skin lightly. "But when I'm really hungry"—his hand slipped from the top of her thigh to the inside, dragging up, up, up until Chloe gasped—"there's nothing like a nice bite right here." He pinched the soft flesh just below the juncture of her thighs. "When I'm *really* hungry."

Without another word, Gavin slid her to the side, leaving her breathless on the bench of the hot tub as he stood and climbed out, sporting an erection that made Chloe think very unprofessional thoughts about her employer.

She wasn't going to whimper. She refused.

But she wasn't going to sleep much either.

GAVIN TOOK a deep breath when he reached the solarium that led to the stairs of his penthouse. Leaving Chloe in the hot tub, wet and ready for him, was one of the hardest things—no pun intended—he'd done in several hundred years.

"You're playing the long game," he muttered. "It's worth it."

Wasn't it?

He'd been wooing the woman for months now, seducing her in slow bites and always leaving her hungry for more. Tonight, when she'd inadvertently brought up turning and then—*fuck* his luck—Gavin feeding from her, he'd nearly lost his mind.

He gripped the erection that threatened to rip his swimming suit and tried to think about anything but Chloe. Outside. On his roof. Hot and wet and—

"I'm a fucking idiot. Why did I leave?" He was just about to walk back outside when the house phone rang.

Walking over to the small desk, he punched in the speaker-phone button. "Whoever this is, you better have an excellent reason for calling."

4

Ben landed at the San Juan Luis Muñoz Marín International at six forty-five in the evening. He had just enough time to catch a taxi, find his rental house, and grab a bite to eat before he was supposed to meet Tenzin in Plaza de Armas in Old San Juan.

He'd chosen the rental house for a reason. It was minutes to the plaza. It was very, very private. It had few windows and an interior patio that opened straight up to the sky. But did Tenzin want to meet him at the house he'd so carefully selected?

Of course not.

Ben wandered around the small square and took in the brightly colored lights, pigeons, and vivid buildings painted yellow, pink, and green. The tourist traffic was light, and he sat on a bench near the fountain, waiting for his partner.

Ben heard the murmured chatter of familiar accents all around him. He felt the knock of memory at the door in his mind, but he ignored it, focusing on the screen of his smart phone while he waited for Tenzin.

She sat down next to him a few moments after dark had fully descended, nudging his shoulder when he didn't look up.

"What does it feel like?"

"What does what feel like?"

"These are your roots. The place where your people came from." Tenzin crossed her legs and threw an arm across the back of the bench. "Nothing?"

Ben finally looked up and around. "It looks like a Spanish colonial city. I've visited them before."

A smile curled up the corner of her mouth. "Fine."

"Do you feel any deep, inspirational flood of emotion when you visit China?"

"I'm not from China."

"Central Asia then?"

"Central Asia is a big place."

Ben frowned. "Where are you from? Do you even know?"

"No." Tenzin looked up at the deep blue sky. "I could probably guess, but I don't want to. It was too long ago."

"Exactly." He looked back at his phone. "I got an email from—"

"Are you actually comparing five thousand years to twenty-five?"

"Do you think I'm twenty-five?"

She narrowed her eyes. "I was guessing. I don't really care how old you are. You're not twenty-five?"

He rose. "Since you don't care how old I am, I guess it doesn't matter. I'm hungry."

"You're always hungry."

Ben reached for her hand. "Some of us have appetites, Tiny."

"We all have appetites. Just not for the same things."

He stopped, turned, and looked at her. It was the first time he'd really looked at Tenzin since they'd arrived. She was wearing a pair of loose black pants and a shirt, her usual, but she had colored strings braided through her hair and her cheeks were flushed.

Ben stepped closer. "What are we talking about here?"

"Appetites."

"Uh-huh."

The flushed cheeks meant she'd just fed from someone. Ben didn't think about who it might be. He didn't like thinking about it.

He couldn't stop thinking about it.

The call of a vendor selling *pinchos* down the street distracted him. "Come on. I'll find some food and then we can walk around."

"It's beautiful here."

Ben glanced around. "Yeah, it's nice."

"That's all? It's nice? Don't you like the colors? The food smells good. The city—"

"Is a city, is a city," Ben muttered. "Cities are all the same."

"Keep telling yourself that if it makes you feel better." She nudged his arm. "You like it."

It's the most beautiful island in the world.

He shoved the memory of his grandmother's voice to the back of his mind. He was here to work. He'd check in on his human relatives when that was finished. If he had time. He'd read the most recent report from his agent on the island, the same agent who'd procured the Jeep for him and Tenzin to drive to Quebradillas in a couple of days.

The report was thorough.

The island was recovering, slowly but surely.

His relatives were well provided for, and his cousin was working again.

His grandmother was healthy and had no idea where her money was coming from.

That was all.

He'd drive west with Tenzin, look for the treasure that probably didn't exist, try not to piss anyone off, then go home with a much-needed tan.

They walked up the street and bought three chicken pinchos from the vendor, then Ben tried to herd Tenzin back to the house.

"Where are we going?" she asked.

"Back to the very nice rental house I found for us. There's already a light-safe room set up and a patio. I want to get some research done tonight."

"Don't you want to wander around?" She bit into the skewer of meat. "You've never been here before."

She had a smear of adobo sauce on her chin.

Ben wiped if off. "No, it's fine."

"It's not like you to be so incurious."

Ben sighed. "Can we just... not?"

"Not what?"

"You're picking at me, Tiny."

"I don't know what you're talking about."

"This is a job." He finished the first pincho and bit into the second. "This is just a job. Can we treat it that way please?"

"No." She stopped in the middle of the cobblestone street. "Look around you. This is a beautiful city. If this was a normal job, you'd be eager to explore. You'd have arrived a week early. You would have jogged every street and probably found a dozen restaurants we just had to visit before we left."

She was right, which meant he said nothing.

"So no. We can't treat this like a normal job for you." She started walking again. "Because it's not. I'm going to explore. I hear music this direction. You can come or not."

Why was she being so stubborn? Usually it was Ben forcing Tenzin to not be a hermit. This newly extroverted vampire was completely unexpected.

"Tenzin!"

She turned around halfway down the block. "What?"

Come with me. Don't leave me alone in this place. I don't like it when I don't know what to feel.

"Keep out of trouble." Ben turned and kept walking to the house.

She didn't follow him.

~

It was only after Ben returned to the house that he realized he'd never given Tenzin the directions. He debated wandering back through Old Town to try to find her. Then he remembered it was Tenzin.

She'd find him. She always did.

Ben pushed two chairs together in the courtyard and dozed in the moonlight, listening to the rustle of palm trees overhead.

~

The TV only showed static. Ben fussed with the bunny-ear antenna, trying to watch his cartoons. Saturday morning was the only morning he got to watch cartoons. His mom was sleeping off the alcohol from the night before, and Ben had the television to himself.

If he could only get a picture.

A fist banged on the door, and Ben went on alert. It didn't sound like any of their neighbors. It didn't sound like the men who sometimes came to his mother's apartment. That heavy fist could only belong to—

"What the fuck, Joey?" His mother barreled out of the

bedroom, down the narrow hallway, and threw open the door. "What the fuck? What fucking time is it, huh?"

"I need the kid today," Joe mumbled, glancing at Ben, who was still in his pj's. They were SpongeBob pj's. Ben didn't really like SpongeBob, but Mrs. Novak had given him the pj's after her grandson couldn't fit in them anymore and they were newer than his old ones, so he said thank you and wore them.

"The fuck you need the kid for?" His mom wiped a hand across her mouth. "We're going to midtown today."

"For what? So he can steal stuff for you?"

"You know he kills in those games. We pick up a little extra money. What's the big deal? He's good at it, and he has fun."

Ben didn't have fun, but he didn't correct his mother.

"My mom is in town," Joe said. "She wants to spend the day with the kid. Take him school shopping or something."

Ben saw his mother's eyes narrow. "She wants to buy him clothes?"

"Yeah."

Ben's mother looked at Ben, then back at Joe. "How long?"

"She'll keep him for the day so he's out of your hair. Cook him dinner tonight. I'll bring him back before bed. My shift is done at nine."

Ben glanced at the old clock hanging crooked on the wall over the TV. Twelve hours with Joe's mom? Sweet. Ben thought about how many cookies he'd eaten the last time he'd seen his abuela. He'd nearly gotten sick from them.

"Fine." She walked over to Ben and bent down. "Go get changed." She leaned closer. "Pick the good stuff, and do *not* take the tags off."

Ben nodded. He ran to change into his nicest clothes. His abuela would be sad if he didn't look happy, so Ben would be happy.

He could do that. He was good at pretending.

~

"I KNOW." The familiar voice came from above him. The only reason he didn't sit bolt upright was because it was a familiar voice.

"You know what?" He cleared his throat and opened his eyes. The moon was still high, and Tenzin was hovering in the air, her body threading through the palm trees in the courtyard.

"You said you were good at pretending."

He felt a sick curl in his stomach. "What else did I say?"

"Nothing else. Just that." She flew down and hovered directly over him. "I know you're good at pretending."

"Uh-huh." He lay completely still.

"You were dreaming."

"It's a thing humans do."

"I know." Her storm-grey eyes went distant. "I think I remember dreaming."

He reached up and fingered a braid of hair with red string woven through it. "What do vampires dream about?"

"Our human lives mostly."

"Do you remember yours?"

"Sometimes." She flipped over and sank into him, laying her body along his, using him as her own personal lounger. "My human life was miserable though. Why would I want to remember that?"

"I don't know." He took a deep breath, inhaling the scent of her, which was as familiar as his own breath. Then he picked up a strand of her hair and started braiding it. "Why does anyone dream about anything? I don't want to remember my childhood, but that doesn't seem to matter."

"Are you dreaming about that?"

"Why do you want to know?"

"You brought it up."

Ben dropped Tenzin's hair and wrapped his arms around her waist. He set his chin on the top of her head. She was exactly the correct height to use as a chin rest, so who was he to argue with nature?

"I'm dreaming about my grandmother."

"Did you pretend with her?"

"Of course. She was a normal person. If she knew what my mom and dad were really like, she would have tried taking me away from them."

"But you've said many times your parents were awful."

He closed his eyes. "They were."

"Wouldn't you have been happier living with your grandmother?"

"Probably? I don't know, Tenzin. I was a kid. Kids don't want to rock the boat."

"Rock the boat." She turned a little. "Make things uncomfortable?"

"Yeah. With my mom, I knew what the rules were. With my abuela? No idea. In retrospect, yes. I would probably have been much better cared for living with my grandmother. I didn't think that way at ten."

"And Giovanni found you when you were twelve?"

"Yeah."

"And he took you?"

"Yeah."

She laid her head over his heart, and Ben felt the settled *rightness* of it down to his bones.

Who else but her? There is no one else.

"You didn't tell Giovanni about your grandmother, did you?"

Ben shook his head. "Not until last year when I needed his help getting information from the island after the hurricane."

"I see."

"He was pissed."

"He would be." Tenzin shrugged. "He has very... decided ideas about family."

"I know. Just like I knew he wouldn't take me if I told him the truth about my family when I was younger. So I didn't."

"You were a very bright child."

"I wasn't really a child anymore."

Tenzin turned and looked him in the eye. She brought a hand up to his cheek and scrutinized his face. Ben felt his heart rate pick up. She had to sense his reaction to her—he knew she wasn't unaware—but he wasn't the only one good at pretending.

"You were a child," she said.

Ben tried to imagine Tenzin as a child. He couldn't. She looked the same now as she did when he'd first met her. He'd turned from a world-weary teenager to a grown man. How had she grown?

Was she more human? Maybe.

Was that a good thing? He had no idea.

Ben asked, "Can we talk about something else?"

"Why?"

"Because I've had about three times as much self-reflection as I ever want. And also we're leaving the city in a few days. We should talk about what we need before we go."

"No." Her lower lip came out. "It's pretty here. I actually don't hate it."

He smiled. "You just enjoy flying over the ocean at night."

"Yes." She stretched her arms up, nearly whacking him in the face with her fist. "Also, there's much less electricity here than most cities."

"That's generally thought to be part of the problem on the island, Tiny. It's not considered a feature. Don't worry. You're on an island. There's plenty of everything here. Ocean. Mountains. Caves where pirates *supposedly* hid treasure."

She turned to him and grinned. "Paradise. Maybe Puerto Rico needs more vampire residents. The lack of electricity and Wi-Fi is delightful. I like the music, and the pirate treasure is also a definite plus."

Ben frowned. "Can you feel Wi-Fi signals?"

"Yes. New York is covered in them. Very uncomfortable."

"Huh."

"It's not as bad in our loft. But on the streets? Awful."

"Is that why you've been going out less?"

"Have I?"

Didn't she realize it? Over the past three months she'd nearly become a hermit. The only time she left the loft was to go flying. She didn't go to visit Chloe at work. She didn't have drinks with Cormac. She'd even stopped wandering through Washington Square to enjoy the street performers in the evenings.

"You've been staying home more," he said, playing with her hair again.

"I didn't realize."

"So maybe it's a good thing we came here." Ben could see that. Maybe she needed to unplug, as much as a vampire who killed technology could unplug. "The house we're staying at in the west runs on solar power. Shouldn't be as intrusive. And no Wi-Fi."

Speaking of houses...

"How did you find this place?" he asked. "I never gave you directions."

"I didn't find the house. I found you."

"You found me?"

"I can always find you."

Ben decided not to ask. If she'd planted some kind of vampire tracking device on him with amnis, he didn't want to know. He just... didn't.

"Okay."

"No more questions?"

"Nope." He sat up and lifted her from his lap, then turned and set her on the chair before he walked back in the house. "Enjoy the night. I need to get some sleep. Research at the national library in the morning, and then I have an appointment with a rare-books contact of Giovanni's in the afternoon."

"What am I supposed to do?"

"Stay here," he said. "There are two light-safe rooms for you, and the angles of this patio should make it accessible for most of the day. No direct light in the interior of the first floor."

"That's it?"

"Read. Meditate." He rubbed his eyes. "I'll bring some books for you from the library, and the maps I ordered should be delivered in the morning. Maybe between the two, you can narrow down the search area a bit." Ben turned. "You do know that these are caves, right?"

"I know."

"And they're underground."

She shot him a look. "I know what a cave is."

Ben raised his hands. "I'm just warning you. I know you don't like going underground."

"I'll be fine."

"Uh-huh." Ben walked into the house. He definitely wasn't the only one who was good at pretending.

5

Tenzin watched him walk inside the house. She listened for the sounds she associated with Benjamin going to sleep. The faucet turning on when he washed his face and brushed his teeth. The rustle of clothing when he changed into sleeping clothes. The soft flip of book pages before a lamp clicked off. Breaths that stretched and grew longer and longer until she knew he was dreaming.

If she closed her eyes, she could hear his heart beating. Hear the furious activity of his body at rest. The biological systems that made him human operated in a beautiful and intricate ecosystem. His digestion and circulatory systems fed his cells the energy they needed to regenerate. His brain slipped into different patterns, allowing his mind to process, filter, and renew itself. All the while, the indefinable spirit that made him Benjamin suffused the space and the air around him.

Who said vampires were magic? Humanity was the most magical thing in all creation. Bright, brilliant flowers that lived for such a short time, yet left such a deep mark.

He will leave a mark.

"No." She spoke her will into the air.

Ben would not leave her.

His fate was other.

Like her, he would join the immortal race, the ones who lived in the darkness, taking their sustenance in the shadows from the bright flowers that fed on the sun.

She had seen it, and it would be. Anything else was unacceptable.

Tenzin didn't examine why. Like Benjamin, she was not a creature of self-reflection. He was hers. One day he would realize it as she did.

What that meant for both of them? They could decide that later.

She flew up into the night and over the city, enjoying the strains of music, human laughter, and traffic that wafted into the night sky like tantalizing scents simmering from an unfamiliar pot.

This city was intriguing. This island was beautiful. Once Ben opened his eyes, he would recognize that.

He just needed to see what was in front of him.

6

Ben spent the next morning avoiding the charms of San Juan and burying himself in the national archives. He was starting to see why his aunt and uncle liked the literary life. Books didn't talk back.

He found a good amount of information on Miguel Enríquez, but nothing that led him to believe the eighteenth-century pirate had secreted a hidden treasure somewhere on the island. There were records of his varied political influence and career as a privateer, books tracking his rise as one of the most influential people in the Caribbean to his disgrace, debt, and poverty at the end of his life.

There was plenty of information, but nothing that set Ben's radar off. According to all available sources, Enríquez had died a pauper after taking refuge in the Dominican convent in San Juan. The government stripped him of his wealth, and he had no heirs who claimed him.

Ben walked out of the national archives and into the sunlight, calling for a car on Avenida de la Constitución. It was only a ten-minute drive back to Plaza de Armas, and he didn't want to walk in the growing heat. His appointment was in a very private flat on Calle de la Cruz, just minutes from the plaza, and he didn't want to be late. The proprietor, an old friend of his uncle's, was opening the shop especially for him.

If anyone knows historic gossip about Dominicans in Puerto Rico, it's August.

Why?

He used to be one.

Ben didn't know the story and he didn't ask. If there was anything he'd learned from his uncle, it was that everyone had stories. If they wanted to share them, they'd tell you. If they didn't, it was none of your business anyway, so butt out. Most vampires played by those rules, but then so did a lot of people, Ben included.

He exited the small car and stretched his legs walking around the plaza. It was nearly noon, and a steady stream of locals and tourists filled the square. Tourists fed the pigeons, and locals sat on the benches in the shade, chatting with friends and sipping cold drinks.

Again, the familiarity pressed in on him. He'd never been to this place before, yet it felt... easy. Like a pair of perfectly fitted shoes. They weren't quite broken in, but given a few days of wear, they would fit him like a glove.

What would his life have been if he'd told Giovanni the truth about his grandmother? The vampire had asked him when he was a child if he had any family he loved. Any he trusted.

Ben had lied. A bit.

He had an affection for his abuela, but did he trust her? He hadn't trusted anyone since he turned eight. Could he have grown to trust his abuela? Probably. But the thought had scared him too much to risk it. Giovanni had offered him a life he could only dream of. And if he was also a vampire? Well, Ben had seen worse.

If he'd told Giovanni about his abuela, would he have grown

up here in San Juan? Would he have a family? Friends? Would he have gone to university or traveled?

His cousin was a park ranger at El Yunque National Park. She had studied biology in Florida before returning to Puerto Rico when her mother became ill. His aunt, whom he'd never met even though she lived on and off in New York, had died five years ago. As far as he knew, Joe had not returned for his sister's funeral.

Ben kept one eye on his watch and another on the pedestrians. San Juan was almost completely recovered from the devastation of the hurricane, but that didn't mean the city wasn't different.

Though the tourists walked through the city with sunny dispositions and light hearts, there was a heaviness Ben sensed around him. It was the reason locals were so easy to spot.

Here today, their eyes said, *gone tomorrow.*

What had it been like before?

Ben would never know.

THE DOOR of the bookshop wasn't marked. A lovely wrought iron 8 hung in the center of the door, but that was the only indication Ben was where he was supposed to be.

Ben knocked and waited. After a few moments, he heard movement within the house. There was a rustling, a pause, then the rattling of multiple locks and chains. The door cracked open, and a large pair of spectacles peered out.

Well, the spectacles were attached to an old man, but they were definitely the first thing Ben noticed.

"Señor Camino?"

"You must be Giovanni's boy." Señor Camino opened the door wider. "You look like him."

"Do I?" Ben slipped inside, and the old man shut the door behind him.

Ben's impression was that Camino knew his uncle Giovanni was a vampire. Maybe he'd been wrong.

"How is the old man?" Camino asked. "I heard he got married a few years back. Hasn't been to see me since I moved from New York."

"So you're from the city?"

Camino nodded and walked farther into a dark apartment stuffed with bookshelves. Front windows were covered, and the living room was entirely filled with books, as was a formal dining room that had been taken over by a library table, a desk, and glass cases. Ben could hear a dehumidifier humming somewhere in the room.

"I was born here, moved to New York when I was a bit older than you. That's where I met your uncle. I was working for the O'Briens then."

Ben let out a breath. Working for the O'Briens meant the old man definitely knew about vampires. "You're a collector?"

The books Ben could see ranged from yellowed paperbacks to leather-wrapped volumes. There was no apparent order, but that wasn't uncommon from what he'd seen with his uncle. Most vampire libraries had their own system known only to the owner or keeper. It made the collection more labyrinthine for any outsider trying to find information.

Camino shrugged as he led Ben down a narrow hallway. "I find things. Not unlike your uncle. We've crossed paths many times. Worked together a few. I hear you're not in the book trade though. You have... other pursuits?"

"Yes, my partner and I—"

"I've heard about her too." Camino turned and smiled. "That's why I made the appointment before sundown." The old man pushed a door open, and a beam of light hit Ben directly in the face.

He hesitated and put a hand up to shade his eyes.

"Come in," Camino said. "Just me here. I keep all the windows in the front covered because of the books. But I thought we could have coffee first. I don't get many visitors these days."

Ben walked slowly into a kitchen that was vivid with color. Large windows filled the back wall, and a set of doors led to a Juliet balcony with green plants hanging from the railing and a large birdcage where two whistling green birds hopped around.

The interior windows of Camino's home looked into a quaint courtyard filled with palm trees and flowers. Laundry lines were strung across the building, and most doors and windows were open. He could hear music coming from another apartment and a soft, ocean-scented breeze suffused the kitchen.

Little wonder why the old man had moved back from New York City.

"I already have the coffee boiling," Camino said. "Do you like *café con leche*?" He turned. "Sit, sit. There are rolls on the table. Make yourself at home."

"*Café con leche* is great." Ben noticed the spiraled rolls on the kitchen table. They were golden brown and dusted with sugar. "*Pan de Mallorca?*"

"You know it?" Camino smiled. "My neighbor makes them." He kissed his fingers. "So perfect."

"My grandmother made them too."

"I wondered." Camino glanced at him from the corner of his eye. "Of course, you have that look, you know? The same as your uncle."

"What look is that?"

"The don't-notice-me look. The I'm-from-here-and-there-and-nowhere look. You're almost as good at it as he is."

"Give me time. I'm a little bit younger." Ben wandered over and watched the birds on the balcony. They whistled when they saw him, their bright red faces following him as he looked out over the courtyard. "My grandmother had lovebirds."

"They are my sweethearts," Camino said. "My little friends to keep me company. They love visitors, but don't let them take off a finger. They go mad for sunflower seeds. You can give them one. But not too many."

"They're like cookies." Ben remembered his abuela saying the same things. *Like cookies, Benjamin. A few is good. Too many make you sick.*

Camino cackled. "You are right. Come sit. Don't let the coffee get cold." He brought over two large cups of light coffee and set them down. He added sugar to his, but Ben took his coffee plain.

Ben sat, grabbed a roll, and tasted it. It wasn't as sweet as he remembered. Then again, he'd been ten the last time his grandmother had fed him breakfast. "These are good."

"A taste of home?"

"No." Ben sipped his coffee. "I'm not from here. I'm from the city."

"Ah." Camino nodded knowingly. "I'm sure it's a story, how you came to be with your uncle."

"Yep."

Camino smiled. "Not a story for today. You and your partner want to know about Enríquez, eh? Not Cofresí? He's the pirate most Puerto Ricans are familiar with. Of course, technically Enríquez was a privateer."

Ben raised an eyebrow. "He was a pirate."

"But a licensed one!" Camino lifted his coffee. "Licensed by the king himself. And he had good relationships with most of the governors as well. An easy truce with many in the navy. Up until the end of his life, he was very, very influential, though he was never truly accepted by the upper classes."

"Why? Because he was a privateer?"

"No, because he was black." Camino lifted a finger. "And illegitimate. Never underestimate humanity's ability to be prejudiced. Miguel Enríquez came from nothing and made himself one of the most influential Puerto Ricans of his time. An incredible story! But he was never accepted by the social elite. His mother was a free black woman. His father was a very well-connected priest."

"I thought his father was unknown."

Camino gave him a sly smile. "And isn't this why you come to me, young Vecchio? You need the real story. Not what is in the books."

Ben smiled for the first time that day. "Yeah. I need the real story."

"Then finish your coffee, and I'll show it to you."

Two BOXES of letters were open on the library table, both yellowed from age but bearing different handwriting.

"These are from a young Dominican who cared for Enríquez during his final days. He was a native of the island, from around Arecibo. And these others are from Matías de Abadía, the governor who orchestrated Enríquez's downfall in his last years."

"Why?" Ben asked. "What did Abadía have against Enríquez?"

Camino shrugged. "Some say Abadía thought he had reached too far for his station. Others say he was a convenient scapegoat for the British after Spain and England made peace. Personally, I think Enríquez wasn't a nice man! He made many enemies during his years attaining power and wealth. Those things come back to haunt you."

Ben laid a letter out on the table. "True."

"The letters from Abadía are interesting." The old man pushed the larger box forward. "Though he'd forced Enríquez to pay fines and settlements to the point of near poverty, he was still convinced Enríquez was hiding the majority of his wealth."

"He thought Enríquez had hidden treasure?"

"Oh yes. And it's also notable that the priest's letters are not very clear on how Enríquez was paying for his stay with the Dominicans. From what the young man said, he was very, very comfortable at the convent."

"Not exactly a pauper's bed, huh?"

"Oh no. He had private rooms. Servants. None of that would have come for free. Enríquez did have a long relationship with the church—"

"Did he know his father was a priest?" An itch formed in the back of Ben's mind. *Something about the priest...*

"It's very likely he did. He and all his siblings had the same father. When he was in trouble? He went to the Dominicans."

"And the convent you're talking about, it's the one right here in San Juan?" Ben spread the letters from the priest out on the table.

"Yes, only a few minutes away. He stayed there until his death."

Ben smiled. "Don't tell me no one has searched the convent in all these years."

"For his wealth? Oh, of course they have," Camino said. "Abadía did. Others have. It was the last place Enríquez lived. But it's been renovated many times. I don't think it's likely any treasure is there."

Ben leaned his elbows on the table. "Do you have any ideas?"

"Me?" Camino's narrow shoulders rose. "What use would I have for gold or silver? I don't collect metal."

"That didn't answer my question."

"These letters here? These are my treasures." The old man leaned forward, his eyes sparkling. "But *if* you were looking for treasure..."

"Which is a fool's errand."

"Of course." Camino shrugged. "Pirate treasure is a myth. But *if* you were to go to the west of the island, you might find those more curious about gold."

"You mean vampires?"

"Oh, possibly. But I don't ask about such things. The older an immortal is, the tighter they hold on to their secrets."

"Secrets like hidden treasure?"

"What treasure?" Camino spread his hands. "Miguel Enríquez died a pauper. Everyone knows that."

Ben smiled at the old man's innocent expression. "There haven't even been rumors?"

Camino considered for a moment. "I will tell you this: you are the first—human or immortal—who has come and asked about these letters since I have lived in San Juan."

"Good to know." Ben smiled. "It's still hard for me to imagine any place on this island is unknown to immortals who have lived here thousands of years."

"Even a little island can have many places to hide," Camino said.

"True."

Camino waited, but Ben remained silent.

"You have an idea," the old man said, "or you would not have come to see me."

"Me?" Ben shrugged. "I'm just doing research."

Camino smiled. "Which is good. As I said, I have no use for

gold or silver. And your uncle has done me more than one favor over the years."

"Thank you." Ben pointed at the box of letters from the young Dominican. "Do you mind if I take pictures of these? Just for my own records? I'd like to share them with my partner."

Camino stood. "Not at all, as long as you don't use a flash."

"Of course."

Ben took multiple pictures of each letter, placing each back in an acid-proof envelope and storage box after he did. He'd been trained by a librarian. He knew not to mess with an old man and his documents. There weren't many, only a dozen or so. But something told Ben the priest's letters held the secret. He carefully photographed each one with a camera he'd brought specifically for documents.

After another hour looking through Camino's personal library and researching Taíno social structure, Ben was ready to go. He could feel the sun sinking in the sky and wanted to get back to Tenzin.

Another cup of coffee and Camino was showing him to the door. "Be careful when you go west," the old man said. "Things in the immortal court are complicated at the moment."

"Aren't they always?"

"This is true. But while some places have one immortal in charge, this little island has three."

Interesting. Novia seemed to think that the only true power in Puerto Rico was Macuya, the cacique. Camino was implying something else. "So there are truly three rulers in Puerto Rico? They're not just figureheads?"

"Three rulers. Three elements. Three peoples." Camino put a hand on his chest. "We *boriqueños* are all of them, are we not? Native and Spanish and African. Made of the ocean and the mountains and yes, even the hurricanes that test us."

Ben felt a stirring in his chest.

Boricua.

What did he know about this place? What did he *really* know? Nothing more than impressions and a bad taste left in his mouth every time he thought of his father. But his father wasn't Puerto Rico. Joe wanted nothing to do with this place.

Maybe that meant Ben did.

"What about the cacique?" Ben asked Camino. "Isn't he the oldest on the island? The most powerful?"

"That is true." Camino looked out the window, and a shadow crossed his eyes. "But I do not fear the cacique. He lives under his mountain and clutches the old ways. I suppose it's good that someone does."

You may not fear the cacique, but there is something you fear.

"Thank you." Ben held out his hand and the old man took it. "You've been a huge help. Your home and your library are beautiful."

"Wait here." Camino disappeared into his house and came back a few minutes later with a white paper bag. "The pan de Mallorca. To take with you."

"Oh, I don't—"

"To remind you of your grandmother," Camino said. "My neighbor will make more for me tomorrow morning. Take it."

Ben hesitated only a minute. After all, Tenzin would be placated if he returned to the house with something sweet. "Thank you."

"And don't forget"—Camino stepped back into the shadowed living room as Ben put his sunglasses back on—"even little islands hide many secrets."

7

———

Tenzin knew Ben had found something the minute he walked through the door. For the first time since he'd seen the treasure map a year ago, he was energized. Eager. Nearly buzzing with excitement.

Finally.

She'd been starting to wonder whether the whole trip had been a mistake.

Which was ridiculous, of course. Gold was never a mistake.

She rose from the hammock hanging on the patio and walked inside, carrying the scent of the night wind with her.

"*Arecibo*," Ben sang. "*Que bonito Arecibo.*"

"What's in Arecibo?"

"It's the home of a priest who cared for Enríquez before his death. A priest who was his confidant. A priest from a poor family not unlike the pirate's own."

Tenzin walked to the refrigerator and removed a carton of mango juice. She poured two glasses and handed one to Ben. "You think the pirate gave his treasure to a priest?"

"No, he gave it to a young man who reminded Enríquez of himself." Ben set the juice and his messenger bag on the kitchen table. "Or rather, he reminded Enríquez of who he would have been if he'd been a better man. I looked in the records Camino had. There's no mention of the priest in the convent records after Enríquez's death."

"He just left?"

"Maybe?" Ben took out his computer and a camera. "Maybe he moved back home. Maybe he had a reason to leave."

Tenzin sat next to Ben as he plugged the camera into the computer and brought up several graphic files with pale scratches of letters on them. "What are these?"

"Letters. I'm going to edit these a little bit to make them clearer," he muttered. "Then we're going to read every word. I'll print them out for you."

"Not necessary," Tenzin said. "Send them to my tablet."

Ben looked at her in shock.

"What?" Tenzin said. "You think I'd travel without Cara?"

Cara was the artificial intelligence program the smart vampires in Ireland had come up with. She was also Tenzin's assistant. Logically, Tenzin knew Cara didn't actually belong to her, but the programmers had made the robotic voice remarkably accommodating and logical, two traits Tenzin valued highly. Cara was far easier to keep on task than Ben or Chloe.

And she knew all Tenzin's favorite music. And YouTube channels.

"Okay, I'll send them to your tablet," he said. "You kept all the firewalls on it, right?"

"Yes. Why are you even asking?"

"Because you took them off once and let a virus into the home network."

Tenzin crossed her arms and smiled. "So you say. Chloe and I still contend you have a secret fascination with the people in the animal suits."

He couldn't stop the smile. "I was not watching furry porn. You're just lucky the virus wasn't a serious one that time."

"Yes, I learned my lesson." She kicked her legs up and stretched them across his lap. "I want a smaller tablet like the one you have. The one I have is huge."

"That's because they have to be to be vampire-proof." Ben put a hand on her ankle and closed his fingers around her small foot, pressing his thumb into her arch.

Mmmfh. She kept her face passive even though that part of her foot was remarkably sensitive. He had no idea.

"Murphy and his team are trying to create a smaller size right now, but to be equipped with the Nocht system and the casing necessary so you don't short the electronics out means the device has to be fairly large."

"Fine." His thumb was moving up her ankle. Tenzin debated removing her foot, but... "Have you eaten tonight?"

"Not since lunch."

"Do you want to go out for dinner?"

She didn't know whether he'd shut down or if the low rumbling that had started in his stomach would win out over his practiced indifference toward the island.

Surprisingly, he looked up with a slight smile. "Yeah, let's go out. I saw a restaurant today that looked good."

"Oh." That was easy. "What happened?"

"What do you mean?"

She cocked her head. "You. This place."

He looked away, though he kept his hand on her ankle. "It's just a place. I've traveled lots of places. There's no need for this one to be any different. It's a beautiful island. We might as well enjoy it." A sly smile crossed his face.

"Okay." Tenzin decided not to push. Eventually he'd have to deal with his human family. It was a necessary step before he... "Wait, what kind of place are you talking about?"

"Local. Friendly." He locked his fingers around her ankle. "Looked like music and dancing."

"Nope." She withdrew her legs.

"Yes." His fingers tightened for a second before he let her go. "I haven't been dancing in ages. It's good exercise."

"Because I need so much exercise?" Tenzin floated off her seat and overhead. The high ceilings were remarkably suitable for her. He'd thought of that, just like he'd thought of the interior courtyard open to the sky.

Ben could be irritatingly thoughtful at times.

"Come on." He rose and held out a hand. "We'll eat fish. Dance a little. Enjoy the music. I know you like the music here."

"I didn't bring a dress."

Ben laughed and caught her foot, dragging her to the ground before he spun her around and looped his arm around her waist. "Since when do you need a dress to dance?" He took a step forward and back that she instinctively mirrored. "See? You still remember the steps."

"I only learned that to help Chloe with her choreography. I'm not dancing in public."

"Says you." Ben spun her around and left her head spinning as he walked past. "I'm changing out of these clothes, and then we'll go out. Come on. We head out of the city tomorrow. We might as well enjoy the nightlife tonight. Who knows? There might even be vampires."

As if she would be that lucky.

Who was she kidding? Tenzin smiled. She was *always* that lucky.

THE PLACE BEN led her to was exactly the kind of place she liked when she felt the urge to be around humans. Hidden from street view by a narrow alleyway, the restaurant was situated in a courtyard lit with colored lights and lanterns hanging from trees. Bright banners hung from the second-floor balconies, and a band played in one corner with couples spinning across the smooth tile floor while others sat at tables dotted around the courtyard.

Servers hustled drinks and plates of grilled fish and savory small dishes. It smelled delicious, and the energy of the humans around her made Tenzin's blood buzz with awareness. She'd fed from a cooperative human the night before, but this much humanity pressed around her made her want to indulge.

Ben bent down and spoke in her ear. "You like it?" The restaurant wasn't so loud that he had to yell, but intimate conversation space it wasn't.

"It's nice. The food smells good."

"I thought so too." His neck was redolent with blood and life. Ben had always smelled of earthy spices to her. Peppers and cumin and saffron. Her fangs ached to taste it.

No.

There were many of Ben's boundaries she happily ignored, but she didn't ignore this one. For his sake and for her own.

He straightened, removing temptation for the moment. "Where do you want to sit?"

"Not too close to the band."

Ben nodded, understanding immortal ears. He waved to a hostess who pointed them toward a table near the bar.

Tenzin glanced up as they crossed the courtyard and noticed the eyes following them. "Immortals," she said quietly.

"Friendly?"

"Observant."

"Expected." Ben held out her chair for her—such a quaint human habit—before he sat across from her. His eyes never left her face. "Anyone you recognize?"

"No, but some recognize me."

"How do you know?"

She shrugged. "There's a look."

"Abject terror?"

She laughed, allowing her fangs to show just a little. She couldn't hide them. Not really. She'd just become practiced at keeping her mouth mostly shut when she was around humans. "Not quite abject."

"But definitely terror." Ben raised an eyebrow. "You enjoy it."

"Vampire fear?" she asked. "Of course I do. It keeps me safe. It keeps you safe."

"You think it's the fear? Not the respect?"

"They're very closely entwined for predators like us." Tenzin reached for the carafe of water and filled both their glasses. "We respect what we fear. We respect the powerful."

"And me?"

"What about you?"

Ben sipped his water. "I'm not more powerful than you are. I'm not more powerful than any of them."

"But you have your own weapons," she said. "Some of which vampires can't even use. Everyone who knows of you in our world can respect that."

"That's good." He glanced over his shoulder at the dancing couples. "We should dance."

"We should eat." She opened the menu.

"We should dance." He rose and held a hand out to her. "Just one."

She glanced at the vampires on the balcony. They were watching. "One."

"Or two."

"One." She allowed him to lead her toward the dancers. Tenzin was wearing black leggings, a red tunic, and worn leather flats that molded to her feet. It was as close to barefoot as she could get. She hated shoes.

She could feel the tile on her soles. Ben was nearly a foot taller than her, but when Chloe had taught them the steps for the dance they were working on, that didn't seem to matter.

Tenzin remembered every step. Of course she did. She remembered most things when she wanted to. They reached the dance floor, and he spun her around. She put one hand in his and the other on his shoulder while he grabbed her waist.

Ben moved them expertly around the dance floor, working in time with the music, his hips shifting to lead in expert rhythm. He seemed to know how the music would change the same way she understood the breeze, instinctively and without a single doubt. As they danced, Tenzin was able to catch glimpses of the vampires in the shadows. Most appeared to be doing what Tenzin was, accompanying human companions as they ate and danced. No doubt some would be feeding later, based on the way they watched the humans below them.

Ben bent down and spoke in her ear. "How many?"

Of course he knew what she was doing. "Four."

"That many?"

"Three are together with human consorts. The fourth is on her own, but she appears to be interested in one of the musicians."

"Which one?"

Tenzin followed the vampire's eyes. "The bass player."

"What is it about bass players?" Ben mused.

"Rhythm. Lack of ego. Good fingers." Tenzin nearly tripped on Ben's feet when he missed a step. "What?"

"Nothing." Color had risen on his neck.

"None of them appear to be dangerous." Tenzin moved closer. "Though that vampire looking at the bassist looks very hungry."

"She's not the only one." He spun Tenzin around in two quick spirals as the band finished their song. "You still got the moves, Tiny."

"As do you." She gave one last glance at the balcony. The vampires had lost interest in the new faces and refocused on the humans with them. "Can we eat now?"

"Yes." He led her back to the table as the crowd clapped and the bandleader cheerfully introduced the next band, a Latin jazz quartet from Ponce. They both froze when they heard the first familiar trumpet solo of "Summertime."

"It's Louis," Ben murmured.

"It's not Louis."

"It's a version of Louis."

"Louis did not play Latin jazz. This is definitely—"

"We always dance to Louis." He tugged Tenzin's hand and spun her back to his chest. "It's the rules."

Tenzin looked up. "Too many." *Vampires.* There were too many vampires, and Tenzin refused—

"Follow me." Ben nodded and led them away from the dance floor, the tables, and the bustle of patrons, into a narrow alleyway off the courtyard where the trumpet cried quietly. A human couple was passionately kissing against one wall. A woman was smoking on a narrow stoop.

He wrapped an arm around her waist and pulled her close. She put her palm over his chest, feeling the steady beat, absorbing it into her cells as if by osmosis. She felt the pounding rhythm of his blood as if it were coming from her own heart.

Tenzin felt Ben's fingers on the small of her back, the pressure tuning her senses. To him. To the air around them. The electricity of the humans and the elements. The water in the humid air. The heat of human blood. The wafting breeze in the palm trees above and the stones beneath their feet.

Time stopped as the song played. They were a single creature in that moment, light and dark, fleeting and eternal.

"They can't see us here," he whispered in her ear.

Tenzin closed her eyes and turned her face into his neck.

Pepper. Saffron. Salt.

Her fangs ached in her jaw, so she kept her mouth shut. Kept her lips pressed together as they moved, suspended in the awareness of his fragility and her need.

How long will you torture yourself? He is a weakness.

The scent of tobacco smoke brought her awareness back. The song was ending. Ben's heart rate had steadied. The kissing couple walked past them with red cheeks and downward glances while the woman in the corner put out her cigarette and tied on an apron.

The song died down, and Ben held her for a lingering minute before he dropped his arms. "We should head back or they'll give our table away." His voice was rough.

Tenzin took a deep breath and focused on the scent of human food coming from the courtyard. "Okay."

"I'm hungry." He cleared his throat and straightened his collar. "Are you hungry? What am I saying—you're never hungry." He grabbed her hand and walked them back to the table where their server stood, scanning the courtyard.

"There you are!" the server said. "I was wondering if you'd left. I didn't see you on the dance floor."

"Sorry about that." Ben glanced down at Tenzin. "We got distracted."

The server laughed and relit the candle on the table that had blown out in the evening breeze. "On nights like this, that happens. Do you know what you want to eat?"

Yes.

"No." Tenzin glanced at Ben, then at the server. "I'll just have whatever he's having."

~

BEN HELD out a bite of fish. "You're in a mood."

She leaned forward and reluctantly took the bite. "I am not."

She was. She'd barely touched her food, and she kept glancing at the balcony above them where the vampires had been. All but the one scoping out the bass player had left.

"They're gone, Tiny."

But she was unsettled. It was an interesting turn. Ben was used to being the unsettled one. But ever since the dance in the alley, she'd been in a mood. Cross. Irritable. Distracted.

He sipped a rum cocktail with mint and lime. "There something you're not telling me?"

"They were watching us."

"Of course they were."

"She isn't."

Ben glanced over his shoulder. The vampire in the corner of the courtyard watching the musicians looked to be around forty, but that meant nothing. She could be young. She could be old.

"You get any sense of her power?"

"Nothing."

"Which means she's either very powerful or not powerful at all."

"Correct."

Ben watched her. She was beautiful, as most immortals were, with long dark hair in thick spiral curls and a round face. Her lips were generous and very red, and her skin was light brown. She'd been darker as a human, but lack of sun and an immortal diet had leached her natural color.

Tenzin had told him once that the paler a vampire was, the more they relied on blood for sustenance instead of taking human food.

Or they were Irish. That was always a possibility too.

"She's ignoring you completely, so that makes me think more powerful and able to shield herself from others," Ben said.

"Yes. That's my guess too."

"Spanish?"

Tenzin shrugged. "There's no way of knowing. She could be a tourist."

"No, she's too beautiful."

Tenzin frowned. "What does that mean?"

"She's a regular here, or she'd be attracting more attention because she's really beautiful." He glanced at the male bartenders. The waiters. "She's magnetic, but they're used to her."

"Good observation." Tenzin picked at the delicately poached fish on her plate. "So she's a regular here. She likes bass players. And she's probably quite old."

"But those other vampires were ignoring her too," Ben said. "VIC?"

Tenzin shook her head. "There's no vampire in charge of San Juan."

"Not even unofficially?"

"Officially and unofficially, Los Tres has the power here and all over the island."

"Says who?" Ben asked.

"Says me and every contact I've checked with, including your uncle."

Ben felt a twitch in his cheek. "You've been talking to Gio about Puerto Rico?"

"Of course I have. He wrote me as soon as the hurricane hit."

After I'd told him about my family. Ben cleared his throat. "What did he want?"

"He wanted to know if you'd told me anything about your grandmother."

"And what did you tell him?"

"I said it was none of his business." She took a bite of fish. "This is good."

"Thank you." Ben was unexpectedly relieved.

"You didn't cook the fish; why are you saying thank you?"

"Thank you for telling him to mind his own business." Why did he care so much that Tenzin had shut Giovanni down?

"You're welcome." She met his eyes. "Why did you lie about her?"

"Because..." *I trusted a manipulative creature of the night over kindness.* "It's complicated."

"Fine." She turned her face back to the band. "Finish your dinner, Benjamin. We've been here too long."

"At the restaurant or in San Juan?"

"Both." Tenzin sat back and looked into the starry sky. "It's time to start looking."

8

Ben was driving the all-wheel-drive Jeep to the west side of the island when he called Chloe. "How's life in the city?"

"Colder than where you are," she said. "Where are you?"

Ben glanced at the sign he was approaching. "Thirty-two kilometers east of Arecibo."

"I don't really know where that is."

Ben smiled. "Out of the city. We're heading to the mountains to meet the VIC here—or VICs. I'm honestly not sure how many we're dealing with at this point—then we go searching."

"For gooooold," Chloe said in a spooky voice.

"Yes, for pirate treasure." The wind whipped his hair and the breeze was cool and damp.

He'd headed out of the city early to avoid as much traffic as possible. He knew he'd run into some; traffic out of San Juan was unavoidable. There was only one main highway on the north side of the island, and it was the most direct route to his destination. With every town he passed, commuters, truckers, and tourists slowly clogged the motorway.

"But before pirate treasure," he added, "we have to make nice with the locals."

ELIZABETH HUNTER

"Who aren't going to object to you stealing their pirate treasure?"

Ben smiled. "Let me deal with that part. How's things in the city?"

"Uh... busy. Good." Chloe was flustered. "I mean, it's good, but I'm busy. The bar is packed lately, and rehearsals for the new show have been kind of tough."

Ben frowned. "Tough how? Is your knee bothering you?"

"No, it's fine. It's... Really, everything is good, Ben. I'm just a bit scattered right now."

"Because?"

"None of your business," she said. "Personal stuff."

Which meant something was going on with Gavin. Ben bit his tongue. "You're right. None of my business. Things are fine at the loft?"

"Construction is actually ahead of schedule, if you can believe that. By the time you guys get back— When are you getting back, by the way?"

"I rented the house in San Juan for a month. I don't want to be gone any longer than that."

"Okay. The main stuff might be done by the time you get back."

"Cool."

"And the finish work will go quickly. You and Tenzin don't exactly live for the elaborate and fussy details."

Meaning their house looked more like an office than a home. Ben had heard the criticism before, from both Chloe and his aunt. He ignored it. "Well, good. I'm tired of having random people around the place. It's not safe."

"I know. I'm spending a lot of time at Gavin's while you're gone."

"Good." Was that good? Ben shook his head. *None of your business.*

"None of the workers have even given me a bad feeling. It's just... weird without you both. So"—she cleared her throat and her voice suddenly went higher—"wrap stuff up and get back home. Can't wait to see the pirate treasure. Okay, gotta go, bye."

She hung up.

Ben frowned at the phone. "Fucking Gavin..."

It never worked out well to have a friend dating a vampire. It just didn't. It had happened too often for him to count in Los Angeles among his school friends, many of whom had been born into families of day people. Young people accustomed to vampires grew up, started to look more attractive to the very handsome old people they worked for, then they got romantically hooked on the alternating danger and security of a relationship with an immortal. Then... they disappeared.

Not *permanently*. No one was disappearing into scary basements or anything. At least not in LA. But vampires tended to be major time sucks.

Ben should know. He was partners with the time-suckiest one of them all.

He was driving to the beach house he'd rented in Quebradillas. The town wasn't far from Lares—where Los Tres were located—and it was in the general neighborhood where most of the Puerto Rican cave systems were. Until they could narrow down a starting point for the Enríquez map, it was better to be in a quiet town that had a few tourists, but not too many.

And while Ben was driving and settling in, Tenzin would be meditating or reading or... something. She'd fly out to the villa that night and join him. In theory. Ben had spent more than one night pacing a room and waiting for Tenzin to show up when and where she'd promised.

And, of course, who was stuck moving the luggage and the books and the computers? Ben, naturally. He left the expressway and merged onto the old highway, which had far more traffic.

Was this his life? Waiting on Tenzin to flit to his side when she felt like it and acting like her personal bellhop the rest of the time? Was the rest of his life going to be a series of similar experiences?

Tenzin gets a wild idea.

Ben chases after her.

He gets drawn in... somehow.

Tenzin flies off.

Ben cleans up the mess after her.

He almost ran into the compact car in front of him as traffic ground to a halt.

"What is my life?" he asked the instrument panel.

What the hell was he doing? He'd always given the mildly judgmental side-eye to his friends who had fallen down the vampire-relationship hole. But he was doing the exact same thing.

And he wasn't even getting crazy-good vampire sex in the bargain.

Ben pinched the bridge of his nose. "I need to rethink my life."

It was probably the twenty-fifth time that year he'd said it.

"What?" A guy in a pickup truck next to him rolled down his window. "It depends on where you're going. You can take road 119 to 485 once we get past town, but I don't think that's going to be any faster."

Ben frowned. "What?"

"Didn't you say you needed to rethink this drive?"

"My life!" Ben yelled. "I need to rethink my life."

The man shrugged and waved a hand to let the car in front of Ben change lanes. "You and me both, man." Then he rolled up his window.

"Well... thanks." Ben tilted his seat back, turned the music to a playlist of Daddy Yankee, and settled in to crawl along the packed highway with the rest of the island.

Tenzin had to wait for hours after sunset to call Giovanni. The younger vampire was four hours behind her in Los Angeles. She set her tablet on the table in the middle of the courtyard. "Cara, call Giovanni Vecchio."

"I would be happy to," the cleverly disguised computer voice replied. The phone rang three times before someone answered.

"Good evening. Vecchio household."

"Hello, Caspar."

"Tenzin!" She could hear the smile in her old friend's voice. "Did you mean to call Giovanni's land line?"

"Does he have another one now?" If he'd switched over to an electronic assistant like Cara, Tenzin would eat her own tongue.

"Well no. But Beatrice does. They're in the library."

"Which one?"

Giovanni and Beatrice were book detectives, researchers, and respected academics in the immortal world. They had libraries in both Los Angeles, California, and Rome, Italy. Beatrice was even recognized as a scribe in Tenzin's sire's territory on Penglai Island.

"They're here in Los Angeles. Shall I get Giovanni for you, or would you rather call Beatrice's mobile number?"

Tenzin debated. She had no idea how much Beatrice knew about Ben's family in Puerto Rico. "I'd like to talk to Giovanni alone."

"Very well."

"Caspar, how is Isadora?"

"Doing very well," he said. "Her hip fracture has completely healed. She's up and walking around. And she hates her physical therapist. But other than that, she's fine."

"I can't imagine Isadora hating anyone."

"This young lady recommended Isadora wear orthopedic shoes and cut back on wine."

"Clearly she is a monster who knows nothing," Tenzin said. "Let Isadora know I will dispatch this person if she requires it."

"I'll be sure to let her know."

"Good."

"And now I shall page Giovanni. I don't imagine he'll be more than a few minutes. Where are you and Benjamin lately?"

"Caribbean," Tenzin said.

"Pirate treasure?"

"Why else do you go to the Caribbean?"

Caspar laughed under his breath. "Some people go to relax."

"I find gold very relaxing," Tenzin said. "It gives me Zen-like tranquility. Like ocean-wave noises on the computer."

"I see."

The phone line went quiet for a few moments. Then a shuffling and a creaking seat while someone sat down.

"Hello, Tenzin."

"Hello."

"You're in San Juan."

"Do you have spies everywhere?"

"Yes."

Tenzin could imagine his face. Slightly superior expression. Aloof. Some might say cold if they didn't know him.

Those who thought Giovanni Vecchio was cold were idiots. Tenzin had seen the fire in him three hundred years before.

She'd selfishly captured some of it for herself when she allowed him to befriend her.

That small fire had grown into a lasting friendship that spread to Giovanni's mate Beatrice, the humans he'd gathered around him, and particularly to Ben.

"How is he?" Giovanni asked.

"What do your spies say?"

"They say he is preternaturally perceptive to the point that he'll hurt himself."

"Not with me around." Tenzin sat in the hammock and kicked a foot out, rocking the woven cot. "He got a lead a couple of days ago. He'd just been to meet an old man you told him about. Anyone I know?"

"I don't think so. Book-world people," Giovanni said. "Someone owed me a favor."

"Are you positive this gold exists?"

"Me?" he asked. "No. My former client is positive though. He isn't sure who drew the map, but he's convinced it's genuine. He'd be going after the treasure himself if it were possible."

"And why isn't it possible for him?"

"Let's just say he's a little too well-known in the area. He would not find a warm welcome on the island."

"So why hire you to find a map he can't use?"

"Why indeed?"

"Oh." Tenzin smiled. "So he knows we're going after it?"

"He seemed almost gleeful at the prospect. I admit, I didn't mention names or specifics, but he's not an idiot. He knows who you and Ben are. It's probable he has an alternative plan to get the gold from you. Be careful."

It wouldn't be the first time Tenzin and a partner had been used for a fishing expedition. It was a solid strategy: have two hired immortals take all the risk, then swoop in and steal the

ELIZABETH HUNTER

prize when victory was inevitable. She'd used that scheme more
than once herself.

Of course, it never worked out very well for anyone who
tried using it on Tenzin.

"I'll be careful," she said.

"So why are you calling?" Giovanni's voice became clipped.
Impatient. "I know it's not to say hello."

"I did say hello though, didn't I?"

"You did. Your phone manners are improving."

"Thank you. I think Chloe is a good influence."

Giovanni asked, "Is this about Ben?"

"Maybe." Tenzin swung herself back and forth in the
hammock. "Where is his grandmother?"

"It's the Rios family home, a semirural place near Río
Grande, which is near El Yunque National Forest. Her parents
lived there and her granddaughter works at the park."

"That's Ben's cousin?"

"Yes. His father's sister's daughter."

"But the sister is dead?"

"Car accident. The grandmother and the cousin are all
that's left of the family."

And the father, but they didn't talk about him.

"Is Ben asking?" Giovanni asked.

"No."

"So you're interfering?"

"None of your business," Tenzin said.

"He's my son. He is my business."

Tenzin didn't say anything. What could she say? They'd
gone through this before. They'd go through it again.

"Are we going to fight about this, my boy?" Tenzin asked.

"I wish..."

Tenzin let the hammock fall still. "What?"

"Decide what you want from him, Tenzin. This indecision isn't like you."

No, it wasn't.

Then again, for the first time in many, many years, Tenzin was unsure of what she wanted.

BEN SIPPED a rum cocktail and watched the ocean as the sun set over the Atlantic Ocean. The villa he'd rented in Quebradillas sat on the hillside with the ocean stretched out before it. Hard waves crashed as the tide came in, and he could see surfers riding in the distance. The ocean glowed deep blue, purple, and orange as the sky changed from one vivid hue to another.

The house was a Mediterranean style painted white and trimmed in bright blue. High walls blocked it from the road, and spacious balconies captured the warmth of the sun. Unlike the narrow, sheltered house in San Juan, it was *not* vampire friendly. Long windows channeled the sea breeze through the house, keeping it cool and bright through the day. Only the back rooms would be sheltered for Tenzin.

Which was fine. If he had to dig through caves looking for pirate treasure, Tenzin could suffer through a breezy, sunlit, oceanfront house.

He took a deep breath and another sip of rum as the sun slipped below the horizon. He'd spent the day gathering supplies in the village and meeting their contact for the house. The bottle of local rum had been a welcome gift he was happy to mix with lime and orange juice from the trees on the patio.

Sun. Rum. And an ocean view?

Okay, maybe his abuela didn't have it all wrong. Puerto Rico was feeling pretty much like a paradise that night.

He had an appointment with Inés, the sister of the cacique, the next evening. Hopefully Tenzin would make it by then. If not, Ben would be going on his own. Since his introduction came via Novia, he didn't need Tenzin to be there. In fact, they'd both decided to downplay her presence unless someone asked.

Everyone in the vampire world knew Ben and Tenzin worked together. Ben was more than happy to let everyone assume this job was for a customer of his or his uncle's, *not* one of Tenzin's own wild schemes.

He let the warm breeze wash over his skin. He'd sat in the sun for most of the afternoon in nothing but a pair of khaki shorts. His skin was noticeably browner. His hair was tangled. He'd trimmed his beard short before they arrived, and his curly hair was pulled back in a short ponytail at the base of his neck.

Ben glanced at his reflection in the mirror and smiled a little. He looked like a beach bum. Yeah, he could get used to that.

He made himself another drink and turned the music down so he could hear the surf crashing. Then he lay on a chaise on the patio and drifted to sleep.

Hours later, she woke him by lifting his arm so she could settle underneath it.

"You smell like sun."

The corner of his mouth tilted up. "Gio says that sometimes. What does the sun smell like?"

She turned her face into his chest and inhaled deeply. Ben could feel her lips against his chest. His heart pounded, but by silent agreement, they both ignored it.

"Salt and a little sweat," she said. "Limes and sugar."

"Our rental agent gave us a bottle of rum."

She wrinkled her nose. "I don't like rum."

"Good. More for me."

She glanced up at him. "You're feeling very satisfied right now, aren't you?"

I could be more satisfied.

"Yes," Ben said. "Beautiful house. Beautiful island. A bottle of rum all to myself."

"And gold." Tenzin grinned up at him, her fangs like twin daggers in her mouth.

Was it wrong for Ben to find that adorable? There was probably something wrong with him. Whatever. He squeezed his arm around her shoulders. "Yes, and gold. How could I forget the gold?"

"I looked through your notes from the old man and the priest's letters. You're right. I think Brother Tomás is the key. And if you're right about what his letters are insinuating, we have the one thing we didn't have before to start this hunt."

Ben said, "We have a starting point."

"Exactly." She tapped her finger along the inside of his wrist. "Do you think it'll be all in Spanish coin, or do you think there'll be some bullion?"

"From what I read about Enríquez's career, it's likely to be a combination of lots of things. He stole mostly from the British. There might be more silver than gold."

"That would be disappointing."

"But still profitable."

"But not gold."

"Don't worry." He patted her shoulder. "I'm sure there will be gold."

"There better be." She snuggled down next to him. "What self-respecting pirate doesn't have boxes of gold sitting around? Cheng has dozens of them."

"*Dozens* of boxes of gold?"

"Yes."

Ben shook his head. "Suddenly your relationship with that

pirate makes so much more sense."

"I do like gold," she whispered. "But he's also—"

Ben clamped a hand over her mouth. "I don't want to know."

She peeled it away. "I was going to say a useful ally."

"Oh. Yeah, I guess he would be." Ben closed his eyes and focused on the waves.

Tenzin said, "You've turned cross."

"I'm out of rum."

"So get more rum."

He curled his lip. "I'd have to move."

Tenzin sighed and sat up. "Fine."

He cracked an eye open. "What?"

"I'll make you a drink." She stood and reached for his glass. "Don't get used to this."

"I wouldn't dream of it."

"What is the drink? Just rum?"

"One orange and one lime, both juiced. Then a shot of rum and a little bit of soda."

She scrunched up her face. "That does sound good."

"It's excellent."

"Except for the rum."

"The rum is the point!"

"Relax." She patted his head. "I'll make you one. And then we'll talk about Inés."

Ben sighed. "Great. Just what I wanted to do before bed, talk about vampires who'll probably end up trying to kill us in the next couple of weeks."

"Don't be a pessimist," Tenzin said. "She might just try to steal from us."

"Excellent point. I don't know why I was feeling so down."

"You've got to stop being so negative, Benjamin." Tenzin walked into the kitchen. "It's not good for your health."

9

They drove over narrow mountain roads the next night, Tenzin sitting uncomfortably in the passenger's seat. They'd decided to keep things as low-key as possible. Ben was driving. Ben was talking. Tenzin would only speak if she had to, and she was going to downplay her role to that of babysitter. It wouldn't benefit them for anyone in Puerto Rico to get too curious.

The Jeep crossed a makeshift bridge, and they lurched to the left.

Tenzin gripped the frame with both hands. "Are you sure you know how to drive this?"

"There's no secret, Tiny. I can drive it."

"Fine." She muttered under her breath, "Four."

Ben couldn't help but smile. "Is that the number of exits you can currently see in the car?"

"Maybe."

"Oh ye of little faith." He reached across and patted her head. "I'll get us there."

"In the mountains. In the dark." She curled her lip. "I hate cars."

"You hate being confined."

"This is true."

They drove past the ruins of a green-and-white house that was half buried by a mudslide, past the roar of a distant waterfall, and down into a small dip in the hills where the town of Lares lit up the night with scattered points of light. Anytime they slowed, the sound of generators could be heard in the distance.

Through the town and back into the hills, Ben drove, looking for the signs he'd been given—a road cutting between two hills, marked with a bright yellow sign and a single name: Valeria.

"You passed it." It was the first thing Tenzin had said in miles.

"I saw it, I saw it." He pulled over to the side of the road, grateful for the three-quarters-full moon. The foliage was dense, thick bamboo and trees lining the sides of the road. He waited, but no one was coming toward them.

Ben turned around and took the road hidden by the trees. It climbed swiftly, twisting back between folded hills and exposed rock formations. They dipped down into a small valley, crossing a flowing stream before they went up and dirt gave way to cobblestones.

"Do you see it?" Tenzin asked.

"I see lights."

"It's beautiful." She leaned out of the Jeep. "Very beautiful."

It was unusual for anything to strike Tenzin as beautiful. She had seen a lot and wasn't usually impressed. The fact that the home of Los Tres impressed her made Ben even more curious.

She was just about to climb out of the window when Ben grabbed the back of her shirt. "Uh-uh."

"I want to fly up and—"

"Another time," he said. "For now we go up to the front door and knock."

She crossed her arms and slumped in her seat. "You're no fun."

"I know. Tonight I'm all business."

"Boo."

"Which will hopefully let us look for your gold a little faster."

She smiled. "Yay."

"So no spying before we actually meet the VICs."

A guard waved Ben toward a dark parking area. He swung left and fitted the Jeep between a Jaguar and a lifted pickup truck with more chrome than anyone needed.

"Remember," he said quietly, conscious that the guard was likely immortal. "Let me talk for now."

"Got it."

"And no violence unless we absolutely, positively cannot avoid it."

"Got it."

Ben narrowed his eyes at her accommodating tone of voice. "Did you bring any weapons?"

She smiled. "Not that they'll be able to find."

She opened her doors and exited the vehicle before Ben could say another word.

Dammit, Tenzin!

Ben left the car and walked toward the flashlight that had guided them to their parking spot. Tenzin fell into step beside him.

"Señor Vecchio?" a voice asked.

Ben answered in English, keen to mark himself as an American. And a guest. "I'm Ben Vecchio. I have an appointment with Inés at eleven o'clock."

The flashlight turned to Tenzin, and the voice switched to English. "Does she know you have a guest?"

"This is my partner. We always travel together. I expect Inés knows that."

"Very well." The guard's clipped accent said Spain, not Puerto Rico. "Follow me, please."

They followed the guard up a curved staircase of intricately patterned tile and white stucco. They reached the top only to find another level with a fire pit and a wide balcony overlooking the hills. Their guard nodded to another standing near the fire where humans and vampires laughed and passed a bottle of red wine.

Or blood-wine. It could have been either.

They walked up another staircase. Then another. Ben was glad he hadn't been slacking off on his morning runs. There was nothing worse than panting when you met immortals. It immediately made him feel like prey.

At the top of the stairs was nothing less than a mansion. White stucco and mirrored glass protruded from the side of a mountain, surrounded by palms and banana trees. Flowerbeds and fountains surrounded the property. The main house was flanked by several outbuildings and smaller houses, most of which were built into the hill they'd just walked up. The architecture nestled into the verdant hill, both foreign and organic.

Ben and Tenzin walked through the front gates and into a party-like atmosphere with twinkling lights, music, and the smell of food and fire. Humans and vampires mingled, but Ben paid no attention to the curious stares. He followed their guard through the interior garden and past two wide wooden doors carved with what Ben recognized as traditional Taíno iconography.

The doors opened, and the delicate strains of a cello poured out of the house. A four-story open-air entryway dominated the space. Though windows were plentiful in the front of the house, the back of the structure was made entirely of glass.

Ben glanced at Tenzin to see her reaction. The small vampire's face had lit up. This house was made for wind vampires. Ben could see several floating on the far side of the room, perched in alcoves that overlooked a sunken living room where the music played.

The back windows exposed the carved face of the mountain where ferns and lush greenery fell down a sheer cliff and a waterfall dropped into a sunken pool.

The pool was occupied by more partygoers. Torches lined the pathways, and a stone bridge crossed from the back of the house, over the pool, and led into the heart of the mountain.

"There," Ben murmured.

"I see it."

Their guard led them past the music in the living room and to the left. An open-plan kitchen dominated that side of the house. A chef in a white coat barked orders at several sous chefs who were plating food before putting it on trays carried by uniformed servers.

Behind the kitchen was a formal dining room separate from the rest of the house. The guard motioned them to one end of the dining room where two place settings faced another one on the opposite end of the long dining table.

The guard left them, closing the door and cutting off the noise from the rest of the house.

Ben turned to Tenzin. "Should I be worried that they led the human into the dining room?"

Tenzin smiled. "Judging from all the humans out there having a good time, I think you're safe."

"This is an amazing house."

"It was designed for vampires."

"Even with all that glass? I was thinking about that. There'll be no shelter at all during the day."

"I imagine many spend the day within the mountain. And there are rooms built below us. There will be underground rivers in this area too."

"There are." A door opened and an elegant immortal woman wearing a flowing yellow dress stepped into the dining room.

A tall man with sandy-brown hair and a neat beard followed her. The man was a vampire and carried himself with a distinct military bearing. The woman was gracious, but her eyes saw everything.

She walked toward them and held out her hand. "I am Inés, sister of the cacique. Welcome to Hacienda Valeria. My companion is Vasco; he is the nitayno of this island."

Ben and Tenzin stood. "Thank you both for your welcome." Ben had heard the word *nitayno* before. Who had said it? Novia. She said a nitayno was something like a general.

"His general is Spanish. A water vampire by the name of Vasco. He's a bit friendlier than most of that group."

Vasco didn't appear very friendly, but both he and Inés shook hands with them, which surprised Ben. Many older vampires preferred not to allow contact with vampires they didn't know.

"Let's move all this, shall we?" Inés motioned to the place settings as Vasco stationed himself near the door. "They set this for a formal dinner, but there is no need for it. Have you eaten this evening?"

"We'd be honored to join you for a meal," Ben said before Tenzin could say they'd eaten at sundown.

"Very well." She clapped her hands, and two human servants entered the room. She directed them to move the place settings together and bring in the meal.

"I thought we'd have fish," Inés said. "I eat light meals when we have a party here."

So she could drink blood at her leisure.

"Of course," Ben said. "Fish sounds wonderful."

The vampire was short but regal. Her skin was the color of iron-rich earth, and Ben had the distinct feeling that soil was the place from where she drew her elemental strength too. Her hair was long, straight, and very black. Inés appeared to be in her midthirties, but her dark eyes and manner told Ben she was far, far older. She had high cheekbones and a wide, generous mouth. Ben wouldn't call her beautiful, but her looks were arresting and he had trouble looking away.

"You're American," Inés said. "Your companion is not."

"She is not."

"I received your letter of introduction two weeks ago," Inés said. "Novia speaks highly of you and your partner." Inés glanced at Tenzin, who was remaining silent as they sat at the table. "I confess, she is not what I had expected."

Tenzin spoke quietly. "I'm usually not."

Inés smiled. "I understand you are here for work."

"I am." Ben started on the carefully rehearsed story. "As I'm sure you're aware, my uncle, Giovanni Vecchio, specializes in retrieval of items that are literary in nature. Books. Correspondence. Things of interest to a specific and very private clientele."

"I understand." Inés paused as a servant set a bottle in front of her. "White wine?"

"Thank you." Ben pushed his glass forward. "While my uncle focuses on the literary side of the business, I assist him when a client is looking for something slightly different."

"Like treasure?"

Ben smiled. "Objects can be valuable for all sorts of reasons. Sometimes sentiment is enough."

"Is sentiment the drive for this particular job?"

Ben put a hand over his heart. "I can't say. As you can imagine, discretion is very important to us, as is client information."

Inés seemed to consider whether or not she'd let Ben get away with it. A slightly amused glint in her eye told him he'd been successful. "And how do I know you're not here to steal from me, Mr. Vecchio? Your reputation is somewhat... inconsistent at the moment."

Because no matter how many times he'd quashed rumors that he'd been behind the theft of a valuable painting last year, they kept slipping out.

To be fair, he had been behind that theft.

"If you know my uncle's reputation, then you know he would not vouch for my traveling so far from his aegis without confidence that I was working for our client and that our client had a claim on the property. I give you my word that any disputes arising from our search will be brought before Los Tres." He felt someone crushing his toe beneath the table. He glanced at Tenzin and offered her a mild smile in return.

"Is that so?" Inés said. "And you are confident in your client's claim?"

"My uncle has checked this person's background very thoroughly."

Because it was Tenzin. Tenzin was their client, and Giovanni knew as much about Tenzin's past as anyone did.

Which meant he knew hardly anything at all.

"Hmm." Inés leaned an elbow on the table. "I will forward your request to my brother. He will likely say yes, simply because he's very confident there are no secrets hidden from him on his island."

"His?" Tenzin asked quietly. "Or theirs?"

Inés turned to her. "His. My brother shares his power from

92

a sense of goodness and fairness for the immortals of this island. But make no mistake: we were here first."

Tenzin nodded and said nothing more.

"I will also warn you, charming young Vecchio, that this sounds to me very much like a treasure hunt."

"Isn't every search for something a little like a treasure hunt?" Ben asked.

Inés raised an eyebrow. "You are not the first treasure hunters to search this island." She smiled indulgently. "And I very much doubt you'll be the last. But I admit I am intrigued by your connections and your unknown client." She took a sip of wine. "Come back in two nights. I will send your request to my brother. If he approves, he will give you an audience and you'll be permitted to meet Los Tres."

"Thank you, Inés."

"Now, enjoy your dinner." She rose and Vasco moved to pull out her chair. "I'm afraid I cannot finish with you. I have another meeting with Vasco tonight."

"Thank you both for meeting us." Ben and Tenzin both rose with her.

"Please stay." She pointed to the food. "Eat. Drink. Join the party outside; we have many human guests tonight. You'll be most welcome. Just don't go into the mountain." Her smile turned cold. "Not if you want to live."

TENZIN TURNED to Ben when they reached the car. "I told you it would have been better to come right after the hurricane." Yanking open the door, she threw herself in the car and slammed the Jeep door shut. "There would have been chaos. Confusion. We could have taken advantage of all that to search quickly, retrieve the treasure, and go. Now we have to meet with some self-important vampire lord who may *give us permission* to search?" She exhaled a derisive snort. "Let him try to stop me."

She devolved into a long string of muttered curses in a language Ben didn't recognize.

Ben started the car and pulled out, waving at the guard who'd escorted them down from the house. "Calm down, Tiny."

"You calm down. It's your fault we weren't here months ago."

He gritted his teeth to contain the sharp retort that wanted to explode. "And if we had been here months ago, we wouldn't have the letters from the Dominican or the governor. There would be no reference point for your precious map. We wouldn't have a comfortable house to stay in. And we still wouldn't have escaped their notice. Don't fool yourself. This island has more vampires than I expected."

It was true. The party at the top of the hill had been chock-full of them, and Ben expected even more lived in the mountain where they'd been forbidden to go.

"You're right." Tenzin looked at him. "Why?"

"Why what?"

"Why are there so many vampires? It doesn't make sense. The island is small. Tourism is down right now. Why are there so many vampires here?"

"Maybe because of the hurricane," Ben said. "Just like you were talking about. Taking advantage of chaos to hunt."

"True. Natural disasters are useful that way."

Ben tried not to shudder at the cold calculation in her voice.

She is a predator.

She is a predator.

She is a very good predator.

"Los Tres is rich, organized, and clearly has pretty wide control of the island." Ben frowned. "So why is the human government such a mess?"

"Because they want it to be," Tenzin said. "Corrupt human governments leave room for vampires to operate unseen in the corners. Think about how black markets grow. A need is recognized. No one in the human world can meet that need. A new source—an illegitimate one accountable to no one—rises. Vampires have worked this way for thousands of years all over the world. They prefer it that way. It makes governments easier to manipulate."

"So modern-day rule of law—"

"Super inconvenient to the way we like to work." Tenzin leaned back in the seat as Ben drove them down the mountain. "We like shadows and secret corners. Corrupt people we can manipulate. People who are afraid of exposure. Afraid of us."

The car fell silent as Ben concentrated on the twists and turns through the mountain. The air was muggy inside the Jeep. Tenzin opened her window and leaned out.

Then... she flew out.

"Tenzin!" Ben slammed on the brakes, but it was useless.

She was gone.

TENZIN FLEW BACK to the party, coaxing the air around into a snug bubble that hid her sound and her scent. She flew high, over the road and through the trees, slipping among the deep shadows of the nearly full moon.

She could see the lights of the party in the distance.

Tenzin flew over the house and back among the lush greenery that grew out of the cliffside overlooking the glittering house. She was cloaked in black, teasing the air to bring her hints of voices and sounds. She was looking for...

What was she looking for?

A feeling. An instinct. The thing that was hidden.

She waited in the stillness for hours as the party ran late and the humans became more and more inebriated. One by one, they were picked off by the predators mingling among them. Two pretty boys followed Inés down the stairs. A full-figured beauty lounged openly near the pool with one vampire attached to her wrist and another to her ankle. Her moans of pleasure went unnoticed by those around her. They were too busy indulging their own appetites.

Tenzin waited and watched.

She felt a presence on the cliff above her. A leaf moved. A rock nudged out of place.

Tenzin launched herself away from the cliffs and spun up, into the darkness. Her clothes whipped against her skin. She rolled into a ball and hid herself under an overhanging fern.

The intruder wasn't as silent as Tenzin. She wasn't as powerful. The wind didn't love her as much.

But it did obey her. A breeze flipped up the fern covering Tenzin's alcove, exposing her to the moonlight.

Tenzin moved again, skipping across the face of the cliff, her toes barely touching the face of the waterfall that poured into the pool below.

She danced up the waterfall and over the crest of the mountain, waiting to see if the other vampire would follow.

She did. Making no attempt to conceal herself, the other wind walker rose in the mist of the waterfall until she was floating across from Tenzin, her spiraling curls misted by the crashing water. Her eyes met Tenzin's.

It was the beautiful woman from the restaurant in San Juan, but all pretense of humanity was gone now. Her rich brown skin was flushed from feeding. Her full lips curled up, revealing glistening fangs.

Tenzin didn't take her eyes off the vampire. She was beautiful and deadly, not at all a combination Tenzin disapproved of.

The wind caressed the flowing dress that wrapped around her body.

Tenzin cocked her head, watching the woman in silence. Would she speak? Who was she? She was powerful; that much Tenzin was certain of. Not as powerful as Tenzin, but the other vampire had no way of knowing that unless she knew who Tenzin was.

They floated in the humid breeze, eye to eye. Neither spoke. Neither moved an inch.

What are you doing here?

Who are you?

Were you watching us in San Juan?

The woman cocked her head as if tuned to a silent chime. She offered Tenzin one last glance before she dove over the crest of the waterfall, flying straight down the cliff face.

Tenzin peeked over the edge, cloaking herself in darkness again.

The vampire alighted on the stone bridge leading into the mountain. Those on the path coming toward her stepped out of the way, one offering a slight bow in her direction.

The wind vampire disappeared beneath the mountain as Tenzin floated into the night.

Who are you?

10

Ben strolled through the plaza in front of the Cathedral of Saint Philip the Apostle in the heart of old Arecibo. A search through city records had proven that the previous church, destroyed by an earthquake in 1787, had been the last posting of the young Dominican who'd taken care of Miguel Enríquez.

Brother Tomás had been born in a small mountain town south of Arecibo and had requested a move back to the city where he'd taken orders just weeks after Enríquez had died. There were mentions in the records of Brother Tomás for a few months, and then...

Nothing.

Ben stopped to grab a coffee at a small stand. The rainbow hues of shops and buildings surrounding the plaza were alive in the bright midday sun. Traffic was slow in the old town, but shops were open and restaurants set out chairs and tables, hoping to catch a lunchtime crowd.

The treasure map Tenzin was obsessed with had shown a city near the junction of three rivers and a church, but one without names. If they were right, then the entrance to the cave system marked on the map was half a day's ride southwest of the cathedral Ben was watching. Half a day's ride was roughly twenty kilometers in the mountainous region they were working in.

From there, they had to look for a variety of karst formations, sinkholes that—with any luck—hadn't filled in, and ruins that hopefully hadn't been disturbed. A large outcropping in the distinct shape of a horse's head. A waterfall. And caves.

And caves were abundant in that part of the island.

Luck and hope. Ben finished off his coffee and glared at the cathedral. *This is why I don't like treasure maps.*

If everything went according to plan, they would gain formal permission from Los Tres the next evening. Then they could start exploring, which would go faster with a wind vampire in the lead, and *if* they found the entrance to the cave system, it could be days before they located the treasure with a map drawn by an amateur. *If* the treasure was still there. And *if* none of the caverns had collapsed.

Tenzin owed him one. Big.

His phone rang. He glanced at the screen, pleased to see Chloe's name. "Hey, gorgeous."

"See, is it too much to ask that all phone calls start out this way?"

"Have you forwarded this request to Gavin?"

"No. He'd just take it as a challenge to start conversations with something far more lewd."

"Vampires."

"I know, right?"

"What's up?"

"I was just curious what the status of Operation *Aaargh* was."

"Operation Aaargh?"

"What else do you call a pirate treasure hunt?"

Well, she had him there.

Ben smiled. "We're supposed to meet with the VICs tomorrow night. Tenzin went rogue after our meeting the other night, but apparently she didn't piss off anyone important because we got an audience with the big boss. Once we have formal permission to start hunting, we can get started. Thanks for arranging the shipping on that equipment, by the way."

"No problem. I just checked. Everything should be at the location you gave me in two days. I didn't even know you had that storage unit."

"Yeah..." Most people didn't know about that storage unit. "It's useful for stuff like that."

"Do those metal detectors really work on gold?"

"Yes. They really do."

"Are you going to wear big goofy headphones while you're using them? Can you send pictures?"

"Probably, and not on your life." He paused while a father and son passed, unable to tear his eyes away from the pair. The little boy was around ten, close to the same age Ben had been the last time he'd seen his father. But unlike Ben and his father, the shared affection between the two was obvious.

The father was gesturing as he talked, clearly passionate about whatever the topic was. The little boy was disagreeing with him, but doing so in a playful way that told Ben he felt safe with his father. Safe to argue. Safe to disagree. They laughed at one point, and the father mussed the boy's curly dark hair.

"Ben?"

"Do you ever miss your parents?" he asked abruptly.

"Wow. Okay, wasn't expecting that question."

Chloe had the opposite of Ben's problem. While his parents neglected him, Chloe's had tried to map out every inch of their daughter's life to their own specifications. The result in both cases was similar. Ben hadn't spoken to his parents since Giovanni had adopted him. Chloe hadn't spoken to hers since they'd disowned her.

"Yeah," she said. "I do."

"Why?"

"Um..." She took a deep breath. "Because they were still my home. Even though it was suffocating, it was still what was familiar. And safe. I know it's hard to understand with them being so controlling, but—"

"No, I get it. I get it completely."

There was silence on the other end of the line. Ben could hear traffic in the background, cars passing and a taxi honking its horn.

"Sometimes," she continued, "I don't think I actually miss them. I miss the idea of them. Or the idea of what parents are supposed to be. Loving. Supportive. Proud."

Present. Sober. Nonviolent.

"That make sense," he said. "You miss the parents you were supposed to have."

"I don't know," she said. "What's does 'supposed to' even mean? Lots of people have shit families. Lots of people have great families. These days it's probably fifty-fifty. I guess I miss what I saw you had with your aunt and uncle. They loved you and you loved them, even if you didn't say it. You didn't always get along. But you really loved each other."

"Yeah." Ben's heart warmed. "You didn't think your parents loved you?"

"I think they are very self-centered and saw me as a reflection of themselves, which means they really didn't see me at all." She laughed a little. "Well, this got way deeper than I planned on. I was just going to tease you about treasure hunting."

"Yeah. And I was just going to tease you about Gavin."

"Hah." She cleared her throat. "So, speaking of Gavin— actually, speaking of your aunt and uncle—"

"Please don't tell me it's Richard again."

"No, as Gavin would say, that's well in hand. But there's another..." Silence on the line. "You know what? Never mind. It's not important."

Ben frowned. "What's going on?"

"I just realized it's kind of Gavin's business and not mine, and I really don't want to break confidence. You know what I mean?"

"Uh-huh." He did know what she meant. And yet he was suspicious. If he wasn't feeling awkward around Giovanni, he'd call his uncle himself.

"Let me know how the meeting goes," Chloe said. "I better get off the phone. Gotta catch a train."

"Stay warm."

"Yeah, yeah, yeah." He could practically hear her teeth chattering. "Jump in a lake, tropical boy. I saw that rum cocktail on Instagram."

Ben smiled. Chloe was only one of a dozen people who followed his private account on the social network. It was the only one he allowed himself, and he half did it for security reasons. If he disappeared somewhere weird, it was handy to leave visual cues for a search party.

"I'll call you tomorrow," he said. "Hi to everyone."

"Hi to Tenzin. Tell her I'm rearranging all her swords."

"Between dating a vampire and messing with her, I'm wondering if you have a secret death wish."

Tenzin flew over the forested hills south of Arecibo the next night, following the rough picture of the map she carried in her mind. She flew high and low, dipping over green fields and rising over hills. The land was dark; electric lights were sparse. The wind sang with verdant promise, rich with water, salt, and the scent of growing things. In the distance, she caught the smell of gasoline burning, but the strongest scent was that of rebirth.

Puerto Rico might not have been a rich island to much of the human world, but Tenzin saw past the petty measures of humans. The land was rich with good soil and plentiful water. And though she sensed human pollutants in the water and the soil, the earth was resilient. This island could be a paradise again.

Humans. Why couldn't they leave places alone?

She dipped down to follow a river, dragging her fingers through the stream as she caught her reflection. Wild hair. Wild woman. What did the humans see when they saw her? A young woman from their limited perspective. Ancient eyes in an unchanging face. She'd braided colorful threads in her hair because she'd been missing home.

I need to leave for the mountains. Soon.

Being on an island rebounding from a great storm reminded her that she'd been in the city too long. She needed wild things and open skies. She needed Tibet. Ben would just have to do without her for a while. She'd finish this job and then she'd tell him. No use putting up with his fussing before it was necessary.

How long had she flown? She flipped head over feet, twisting over the forest and upward into the warm night air. The cloth of her pants twisted around her ankle, irritating her. With a shimmy, she discarded the human clothes. Encouraged by the wind's embrace, she stripped her shirt off and allowed her element to carry her.

Tenzin let out a sigh of relief as the wind caressed her skin.

She could feel more now, sense the expanse around her, the dimensions of the earth and the sky. She closed her eyes and felt the contours of the land, the filtered moonlight through the trees. The drop of stone where the earth had closed in on itself long ago.

There.

Tenzin smiled and flew lower. The sinkhole on the map fell into the forest just past the rocky outcropping in the shape of a horse's head. She hovered over the sinkhole for a few moments before she allowed herself to drift down. She could hear animals in the brush fleeing from her. Birds and small rodents scattered.

All could sense the presence of a predator.

Tenzin landed barefoot in the center of the sinkhole. It was an old formation, its walls covered in lush green ferns and bromeliads. Tree roots clung to the rock as life reached upward to the sun.

She turned in place, inspecting the margins of this remote area. She could sense no human presence. There was no scent or visible trace of them.

Excellent.

Water fell somewhere nearby. She floated over the land, searching for it.

There.

The waterfall was underground, the stream tipping over the edge of the rocks and following a narrow opening along the edge of the sinkhole. Moss and algae grew along the channel. Tenzin lay on the ground and ducked her head into the moss-lined hole.

The darkness was immense.

Perhaps during the day some trickle of light reached the chasm, but at night even a full moon would have been obscured. Nevertheless, Tenzin could feel the expanse below her. Under the surface, a honeycomb of caves twisted, each sending a slightly different scent to her nose. In that direction, water. In another direction, the smell of rotten eggs. In another, bat guano. And mixing in among those smells, the chalky smell of old bones that told Tenzin a predator had once used a cave for shelter. Judging from the age and smell, she guessed it had been a vampire.

Interesting. Possibly problematic. Then again, not all immortals were interested in gold. Some barely gave it notice.

Tenzin wondered if there were stories about a creature in these caves. She'd be sure to ask Ben if he'd studied the local folklore.

Despite her necessary caution, she felt the fluttering thrill of discovery in her gut. She'd found the cave. It was here. She had found the entrance and she had a map.

Within days, a new cache of gold could be hers.

But for now—she flew up and into the night sky, twisting in the sea breeze—she could wait.

BEN WAS SITTING IN A LOUNGER, reading a book under a lamp, when he heard her land. "Hey," he said. "Did you have any luck?"

"Yes. I did."

He glanced up, then down, then up again when he saw her. His eyes went wide.

Naked. So much naked. It wasn't the first time he'd seen her naked, but it had been a few years.

Tenzin's body was slim and anything but boyish. Her hips were wide and her waist narrow, her breasts small and round. She had tattoos, one thing he'd never forgotten. They were fine lines and crosses between and beneath her breasts, running down the center of her body and splitting at her navel to frame a soft belly.

He cleared his throat and forced his eyes away. "Uh... did something happen to your clothes?"

"Oh." She sounded surprised. "I couldn't find them."

"And you lost them how?"

"Well... Honestly, I didn't look. I forgot. They were annoying me and the air was nice and warm. Why are you being puritanical?"

"You mean why am I not staring at you while you're naked?" His heart pounded. He wanted to look. Oh, he wanted to look. Not that he needed to. Some things you didn't forget. Ever. "Uh, just trying to be polite."

"You're ridiculous." She walked to the edge of the balcony. "Being naked is the natural state of humanity unless our bodies need shelter from the elements. Do you think the indigenous people on this island wore clothes?"

Ben kept his eyes on his book. "Anthropologically, I'm sure you're right. Can you put some clothes on anyway?"

She walked over to stand right in front of him. He couldn't avoid her. Her feet were muddy. Her knees covered in dirt. She looked like she'd been crawling around on the ground.

"Tenzin, what—?"

"Why?"

"Why what?"

"Why should I put on clothes? I'm comfortable like this."

He looked. He couldn't help it. His eyes ran from her feet, up her legs, over her pubis and belly, her breasts, her arching neck, until he was looking into her eyes. He felt an unexpected spike of anger twisting within the furious desire her body ignited.

He hadn't taken a lover since the last disastrous woman who'd lied to him. He'd been a monk. Drinking less. Pouring himself into work. Focused only on rebuilding his reputation for himself and his family.

"You want to do this right now?" he asked in a hoarse voice. "Really?"

She said nothing, her grey eyes staring into his.

"Put some fucking clothes on, Tenzin. Because I'm a man and you are attractive, and if we're going to work together, you need to wear some fucking clothes so I can concentrate."

She held his gaze for another beat, then she walked past him into the house and shut the door without a word.

Ben closed his eyes and let his head fall back against the lounger.

Why are you doing this to yourself?

What are you doing?

What do you think is going to happen?

A few moments later, she walked back out to the balcony, clad in a black caftan that covered her body but hinted at the form beneath every time the breeze blew.

Fuck me. It's almost worse.

"Okay, you found what? The horse head?"

She pulled up a footrest and perched next to him. "I found the horse head. I found the sinkhole. I found the cavern."

Ben blinked. "Holy shit."

"Yes. The good news is, I didn't sense any human activity around the caverns. No signs or scents of them. The nearest road is quite a ways away."

"Which means you'll probably have to fly me in."

"Maybe. But there appeared to be hiking trails."

"And the bad news?"

"There's been a vampire there. Not recently, but I can smell her kills."

"Her?"

Tenzin shrugged. "Or him. I couldn't tell. The energy was too old."

"So there's been a vampire. How deep into the caves?" Ben calculated the odds of another vampire finding the exact same cave system by coincidence. Honestly, it wasn't that far-fetched. How many isolated cave systems could there be on an island?

"I couldn't tell how deep the other vampire went; I didn't go into the caverns themselves. There's no light, which means I couldn't pick anything up. We'll have to go with your equipment."

"Wind vampire?" he asked. "You said it was pretty inaccessible."

"Maybe? It's hard to tell. An earth vampire could theoretically get into the area, though the cave systems are limestone, which isn't easy to manipulate without damaging it. Just to give you an idea, Lucien can work with limestone; Carwyn cannot. That's the age we're talking about with earth vampires."

"So not very likely to be earth. And Macuya is earth, right?"

"Yes. So water or wind vampire would be my guess. Either are equally likely. There is a lot of water on this island. The underground rivers here are far more extensive than the humans realize."

"So there's been a vampire in the cave, but it might just be a useful hiding space. How extensive was the scent?"

She smiled. "You're very bright. Not extensive at all. I only sensed the vampire in one direction, which meant it hadn't really explored. We won't know more until we get down there with the map and some equipment."

"And we don't want to do that until we get formal permission." He tapped his chin. "Tomorrow night."

"I'm telling you, Benjamin, these self-important immortals aren't going to stop me from finding this treasure," she muttered. "I don't care what they say tomorrow. I'm searching that cave."

"Calm down," he said. "I'm sure it'll be fine. You're right. They are self-important. You think they believe there's anything about this island they don't know? They'll let us search because to deny it would be as good as admitting there are secrets here they don't know the answer to."

"Good point."

"So chill out, let me do the fancy talking tomorrow, and we'll keep everyone happy for as long as we can."

11

The house in the hills was lit with torches the next night when Ben and Tenzin arrived. There were no humans there, but dozens of vampires lounged around the patios and perched along the cliff face. Water vampires floated in the pool and stood under the waterfall. All watched silently as Ben and Tenzin walked across the grounds.

Ben kept an eye on Tenzin, mindful of her discomfort at being underground. She was a creature of air. She wasn't meant to be confined. She'd switched from her loose pants and dresses that night to slim black leggings and a fitted tank top. She looked like danger in a compact package.

Good. It was the impression Ben was hoping she'd go for.

Ben, on the other hand, decided to present himself as the academic. Let the vampires be reminded of his uncle, the notorious fire vampire. He wore a white linen shirt and black pants. He wasn't wearing a tie, but he'd donned a summer-weight black jacket with turned-up cuffs, and his hair was slightly mussed. He'd been tempted to wear glasses, but he didn't want to push it.

Inés eyed them with some amusement when she met them at the front door. But she led them wordlessly across the grounds and back to the mountain. They crossed the footbridge and walked into a large tunnel lit with more torches. Music echoed down the hallway, the beat thumping with a syncopated rhythm Ben associated with the Caribbean. Drums echoed down the hallway.

"Address the cacique as Cacique Macuya. His two queens are Cacica Valeria and Cacica Jadzia. You may address them as such. All three are fluent in English and Spanish. I will introduce you in Spanish since that is the language of the court, but you may feel free to speak English as you are visiting Americans."

"I'm not American," Tenzin said.

"That may be, but the caciques do not speak any Asian languages," Inés said. "You may use English."

"We'll use English," Ben said swiftly. "Thank you, Inés."

They entered a wide cavern with painted walls and arching bridges that looked half natural, half man-made.

"Vampire hewn," Tenzin muttered.

An earth vampire had created or expanded a natural cavern to accommodate what looked very much like a royal court. Drummers and dancers performed in front of three raised thrones on a dais, the dancers twisting themselves into configurations that left no question they were vampire. The air smelled of flowers and smoke.

The center throne was occupied by a man of medium height with dark brown skin similar to Inés and an elaborate feathered headdress of blue and gold. Gold links were around his neck and wrists. More gold decorated his ankles. He was bare-chested and muscular.

To his right was an elegant woman with pale white skin and reddish-brown hair pulled into a braid that hung over her shoulder. Instead of feathers, flowers decorated her hair, and her dress was a simple sheath in deep blood red.

To the man's left was another woman, a very familiar woman.

"Do you see?" Tenzin muttered in Chinese.

"Mm-hmm."

The woman to the left of the cacique was the same woman they'd seen in San Juan, watching the musicians in the restaurant. Dark unconstrained curls formed a natural crown on her head, complemented by flashes of gold around her face. She wore a strapless dress of vivid aquamarine blue that clung to her body.

All three of the figures on the dais were regal in completely different ways. All watched the dancers in front of them while other vampires hovered around them, whispering in their ears or serving them in some way.

A king and two queens.

Los Tres.

Inés had paused at the entrance to the cavern to give Ben and Tenzin a moment to take in the grandeur, but after a few beats she walked forward and they followed. As she approached, dancers bowed and fell back. Drummers turned and lowered their volume. The mood in the cavern shifted from excitement and celebration to focused curiosity as Ben and Tenzin stepped forward.

Ben mentally took stock as they walked through the crowd.

Fifty vampires at least. At least ten hovered overhead.

One known exit. Unknown caverns and tunnels leading farther into the heart of the mountain.

Weapons surrounded the room. Curved blades and stone-tipped staffs carried by no less than a dozen guards.

Basically, if Los Tres decided to kill them, Ben was shit out of luck, even with Tenzin at his side.

They walked through the middle of the crowd, the room growing more and more quiet as they approached the thrones. Tenzin whistled three notes, the familiar opening to a Hollywood Western showdown.

Ben glared at her.

"What?" She shrugged. "Tension."

"My brother, Macuya." Inés stopped in front of the thrones. "Valeria and Jadzia. I present to you Ben Vecchio, nephew of Giovanni Vecchio, scribe of Rome and son of Kato. Accompanying him is his partner, Tenzin, daughter of Penglai and Commander of the Altan Wind."

Ben whispered, "They left out the 'Scourge' part."

"I asked her to," Tenzin said. "I'm trying to seem more approachable."

"Really?"

"No."

Macuya, Valeria, and Jadzia rose. Inés stepped back and motioned Ben and Tenzin forward.

Ben dipped his head to the cacique but kept his eyes on each figure as he greeted them. None of the three acknowledged him with more than a noncommittal glance, but they nodded at Tenzin when she copied his gesture.

It was yet another reminder that Tenzin occupied a rare place in the vampire world no matter how much she was a personal thorn in Ben's side. To most vampires, especially older ones, she was royalty and was treated as such.

"Cacique Macuya, Cacica Valeria, Cacica Jadzia." Ben let his eyes linger on Jadzia for a moment, let her know that he recognized her. "Thank you for this opportunity to visit your island, and thank you to Inés for the introduction."

Macuya sat in his chair, followed by his queens. "You are American."

"I am."

"You come here for your work?" He glanced at Inés. "You come here to find something?"

Ben chose his words carefully. "My uncle and I have been hired by a client to search for an object of personal value that the client believes exists on this island."

"And does this object belong to your client? Or are you trying to steal from my people?"

Thank you for asking that second question. "The origin of this object is not Puerto Rico, Cacique. I would not steal from your people." Which was true. Most of the treasure was likely of either Spanish or English provenance. "We believe our client has a strong claim."

"And you can't tell me what you're looking for?"

"The confidentiality that our clients expect forbids me, Cacique. As an immortal of considerable power"—never hurt to tack on some flattery—"you realize how even a minor object of personal interest can be used against an immortal. Confidentiality is vital to my uncle's and my work. We guard it zealously, as we would if you ever had need of our services."

The vague mention of services intrigued the vampire. Ben could see it in his eyes.

Interesting.

"So if I allowed this search," Macuya said, "it would be a great favor to your uncle, would it not?"

Giovanni had prepared Ben for this. Favors weren't handed out lightly in the immortal world. He had to be careful how he responded.

"Your consideration would be greatly appreciated," Ben said. "And your cooperation would be remembered should your path cross my uncle's or anyone under his aegis."

Ben could tell it wasn't what Macuya wanted to hear, but it wasn't nothing either. Giovanni Vecchio and his mate, Beatrice De Novo, were two vampires of immense reputation and power around the world. Being on their radar in a positive way wasn't a bad position to be in.

"This... object," Macuya said, "is of sentimental value?"

"Yes," Ben said. "I can tell you it is something the client values personally and they are very attached to it."

Which was one hundred percent true. Tenzin was really, really attached to gold. All gold. But especially gold she could obtain by dubious means.

Ben glanced at Tenzin but saw her staring at Jadzia and Valeria in turn. He looked back at Macuya to see the vampire had been distracted by a wind vampire turning over his head. The woman was dressed in nothing but body paint and feathers. Macuya was entranced.

Inés stepped forward. "Cacique?"

Macuya looked at his sister with a frown. "What?"

"Does the young man have permission to search for this object in your territory? Do you wish to consult with your queens?"

The vampire let out a great sigh as if his sister had annoyed him by asking the question. He glanced at Valeria and Jadzia, who clearly had something to say. Jadzia opened her mouth, but before she could speak, Macuya waved a careless hand in Ben and Tenzin's direction.

"Go," he said. "It's fine. Search for your trinket. If you have any problems, contact Inés."

Ben made quick work of his exit. "Thank you, Cacique." He turned to each queen. "Thank you, Cacicas. May you have a delightful evening, and we appreciate your cooperation."

He backed away from the dais as the music picked up and the dancers filled the cavern again. The wind vampire twisting above Macuya's head was dipping down now, teasing the vampire lord as he tossed flowers toward her. She caught them and laughed.

Valeria was already consulting with a familiar male vampire in a red tunic that matched her dress. It was Vasco, the nitayno they'd met two nights before. He knelt beside Valeria, nodding as she whispered in his ear.

What was Valeria doing consulting with the general?

While Ben was contemplating, Jadzia—the vampire they'd seen in San Juan—watched them. Her eyes were glued to Ben and Tenzin before they turned and exited the cavern. Even as they walked up the sloped tunnel and toward the moonlight, he could feel her gaze in the center of his back.

"I SAW HER THE OTHER NIGHT," Tenzin said. "Not in San Juan. After that."

"Who? Jadzia?" Ben wrenched the steering wheel to the side to avoid a dog that ran across the muddy road. "When was this?"

"When I flew out of the car."

"Two nights ago?"

"Yes. I encountered her near the waterfall. She found my hiding place. Followed me. She confronted me but said nothing about who she was or her role here."

"That's interesting." *Very interesting.* They were driving down the mountain, and Ben was eager to return to their rental house. The package Chloe had arranged would be arriving in the morning. He needed to get some sleep. "So you didn't know she was one of the queens?"

"They're not queens," Tenzin muttered. "Didn't you sense that? He doesn't even pay lip service to them. They're... tokens. Objects he considers his."

"So Novia was right. Macuya is the real ruler."

Tenzin frowned. "I think it's more complicated than that. They clearly play a role, as does Inés."

"I definitely sensed that. I'm betting she's the one who keeps things running around there."

"Valeria is a strategist. She watched you, Macuya, Inés, me. She watched the reaction of the court to our presence—which was generally positive, by the way; they found you amusing—and she is calculating. Whatever plans she has, she works on them behind the scenes. And Vasco is loyal to her."

"And Jadzia?"

"Intense," Tenzin said.

"Intense?"

"Yes, and also calculating," Tenzin said. "Much harder to read. She's very smart. I would say she is the smartest of all of them, just on first impression. Though Valeria is also highly intelligent."

"And Macuya?"

"Intelligent also. But... lazy? No, he's not lazy. He's been in power too long. He's... comfortable. Overly confident. He expects his people to love him."

Ben always loved talking vampire dynamics with Tenzin. "And do they?"

"Some do, but not the ones who should love him most. Not his queens." Tenzin crossed her arms. "And that could be a problem."

"Who is the most likely to cause us problems?"

"I would say Inés if I hadn't seen Jadzia open her mouth. She has thoughts on why we're here. You managed to create the impression in Macuya's mind that we are after some collectible trinket—well done, by the way—but she saw through you. She knows you were being evasive."

"Of course I was being evasive. You know what? If I walked in there and said, 'Hey dudes, I'm going to go find a bunch of buried treasure and keep it all for myself,' they'd laugh at me and then probably eat me. But not a single one would believe I was going after treasure. They're too arrogant. They would automatically think if there was treasure on this island, they'd have already found it."

"They might have."

"At least you're finally admitting it," he muttered. "We'll be fine, Tiny. I think we'll find something. Did you check the car for bugs, by the way?"

"Yes. I found four, but I crushed them. They were the only ones."

Tenzin's sensitivity to electronics definitely came in handy anytime they had to search for listening devices. Not even Patrick Murphy's company had come up with one she couldn't sense. Ben knew that because they sent all their new tech to Tenzin for testing. So far, every bug had failed.

"So tomorrow the equipment should get here," Ben said. "And the night after that we take the Jeep out to the forest. I'm expecting a hike. Are we camping? Where are we setting up a base?"

"If we hide the Jeep, you can probably camp in the sinkhole without anyone catching on that you're there. I can stay in the caverns during the day. Be prepared for the damp though. Lots of water around there. Waterfalls, streams, springs. It's remote, so bring food. No fires. We don't want anyone to come by."

"Gas stove it is," Ben said. "Everything we need should be in the shipment."

"And your cousin?" Tenzin asked.

Ben frowned. "My cousin?"

"You realize she's working at the Camuy Caves right now, don't you? That's not very far from this site."

Ben blinked. "What? No."

"Your little spy didn't tell you about her transfer? It's just temporary while they're doing some administrative updating. Apparently she's brilliant with computers."

He was speechless. "What...? I mean, how did you—?"

"How did I know she was doing this project when your spy didn't?" Tenzin shrugged. "Easy. I asked your abuela. She's very nice, by the way. Her coffee is excellent."

Ben yanked the Jeep to the side of the road and put the vehicle in park before he turned to Tenzin. "Explain," he said. "Now."

"On the side of a single-lane mountain road?" she asked. "Wouldn't you rather go find some food? Or go home? Let's go home." Before Ben could respond, she opened the door and flew out. "I'll see you at home!"

Ben gritted his teeth, started the car, and pulled it back onto the road, trying not to speed as he drove toward Quebradillas.

Interfering little pain in the ass.

Tenzin was going to pay for this.

By the time he got home, Tenzin was nowhere to be found. Ben flipped on every light in the house, then flipped them off again to not waste power. He searched every room. Then he gathered the most recent file his agent had sent him and went out on the balcony to read and listen to the sound of the waves.

Liza Ochoa Rios, daughter of Juana Rios and Eduardo Ochoa. Her parents had divorced when she was three and her father had moved to Florida, leaving Juana and Liza to move in with Ana Lisa Rios, Ben's grandmother. Though they had lived in New York on and off for Juana's education, they always returned to Puerto Rico. Juana was his father's older sister, and she'd been a teacher. She'd passed away after a horrible car accident three years earlier.

Liza had moved back to Puerto Rico after she'd graduated with a degree in environmental science from a university in Florida. She'd already been an intern in the national park system during school. When she'd applied to work at El Yunque National Forest, she'd been hired quickly.

She took care of her grandmother, who kept a small farm on the edge of the park. It was the same place her great-grandparents had lived, and her abuela loved it. They kept chickens and goats. Liza and Ana Lisa grew most of their food and kept seeds from one year to the next.

They had not suffered as much after the storm because Ana Lisa had known how to replant their garden after the storm and their fruit trees had survived. Their home was a gathering place for most of their neighbors. It was old, sturdy, and hadn't suffered much damage.

Ben had gotten all that from a deep background check done by the agent Giovanni had recommended.

Ana Lisa was resourceful and tough. A devoted grandmother, friend, and neighbor.

And Liza, his cousin, was a rule follower. A high achiever. A good citizen.

Ben was none of those things, and he was her only cousin.

He'd never met Liza. He wondered if she even knew about him. Probably. Ana Lisa Rios wasn't a woman who hid things. Unlike his father. Unlike his mother. Unlike everyone in his family, vampire or not.

Ben lived in a world of secrets, and his cousin didn't belong there.

Tenzin landed on the edge of the balcony an hour after he'd arrived at the house. He'd had time to calm down, but his decision hadn't wavered. Not even a little bit.

"I don't want you near them," he said quietly. "Not Ana. Not Liza. Leave them alone."

"I only spent a little while with your grandmother, and I altered her memory afterward. She's not going to be suspicious."

"That's not the point."

"So you're going to just pretend they don't exist?"

Ben was silent.

Tenzin narrowed her eyes. "They're your *family*."

"No." He closed the file. "They're not. I had the chance to make them my family when Giovanni asked me. I chose something different. They didn't. And I refuse to bring them into this world, not even to the edge of it."

"I think you're being stubborn and stupid."

"Because I'm not doing what you want?" He shook his head. "Too bad."

Tenzin scowled at him.

"Listen, most of what I said to Macuya and that vampire court was bullshit. You and I both know it. But part of it wasn't. A minor object of sentimental importance can be used against someone in your world. Any attachment can be turned against you. A person?" He shook his head. "They're not targets right now. Nothing about them makes them targets. And I refuse to bring them closer. Don't pretend you don't know why."

"You brought Chloe closer."

"And you think I don't question that every day?" Ben asked. "You think I don't blame myself?" He scooted to the edge of the lounge chair. "Listen, you and I both know that someday something is going to happen to her. She'll be used as bait or leverage or... God knows what."

"I will kill anyone who attempts it," Tenzin said, her voice utterly cold.

God, she was so damn loyal. It wasn't easy to gain Tenzin's loyalty, but once you did, you had a friend for eternity. That alone made it hard to stay mad at her.

"I have no doubt you would, Tiny. But there's no guarantee

Chloe wouldn't be hurt in the process. Someday something will happen to *me*," he continued. "With all my connections, all my training, all my precautions, something *will* happen to me. I've lived in your world long enough to know. Humans don't usually live to old age."

Tenzin stared at him. "You know what the solution to that is."

"I know I don't want it."

"Keep telling yourself that." Tenzin walked toward him. "What do you think your life is going to be, Benjamin? Are you going to make your fortune, retire from vampire life, and marry a nice human girl from the suburbs? Have three kids and coach baseball on the weekends?" She leaned down and braced both hands on the arms of his chair. "Do you really think that's your destiny? You would be bored to death."

"I don't know what my destiny is," he said. "And neither do you."

"I think I have a better idea than you do." Tenzin stood. "This isn't *my* world, Benjamin. It's *our* world." She walked to the edge of the balcony. "But for now I'll respect your decision about your family. You're right. We don't have any power in this place. Either of them could be leverage."

She fell back into the darkness, and Ben heard her take to the sky. Then he picked up his files, went inside, and locked the door to his room before he got some sleep.

Tomorrow would be a long day.

12

Ben pulled up to the small surf shack east of Arecibo and waited in the Jeep. The sun was baking the private cove where the bungalow sat, turning the pale sand a shimmering gold. He waited for fifteen minutes, long enough to count the cars passing on the road in the distance. After he'd heard the third one pass, he opened the car door and walked to the house.

Opening the kitchen door with the key he'd been given, he saw the pile of boxes in the middle of the room. They were stacked, plain brown cardboard with a familiar smile on the side, nothing that would arouse suspicion if anyone were to pass by and peek in the windows.

He opened each with a box cutter he found in the kitchen drawer, then carefully resealed them and took each out to the Jeep. Camping equipment, caving equipment, and his metal-detecting kit. All of it was there, along with a page of directions his agent had left for their exit from the island.

Within fifteen minutes, he was finished packing everything up. Within twenty he was back on the main road, leaving the small house locked and waiting, surveillance cameras set and programmed.

He drove back to the rental house in Quebradillas and put the Jeep in the garage. There was no use unpacking it when all the equipment was just going out that same night. He ate a small lunch, dragged a lounge chair into the shade, and tried to take a nap. The balcony was bathed in sunlight and would be for hours. He was as safe as he could be.

He slept.

"What are you doing, José? Your father and I didn't raise you this way. What kind of life is your son going to have if you keep drinking like this? If you keep shoving your responsibilities away!"

"Ma, I told you my name is Joe. Stop calling me fucking José. You think we're still back on the island or something."

"José! Joe! Whatever you want to call yourself, you cannot let your son stay with that woman."

"That woman is his mother."

"And you're his father."

"So she says."

Ben heard a slap.

"Watch your mouth. That child is the spitting image of you at that age. Don't lie to me. He should be with *us*. With his family. Not with a woman who's using him to steal! What kind of life is that for him? How can you allow this? Does he even go to school? I can see how bright he is. What are you doing for his future?"

"It's not my decision, Ma. I give her money when I can. Look at this place; you think I'm rich or something? What do you want? You think I should take the kid from his mother? She feeds him, okay? I never seen him with bruises or cuts."

Not unless you put them on me. Ben slumped against the

back of the door and listened to his abuela and his father arguing.

This wasn't good. He didn't want anyone to argue. And they were talking about taking him from his mom. That was... not a good idea. Ben was the only reason his mom ate. She'd be out of control without him.

He eyed the locked window that led to the fire escape. Joe's apartment was on East 116th and 2nd, not too far from the 116th Street station. He could catch the green line there and go south. He'd be back at his mom's place before dark.

"If you don't do something about him, then I will," his abuela said. "This cannot continue. I refuse. I *refuse*. Benjamin is my grandson. He deserves better than this. He deserves a family. Stability. Safety. And if you're not willing to do something, then I will do something, José. Do not test me."

"Don't you make trouble, Ma. Don't you dare—"

The voices stopped when Ben used a blanket to punch through the glass in Joe's bedroom. It really hurt, but he didn't stop to think about it. He grabbed the jacket he'd come in and a metro card off Joe's dresser. Then he scurried down the fire escape as Joe and his abuela stuck their head out the window.

"Ben!"

"Benjamin, stop!"

He didn't stop. He couldn't.

BEN WOKE, flexing his hand, the pain of breaking glass still real from his dream. He could feel the bruises forming, the tiny shard that had wedged between his knuckles, getting infected a few days later. His hand had been so stiff he'd nearly been caught picking pockets that week.

He deserves better than this. He deserves a family. Stability. Safety.

Whether his grandmother knew it or not, those words had carried him through the roughest parts of his childhood. When bigger kids picked on him or hurt him, he felt sorry for them, because probably no one thought they deserved better. But Ben deserved better. Even though he never saw his grandmother again, he knew he deserved better. His abuela was an honest woman; she wouldn't have said it if it wasn't true.

It was strange what stuck in your memory. Ben remembered every kick his father ever gave him, every punch that Joe managed to land. He remembered the way his blood looked on a broken mirror and the sound of a bone breaking.

He didn't remember all the times his mother had used him to steal, how many wallets he'd stolen, or how often he'd slipped food or money in his pockets. He didn't remember all the lies she'd told him. He never knew what was real or what was the truth.

Or maybe he didn't want to know.

His mother told him she'd been an artist and an actress. She'd met the king of Lebanon and performed in an international dance company. She could sing; he remembered that. Her voice was the only angelic thing about her.

She said she'd come to New York because a German count wanted to marry her, but when she arrived, she decided she didn't want the life of a royal and so she cut the count loose, choosing to write her own story—mostly fictional—in the East Village of New York City.

She was a grifter, Ben realized with the clarity of hindsight. And he suspected she was pretty good at it until she got drunk. After that, the lies started to fall apart.

Why am I thinking about them?

It was funny what the mind recorded. Ben didn't remember

the wounds his mother had given him as clearly, maybe because violence always carried a hint of surprise to him. No matter how many times his father raised his hand, Ben never expected the hit or the punch.

But he did expect the lies.

Everyone lied.

Except his abuela.

He watched the sky turn colors and the sun sink down into the ocean. He rose to his feet, waiting for the rush of awareness her presence brought.

Everyone lies.

Even her.

Especially her.

Then again, Ben had a bad habit of getting attached to women who lied.

TENZIN FLEW AHEAD, leaving Ben to drive to the crater where the sinkhole had dropped the floor from under the forest. He'd drive as far as he could, then park the car and send up a flare so Tenzin could find him.

After that, they'd cart the equipment through the forest and down the sinkhole, making camp where no one would see them. Then the search would begin.

He drove from asphalt to gravel, gravel to mud. Rocking back and forth on rutted roads, Ben wondered if Tenzin was circling overhead or waiting patiently at the site.

He was guessing the circling thing. She'd been as excited as a kid at Christmas when he'd tapped on her door at nightfall.

Gold. That crazy little vampire really was nuts about it.

"Hey, Cara."

His phone came to life from its perch on the dashboard.

"How may I help you?"

"Call Chloe."

"Calling... Chloe." The line rang three times before she picked up.

"Everything get there safe?"

"Yep," he said. "You're the best."

"I know. I really am. So what's the plan now?"

"Find the stuff. Leave the island."

"So... home by the weekend then?"

Ben smiled. "Yeah, for sure."

"Good. Then you'll be able to see your aunt and uncle while they're here."

Ben blinked. "Gio and B?"

"Yep. Kind of a long story, but... they're here for a while and they're staying at the loft. I didn't figure you'd mind."

"No, of course not." Well, that was... weird. "Chloe, does this have anything to do with Gavin's thing you didn't want to talk about?"

"Maybe?"

That was a yes.

"And you're sure you can't tell me what's going on?"

She sighed. "Very sure about that."

"Okay. Well..." What to say? "I guess just let me know what's going on when you can."

Ben forced himself to remember that Gio and Gavin had been friends far longer than Gavin and Ben had been friends. It was hardly unusual for them to be involved in each other's problems.

"Tell me about the VICs," she said quickly. "Anything weird?"

"So many things," he said. "But maybe not that weird for old vampires. They're old and powerful and they like weird traditions like bowing and polygamy."

"You and your crazy shenanigans," Chloe said. "Polygamist vampire royalty? What will you do to top this?"

"I don't know, maybe find some pirate treasure?"

"Sounds like fun to me." There was noise in the background. "Listen, I better go. Since your uncle is here, is there anything you need help with researchwise?"

"I'll let you know if I can think of anything. Keep in mind, where we're going is pretty remote and we'll be working underground. So don't worry if you don't hear from us for a while."

"Wait, what's a while? Does your uncle know? Give me an idea of—"

The phone cut off as Ben reached the top of a hill. He glanced at his phone.

No connection.

"And there we go," he whispered. There wouldn't be much more than hints of mobile service for miles. Hopefully Chloe wouldn't worry. After all, he had Tenzin. What other protection did he need?

THE ROAD STOPPED in a small clearing people clearly used for parking. There must be a trailhead nearby. Ben stopped the car and reached for the flare gun in the side compartment, hoping he'd gotten within a mile or two of the search site.

Pointing the gun up, he fired.

A bright arcing red flare shot into the darkness, startling birds from the trees. In a few moments, Tenzin appeared near the edge of the clearing, her hair tied back, wearing slim leggings and a fitted tank top again. He'd brought her coveralls for the cave but had no idea if she'd wear them or not.

She was vibrating with energy. "Finally."

"How close did I get?"

She walked over and opened the back of the Jeep. "About as close as you can get in this thing. You're less than a mile from the crater."

"Cool." He slung on the backpack he'd packed with personal items, then took stock of the boxes. "How many of these can you get?"

Tenzin shrugged. "All of them. They're not that heavy."

"You want me to just start hiking?"

"Sure. I'll bring the stuff. You have a note for the car?"

"Yep." Ben took out a note wrapped in a plastic bag. *Out of gas. Be back soon.* He tucked the note under the windshield and walked back. "Just lock it up when you're done and we should be good."

"Okay." She caught the keys and hoisted the first box with a smile. "See you when you get there. You have the coordinates?"

Ben lifted his GPS in one hand and a map in the other. "I got it. See you there."

"See you."

The night was damp and a soft drizzle fell from the sky as Ben began his hike. He cut through the forest, watching for unstable ground. According to the hiking guide he'd found, this area was prone to mudslides and sinkholes.

There wasn't much of a trail, but the forest was more open than he'd expected. There was no cutting necessary, and most of the ground was damp but solid. They'd had rain two days before, but the days since had been dry and warm.

Ben trudged in the darkness, his hand occasionally going to the knife at his waist. There weren't a lot of large predators in Puerto Rico unless you counted the unusually high number of vampires on the island. He occasionally heard the sound of Tenzin flying overhead.

Little troublemaker. If she weren't so damn excited, he'd try to stay mad at her. Ben was still unconvinced that anything was in these caves. He had no way of gauging the accuracy of the map, nor did he have any confidence that no one on the island had discovered this cave in nearly three hundred years.

And why had the Dominican buried it out here anyway? Was this really the best place to hide the treasure of Miguel Enríquez?

Too many questions. Not enough answers. He hated going into jobs like this. They never went well.

He ran into a wall of vegetation going up a small rise. He could see on the GPS that the sinkhole was just past it, so he got out the machete he'd stored in his backpack and hacked. Fifteen minutes of steady work created a tunnel wide enough for him to squeeze through. He twisted his body through the vines and branches only to feel the ground fall away under his feet.

"Shit!"

He slid down a steep slope, his arms flung wide, trying to grab anything to stop the fall. He slid on his side, his backpack throwing him off-balance. His jacket tore and the grit and stones scratched his torso. Mud filled his mouth as he tried to yell for help. He glanced down the slope and saw a small tree rapidly approaching. It was near the edge of what looked like a cliff. Nothing but blackness spread out beyond it.

Ben rolled toward the small tree. He reached for it, fingers catching and holding on just before he slid over the cliff. His body and backpack jerked to a stop. He gasped for air and tasted dirt and blood.

He lay on the edge of the sinkhole, his mind and body reconnecting. Now that his momentum had slowed, he could scramble up the side of the slope. He struggled out of his backpack and stuffed it above the tree, then he sat up gingerly and pulled his jacket down over his scraped ribs.

Ben tried to see what was in front of him, but he only got the vague impression of empty space and darkness. He reached into the front pocket of his backpack and withdrew the headlamp he should have been wearing before he slid down the hill.

Of course, there was no guarantee he still wouldn't have fallen, and then he would have lost the headlamp as well as his dignity.

Flicking it on, he scanned the slope he was perched on. A steep angle, for sure, but not unmanageable if he hadn't lost his footing. He needed to walk parallel to the edge and hope he could gradually work his way down. There had to be a way into the sinkhole that didn't require ropes. They had them, but they were all in the boxes Tenzin was carrying.

"Hey." Tenzin appeared on the edge of his light, hovering above him. "What happened?"

"A steep hill happened." He struggled to his feet. "How do I get down to the bottom? How far is the bottom?"

"The bottom?" She frowned and floated away from him. Then she put her legs down and stood. "You mean this bottom?"

Ben walked to the edge where the tree had caught his fall and looked down.

Four feet down, just past the light, was the dark, rocky bottom of the sinkhole.

"Yeah." He reached for his backpack and hopped down. "That bottom."

Tenzin walked beside him as he began to cross the uneven ground. "Should I not ever mention this again?"

"Yeah, that would probably be a good idea," he muttered. "Where's the stuff?"

"Just over here." She skipped ahead. "I already set up lights in the cave. There's a wide opening once you get past the first entrance if you want to set up a tent there."

"Let me look, because what you said makes no sense to me."

He was grumpy and tired and aching. His ribs hurt. He didn't think he'd broken any, but they were definitely bruised.

He just wanted to make camp and get some sleep. He'd explore the sinkhole crater in the morning.

"Here." Tenzin walked to the edge of a waterfall and crouched down. "This is the entrance I initially saw." Then she stood and walked to the left, hopping down a tumble of rocks covered in moss. "But if you go in this side, there's a natural ramp."

She brushed a fall of ferns away, and Ben followed her.

"Look," she said. "See what I mean?"

Beyond the narrow opening covered by ferns was a short tunnel that sloped down to a wide cavern. It had been formed by water and time, a cave behind the falls that had formed where the sinkhole ended. Ben looked up and saw a sliver of stars through the sheer curtain of water. During the day, the sun would shine onto the edge of the cavern. At night, it created a hollow insulated from the wind.

"Excellent." He turned in place. The ground was rock, but there were parts of it that were smooth enough for a tent. The waterfall was too big to sleep next to without getting soaked, and he didn't want to sleep in any of the three tunnels he saw branching off the main cavern. "If I set up here, we'll be completely hidden from overhead." Which was a good thing since wind vampires were a thing that existed. "The supplies?"

Tenzin nodded to the entrance tunnel. "We'll have to bring them in one box at a time. There's not much room to fly down here."

Ben watched her. "And are you going to be okay with that?"

Her eyes turned sharp. "Did I panic when we were meeting Los Tres?"

"That cavern was bigger than this."

"I'll be fine."

"Are you ever going to tell me why you hate being underground so much?"

Tenzin paused, and something about her expression made Ben wish he hadn't asked.

"I'm a wind vampire," she said. "This isn't my element. Come on. Let's get the boxes moved in. You need to get some sleep."

13

Ben woke in the dim light of his tent, his back resting on a thick air mattress that cushioned his body from the rock floor of the cavern. They'd set up camp the night before and settled into their respective shelters, Tenzin creating a pallet under a tent farther back in the cave and Ben placing his nearer to the light.

He'd slept well but woke with aching stiffness in his ribs and back. His legs were bruised, but his knees were fine. He lifted his shirt and checked the blue and green marks on his torso. He had cuts and bruises, but no piercing pain.

He flipped open the first aid kit and downed four ibuprofen with a gulp of water. It was cool and damp in the cave, but not cold. He wore long sleeves and a loose pair of pants he'd switch out for a thermal base layer and coveralls when they went into the tunnels.

He unzipped his tent and slipped on the heavy rubber boots he'd packed with their supplies. They were waterproof and had excellent grip. He was expecting cool, damp conditions with possibly a lot of moss.

Morning light streamed into the cavern, sparkling through

the waterfall, its reflections dancing off the cave walls. Ben looked over his shoulder to see Tenzin, not in her tent but sitting cross-legged on a pallet, staring at the dancing reflection of the water on the wall.

He walked over and sat beside her. "It doesn't hurt your eyes?"

Direct sunlight was a no for any vampire, but reflected sunlight wouldn't hurt them. Too much of it could make them uncomfortable though.

"No," she whispered. "It's beautiful."

It was sun reflected off water. He'd hardly even noticed it. But she was right.

"It is," he said. "I'm going to get some food. Do you want anything?"

Her eyes didn't leave the cave wall as she shook her head.

"Okay." He glanced at the three openings. "Any idea which tunnel we should start with?"

"I need to look at the map again," she said. "And I need to smell the caves."

Smell the caves. Ben shook his head and walked back to the camp kitchen he'd set up the night before. It was nearest to where the sunlight touched the water, and moss and algae covered the rocks behind it. Anywhere the light touched, green bloomed.

He boiled water for coffee and heated a packet of prepackaged chicken stew. With crackers, it made a decent meal. He walked out of the tunnel and up to the floor of the old sinkhole.

Everything was green kissed by gold. In the morning light, vines fell from the walls, and the air smelled of earth and moss. It was warmer in the sun. He sat on a rock in a sunbeam and enjoyed the sight he'd missed the night before.

It wasn't a particularly deep sinkhole. It was old and most of the walls had tumbled in on themselves, creating steep slopes toward the rocky bottom. Only one side was still sheer. That was where the waterfall cascaded. It dropped down under the earth, creating a mist that kept the bottom of the sinkhole damp even though the days had been sunny.

Ben walked back into the tunnel and entered the liminal space of the cavern. Though it was midmorning, he felt his nights and days blending together. He could get lost here. They weren't underground, but they weren't on the surface. It didn't feel like daytime, but it definitely wasn't night, when the cavern had been pitch-black and cold. The bonus to the lack of direct sun was both he and Tenzin would be able to search around the clock. The disadvantage was a loss of any sense of time.

"Eat when you're hungry. Sleep when you're tired." It had been his uncle's advice when Ben told him he'd be treasure hunting in a cave.

There was no sign of any other human in the cavern or in the sinkhole. No trash or marks. No fire scorches or footprints. It was as if the cave was new and ancient at once.

By the time he finished eating and cleaned up, Tenzin was sitting at the mouth of one tunnel, staring into the blackness with a copy of the map in front of her. Ben sat beside her, his body aching, and glanced at the document in the clear plastic sleeve.

It was a simple map. Whoever had drawn it was clearly not a cartographer. Though the writing was clear, the sketching was rudimentary, and they had no way of knowing if anything was to scale. It was a map drawn by an amateur, possibly only for his own reference.

But in its simplicity, it was also blessedly clear. Once Ben and Tenzin had understood the church and town were Arecibo, everything else about it made sense. The only potential problem was that the priest had drawn a branching map that didn't encompass the whole of the tunnels. Tomás had simply listed the turns. Which meant if they missed one or if Tomás had missed one, they were shit out of luck.

And there was no mention—none at all—of three different tunnels.

"We might have to do this three times," Ben said.

"I don't think so." Tenzin turned her face to the tunnel on the far end of the cavern. "That's the tunnel that smells like bones. The vampire was there."

"That means nothing, Tenzin. A vampire could have been there, used that cave, and not even seen Enríquez's gold. Or he could have seen it, taken it, and left us nothing."

She stared at the tunnel. "I don't think it's that one."

Ben sighed. "Okay." She wouldn't listen to reason. Not if her mind was made up.

"Which leaves these two," Tenzin said. "This one smells of earth." She nodded to the center tunnel. "This one, water." She motioned to the left.

"You think earth?"

"I think the rivers are unlikely to have changed course signif-icantly over the past two hundred years. Not underground. So Tomás would have avoided them. I'm betting he went for the driest tunnel, not the one with a risk of flooding."

"Makes sense." Ben stood. "So when do you want to start?"

"Now."

BEN UNPACKED the caving equipment first. He wanted to explore the tunnel to set pitons, ropes, and lights before they brought out the metal detector.

He could feel a low level of tension coming off Tenzin, like a buzz in the air.

"I'll go first," he said, adjusting his helmet and headlamp.

It wasn't his first time in a cave, but he wasn't an experienced explorer. "Let me set up some lights and lines before you start in. If it's even, we'll be fine. If it's not, I'll have to bring heavier equipment from the Jeep and it's going to take a lot longer."

"I'm fine."

"I didn't say you weren't." He stepped in front of her. "But let me go first. You can follow right after me if you want. But let me go first."

She crossed her arms but said nothing. She'd been unusually quiet.

A silent thread of worry took root in his belly. He hadn't been around Tenzin many times when she felt truly uneasy. Even in the middle of a battle, she was in her element. But here? Under the earth, cut off from the sky where she thrived?

Ben stepped into the center cave, flipping his helmet light on low and checking the flashlight hanging from his tool belt and the lump of glow sticks in his pocket. Even on low the helmet light nearly blinded him, but he let his eyes adjust and took his first steps inside. The line of parachute cord lay over his shoulder. He'd tied one end to a stake at the mouth of the tunnel. The other line he'd anchor at various points when he had the chance.

It was a narrow passage roughly three feet across, bordered by rocky walls and a somewhat even floor. The height of the tunnel ranged from four feet to immeasurable black. He stepped up and over a tumble of rocks, heading into the unknown.

"It looks pretty even," he yelled over his shoulder. "No evidence of rock slides. No drops."

He heard nothing from Tenzin, but he kept walking. He carried his own copy of the map in his hand, referencing it every time he came to a turn.

At each juncture, he hammered a piton in the limestone and

strung the cord through the eye to keep track of his path. All told, there should have been nine turns.

He reached the first, anchored, and turned right.

He reached the second, anchored, and turned right again.

The third, after the anchor, he kept to the main tunnel going straight. It was a honeycomb of tunnels beneath the surface, but evenly sloping and mostly clear.

Left again.

Right.

Right.

Left.

Right.

He felt his heart rate begin to spike. He wasn't thinking about how far underground he was. He wasn't thinking about how deep into the earth he'd crawled.

He was thinking about gold. One last turn and he'd anchor his line, hang a lantern, then go back for his metal-detecting equipment. He could almost taste the gold in the dusty, damp air.

He came to the last turn, which... wasn't.

"Shit."

He checked the map again. Looked up.

Dead end.

After turning in place a few times, Ben began the walk back out of the tunnel. He left the cord where it was, but in the back of his mind, he was convinced he'd missed a turn, missed a branch, missed something that would have led to the correct cavern.

Tenzin was waiting. "Well?"

"We'll have to walk it again." He fidgeted with his extra flashlight. "I'm pretty sure I missed a turn."

"What was at the end? Did you make all the turns? What did you find?"

"Nothing." He flipped his flashlight on to check it and stuffed some extra glow sticks in his front pocket. "It was a dead end."

"That can't be right."

He cocked his head. "Because we didn't find it our first walk in? You've got to be joking. We rewalk it. Then we walk it again. Then we use the metal detectors. I'm not giving up, Tenzin. But I am saying we need to be on top of this and realize it might be one of the other tunnels."

She shook her head. "I'm telling you—"

"I know. I know. You're positive this is the tunnel."

"Exactly. The priest may have made a mistake drawing the map. We can't give up."

"I'm not going to." He strapped a different-colored cord to his waist. "I'll take the metal detector next time. Let me walk it once more now that I have a feel for the place. I probably missed something last time."

"Yes," Tenzin said. "You can be careless when you're excited."

He rolled his eyes. "Thanks for the vote of confidence."

"You're welcome."

THREE MORE ATTEMPTS at exploring the cave exhausted Ben's energy for the day.

"I'm done," he said, unzipping his coveralls. "I'm cold. I'm bruised. This is going nowhere. We'll have to start again tomorrow."

"We're not giving up," Tenzin said, staring at the mouth of the tunnel.

"I'm not saying we're giving up, but I'm taking a break. We have to be methodical about this, or we could miss the right path by a few feet. We go back tomorrow, start at the beginning, and slowly eliminate possibilities. Keep the first line for a reference point."

Tenzin nodded. "And I'll keep looking."

Ben watched her from the corner of his eye. "I'm not sure about that, Tenzin."

"Why not? I'm not going to sleep."

She'd been edgy all day. He knew being underground made her nervous, whether she admitted it or not. She became more disconnected. Less... human.

"I just don't think it's good idea for either of us to be alone down here with no backup. Give both of us a break. I may sleep for a few hours and be ready to look again."

"Fine."

She said it, but her tone of voice told Ben she was humoring him.

He walked over and crouched in front of her. "Don't go in there without me. I'm asking you as your partner and your friend."

Tenzin was silent.

"I don't know why you hate being underground so much, and I don't need to know unless you want to tell me. But I know it's not a good idea. So just... don't."

Her eyes flashed. "You presume, Benjamin Vecchio."

"Yeah, I do. But only because I've seen what tight spaces underground do to you. I've seen it in more than one place, so don't stress me out for no reason other than your stubbornness. Please."

"Fine."

This time her voice was less patronizing and more annoyed. That was fine. Ben could deal with annoyed. What he couldn't deal with was a murderous vampire disassociated from her more human instincts.

"I'm going to eat something and then sleep. Do you want anything to eat? Maybe just something warm? Blood? Blood-wine? I brought both."

"No." Tenzin rose and returned to her pallet near the water tunnel. "Come get me when you're ready to work again."

Ben bit his tongue and walked back to the small kitchen he'd set up. He heated a package of chili and opened a bag of corn chips. A shot of whiskey added to his tea and he was feeling nearly human again by the time he crawled into his tent.

He opened the file of Tomás's letters again and started rereading from the beginning. He read about the last days of the privateer Miguel Enríquez and the anger and bitterness the man felt about his fate. He had been powerful, rich, influential, even if he wasn't popular. It was all gone. At the end of his life, the powerful man vented his bitterness on the priests he'd supported so diligently early in his life. Priests who cared for him out of moral obligation and divine vow.

He was a bastard of indeterminate birth and questionable moral compass, neither at home in proper society or the class of criminals he brushed against.

Was it any wonder Ben had avoided looking in a mirror that reminded him of his own uncomfortable truths? He fell asleep with the priest's letters on his chest, the sound of dripping water in the distance and a voice singing softly in the darkness.

"You're a little bastard."

Ben looked up from his bowl of cereal with caution. It was morning, but his mother already sounded drunk. Maybe she'd been drinking already, or maybe she hadn't gone to sleep the night before. It was impossible to tell. Ben had figured out how to put a lock on his door at age seven and had been locking himself in at night ever since. Once he was in his room, he didn't leave until the light came.

"Do you know what that means?" she asked him, slurring her words. "To be a bastard?"

"Uh-uh." He resumed eating with one eye on her as she leaned against the counter.

He knew what it meant when people yelled it on the street at each other, but he didn't think that's what his mother was talking about.

"It means," she said, "that your parents weren't... weren't married when you were born."

"Oh." Ben kept eating. He finished one bowl and poured another. The cereal didn't fill him up, but he liked how crunchy it was. He should probably buy oatmeal the next time he went to the bodega. When Mrs. Novak made him eat oatmeal, he was full for hours. But it didn't crunch. He liked the crunch.

"But I wasn't married to Joe." His mother opened the fridge, stared inside long enough for the kitchen to get cold, then closed it without taking anything out. "I'd never marry Joe."

Of course she wouldn't. His parents couldn't stand each other. He learned early where babies come from, and it still confused him that his parents had ever liked each other enough to do *that* even once.

"So you're a bastard," she said again. "A *bastard*." Louder. "Do you care?"

Ben shrugged. "Not really."

Lots of his parents' friends weren't married, so it wasn't like Ben was the only bastard on the block. Carla was probably the only kid in the building with two parents at home. Well, Austen had two parents sometimes, but they fought a lot, so his dad was only there a little bit. But Ben thought they were married. Probably.

"Does it matter?" he asked, not looking at his mother.

"I guess not." She slid down the counter and sat on the floor, her back propped against the cupboards. "My parents were married."

"I think Joe's parents were too." Ben was sure of it actually. His abuela talked about her late husband a lot. She even told Ben that he reminded her of his grandfather, and Ben had felt unaccountably warm and proud of that. Why? He had no idea. He'd never met his grandfather and he never would. The old man had died before Ben was born.

"Joe's parents...," his mother muttered, and a dark look came to her eyes.

Ben quickly finished his second bowl of cereal, drank what was left of the watery milk, and cleared his dishes. He shouldn't have brought up his abuela. His mother only got pissed off when he did that.

"You shouldn't see her anymore," his mom said. "She... what's she ever done for you, huh?"

Fed me. Bought me clothes. Took me to movies. Made cookies.

"Nuthin'," Ben said, quickly exiting the kitchen and making his way to the living room. He turned on the TV and switched the channel to one of the shows his mom liked to watch. Something on MTV with lots of flashy cars and houses. That would distract her. He'd been planning to watch cartoons since it was Saturday, but he didn't want the headache.

He'd let his mom fall asleep on the couch, then he'd go out. The weather was okay this morning. Maybe he'd walk over to Washington Square and lift some wallets from the tourists. If the dancers were any good, the pickings were easy, easy, easy. And if he got enough cash, he could go to a movie or something. Maybe he'd hang out in the park and eat hot dogs all day.

Anything but stay at home.

Anything but that.

14

Tenzin listened to him sleeping. Ben talked in his sleep, far more than he probably realized. He also spoke various languages. English mostly. Spanish second. A surprising amount of Arabic, notably curse words.

She unzipped his tent and watched him. He had the priest's letters on his chest and had kicked off some of the blankets. She re-covered him, knowing how cold human blood could get underground.

I don't know why you hate being underground so much, and I don't need to know unless you want to tell me.

He didn't want to know. Ben was remarkably adept at avoiding ugly things. He reminded Tenzin of herself that way. Why dwell on ugly things if it wasn't necessary? Why ruminate on the past when you could remake yourself in the future?

Tenzin had asked Ben why he hadn't told Giovanni about his grandmother, but she already knew the answer. She was curious what he'd say, but she knew.

It was easier.

It was always easier to leave the past behind. Forget it. Cut off the disease. Start fresh. Start new. It was a technique she'd used many times. Mostly it worked.

And when it didn't... you became an inhuman monster who reverted to her most animalistic instincts. That happened sometimes too.

Not the most desirable option.

It was why she'd agreed to wait for Ben even though she was certain the treasure wasn't in the tunnel they were searching. She was nearly certain of it. They'd tried. The map was clear. Perhaps the rivers had shifted. Perhaps they were imagining the mind of the priest wrong.

Water.

Holy water.

He was a native of this place. He was familiar with the tunnels and the caverns. Maybe he knew the treasure was safer where humans would avoid it, where it was surrounded by water. It was treasure stolen on the water. It could be stored near it too. The underground rivers had their own labyrinthine passageways, enough to discourage most treasure hunters.

That was it. That was the truth.

They were looking in the wrong place.

BEN MAPPED each attempt in a notebook as he explored. Attempt five? No luck. Attempt six? Dead end after turn four. Attempt eight nearly took his head off with an unexpected drop that left him with a lump on his forehead.

He was taking notes, grabbing an energy bar, and crossing off previous map attempts when he noticed that Tenzin wasn't staring at the earthen tunnel anymore. She was staring at the center tunnel. The watery-smelling one.

"Tenzin?"

"I was wrong."

Did it break your brain to say that? Ben rolled his eyes. "You think it's the center tunnel? Why not the one that smells like bones?"

"Because a vampire that close to gold would have noticed it." She turned to look at him. "Do you think I'm making that up? Each gold alloy has a distinctive smell. A vampire would have to be an idiot not to smell it. I don't know why that's so hard to understand."

Ben kept his temper in check. Barely.

"Well, since it's literally the first time you've ever mentioned that little fact, I don't know why I'm supposed to have known that. Why the hell would I know that gold has a scent, Tenzin? It's a nonreactive metal." Okay, his temper had shown through a bit on that last question.

She ignored him and stared at the tunnel. "Pure gold is nonreactive. But most gold for coinage was alloyed, which means it has a scent, even if humans are too dull to sense it. I thought everyone knew that."

Bullshit.

She was just trying to piss him off. He closed his notebook and opened another one. "Great. Wonderful. Okay, we're starting over. Where's the map? And where's the extra rope?"

"I'm going on this try."

"No, you're going to let me map it out first and see if there's a chamber that would be logical to keep a treasure in. There's no telling—"

"What's down there?" She nodded. "Exactly. That's why I'm going. If you get into trouble, it'll be better if I'm there."

"Because you're so great underground," he muttered.

"If you'd let Carwyn change you, you'd be an earth vampire and we wouldn't have to worry about all this, would we?"

Tenzin put her hands on her hips and rose a foot off the ground. "But you can't do that, can you? You can't think of anyone but yourself. Do you know how much easier it would be to do this kind of work if we had a wind vampire and an earth vampire?"

"You seriously fucking want me to change into an earth vampire so we can hunt more treasure?" Ben didn't know why he was shocked. It was near-perfect Tenzin logic.

What is good for me?

What will make me richer?

What will give me exactly what I want?

Okay, do that.

He shut his eyes and took a few deep breaths. "You're certifiable."

"Yes. But I'm not wrong."

He unzipped the heavy coveralls and yanked the sleeves down, stripping to the waist. "Why did you even want to do this with me if you're going to be such an asshole? You want a vampire partner? Go find one! Leave me out of it."

She scoffed. "As if you wouldn't go crazy without the challenge. You need this, Ben. Just as much as I do."

"I don't need this." He flung his arms wide. "I don't need all this shit. I don't need treasure maps and... and getting dragged to places I hate. I don't need you shoving my shitty childhood at me. Have I ever done that to you?"

"No. I don't tell you anything about my past for a reason."

"Fuck you!" He marched back to his tent, tossed the notebooks and ropes to the side, and left the cavern, walking into the light and letting the sun pour over him, well out of reach of Tenzin's antagonism. He climbed out of the sinkhole and stretched on a rock that lay near the edge. The stone was warm on his back, and the sunshine hit his skin, leaching into his bones like water soaking into dry earth.

He slept in the sun, reminded of a summer in Tuscany on

his uncle's estate when the immortal world had overwhelmed him and he couldn't take any more. He'd been sick of it then. Had his cynicism only gotten worse? He thought he'd be able to do good things, retrieve what was lost, find memories and forgotten dreams, make decent money along the way. He'd had grand ideas of what this business would be. Intrigue and mystery and grateful clients.

What had happened in New York the year before had soured all that. In one fell swoop, he'd become the bad guy, not the good one. His reputation hadn't taken a hit—ironically, it had probably given him a certain legitimacy in the vampire world—but his own sense of self and of the man he was making had been shattered.

He'd been trying to walk a narrow line, and he fell. He'd been blinded by a good story. He'd been out-conned. He'd turned into the thief his mother had wanted him to be.

Was he mad at Tenzin or at himself? She hadn't changed, not in any significant way. He'd known what he was getting, going into business with Tenzin. He'd walked in with clear eyes.

Ben walked back into the cavern and straight to her. She was staring at the watery tunnel with an intent gaze. Ben sat on the rock behind Tenzin, wrapping himself around her and setting his chin on the top of her head. "This place is getting to me."

"You let your past control you, Ben."

"Sometimes."

Her shoulders relaxed. "You're just so..."

"Stubborn? Fastidious? Deliberate?" All epithets she'd thrown at him in the past.

"Human." She turned her head a little, and Ben could see her fangs, the ever-present reminder of how inhuman she was. "You're so *human*."

Ben let out a breath. "Yes. I'm never not going to be human."

She put both her hands on his arms where they crossed over her torso. "You keep saying it. But I don't think you believe it any more than I do."

"You can't really see the future, Tiny. There's a lot of magic in the world, but there's no such thing as precognition."

"If you've seen enough of the past, you can always see the future."

"Why? Because history repeats itself?"

"Yes. And people don't really change. Not much anyway."

Ben sighed and lowered his cheek to press against her neck. A slow, irregular heartbeat touched his skin. "You don't want me to be less human," he said softly. "If I were less human, I wouldn't be me."

She put her hand up to his rough cheek. "You think that. But who you are isn't limited to your biology. This body you carry is only one expression of yourself. It is, in the end, incidental. The crumbling chest, not the enduring gold inside." Her fingers teased the curls of hair at his temple. "I have... become attached to many people in my life. Human and vampire. When I care for a person, I desire the gold, not the crumbling chest."

Do you desire me?

He closed his eyes and didn't speak it. She cared for him. Ben knew that. In fact, if pressed, she would give him her love. She loved Giovanni. She loved Beatrice.

He wanted to be more.

But he wouldn't say it. He couldn't. It would ruin everything.

"Come on." He sat straight and squeezed her shoulders. "Let's do this. You and me. We stay together, and I'll get more rope so we can start mapping the second tunnel. If it's there, it'll go faster with your nose."

THEY STARTED the same way they had with the first tunnel, but the attempt went wrong quickly. They ran into a dead end at turn three. They went back. They started from the beginning. Ben got a new notebook and the second attempt went to turn eleven before they ran into a cavern instead of a tunnel.

There were more streams and obstacles in this section of the caves. The waterfall from the sinkhole ran into a stream that flowed under the rock they were walking on, sometimes giving way in sections they had to tiptoe across.

Water led to erosion. Erosion led to cave-ins. More than once Ben and Tenzin had to stop and get shovels to dig out a partially blocked passageway. Three times, Ben had to stop and snap Tenzin out of a daze when she seemed to be getting lost.

Ben felt a little more secure that this tunnel was taller than the last earthen one. The path broke open into large caverns more often, which made navigating more difficult—caverns weren't marked on the map—but also seemed to put Tenzin at ease.

There was only one time he'd truly gotten nervous.

"Tiny, hand me the shovel." He was walking ahead of Tenzin, his headlamp flashing against dripping walls on both sides. This section of the tunnel appeared to be pure limestone, which eased his mind, but there was a section ahead of them where the map might have indicated a turn that was partially blocked by a mudslide.

Tenzin passed the shovel forward, then perched on a rock near the tunnel wall. Ben tested the edge of the mud. If it was solid, he didn't want to disturb it. If it was crumbled, it likely wasn't structurally significant.

Or so he was guessing.

Part of him was really wishing they did have an earth vampire with them.

"Hey, Tenzin."

"Yes?"

"If we ever look for anything underwater, we're taking a water vampire with us."

She tossed small stones against the limestone. "I wouldn't dream of doing anything otherwise. You know, it's interesting that you brought that up."

"Oh?" He poked higher. Still crumbling. Still soft.

"Yes. Cheng sent me a letter a few months ago—" A slick, shifting sound cut off the rest of her words.

"Tenzin!" Ben turned to see a chunk of mud had broken away from the wall near the top of the tunnel and slid down, partially burying Tenzin. The mud exposed limestone above it. Ben didn't see any danger of further collapse, but the mud had shoved her to one side of the tunnel, nearly covering her face and part of her torso.

She was frozen, her eyes wide and her fangs bared.

"Fuck." Ben crouched down and started to clear the mud from around her. "Good thing I made you put on these coveralls." He stopped when he heard the growl.

She was staring at him, and there was no hint of recognition behind her eyes. Despite his careful training, Ben's heart began to pound. "Tenzin?"

Her head tilted to the side, and she leaned forward, mud falling around her as she breathed him in.

"Tenzin." His voice was louder, sharper. "Tiny, snap the fuck out of it."

Her lip curled up, and he saw her fangs gleaming in his headlamp. Her eyes were on his neck.

Shit shit shit.

Ben forced himself to take deep breaths and calm his heart. Then he unzipped his coveralls and stripped off the shirt underneath.

Tenzin stopped growling. Her mouth dropped open and her fangs grew even longer.

Why the fuck is that hot?

There was something wrong with him.

Her eyes moved from his neck to his torso. He could feel her gaze like a physical touch.

"You like the view?" he muttered. "Yeah, I know you do, little liar."

For the first time since the earth had fallen over her face, she looked into his eyes.

"Hey there, pretty monster," he murmured, taking his shirt and wiping the side of her face with it, clearing the mud from her eyes, cheek, and mouth. Using his familiar scent to bring her back around. "Hey, Tiny. It's me. I'm not dinner; I'm your friend."

She turned her face and breathed in the scent of his shirt. Despite the cold temperatures underground, he'd been sweating under his coveralls. That shirt would be ripe with his sweat and pheromones.

Old advice from his uncle echoed in Ben's mind like the sound of rushing water bouncing around the tunnels. *Remember, Benjamin. When we lose our human instincts, we react like predators. Even the most controlled of us can fall victim under the wrong circumstances. We have to be reminded of who we are.*

"Hey, Tenzin."

She was still smelling his shirt. Her eyes had moved from his body to his face. She was examining him, but her fangs had eased back and her expression was more human.

"Remember me?"

From one second to the next, she returned. "Yes."

Tenzin swiped Ben's shirt from his hand, cleaned her face with it, and tossed it back to him before she turned and walked out of the tunnel.

After she left, Ben sat on the floor and took three long breaths.

Close. Too close.

He stopped searching after that. They had set pitons and ropes for much of the cave, marked drop-offs with flags, and cleared the main tunnel from two mudslides. Ben was losing hope that anything of substance would be found in the cave, until he walked out and saw a red flag stuck in the ground near the first turn.

He walked faster. "Tenzin?"

When he exited the tunnel, he saw her, bent over the pool where the waterfall fell, sweeping something back and forth.

She looked up with a huge grin on her face. "I told you. It smells different."

THEY LOOKED at the two profiles on the face of the coin Tenzin held in the palm of her hand.

"Gold," Ben said. "William and Mary one-guinea gold piece. Turn of the seventeenth century. Great condition. This would be worth a lot to collectors, more than just the gold's value."

"I could be convinced to part with it for the right price," Tenzin said. "That fits with when Enríquez was raiding British ships, correct?"

"Yes." He tried to look closer, but Tenzin closed her hand around the coin. "Tiny."

"Fine." She handed it over. "But this one is mine."

"You found it." He held it up to examine it better. "Where?"

"It was about three inches under the mud. See? I told you that was the right tunnel."

"You said the dry one was the right tunnel."

"I'm pretty sure you said that."

"Yeah, no." He cocked his head. "You found it quickly."

"For the last time, my hunting instincts were roused and gold smells—"

"Different. Yeah, I know. The problem is, we need to figure out a way to rouse your hunting instincts so you can sniff out this gold without my becoming dinner along the way."

"Huh." Tenzin sat back and stared at the waterfall. "Yeah, I have no idea."

"That's helpful."

She shrugged. "It's been a while since I fed, so that probably helps."

It doesn't help my neck.

"Okay, so... you wait on eating until we find the treasure. I can't say I love that idea, but it does have logic on its side. We could try you searching alone—"

"No." She stood. "That's not a good idea."

The look on her face was raw. Wary. It was so rare for Tenzin to concede any weakness, Ben didn't know what to say.

"We'll go together." She looked into his eyes. "I won't kill you. I don't think I'd be able to even if I wanted to."

What does that mean? You nearly did half an hour ago.

"Okay, we go together." He stood, handed the coin back to her, and zipped up his coveralls. He'd started to get a chill again. "I'm going to warm up, sit in the last of the sun for a while, and then get some food and sleep."

"Sounds good."

"When we're ready to work again, we'll focus on the tunnel where you found the coin. And I'll try to shut up and let you use your nose."

"Good idea."

And we're not going to mention what happened before in the tunnel at all, are we?

Tenzin's eyes held his, and they did not reveal a thing.

Ben nodded. "Right."

15

Ben woke before it was light. He glanced at the clock on his phone; it was only five in the morning.

Sleep when you're tired. Eat when you're hungry.

He'd lost track of how long they'd been in the cavern, but his phone was nearly dead. He'd forgotten to use his solar charger the day before, and very little power was left.

Tenzin unzipped the tent before he could sit up.

"Hey." She was buzzing with excitement. "I heard you wake up."

His voice was hoarse when he answered. "It's early."

"I set up the work lights already." She slipped inside the tent and sat cross-legged on the floor. "It's warm in here."

"Yeah." Ben rubbed his eyes.

"You produce heat when you sleep. It makes the ambient temperature more comfortable."

He took a deep breath. "Tiny, did you have a reason for barging in here?" Not that she usually needed a reason.

Boundary issues. They had them.

"I'm..." Tenzin frowned at him.

"What?" He needed to piss. He wanted to get dressed. He

wanted coffee, and he had limited patience for her chatter this morning.

"I am sorry I lost my awareness yesterday."

She was apologizing? That almost never happened.

"There was a moment where I lost track of myself. I don't believe it will happen again. I will be more aware—"

"It's fine," he mumbled. "I know you don't like being underground."

This time she was the one who let the silence stretch. "You don't want to know why?"

He wanted to challenge her, but what was the point? *"There is no meaning in pain."* How many times had he heard her say it? Asking would relieve his own curiosity, but it would do nothing for her.

"If you ever want to tell me," he said quietly, "I'll listen."

She nodded. "Thank you. But no."

"We'll stick together today. Are you still sure it's better for you not to feed? I brought blood and blood-wine."

She curled her lip. Tenzin hated preserved blood. "I'll be fine. Especially now that I know what this gold smells like. I'll be more focused."

"Does each gold smell different?"

"Yes. Slightly. Different alloys. The less pure it is, the stronger it is. If that makes sense."

"It does. So pure gold—"

"I can still smell it, but it's faint."

"Okay." He was trying to figure out the scientific basis for gold smelling like anything at all, but he figured if Tenzin could use her nose, then why question it. He was still taking his metal detector.

"The tunnel where I found it isn't deep."

"So... you ignored me and went exploring?"

"No. But the air doesn't smell stale, and I can't hear any water from the entrance."

"Okay, give me half an hour." He really needed to pee.

Tenzin wasn't moving.

"I need to piss, Tiny."

She rolled her eyes and rolled away from the tent flap. "Human."

"Yep. Are you staying in here?"

"Yes, it's warm." As soon as Ben vacated the air mattress, Tenzin rolled over and bounced on it. "I want one of these."

"You don't sleep." Ben yawned when he stood up.

"I still want one."

He shook his head and walked to the entrance of the cavern. Stepping outside into the sinkhole, he felt the air change. It was warmer. Softer. A little drier, despite the humid air. A breeze touched his skin and lifted his spirits.

"Tenzin!" he shouted.

"What?" Her voice was tiny from underground.

"The sun isn't up yet. Why don't you come outside and get some fresh air?"

"You know I don't actually need to breathe, right?"

"Are you a wind vampire or not? Get out here." He walked behind a tumble of rocks to pee. "Get some altitude. It'll be good for you."

A barely mumbled "fine" was his only warning before she zoomed overhead and into the air. Ben didn't even have his pants zipped up.

"Tiny terror," he muttered.

Tenzin flew in loops overhead, like a bird stretching its wings. He heard her breathing deeply and speaking in her own language. What was she saying? Who was she speaking to? More than once, Ben suspected it was the voices within herself, but who was he to say?

She stretched herself in the air for ten or fifteen minutes while Ben stretched out on the ground and stared at the slowly lightening sky. The pearl-grey dawn was creeping toward them, and Ben knew she'd have to return to the cavern before the sun breached the horizon.

For now, let her fly.

SEARCHING the tunnel where Tenzin had found the gold coin proved more complicated than initially predicted.

"Are you getting anything?" he asked.

"No. You?"

Ben swept the metal detector slowly over the second small crevice off the main channel. "Nothing."

It was still bothering him that none of this was even vaguely approaching the directions on the map. That map might have been written by an amateur, but it was an amateur who had taken care to mark specific topographical features and points of interest. How could a treasure map lead them so carefully to the tunnels where the gold was stored and then be so completely off when it came to specifics?

It didn't make sense to Ben, but Tenzin insisted on following her nose, and she wasn't willing to deviate since she'd gotten a taste of the treasure.

"This way," she said, motioning Ben toward a narrow passage to the left of the main tunnel.

"Are you sure?" Ben swept his light over the ceiling. Water dripped from the limestone more readily than the rest of the passageway. He could hear water in the distance. The ground was muddy.

"Yes, I'm sure."

Tenzin walked ahead of him, the light from her helmet

giving him a point to follow. He bumped his helmet twice; the passageway was low. He followed her light and her voice, moving deliberately deeper into the cavern. The water was growing louder. The ground sloped down. He no longer had to duck to move forward.

"Tenzin?"

"What?"

He followed the faint echo of her voice. Ben ducked under a low arch and stepped sideways through a narrow passage, then he heard the echoes grow.

Loud. Louder. The sound of water was nearly deafening.

"Tenzin?" he yelled into the darkness. He couldn't see her light anywhere. He couldn't hear her footsteps. His voice echoed off a high ceiling. Where was she? "Where are you?"

"Here!"

He swept his flashlight back and forth three times before he saw her, perched in a corner of the cavern, her head uncovered.

"Where the hell is your helmet?"

She waved toward the ground. "Somewhere. I think I dropped it in the water. Careful."

Ben unclipped the flashlight from his belt and pointed it at the ground. Running through the middle of the cavern was a deep crevice where the sound of water was loudest. It was only one of the many underground rivers and streams of Camuy. The narrow crevice wouldn't be hard to cross, but who knew where it went or how far the fall was if he slipped.

"Okay," he said, carefully stepping to the side of the stream. "Is that why you're flying?"

"I can smell fresh air." She poked at the ceiling. "I think we're close to the surface here."

"We were walking down."

"Were we? Passages underground can be deceiving."

"That's true." Ben carefully tossed his backpack and metal

detector across the crevice and braced himself on a sturdy boulder before he hopped across. "What do you think? Have you looked at the ground in here? Any signs of disturbance?"

Not that there was likely to be visible disturbance after a few hundred years. With this much water in the cave, erosion was inevitable. He could feel water dripping overhead too. Tenzin was probably right that they were nearer to the surface than it seemed.

Ben looked around the cavern. Rocky walls shaped like an inverse cone led to nothing but darkness. He couldn't see the ceiling in this section of the cave. It was nearly perfectly round, and the ground was rocky. There was no moss. No light had ever touched it. But signs of life still existed in the pale fish darting in the stream.

"The world is an amazing place," he murmured.

"Yes." Her voice was still coming from overhead, but this time from the opposite side of the cavern. "Can you hear the rain? It's raining above us. I can smell it and hear it. We're so close." She let out a quiet grunt.

"Tenzin, what are you doing up there?"

"I'm..." She grunted again. "Testing."

"Testing what?"

"The rocks."

"Bad idea!" he shouted. "Stop. Seriously, what are you thinking? You're pushing on the rocks? Do you want a cave-in?"

"It's not going to cave in."

A sliding sound across the cavern caused Ben's heart to stop. He pointed the flashlight in the direction of the noise and looked, but he could see nothing. Then he pointed it up at the ceiling. Tenzin was poised at the top of the cavern, poking the limestone with the walking stick he'd given her to help navigate the rocky floor of the tunnel.

"Stop it," he said quietly. "Right now."

"That wasn't because of me."

"Do you know that? You're suddenly a cave logistics expert?"

"And you are?"

"I've studied it more than you!" He tossed his backpack back across the crevice, along with his metal detector. "I'm going back."

"Don't be a spoilsport," she said. "Ben, you haven't even used your machine. As long as we're here, you should at least use your machine."

"Some of us can die, did you forget that?"

She flew down and landed beside him, picking up his metal detector.

"Don't." He swiped it from her. "You'll short it out."

"Fine! Don't let me help. I was just exploring. Remember when you liked to explore? Back when you had a sense of humor?"

He turned on her. "Since when have you wanted to explore underground? When did that become a thing? You think this is a game?"

He spun back toward the passage where they'd entered the wider cavern and squeezed into the passageway, not bothering to remove his backpack. He bent to pick up his metal detector, narrowly avoiding hitting his head on a jutting limestone protrusion. He heard Tenzin behind him.

She was stewing and muttering under her breath, but Ben didn't care. Poking and prodding at a cave? Was she insane? They were going through a section of cave that was more earth than limestone. They were already doing enough damage leaving the marks they were. These caves were isolated ecosystems, delicately balanced; a single new factor could cause...

A rumble that seemed to come from every direction.

Ben's heart seized.

"Tenzin," he whispered. "Go back." Back to the limestone. Back to the fresh air. "Tenzin, go back!"

Too late. The first clump of mud hit him on the left shoulder as he was turning. The second knocked him to his feet as the tunnel began to collapse.

BEN WOKE with the taste of earth in his mouth. Mud had closed around him, but it wasn't solid. He could breathe. He wasn't crushed. He felt for his flashlight but couldn't find it. He reached for his helmet and found it still attached to his head. With a few shakes, the light turned on.

"Tenzin?" He tried to move his head. He was on the ground and his legs were covered, but he thought he could crawl out with a little help.

Crawl out of the mud. Take stock of your surroundings.

Don't panic. Your chest will expand and you'll be more stuck than you were before.

"Tenzin, where are you?"

Dear God, don't let her be under the collapse. He tried to move his head, but his range of motion was too limited. He carefully shimmied back and forth until he'd freed his legs. He was sitting up and searching for his flashlight when he heard a shifting sound to his right. He moved his head in that direction, only to see Tenzin crawling on all fours. She was coming toward him, covered in mud and bleeding from her cheek. She froze when the light shone in her eyes.

"Shit. Sorry." He angled his headlamp down. "Are you okay? What happened to your cheek?"

She didn't say a word.

"Tenzin?"

This was not good.

Ben crawled to her, but her eyes were blank and unfocused. The pupils were dilated and fixed, but she wasn't growling. She wasn't panicked. She didn't seem to be aware at all.

"Hey, Tiny. It's me. We're underground, but we're okay. We're going to get out." He reached up and brushed the mud away from her mouth and cheek. He left a hand on her cheek. "Talk to me, okay?"

She turned to him, her mouth dropped open, and a rasping sound left her throat. It kept going and going. Her eyes were fixed and her face was frozen in terror.

Ben's heart raced when he realized what was happening.

Tenzin was screaming. And it was completely silent.

"Wake up," he begged her. "Tenzin, please." His heart ached. Watching her scream was the most powerless he'd ever felt in his life. "Tiny, wake up. It's me. I'm here. We're okay. Just wake up." He pressed his cheek to hers and put his arms around her. "Please. Please."

The screaming stopped when her skin touched his. She shuddered, then grew still.

She crawled over his legs, straddling him. She pulled back and Ben loosened his hold on her.

"Tenzin?"

She still wasn't speaking.

Ben didn't get truly nervous until she knocked his helmet away. He could barely see her in the dim reflected light. A faint growl came from her throat.

Shit.

She'd gone into the cave hungry, and she'd been caught in the mudslide. Her eyes were glazed with bloodlust, and there was no hint of recognition as she stared at him.

"Tenzin?" He swallowed hard.

She leaned forward, smelling his neck. She still wasn't talking.

She was hunting.

Time to panic.

He reached up and unzipped his coveralls, hoping his familiar scent would wake her from the bloodlust. He spread the canvas wide, exposing his T-shirt to her. His neck was bare. He could smell his perspiration and her hunger in the mud-filled passage. Ben put both his muddy hands on her cheeks.

Tenzin froze.

"Hey there," he whispered. "Remember me?"

She paused.

"It's me. It's Ben."

She leaned forward again, filling her lungs with his scent. He felt her lips at his neck. Her nose dragged along the line of his jaw, following his pulse. He could feel a buzz of amnis along his skin.

He tightened his fingers on her cheek. "Don't use amnis on me. That's not allowed, remember? Wake up, Tenzin. Please wake up." Tears came to his eyes when the fingers touching his neck went numb. She wasn't waking up. She wasn't hearing him. "Tiny, it's Ben. It's me. Don't do this."

He tried leaning away from her. Eventually he was lying prone and Tenzin was crouched over him. Trying to escape from her would be useless.

He was prey, and she was a far faster predator.

"Tiny," he kept repeating. "Tiny, it's me. It's Ben."

His head was swimming. He was dizzy and euphoric at the same time. Tenzin paused, and Ben thought he heard a sound close to awareness come from her throat. It was somewhere between a sigh and a cry.

"Tenzin?"

The cry turned into a low growl, she took another deep breath, then her fangs struck his neck.

"Ahh." Ben's back arched. "*Fuck.*"

The pain of her bite wasn't what he'd imagined.

It was *so much better.*

The piercing of her fangs into his skin hit Ben like the onset of the most powerful orgasm he'd ever felt. Her mouth on his neck, pulling his blood like a direct line to his cock. Her body over him, her breasts pressed into his chest. The pleasure so intense it was near pain.

"Fuck, fuck, *fuck!*" Ben arched up and into her, grinding his erection between her legs as she straddled him. His hands moved to her ass, grabbing her curves and pressing them closer.

She was feeding from him, and it was no gentle bite.

It was pleasure. It was pain. It was heaven and hell and she was drinking his blood and he wanted it. He wanted her to devour him. One hand moved from her ass to her breast and he squeezed. He swept his thumb over her erect nipple and turned his head so she could go deeper. His other hand gripped her hair, pulling her mouth from his neck. He could feel his flesh tear, but he ignored it, dragging her bloody mouth to his.

The taste of blood in his mouth conjured a dream. They were locked together, her blood in his mouth. His blood in hers. Their bodies moved as one. In the back of his mind, the image spun as lights flashed behind his closed eyes.

Her mouth was everything he wanted. He cut his lips on the curved fangs. She sucked his tongue into her mouth and bit down, drinking from him as he moaned under her.

Yes.

Take it.

Take me.

I'm yours.

I've always been yours.

She released his tongue. His mouth. Ben turned his head as Tenzin bent to the other side of his neck. He gripped her hair tighter, and his arm went around the small of her back, cradling her as she killed him.

"It's okay," he whispered. He could feel the blood pooling at his neck even as she drank from the other side. "I know..." His breath caught when he felt her tongue lapping at his neck. "It's okay, Tiny."

He swallowed hard. He was going to pass out. Tears slipped from the corner of his eyes, mingling with the rivulets of blood. He smoothed her hair back from her face and tucked it behind her ear as his fingers went numb.

"It's okay, Tiny."

Darkness took him.

TENZIN CRADLED the body beneath her, the pleasure of the blood near blinding. She lapped at the neck, one hunger sated while the other raged. She was empty and he filled her, but it wasn't enough.

She wanted more. She wanted to taste his skin and ride the hard erection pressed between her legs. She was blinded by the taste of his blood in her mouth. Familiar blood. Unfamiliar blood. Sweet and hot.

She'd woken in the darkness with the taste of earth in her mouth. She'd risen from the dirt, scraped away the tomb around her, every instinct aroused. She smelled the scent of prey in the darkness. Followed it to the male beneath her.

She drank and she wanted more.

He held her close, and the hands were familiar. The touch of his fingers was gentle at her temple. They didn't strike. They didn't grip or break or twist or hurt.

Gentle.

Familiar.

"It's okay, Tiny."

Benjamin. She let out a long breath. *My Benjamin.*

Tenzin blinked and sat up. She could see his pale skin in the darkness, see the pool of blood at his neck and the raw fang marks in his neck. His lips were covered in blood. His blood.

"No."

His eyes were closed. His pulse slow.

Tenzin tasted the blood in her mouth, felt the sticky iron-rich liquid on her lips.

She sprang to her feet and screamed. "No!"

Tenzin knelt down and put her mouth to his neck, sealing the deep wounds she'd left with her fangs. She poured her blood into the bite marks, cleaning them before she wiped his cool skin with her sleeve.

"Benjamin."

She would not panic.

"*Ben.*"

This wasn't how it would be. It couldn't be.

No, this would not be.

Her heart thumped twice, and Tenzin took careful stock of how much blood she'd drunk. She was sated, near bursting with it. For her, as old as she was, that meant she'd probably drunk no more than two pints. She lifted the light and looked at the blood on the ground. At most a cup more.

Two and a half pints.

He would not die. There was no reason for him to die. He had passed out from shock, not from blood loss. From the cold. She needed to get him out of the cave and get him warm. After that, he'd be fine.

Fine.

"Don't wake up," she muttered. "Just... don't."

If she were lucky, he'd remember nothing except her biting him. He'd be mad at her, pout for a reasonable amount of time—

at the most, she was estimating two years—and then they could move on.

Tenzin ignored the aching between her legs and the raw sexual hunger Ben had roused. She tried to banish the rich taste of his blood, but it had entered her bloodstream. Her head was filled with the scent of him now. It invaded her mind, tormenting her.

You want him.

Take him.

He will be yours.

He wants you too.

No, it didn't work that way. Not with Ben.

Another whispering voice taunted her at the back of her mind.

Kill him now.

He is a weakness.

Kill the weakness or it will destroy you.

No.

She was not that creature anymore. She was more. He had made her more. She was a friend. A protector. She was a partner.

"It's okay, Tiny."

She'd been killing him, and he'd offered her reassurance. Tenzin swallowed the scream that wanted to escape her throat. She zipped Ben's coveralls and covered him with the foil emergency blanket he'd stuffed in her pocket.

She walked to the side of the tunnel leading back to the cavern and punched her arm through the mud with all her rage. Her arm went up to the shoulder, but her hand didn't reach air on the other side. That side was blocked thoroughly.

She walked to the other side. The tunnel was only partially covered on this end. She would go back to the larger cavern and find a way out. She'd smelled fresh air. She could work with that.

She left Ben in the tunnel, covered by the blanket, and flew back to the tunnel holding the headlamp under her arm.

Don't wake up. She glanced back at the tunnel, knowing he'd be terrified if he woke in the dark. *Just don't wake up.*

Tenzin flew over the rushing stream and up, weaving between the rocks dripping down from the ceiling of the cave. She followed her nose to the source of the fresh air and reached out with her elemental energy.

There.

A channel through the rocks, broken and twisting where the water leaked down. Tenzin floated down below the crack and called the air around her.

Come to me.

You are mine.

Mine to command.

She closed her eyes, felt her body accept the space around and within her, and called the wind to her bidding.

The rocks cracked and groaned, powerless to the rushing currents that beat upward like a hurricane rising from within the earth.

Tenzin lifted her arms, Ben's blood fueling her, her hair rising upward with the current, as the tiny crack grew wide. Wider.

The earth groaned and a chunk of limestone fell away, revealing a spear of direct sunlight Tenzin had to dart away to avoid. The rocks fell into the bottom of the cavern, crashing into the stream.

She flew back to the tunnel and lifted Ben, dragging him back to the larger cavern. She propped him against a wall, covered him with the blanket again, and sat down to wait for dusk, hoping he'd take a nice long nap. From the angle of the sun, she only had two or three hours to wait.

She glanced at Ben's pale skin and red neck. She dragged her eyes away from the line of his jaw and the defined muscle where his shoulder met his neck. She still wanted to sink her teeth into it. She closed her eyes and tried to will the image away, but his blood had infected her and it was all she could think about.

Dammit.

She was going to have to call Giovanni.

16

The first thing Ben noticed was the massive headache pounding between his temples. He was lying on something soft and he was warm. He was dry. He could hear a Spanish voice talking on the radio in the distance, and for a moment he was back at his grandmother's house with the smell of chicken, garlic, and coffee filling the air.

He blinked and opened his eyes to filtered sunlight streaming through the window of a house.

Where was he?

Who was with him?

How had he gotten here?

Don't do this, Tenzin.

His hand went to his throat. It was sore, but it wasn't bleeding. In a rush of memory, he felt her mouth sucking his neck. The blind hunger of their kiss. Blood pouring out of him and into her. Her breast in his greedy palm. The soft angle of her body cradling his cock and his hand gripping her hair.

His body reacted to the memory and he sat up in a rush, only to feel his head swimming and his stomach roll.

Ben groaned and lowered his head into his hands.

Where am I?

A dog barked somewhere in the distance, and Ben looked around the room. It looked like a bungalow or cottage. A single room with a bed in the corner, a kitchen near the front door, and a couch where he was lying with a light blanket thrown over him. Public service announcements hung on one wall. Antilittering slogans in Spanish. A large map of the island with red and yellow highlights.

A screen door slammed again, and Ben heard the sound of a dog. Panting, it ran around the corner and slid across the old wood floor, coming to a tongue-lolling halt with its head near Ben's crotch.

"Hey. Whoa." He diverted the canine's head from his lap and gave his ears a friendly scratch. "Hi, there."

Footsteps came around the corner, and Ben looked up to see a young woman in a uniform walking toward him.

"Hi." She smiled a little. "Oso was barking, so I thought you might be awake."

Ben blinked. The woman was wearing a light green shirt and brown uniform pants made of canvas. A badge hung on her pocket, which was covered with an official-looking gold emblem. Her hair was tied up in a neat bun, and two simple gold hoops hung in her ears.

She looked familiar. Very familiar.

Damn you, Tenzin.

Ben didn't know how Tenzin had gotten them out of the cavern or why she'd left him alone, but for some reason she'd decided to be a pain in the ass even in her absence. She had to have known. It was impossible that it was a coincidence.

"I'm Liza Ochoa Rios." The woman held out her hand. "I'm a ranger at the park here. How are you feeling?"

~

BEN SAT AT THE TABLE, drinking *café con leche* across from his cousin, who didn't know she was his cousin. Her dog sat next to her, a giant mutt of indeterminate heritage who lived up to his name. He was dark brown and had a goofy smile. He looked far more like a small bear than an island dog.

"I found you lying on the side of the road. I'm not sure how long you'd been out there. Is that your Jeep over by the trailhead?"

"Maybe?"

"You know, I don't have any interest in making trouble for you, but the park isn't officially open yet. We're still doing a lot of cleanup on the roads and infrastructure. You're not supposed to be here. It's not safe."

Ben shook his head. "Sorry." His voice was hoarse. "I must have gotten some bad information. I didn't realize."

"So that is your Jeep?"

He nodded and tried not to stare at her. He'd seen pictures taken from a distance, but up close she looked so much more like their grandmother than he'd realized.

"Do you remember how you got on the trail?" Liza asked. "I nearly ran over you."

"I don't..." He took a sip of coffee. "I don't remember much. I know I have a rental house in Arecibo."

"You go out partying with anyone?"

"Not that I can remember. And I don't do drugs if that's what you're wondering. I was going hiking with a friend, but she can be... kind of flaky. We had a fight. Kind of."

Where are you, Tiny? When this is over, I'm gonna kill you.

"Huh." Liza didn't look like she believed him. "And those marks on your neck?"

Ben put a hand over the marks in question. He tried to act

surprised, but he didn't know if he pulled it off or not. The memory of Tenzin's mouth was too vivid.

"No idea," he said. "An animal bite maybe?"

"Don't know any animals with a bite like that."

"I wish I knew," he said. "But I really can't remember much."

He remembered everything.

Everything.

It was near dark outside, and the sun was covered by clouds. Rain poured down on the tin roof of the cabin.

"The roads are a mess right now," Liza said. "This storm came up really suddenly. You've barely woken up, and you still look kind of pale. We'll have to hike to your Jeep, so I'd really rather you stay here for a while. You could probably make it back to Arecibo tonight, but it might be close with the mud. I'd hate for you to get stuck and end up on your own out in the forest."

It was tempting to flee, but Ben also had to admit he was burning with curiosity about his cousin.

"I'll stay. I can sleep in your truck or something," he said. "If you're not comfortable with my sleeping on the couch."

Liza smiled a little. "I'm not worried about you. I already searched you for weapons, and you don't have any. Besides, Oso stays in the house at night, and no one messes with me as long as he's around."

Ben didn't doubt it. For all his friendly licks, the dog hadn't left her side the entire time Ben had been awake.

"I appreciate it. Thanks."

"What's your name? You didn't have any ID on you."

"Sorry. It's Ben. Ben... Vecchio."

"Nice to meet you, Ben. The kitchen is pretty basic here, but I made enough dinner for both of us. Hope you like *asopao*."

"Yeah." He nodded. "I love it."

~

"So how do you like being a park ranger?" Ben was digging into the bowl of chicken stew with chorizo and rice. It was exactly as he remembered it from when his abuela made it.

"I love it." Liza smiled. "Right now it's complicated. We have a lot of work just cleaning up, and the power grid—" As if on cue, the lights flickered out. "Yeah, I'm sure you've been able to tell it's still a mess. But I don't need much, and my real house has solar panels, which are great."

The lights flickered on again.

"You have a generator here?" Ben asked.

"We're only supposed to use it for emergencies. Other than that, lanterns and candles."

"You must love it on the island," Ben said. "To stay with all the problems. Were you born here?"

"I was, but I went back and forth between here, Florida, and New York growing up. Did my degree in Florida, then came back here."

"You were here during the hurricane?"

She nodded. "Yeah. On the other side of the island though. I'm only in Camuy for a short-term assignment. I live near El Yunque. You know—?"

"Yeah," he said. "I know where El Yunque is." *I know where your house is. I know how much your bills are and how many eggs your chickens are laying right now.*

Better to not tell her that.

"For a while I thought about leaving. Our house was okay— we only had like one leak in the roof, which was insanely lucky —but our garden was just..." She made a sweeping gesture. "Everything was gone. Only the trees left, and they were stripped bare. But my grandmother wouldn't go anywhere else."

Ben tried to keep his voice even. "Your grandmother?"

"Yes. She loves it here." Liza smiled. "The most beautiful island in the world. That's what she calls PR. Hit by a hurricane or not. She'd never live anywhere else." She glanced at him. "You have family on the island? You look—"

"I'm Italian," he said quickly. "New York."

"Ah." She nodded. "No offense, but you don't sound too New York."

He smiled. "I went to high school in LA. But I'm living back in New York now."

"Everyone's gotta go home eventually, right?" She took another bite. "And if you're my grandmother, you never leave home. Not if you can help it. My mom and my uncle went away, and I think it just about killed her."

Ben's heart jumped. "But they're back now?"

Liza smiled sadly. "My mom came back before she passed. My uncle didn't. He lives up in your neighborhood."

You have no idea how right you are.

"My mom and I lived in New York on and off over the years. I never liked it much. Too cold in the winter."

"So you're back. Your grandma must love that."

"Yeah. And she takes good care of me. She's an amazing cook. And we have a great neighborhood. Everyone looks out for each other."

"That's awesome."

"Yeah." Liza nodded. "It might not be the richest island out there, but that's one thing we definitely have. We take care of each other. Take care of our neighbors."

Ben finished his dinner. "Well, you definitely took care of me. And I'm really grateful."

"No problem." She frowned at the red marks on his neck. "I just wish we knew what kind of animal might have done that. Those bruises are so strange."

Ben swallowed the lump in his throat. "It's a mystery."

"No kidding."

Tenzin, Tenzin, Tenzin. You have some explaining to do.

BEN DIDN'T FEEL like sleeping so soon after waking up, so Liza put on the television while he cleaned the kitchen. He washed and dried the dishes, put them away on the open shelves of the small cabin, then walked outside to get some fresh air.

He looked up into the misty, pitch-black night. A light rain was still falling, but that wouldn't bother her. Was she back at the cavern? Back at the house in Arecibo? San Juan? Already headed back to New York?

No, she wouldn't leave. She'd still be focused on the treasure. She'd left him on someone else's doorstep and kept hunting for her precious gold.

For the twenty-sixth time that year, Ben asked himself what he was doing with his life.

He and Liza were watching a local news show out of Arecibo when someone knocked at the door. Ben went on immediate alert, as did Oso.

Liza stood and hit the remote control to mute the TV. "That's weird. It's late."

"Let me answer it," Ben said.

Liza patted her hip and Oso came to her. She smiled. "You really think it's an ax murderer or something? This is Camuy, not New York. It's probably someone lost in the forest like you. A car stuck in the mud. You never know."

Ben knew she was right, but he still stood and followed her around the corner, hanging back while she answered the door.

"Buenas noches, necesitas ayuda, Señor?"

"Hi." A familiar voice in a careful American accent came

from outside. "I'm hoping you might know something about my nephew. My name is Giovanni Vecchio."

GIOVANNI TOOK the towel Liza handed him and rubbed it over his soaking-wet hair. "Thank you so much."

Ben's adoptive uncle was a vampire turned during the height of the Florentine renaissance, chosen by a madman to be the ideal of human achievement physically, intellectually, and supernaturally. He was a fire vampire with the looks of a super-model and the brains of a rocket scientist, and Ben expected women—*all* women—to react to him.

The fact that it was his cousin this time did make it a little weird.

Liza's cheeks were flushed. "You're welcome. It's nothing. I'm just glad you showed up. I mean, I'm glad Ben isn't all alone out there."

Ben stared at Giovanni. "I didn't know you were coming."

"It was a last-minute thing." Giovanni glanced at him from the corner of his eye. "She called me."

"Did she?"

Liza looked between them, halfway between confused and amused. "Your friend?" she asked. "The flaky one?"

"Flaky." Giovanni nodded. "That's definitely one word for her."

"I'm not going to lie," Liza said. "I don't think too much of people who leave their friends alone in the middle of the forest. I think your... Sorry, did you say your *nephew*?"

"Yes," Giovanni said.

"You look more like brothers."

Well, that was flattering. Ben smiled. "We get that a lot. It's an unusual family."

"Huh." Liza looked skeptical again. "Well, Ben is better off with you here than a flaky friend."

"Indeed." Giovanni took the cup of coffee Liza poured for him. "Though she did drop me off by the Jeep. So we have that. It's how I got here."

"No problem with mud?" Liza asked.

"Nothing I couldn't handle. I was checking anywhere that looked promising along the road on the way back to town. Was going to go to the park headquarters in the morning if I couldn't find any sign of this guy." Giovanni leaned across and slapped Ben's shoulder. "He's the worst about not charging his cell phone."

"You have to be careful out here. It's a small island, but there are still a lot of wild places."

"Luckily, the roads are in good shape. A few obstacles now and then. You just have to go slow."

"Good." Liza clapped her hands together and looked at Ben. "So you can sleep in your own bed tonight. That will be a relief. This couch isn't all that comfortable. It should only take an hour or so to get back to Arecibo."

Ben knew it was better for him to go, but he was unaccountably annoyed with his uncle for showing up and interrupting his time with his cousin. It was possible he'd never see her again.

"Yeah." Ben glanced at Giovanni. "That'll be great."

"But please," Liza said, "finish your coffee before you go. Have you eaten tonight? I have some chicken stew left if you'd like some."

Giovanni looked at Ben, then Liza. "That would be amazing. Thank you."

They spent an hour visiting after that, Giovanni teasing out more and more details about Liza's life and her family. Ben sat in awe of the charm offensive. He didn't know if he was more grateful or annoyed that his uncle was flirting so shamelessly with his cousin. It was a harmless flirt, but still.

Giovanni got her to talk about her work in El Yunque and the progress reopening the park after Hurricane Maria. He got her to talk about the farm and tell funny stories about her grandmother. He also got her talking about some of the folk tales in the Camuy region.

"You're a folklore researcher?" Liza asked. "That's amazing. Do you work for a university? Something like that?"

"I do lecture sometimes," Giovanni said. "But I'm hired mostly for private research. To be honest, it pays better."

"Really?"

"Really." He leaned toward her. "So what about the Camuy Caves, huh? Any dark and mysterious tales around here? Ghost stories? Mythical creatures?"

"Well, you know the pirate beach in Puerto Hermina, right? There are lots of stories around that."

"But nothing around here?" Ben asked. "Nothing unique to the mountains?"

"Well..." Liza cocked her head. "Actually, there's the demon of Camuy. But that's an old, old story. Some people say it goes back to the Taíno."

"What's that one?" Giovanni said. "The oldest stories are always the best."

"I think it's just one of those things to keep kids in at night, you know?" Liza laughed. "Don't go into the hills at night or the demon of Camuy will drag you into the caves and drink your blood. That kind of thing."

"Huh." Ben said, pasting on a smile. "Kind of like the chupacabra in Northern Mexico?" He glanced at Giovanni, who was wearing a similarly mild expression.

"Exactly like that. We have the same myth here." Liza

looked at Giovanni. "I mean, don't most cultures have stories like that to keep children from wandering at night?"

"Of course." Giovanni spread his hands. "And in a place like Camuy, with so many caverns—so many of which have water in them—it would be prudent to keep children from wandering into the unknown. A story about a demon who drinks your blood would do the trick."

"Oh, I don't know if it would have scared me off as a kid," Ben said. "Who believes stuff like that?"

"Always a cynic, huh?" Liza asked. "Even as a child?"

"Always."

Giovanni stifled a smile. "You were a reckless child, Benjamin. Especially when there was something particular you wanted."

"You have to go after what you want," Ben said. "Even if there are risks."

"If I didn't know better"—Liza rose and took Giovanni's bowl and spoon—"I'd say the Camuy cave demon got your neck. I sure as heck don't know what else could make those marks."

Shut up, Giovanni mouthed at Ben when Liza's back was turned. *Just shut up.*

"Whatever it was," Giovanni said, "he was lucky you were around to pick him up."

"Just doing my job."

"And now we should go. We've inconvenienced you long enough, and I'm sure you'd like to get some sleep."

Ben and Giovanni rose. Ben scratched Oso behind the ears and walked over to Eliza. He gave her a hug. "Thanks. Seriously, thank you."

"You're welcome." She smiled at him and shook Giovanni's hand. "Be more careful, okay? And if you're ever in El Yunque, stop by the visitors' center and ask for me. I'll be back next week, and I'd be happy to show you around a park that's actually open, okay? Just stay out of this one until it's safer."

"Got it."

Ben and Giovanni gathered the dirty coveralls Liza had hung in the shed and waved as they climbed in the Jeep. It was ten minutes later, bumping down the road north to Arecibo, when Ben finally asked the question that had been burning in his gut since Giovanni arrived.

"Okay, where the hell is she, and why the *fuck* did she leave me alone and unconscious in the forest?"

17

Giovanni didn't answer right away. He drove the Jeep down the road for another half mile or so before he pulled over in a less muddy patch and got out of the car. Ben automatically hopped out and walked around the front to take over driving. His uncle was a fire vampire. Expecting a modern car to not short out when he drove it was asking for disappointment.

Giovanni met Ben in the front of the car and jerked him to a stop. His mouth set in a hard line, he jerked Ben's chin to the side and inspected his neck in the glow of the headlights.

Ben felt like he was fifteen again, his uncle inspecting him and Ben coming up short.

"Gio—"

"Shut up." Giovanni turned Ben's head to the other side and inspected the angry red marks on that side too. He put both hands on Ben's neck, his thumbs resting on Ben's pulse for a moment before he pulled Ben into a hug. "I'm very angry with her right now."

Ben let his shoulders relax in the fierce protectiveness of

Giovanni's embrace. "We were underground. There was a cave-in. You know how she gets when—"

"She told me." Giovanni pulled back. "Did you know she hadn't fed?"

Ben opened his mouth, then closed it.

Giovanni must have seen the truth on his face. He pushed Ben back. "*Non capisci una fava!* Did I raise an idiot?"

"Hey. We were trying to find the gold, and when she'd had a close call the day before, she was able to smell—"

"This happened twice?" His uncle was incredulous. "You had a close call one day and you go underground with her the next day? And you *knew* she hadn't fed?"

Ben didn't know what to say. In retrospect, it sounded exactly like the stupid idea it was. "We were underground. At the time—"

"You're as foolish about gold as she is," Giovanni said bitterly. "And this will end in tragedy. And remember, Ben, when it ends in tragedy, it isn't only the two of you who will be affected. Do you think I would ever be able to forgive her for killing my son?"

Ben swallowed the lump in his throat and blinked back tears. "She's not going to kill me."

Giovanni said nothing for a long time. They stood across from each other, mist falling around them in the glow of yellow headlights.

"Get in the car," Giovanni said quietly. "We're driving back to San Juan tonight and we don't have much time."

Ben climbed into the driver's seat and buckled his seat belt. He waited for Giovanni to close his door before he put the Jeep in gear and started driving.

His uncle was pissed. So pissed Ben could feel the heat from his skin across the car. It took a lot to make his tightly controlled uncle snap, but apparently he and Tenzin had managed.

"I'll be more careful," Ben said quietly. "I'm sorry I worried you."

They drove through the muddy forest and reached the main road in under an hour. Once they were back on gravel, Ben picked up speed. By the time they were back on the highway, his uncle had cooled off enough that Ben risked a question.

"Why are we going back to San Juan?"

"Because you've overlooked something about the map. Something very obvious."

"But you're not going to tell me what it is, are you?"

"What would that teach you?" Giovanni glanced at him from the corner of his eye. "We're going back to Camino's flat. I've already called him. He's expecting us tomorrow evening."

"Camino's house?" What had Ben missed in the old man's library? He'd studied the letters. Taken copies of correspondence. He'd tracked Tomás's home to Arecibo and found the start of the map. Was there something the old man was hiding?

"Tenzin is in San Juan," Giovanni said. "You two need to talk."

"We need to," Ben muttered, "but we won't. She doesn't do that. You should know that better than anyone."

"Because she doesn't talk to me?" Giovanni crossed his arms. "You're not me. Sometimes I think she treats you more like a peer than she treats me. Explain that one."

"I can't."

"Neither can I." His uncle paused as Ben passed a large truck heading east. The rain had grown heavier; it beat against the windshield and fell in sheets when they drove under overpasses.

"It's changing," Giovanni said quietly. "It was always going to change, because people change. She's not who she was, and neither are you. You've changed each other."

"I know." Ben flashed to the memory of Tenzin above him. Her breasts pressed to his chest. Her mouth at his neck. His hands pulling her closer as she bit.

Would he have let go if she'd released him? Or would he have pulled her closer still?

"You have to decide what you want," Giovanni said. "And so does she."

THEY PARKED the car in a paid lot a few blocks away from the house and walked through the streets of Old San Juan an hour or two before dawn.

"I have your keys." Giovanni tossed them in his direction. "I'm not sure how much of your gear is left at the caves. Most of it, I think. Tenzin just grabbed what she thought was most valuable."

"So God knows what's actually here and what's been left?"

"Pretty much."

Ben glanced at him. "Did you go?"

"To the cave? No. I'm angry as hell at her, and I don't want to push it."

Ben thought about telling his uncle not to be angry, but he didn't think it would make much difference. And he was mad at Tenzin too. Not for biting him during the cave-in, but for leaving him alone in the forest.

He unlocked the door and entered the house, which smelled like lamb polo and saffron tea.

She made your favorite dinner.

"Tenzin?" Ben set his keys on the counter and walked

through the house. She was nowhere to be found. He sighed and stuffed his hands in his pockets.

"Typical." Giovanni crossed his arms over his chest. "She'll be back before dawn."

"Right. I'm going to take a shower," Ben said. "Then I'm going to eat and go to sleep. There's an extra light-safe room down the hall on the left."

"Is there a dead bolt?"

"I installed dead bolts and alarms on all the bedrooms as soon as I got here."

"Thank you."

"No problem." Ben knew his uncle wasn't being paranoid. As unlikely as it was that anyone would come into their home during the day when Tenzin was awake, Giovanni lived a life of caution, and he was vulnerable during daylight.

"Good night, Benjamin." His uncle clasped him by the neck again and kissed his cheek. "I am phenomenally relieved you are healthy and I don't have to kill anyone."

"Good night." Ben swallowed that familiar lump. He didn't deserve having anyone care about him that much.

You're a little bastard.

He shut the door of his memory and walked to his bedroom. He stripped off his muddy clothes and started the shower, turning the water as hot as he could stand. For the first time he looked in the mirror and understood why his uncle was so angry.

His neck looked like it had been gnawed on. The fang marks had healed over—vampire blood could seal wounds—but broad, angry welts were left on both sides of his neck. There would be bruises. Fairly massive ones if he had to guess. Probably no scarring though. He flipped off the lights in the bathroom. The fluorescent was too bright. Darkness was far more comfortable to his eyes.

Her fangs in his neck. His cock between her legs. Hunger so acute it was painful. One sated, the other still raging.

Ben stepped into the shower, trying to ignore the reaction of his body to the memory, but in the dark warmth of the shower, it was all he could think about. It was the single most erotic encounter in his life, and it had nearly killed him.

He gripped his erection as the water poured over him, reliving every moment.

Her breast in his hand. Her nipple hard under his thumb when she bit his tongue and swallowed his blood. His cock hard between her legs.

When he climaxed, a near-silent groan left his throat. He could feel her teeth in his neck.

Ben pressed his forehead to the cool tile and let out a long breath, then he washed himself from head to toe, rinsed off, and dried himself with the soft cotton towels hanging in the bathroom, wincing a little when he had to touch his neck.

He left the bedroom and slipped on a pair of sweatpants he'd left in San Juan. Most of his clothes were in Quebradillas, but he'd been careful to leave a few things there. You never knew when you'd need to stop by a safe house. He walked shirtless out to the kitchen, served himself some polo from the pan on the stove, and ate on the patio, looking up at the stars breaking through the clouds.

He was nearly asleep on the lounge chair when he sensed her. She was perched on the roof, hidden by the palms.

"You left me alone in the forest," he said quietly.

"I left you with a human. One I knew was safe."

Ben didn't say anything.

"She took care of you. If you needed human medical care, she would have known. Rangers are trained in that sort of thing."

"You left me."

Tenzin was silent for a long time. "You needed to be with humans."

I needed you. He didn't say it. "Did you go back to the cave?"

"I needed Cara to call Giovanni."

"You told on us."

"We need his help. He said there's something on the map we're not seeing."

"Yeah, he told me the same thing."

With the safer topic of treasure hunting between them, Tenzin floated down from the roof and sat across from Ben on a lounger. "What did we miss?"

He drank in the sight of her. She was wearing a floating black tunic and skintight leggings. Her lips were red and her cheeks flushed. This time he knew it was from his own blood. Ben took a deep breath and willed his body not to react.

You're acting like a horny teenager.

"I don't know, but we're going to Camino's library tomorrow night." The sky was turning pearl grey. "You should get inside."

"Are you angry with me?"

Ben let out a hard laugh. "Yeah."

"Because I bit you?"

"I know what you are, Tenzin." He locked his eyes with her. "We were both being reckless. I'm not angry about that."

"You're angry because I left."

"Yes."

He couldn't read her expression. It was carefully and deliberately blank.

"How much do you remember from the cave?" she asked.

Ben weighed his options. "I remember waking up in a strange house without my partner."

"And that's all?"

His voice dropped. "Is there something else I *should* remember?"

Her eyes gave nothing away. She had to know he wasn't telling her everything, but she wouldn't be the one to say it, and she'd never know unless he told her.

Let her wonder. Ben knew it was the only satisfaction he'd get. Wondering might just make her a fraction as crazy as she made him.

"I need to go inside." Tenzin stood. "The sun is about to rise. I'll see you at nightfall."

She walked inside. Ben could hear the door to her room shut and the lock turn.

And that was that.

Tenzin didn't go to Camino's library with them the next night. Giovanni wouldn't let her. "Stay here," he said. "Don't bite anyone."

Tenzin's mouth dropped open in indignation, but a look at Ben shut her up. He shrugged and followed Giovanni out the door.

"Is that because you're still pissed at her?"

"Not really," Giovanni said. "Camino is afraid of her."

"Why?"

"Because he knows who she is."

They walked the few blocks to August Camino's apartment, waiting after they'd rung the bell. A familiar shuffling behind the front door. A crack opened, and a familiar face greeted them.

"August," Giovanni said. "It's good to see you."

Camino laughed and opened the door wide. "Giovanni Vecchio." He opened his arms and the two old friends embraced. "It's good to see you, my friend. And young Mr. Vecchio, welcome back. I have more bread for you."

"Thank you, Señor Camino."

He waved both Ben and Giovanni into the house. Warm lamps lit the whole of the library room, but they followed Camino back to the kitchen.

The old man looked over his shoulder. "You're looking good for your age, Vecchio."

"So are you."

Camino cackled and opened the door where the chirping song of his lovebirds greeted them. Ben walked over and greeted them, picking up a sunflower seed and offering it to the female. She gave a flirtatious head bob and snatched it away.

"Sit," Camino said. "It's not too late for coffee, is it?"

"Never. After all"—Giovanni glanced at Ben—"we're just starting our day."

Camino must have noticed the red marks on Ben's neck, but he said nothing about them. "I understand you have more questions about Enríquez."

"Of a sort," Giovanni said. "I'd really just like to examine some of his letters."

"The priest's or Enríquez's?"

"You know, I think we should see both." Giovanni glanced at Ben. "Don't you, Ben?"

"Is this going to be a valuable learning experience?" Ben asked.

"Isn't everything?" Camino said.

Ben lifted the cup of coffee Camino had poured. "I can see why you two are friends."

Giovanni smiled. "Did he tell you what he was looking for?"

"No," Camino said. "But I can guess, of course. There is a look treasure hunters have."

"And who else is that interested in Miguel Enríquez?"

"These days?" Camino rose. "You'd be surprised."

Ben and Giovanni exchanged glances.

"Have you had company, August?" Giovanni asked, following the old man back to the library.

"Ah, my friend. I have to respect confidences, do I not?" He looked over his shoulder. "If I do not respect others, how can you know I'll keep your business private?"

Ben gave Giovanni a look that said *he has a point*.

Giovanni frowned a little. "All we need is Enríquez's letters along with the priest's."

"And so you will have them." Camino lifted a box from below the library table. "The priest's." He turned and wandered into the bookcases and came back with a much smaller box. "And Miguel's own hand."

Giovanni took a copy of the map out and laid it on the table between the two boxes.

Ben glanced at his uncle. "So you kept a copy for yourself too?"

The corner of Giovanni's mouth turned up. "Of course I did. So, August, did my nephew share this little treasure with you?"

Camino's eyes went wide, and he lifted reading glasses to his nose. "He didn't. Selfish boy. How very interesting."

"What was that you were saying about secrets and confidences?" Ben asked, leaning over the map to pull the chain on the table lamp, flooding the area with light. "Gio, are you sure—?"

"It's fine." Camino waved his hand. "Your uncle knows he can trust me."

"Look at the map, August. Do you see where he went wrong?"

"Possibly," Camino muttered. "Was he under the impression that the priest—"

"Yes."

"Oh, so he's never seen any original writing from—?"

"I don't think so. I was assuming he'd ask if you had any here, but I obviously shouldn't have assumed." Giovanni glanced at Ben.

"Are you going to tell me what you're talking about?" Ben asked. "Or just talk about me like I'm not here?"

His uncle waved Ben over and opened the two boxes. He carefully lifted a clear plastic sleeve with a yellowed letter from the priest's box. Ben had seen those before. Then Gio opened the smaller box and brought out a compact, leather-bound journal. Placing it on foam wedges Camino set out, Giovanni stepped back.

"Look," he said. "Here is the journal of Miguel Enríquez."

Ben bent over and started to read. It was more of a ledger than a journal. It detailed names and had small figures next to each. Ben turned the page. Supplies for the trip. Precise amounts of water and dried fish. Line after line of—

"Oh damn." It was a distinctive capital *L* that caught him. Ben's eyes darted from the journal to the map and back to the journal. Back to the map.

He was an idiot.

He leaned on the library table, his head in his hands. "The priest didn't draw the map."

"No," Giovanni said. "Enríquez did. He gave the map to the priest, but Enríquez himself drew that map."

"Which means... the priest never had the treasure." Ben's mind whirled. *What did it mean?*

"I don't think we can assume either way. We *know* Father Tomás had the map; that doesn't mean he had the treasure. Of course, that doesn't mean he *didn't* have it either."

"But he disappeared from the church records shortly after

Enríquez died. If he didn't have the treasure, if he just had the map, then why—?"

"At least now you're asking the right questions," Giovanni said. "This is why you never ignore original documents, Ben. I assumed you'd ask to see a sample of Enríquez's writing when I sent you to August, but you were chasing the chasers, not looking for the source." He turned to Camino. "Thank you, August. I think that's all we need."

"You are welcome anytime."

What did it mean? What did it mean? As Giovanni bid their farewells to the old man, Ben's mind whirled.

Did Tomás ever find the treasure? Was it in the caves anymore? Had anyone else seen the map and sent someone after it? They had to have been in the right cave. A gold guinea like the one they found wasn't going to just randomly show up in a cave in Puerto Rico. But maybe the coin they'd found was just a remnant of something already gone?

"Come on." Giovanni clapped a hand on his shoulder. "Let's get Tenzin and go out to eat. We need a crowd. You always think better in a crowd."

18

_____

They returned to the restaurant in Old San Juan with live music on the patio. A different band was playing, one with a faster beat, but the atmosphere was the same. Humans in the courtyard, vampires on the balcony, and a few mixed with the crowd.

Giovanni, Ben, and Tenzin gathered furtive looks from a number of immortals as they sat and ordered on the patio, but most gave them only a small nod before they returned to the more pleasurable task of finding a willing human for the evening.

Ben kept an eye out for anyone familiar. "Did you get an introduction?" he asked quietly. "Does anyone know you're here?"

"No."

"How did you get here?" Tenzin asked.

"I do own a plane," Giovanni said. "Occasionally I use it myself instead of loaning it out to the rest of the immortal population. Can we focus on you two?"

Ben looked at Tenzin, who shrugged.

"What did you find out at the old man's?"

"The map wasn't drawn by Tomás," Ben said. "It was drawn by Enríquez."

Tenzin narrowed her eyes. "Really? Well... that changes everything."

"Does it?" Ben spread his hands. "How? I've been trying to figure that out."

"I don't know yet, but it does."

"Good to know you're just as lost as I am."

Ben thanked the server when she put the fried snapper in front of him. He took a long drink of his rum cocktail and thought longingly about the view from the deck of their rental house in Quebradillas. "Gio, how long are you staying?"

"Long enough that I'll probably have to present myself to the VICs here," he said, picking at the roasted chicken he'd ordered. "How are they?"

"Interesting," Tenzin said. "It's a trio. On the surface, the male earth vampire appears to be most dominant, but there are dynamics that are not obvious to me. The two females are a water vampire and a wind vampire. There is"—Tenzin stopped to take a drink of her water—"something happening."

Giovanni asked, "What?"

"I don't know." Tenzin made an irritated face. "They're smoke from a volcano and just as predictable."

Which meant not predictable at all.

Giovanni looked at Ben. "What do you think?"

"The same. There's something going on, but it's hard to tell what. There's a sister too. She's actually more the day-to-day administrator if I had to guess."

Giovanni leaned back. "Okay. So that's interesting. I don't think it has much to do with us though. Am I wrong?"

"Maybe, because one of them is watching us right now," Tenzin said, looking from the corner of her eye. "One of Los Tres."

Ben didn't follow her glance. Neither did Giovanni.

"The one we saw here before?" Ben asked.

"Yes."

"Jadzia," he said under his breath. "The wind vampire."

"Mm-hmm."

"Is she with anyone?"

"A human. She's not actively watching us, but she noticed Giovanni."

"Damn," Ben's uncle said. "That's inconvenient."

Ben noticed movement from the balcony. He glanced up, then quickly looked away. "We may have more problems."

"Who?" Tenzin asked.

"The other woman in Los Tres. Valeria. She's here too, and she's definitely not alone."

Tenzin locked her eyes with Ben's. "Who?"

"I'm not positive." Ben switched to Chinese and kept his voice nearly silent, knowing both the vampires would be able to hear him. "But I think it was the general—the one who was consulting with Valeria when we left."

"What was his name?"

"Vasco."

"Yes, the one who was loyal to her. That makes sense," Tenzin said.

"None of this makes sense." Ben glanced up and saw the three vampires, Jadzia, Valeria, and Vasco, were all on the balcony now, along with someone else who was very deliberately staying in the shadows. "Why are they here?"

Tenzin sipped her wine. "It is a very nice restaurant."

"The music is very good." Giovanni gave her a smile. "Tenzin, you want to dance?"

She laughed, but it was fake. "Not with you."

Ben looked between the two of them. "Are you two serious right now?"

"As serious as we can be." Giovanni was wearing his plastered-on smile. "Think, Benjamin. They may not understand us, but they've heard their names. They know we've seen them and they've seen us. The last thing we need to look like we're doing is plotting to take a fortune of gold off the island. So..." He smiled bigger. "Look happy."

Ben smiled. "Right." He glanced at Tenzin. "She's not looking happy."

"If I smiled, I'd scare the humans."

"Fair point." He glanced up at the balcony, but the vampires were no longer looking at them. "Why are they here in San Juan?"

"I don't know, but didn't Camino say he'd had company recently?"

"You think it has to do with any of them?"

"I don't know." Giovanni took another bite of his chicken. "But I think I might need to pay August one more visit before I leave."

THEY WALKED BACK to the house slowly, careful to catch any tails that might have been set on them. None appeared. It didn't appear that Giovanni, Ben, and Tenzin were attracting any more attention in San Juan than they had been before they went caving, which reinforced Ben's impression that no one had discovered the cave before and no one was likely to guess their movements. It boded well for the success of their job.

By the time they'd returned to the house, it was near midnight.

"August will be sleeping," Giovanni said. "We'll have to catch him tomorrow night."

"I need new clothes," Ben said. "I only have these."

"And the ones from the cave," Tenzin said.

"They're dirty," Ben protested.

"There's a machine," Tenzin countered. "Use the machine. Aren't you always telling me to use the machine? Take your own advice."

"Fine." Ben hated doing laundry, but Tenzin was right. He took his clothes to the small laundry room and tossed them in the washing machine. Then he glanced up. There were three narrow cabinets overhead. He opened the far left cabinet. Nothing. The center cabinet. Nothing there. Would he have to go out for laundry detergent? Were there even any shops open this time of night? Maybe a twenty-four-hour drugstore was open somewhere.

He opened the third cabinet and was relieved to see a box of powdered detergent. He took it down, shook it to break up the clumps inside, and poured a little into the washer before he reached up and put the box back.

His hand was still on the handle when the thought hit him.

Why hadn't they looked in the third tunnel?

Because according to Tenzin, it smelled like the dead. She thought it had been used by a vampire.

But Tomás hadn't written the map. Enríquez had. And Tomás had disappeared soon after coming into possession of the map. Maybe Tomás had found the treasure. Maybe he hadn't.

Or maybe he'd never left the cave in the first place.

They needed to search the third tunnel.

"WHAT IS THIS THEORY?" Giovanni asked him as they walked to August Camino's apartment the next night. "The third tunnel?"

"Tenzin was convinced the third tunnel, the dry one that

branched off to the right, wasn't the correct tunnel because a vampire had used it." Ben kept his voice low as they walked. "She said a vampire using it would have smelled the gold, so it had to be one of the first two—you know, at the time it made sense, but now I think she was just bullshitting."

"Yes, you have to be careful about that. She'll get a thought in her head and focus. Sometimes she focuses so much that she loses sight of the big picture or any alternate avenues of thought. And she can be as stubborn as a mule when she gets in that kind of mood. You have to coax her out of it."

"I've noticed."

They reached the building in minutes and climbed the stairs. Ben started to knock, but Giovanni stopped his hand before it reached the door.

"What's—?"

"Blood," his uncle whispered. "I smell blood." Giovanni's face was bleak. "A lot of blood."

Giovanni reached for the doorknob and turned it. There were no locks. No chains. The door swung open without a creak. The darkness they stepped into was immense.

No lamp lit the front room. No sound greeted them.

Giovanni carefully shut the door as Ben switched on a lamp. A dim, gold light scattered shadows through the forest of bookshelves that made up the library of August Camino. Ben followed Giovanni as his uncle walked silently through the maze.

They were halfway into the library when Ben smelled what Giovanni had at the door. Blood. The copper-rich tang of it filled the air, making his nose twitch. Two thin legs were sticking out from under a library table.

"Oh, August." Giovanni's voice was aching. "Who has done this to you, old friend?" Giovanni knelt on the carpet and poked his head under the table to investigate.

The old man hadn't died where he lay. Dark brown smears marked the ground where something had been dragged. Ben followed them back to the source, which lay in front of a wooden cabinet with the door hanging open. There was a safe bolted to the ground inside, sitting undisturbed by the pool of blood at its feet. There was no blood on the safe. No marks or dents. Papers were strewn on the ground and books had fallen from the shelves around it.

There had been a struggle. Someone had wanted the safe open, and Camino wouldn't open it. Whoever had wanted the safe hadn't bothered to try to pry it open. They'd simply killed Camino and left.

Impulsive thief? Or did they plan to come back to retrieve the safe? It was a fairly simple combination lock. With the right tools, Ben could crack it in minutes. Of course, he didn't have the tools with him.

"Did a vampire kill him?" Ben asked quietly. Vampires weren't the best at cracking safes. They tended to try to break through barriers, not finesse them open.

Giovanni said, "Yes."

"There's a safe here."

"Is it open?"

"No. It doesn't even look like it was touched."

Giovanni walked away from Camino's body and toward Ben. "Let me."

"Do you know—"

"Unless his habit has changed over the years, I know the combination." He glanced at Ben and pointed at Ben's phone. "Look on your phone. Find the lottery numbers from last Saturday."

"Which lottery?"

"The New York one of course."

"Dude, there's like a dozen of them." Ben lifted his phone.

"Are you talking New York State? The multistate ones? Which?"

Giovanni huffed out a breath. "Is there one that draws on Saturday?"

"I'm sure there is." Ben started to search the internet from his phone. "Uh... Powerball. Lotto. Pick Five—"

"Lotto. Is that specific to New York?"

"Yes." Ben tapped on his phone. "New York lotto. Every Wednesday and Saturday."

"Tell me the last three numbers from the last Saturday draw."

"Twenty. Fifty. Fifty-four."

Giovanni quickly spun the lock, but it didn't open. "The Saturday before that."

"Seventeen. Forty-six. Fifty-six."

That didn't work either. Giovanni frowned. "He'd never go two weeks without changing the combination."

"What about bonus numbers? Would he use them?"

"Possibly. Give me the first set again, but with the bonus number."

"Fifty. Fifty-four. Forty-six."

The lock clicked and swung open just as Ben heard footsteps at the door. "Shit. Someone's here."

"I hear them." Giovanni grabbed the stack of files crammed in the safe along with a small leather bag. He stuffed the bag in his pocket and shoved half the files at Ben as well as a leather-bound book with bloodstains on the cover. "Take these. We'll go out the kitchen." He closed the safe, spun the lock, and wiped the area around the lock with a handkerchief from his pocket. "Go, Benjamin."

"We're just going to leave him here?"

Giovanni's expression was halfway between angry and

confused. "What do you suggest we do with him? That's likely to be the police at the door."

Someone pounded on the door. "Señor Camino? Señor August Camino?"

Giovanni shoved Ben toward the kitchen. The swinging door nearly slapped Ben on the back of the head. There was more disturbance in the kitchen, and Camino's lovebirds started shrieking when Giovanni and Ben entered the room.

"We can't leave them," Ben whispered.

"The birds?" Giovanni was incredulous. "Ben, the birds—"

"Just don't." Ben shoved his stack of files toward Giovanni, then he threw the cover over the birdcage and unhooked it from the stand. "Go out the balcony. I was here before; it connects to a fire escape."

Giovanni cracked open the french doors and stepped onto the balcony. Ben waited for him to start climbing down before he stepped outside with the unwieldy bird cage.

What the hell are you doing, Ben?

The birds hadn't stopped shrieking. They hopped around the cage, making it swing wildly as he held them.

Giovanni ambled down the fire escape in the darkness with the grace of an immortal. Ben followed him, trying not to whack himself in the face with the two angry birds. He heard windows opening and voices shouting into the night, but the apartment windows stayed dark, and Ben knew the night was too black for him and Giovanni to be identified.

When they reached the ground, Ben continued following Giovanni, darting between trees and ducking under clotheslines as the shouting in Camino's apartment grew louder. It was the police. A neighbor had called when Señor Camino hadn't opened the door. They had found the body.

Ben asked, "How long—?"

"I think late last night or early yesterday morning."

"And you're sure it was a vampire?"

"I'm sure. I got their scent."

"They?"

"Yes. A man and a woman."

They walked toward the high fence at the back of the court-yard, opened the gate, and stepped into the flow of evening pedestrian traffic in Old San Juan.

"The birds." Giovanni grimaced. "Ben, what were you thinking?"

They are my sweethearts. My little friends to keep me company.

"Camino wouldn't want a stranger to take them," Ben muttered. "I'll figure something out."

"They can't go back to New York."

"I know."

"If you'd just left them there, someone would have—"

"I know, okay?" He should have left them there.

He couldn't have left them there.

They took a circuitous route back to the house, watching for anyone following them, but in the hubbub of Friday night, no one noticed two men who could have been locals walking down the street with a covered birdcage and an armful of paperwork. They reached their rental house without any incident.

Ben set the birds on the patio and made sure they had food in their dish. He refilled the water that had splashed out and checked the paper lining the bottom of the cage. The longer they were sitting in one place, the more they settled.

Tenzin was outside before he could leave the birds. "You brought home birds. In a *cage?*"

"I know you don't like—"

"Caging birds destroys their nature, Benjamin."

"I understand that, but—"

"Birds in cages cannot fly. It is in a bird's nature to fly. Caging them denies their—"

"Shut up!" He felt his anger spike. "I understand that you find caging birds morally reprehensible, but these are tiny domestic birds raised to live in cages, birds who have never had to fend for themselves, and their person just died." He took a slow breath. "So can you just *not* mess with them, please? Just leave them alone until I can find someone who will take care of them."

Tenzin's face went blank. "Their person died?"

"Yes."

"The old man?"

"Yes."

She was silent for a long time. "Where's Giovanni?"

"Inside."

Tenzin disappeared into the house, and Ben spent a few more minutes watching Camino's birds. They were quieter, but they were still puffed up and nervous, hopping around their cage and keeping close together.

"You're safe here," he said. "I'll figure out a safe place for you."

The birds huddled together.

"I'm sorry about Camino." Ben reached into their cage to grab a sunflower seed to give them, but the larger bird hopped over and bit at his finger. Ben pulled it back, shaking it as the bird glared at him and jumped back to his mate.

Ben rose and walked inside to see Giovanni at the table, hunched over the papers and the book he'd grabbed. Tenzin stood on his left, and her arm was around his shoulders.

"Are you sure?"

"Positive."

"And there's no way he could have been a threat?"

"He was ninety-two, Tenzin. He'd been retired for nearly

fifteen years." Giovanni sighed. "It's so unfair. He loved it here. He'd talked about retiring to the island for years."

"He lived a good life, my boy. A long life. Especially for a human in our world. He was respected and he will be remembered with honor."

"I'll have to inform O'Brien, and it will have to be soon. As far as I know, he was still under their aegis. This will not go over well. August and Cormac were very close friends."

Ben stepped toward them. "It would help if you could tell Cormac who the murderer was."

"If I can get close enough, I'll recognize the scent."

Tenzin looked at Ben. "Ideas?"

"It was a male and a female," Giovanni said. "Both vampires."

"Jadzia or Valeria?" Ben offered. "But they would know Camino was powerfully connected. Why would they risk it? And who could the male be?"

"The general? Vasco?"

"There's no way of knowing without Gio meeting them. And what proof do we have? It's not like there aren't plenty of vampires in San Juan."

"Agreed," Tenzin said. "But why are they here instead of in the mountains? It has to be for some special purpose."

"Like these papers?" Giovanni asked. He spread them out across the table, setting the bloodstained book to the side. "August kept files for his own safety. Some would consider them blackmail files, but he only ever used them for personal security. He was too smart not to have leverage."

"So these contain information about vampires in power?"

"Yes. It wasn't a secret that he had them, but he didn't broadcast it either."

"But the politically well-connected would know? Like Los Tres?"

ELIZABETH HUNTER

"Most likely."

"If there are rivalries going on—"

"Someone might have wanted them for the same reason August had them," Giovanni said. "Leverage."

"Interesting." Ben picked up a thick file marked C. O'Brien.

Giovanni snatched it back. "Not your business."

"Is it yours?"

"I'll be returning anything related to Cormac's people as soon as I return to New York. I don't expect you to look at any of them. August gathered his own intelligence over the years. It doesn't belong to you."

It was a twisted kind of honor, but it made enough sense for Ben not to push it. If Ben found something to hold over the O'Briens on his own, Giovanni would respect that. But stealing the confidential files of a dead man was another thing.

But there were other files in that safe. Things that didn't relate to Cormac O'Brien. Things that might relate to whoever killed him.

Tenzin had picked up the bloody book. "What is this?"

"He was holding it when I found the body."

"Hmmm." Tenzin paged through it. "It's a book of folk tales in Spanish. It's old."

Giovanni frowned. "He must have been reading it when someone came to the door. Odd that he would—"

"No." Ben couldn't believe there was something his uncle hadn't caught that he did. "No, he crawled to it, Gio. Didn't you see the blood? He was killed near the safe, but he crawled to the bookshelves. Are you saying he had *this book* in his hands?"

"Yes."

"Then... he was crawling to it. He grabbed it for a reason."

"You're right." Giovanni blinked and some of the grief fell from his eyes. "He was dying, but he managed to get this book

210

and hold it. What was so important, August?" He reached for it, and Tenzin handed it over. "We need to read this and read it carefully."

A pair of sandwiched files caught Ben's eye. "And any of these files not related to the O'Briens, we need to examine too."

Giovanni opened his mouth, but Ben cut him off before he could protest. "I'm not looking for gossip, Gio. These papers might answer some very important questions about who killed Camino." He reached for the folder. "For instance, why did he have a file on a pirate who's been dead for three centuries?" He opened the cover. "And why is a there folder with Jadzia's name stuck inside?"

19

They took a break from sorting through Camino's files a few hours before dawn. Ben heated some soup he found in the pantry while Tenzin and Giovanni had a whiskey and plotted their next move. Ben watched them in silence. It was always interesting to see their dynamic, see how Tenzin worked differently with Ben's uncle than with Ben.

"There's no way I'm going to get away without presenting myself," Giovanni said. "Especially not now."

"You showed up in San Juan and then a human winds up dead because of a vampire. And it was a human you were known to consult with," Tenzin said. "So yes, unless you want rumors to start, you need to make yourself known."

"August and I were friends, not rivals."

"We know that." Ben sat down at the table with his food. "Did they? And is it safe? With the information in that file, Jadzia is the likely killer."

"Or Valeria," Tenzin said. "She could have wanted to keep the information for herself as leverage."

"If Vasco was the other scent," Ben said. "Then Valeria is the more likely killer. Vasco is her lover, not Jadzia's."

"Are we sure about that?" Tenzin asked. "You know things can get interesting in vampire courts."

Old vampires—at least those who tended to be in power—generally fell into two camps that Ben had seen. Either they were paired with a very long-term mate who was nearly symbiotic, or they didn't approach anything close to monogamy.

In the former, immortals tended to view anything relating to sexual relationships as a near sacred covenant. Human partners —if they existed—were guarded zealously. Vampire mates were blood-bound and loyal to death.

In the latter, political matings were common and often transitory. As were lovers or harems for both men and women. Open relationships were the norm, as were casual affairs. Sex was traded freely; blood was *not*, as sharing elemental energy created vulnerability.

"Ben, what is your impression?" Giovanni asked. "Would the cacique care if his wives took lovers?"

"I'm going to say yes. He seemed like the possessive type. And his sister was too. She saw her brother's claim on the throne as the rightful one. The wives were tokens as far as she was concerned. I think both of them believe Macuya is the rightful ruler. Jadzia and Valeria are his nods to sharing power with other groups on the island. I don't think he'd be okay with them having other relationships."

"Interesting."

Tenzin asked, "Why didn't you ask me?"

"Because you're not as good at reading human motivation as Ben is," Giovanni said. "Know your limitations, Tenzin."

"But they're not human. They're vampire."

Giovanni smiled. "We're still human, Tenzin. Every single one of us, whether we want to admit it or not."

Tenzin huffed. "I still say Vasco could be a lover to one or both of them. Macuya might not care."

"And I'm saying that Vasco might be a lover to one or both of them," Ben said. "But Macuya would *definitely* care."

"So we tread carefully. Valeria, Jadzia, and Vasco all saw us at the restaurant, and they know we saw them. Whoever killed August doesn't necessarily know we found his body, and they have no way of knowing that we have the contents of his safe." Giovanni wiped a hand over eyes that looked weary. Since he was little affected by the dawn, Ben knew his uncle was feeling loss, not physical exhaustion. "Only we know what was in there."

"And possibly Jadzia."

Tenzin said, "She probably suspects. She doesn't know."

"The letters between the priest and Enríquez," Giovanni said. "Did August show them to you before?"

Ben said, "No. It's pretty obvious that Enríquez thought he was going to manage to escape Abadía, even at the end."

"Why wouldn't he?" Giovanni asked. "He'd escaped before. Many times."

"Tomás was his backup plan," Tenzin said. "Of course, it's obvious he did feel some fondness for the young man. He left him the map."

Ben looked at Giovanni. "But you didn't know anything about the Enríquez letters?"

Giovanni shook his head. "Not even a rumor. I knew August had Enríquez's journal, but I'd never heard of any letters. When I was hired to look for the map, the client told me a Dominican priest was the likely place to start, which led me to ask for August's help, but he never..."

"And who is this client?" Ben asked. "Still can't tell us? How do we know he's not the one who killed Camino?"

"He wouldn't step on this island," Giovanni said. "And he wouldn't kill August. That's all you need to know about the client right now."

How about later? Ben ate his soup. He knew better than to push his uncle when Giovanni was in a mood. "The letters were new to all of us. So why did August keep them secret?"

"Leverage?" Giovanni guessed. "But against whom? Enríquez is dead. Could Tomás still be living?"

"If he is, he's created a new identity."

Giovanni shrugged. "Vampires do it all the time."

"So Tomás could be living," Ben said. "And in all this time, he's never gone after the treasure? I don't buy it."

Tenzin said, "We need to go back to the cavern. We need to search the last tunnel."

Ben tried not to gape. He'd thought he was going to have to finesse the mule down the road, but she seemed to be trotting down the path on her own.

Better put up a token resistance before she got suspicious. "I thought you said it was a dead end?"

Giovanni glanced at him, clearly trying not to smile. "Didn't you tell me it wasn't worth the time, Ben?"

"I don't think it is. If a vampire was using it—"

"A young vampire might not have smelled anything," Tenzin said. "Especially if it was in the throes of bloodlust. We definitely need to check the third tunnel."

"If you think so," Ben said. "But I don't know if we're going to find anything."

"If nothing else, we might find bones," Tenzin said. "It definitely smelled like death. But old death."

Ben tried not to grimace. "Oh goody."

"Or we might find treasure."

"My client was fairly sure the map was accurate and the treasure hadn't been disturbed," Giovanni said. "For whatever that's worth."

"Not much when we don't know who your client is," Tenzin said.

Giovanni shrugged. "Oh well. Ben, have you managed to work out how you're going to transport the gold to New York?"

"Yes." Ben glanced at Tenzin. "Why do you ask?"

"How? Air? Water?"

"Water," Ben said. "I have a boat."

"Yes, it's a good thing I brought the plane," Giovanni muttered. "Water was never going to work."

Ben frowned. "I had it set up, Gio. I'm not an amateur. I'd already contacted a private yacht company and—"

"I'm not saying your plan was bad," Giovanni said. "I'm just saying it wouldn't work for this particular job."

"Let me guess," Ben said. "Because of the mysterious client?"

"Let me worry about the client." Giovanni pointed at Ben. "You have something far more important to figure out."

"What?"

"What the hell are we going to do with those birds?"

BEN WENT to bed before the vampires did. Tenzin watched him walk inside, waited for his door to close, for the locks to engage. She turned to Giovanni.

"You didn't tell him."

"Tell him what?"

"Why you really came down here."

Giovanni looked perturbed. "You called me and confessed to biting my son. You left him with a strange human—"

"I left him with his cousin."

"She doesn't know that," Giovanni hissed, his fangs down. "She doesn't know who he is. She's not a doctor. She could have seen him as a threat and left him out in the cold. He could have died, so don't"—Giovanni was nearly shaking with anger

—"*don't* tell me he was safe. You risk yourself and him when you're reckless like this. And if he dies—"

"He's not going to die."

"And you're willing to guarantee that?" Giovanni said, his voice a low threat. "You personally?"

Tenzin refused to meet his eyes.

"Don't think I don't see how things are changing. Don't imagine for a minute Beatrice and I aren't aware."

"And what?" Tenzin looked up at the moon riding high in the grey predawn sky. "You don't approve of something you're imagining in your head?"

He didn't answer her. Annoyed, she looked at him, but far from the anger or disapproval she was expecting, Giovanni's face was open. Loving. His strange blue-green eyes had kept her from killing him once. They'd reminded her of the child she'd lost. They continued to disarm her, even hundreds of years later.

"We love you both," he said, "but you have to realize that in this game, you hold all the cards."

She gave him a slight laugh. "Do you really think that?"

"Are you saying it's not true?"

Because it was Giovanni—and only because it was him—she allowed herself to speak the truth. "Only three living people have the ability to undo me, my boy. And only one has ever made this dead heart feel even a little bit human. You say we're all human, but you forget how long I've been a monster."

"You're not a monster."

"But I am," she said. "Far more than you've ever been willing to admit. The odd thing is, even with all your years and all your wisdom, I think he sees me more clearly than you do."

"I see you."

"But not like he does. You see, it's still a mystery to you, but I know why he didn't tell you about his family here. I know why he went with you when he was young. And I know why he will stay with me in the end."

"Are you going to share or keep me guessing about my own son?"

"He is more at home with monsters than with humanity."

Giovanni said nothing.

"All this is only preparation for the life he's meant to have. For the life you know he's been training for, whether he'll admit it or not. He'll choose this—choose us—in the end."

"You're overconfident," Giovanni said. "And it may doom you both."

"Are you going to tell him why you're here?"

Giovanni looked away. "You're tapping on a hornets' nest, and Ben doesn't know it."

"You were already in New York. You were on the way here as a favor to Cormac."

"How do you know that?"

"I have my own sources. So as Ben would say, stop bullshitting me."

Giovanni was silent for a long while. "Someone in the court has made overtures to Novia. Overtures that have been met with approval."

"Are you saying New York wants to back a coup in Puerto Rico?"

Giovanni's voice dropped to barely over a whisper. "I'm saying that many in the broader world have noticed how unresponsive the immortal leaders of this place have been to the needs of the people here."

"We're vampires. We don't involve ourselves in human politics. Disasters happen. Human tragedy happens. We're not here to solve that. It's not our business, and it's not in our nature."

"Some agree with you. Some don't. But it's not only the humans who are suffering."

So Cormac was backing a coup in Puerto Rico. Hmmm. It was interesting. And possibly messy.

"Can't it wait until we finish our project?" Tenzin asked.

"Not if you want my help moving all that gold."

She tried not to pout. "You know, if coups keep happening in places I visit, I'm not going to be very welcome in much of the world."

"I think it's really odd you think you're welcome now."

"What are you talking about? I'm delightful."

"You're dangerous." He smiled a little. "And sometimes you're delightful."

THE TWO LOVEBIRDS were huddled close together the next morning, but they were making happy cooing sounds instead of angry whistles or shrieks. One seemed to be feeding the other one, and water and seed were scattered on the floor of their cage.

Ben had found some spare newspaper under the sink in the kitchen, and he was changing the cage liner when he heard Tenzin speak from the shadows.

"Cara showed me bird videos on YouTube."

He glanced over his shoulder. "Is that so?"

"Yes, lovebird videos. I know everything about them now."

"Everything?"

"Admittedly, it was not a full ornithology lesson, but I do feel adequately prepared to care for them should the need arise."

Ben couldn't stop the smile. He stood and walked back in the house. "I don't have any plans to keep the birds, Tiny."

"Then why did you take them?"

"Because he was a nice old man and he loved these birds. He

didn't have any family. The police would probably have taken them to an animal shelter. I didn't think a stranger should have them."

"Do you think Giovanni is going to want them?"

Ben gave her a look. "I'm not stupid. He's a cat person."

"You don't want them. He won't take them. So who is going to care for them? Are you going to set them loose?"

"I don't think they have it in them to be wild," Ben said. "And they're not native to the island. I have an idea, okay?"

"Fine." She paused near the doorway down the hall. "But should the need arise, I can care for them. I've watched YouTube."

The resentment he'd been feeling for a few days softened. "Thanks, Tenzin."

"You're welcome."

They were driving back to the cavern in Camuy tonight. Ben had already tried to call the ranger station there, but he'd been informed that Liza Ochoa Rios was back to her regular assignment that morning.

Which means she's close.

Ben put the birds in the back of the Jeep and covered them. They were agitated again, but they didn't nip at him. He buckled the cage in so it wouldn't slide around, then he started on the road toward El Yunque National Forest.

It was a little over an hour to get from San Juan to the area where Ben thought he'd be able to contact Liza. He knew she worked in computer systems, so he was guessing she'd be in the main visitor center. Of course, a quick search online told him the main center was still closed, but a temporary hub had been opened in the town of Palmer nearby. Ben headed there, hoping he'd be able to find his cousin or someone else who could help.

As he left the city and drove deeper into the country, the landscape changed dramatically. Lush forests had recovered from the storm. Though he could still see debris in many places, the heavy rain had led to wild and abundant growth in the trees and undergrowth.

Bright shopfronts were buzzing with activity. Ben checked his phone and was surprised to realize it was Saturday. He'd lost track of time days ago, but the island hadn't. The sun was shining and families were out and about. Shopping, eating, and enjoying the beautiful weather.

There were far more tourist traps on this part of the island, but Ben could also see the tapestry of everyday life. Animals barking behind fences and neighbors calling to each other. Two old men talking in front of the hardware store. Mothers chatting in front of the market.

His grandmother lived nearby.

She had a large house with a garden. Chickens and goats. She grew vegetables and canned tomatoes. She fed her neighbors, just like she'd fed Ben all those years ago. There were probably little kids sitting at her kitchen table right now, eating cookies and listening to a radio program or a TV show.

Good. It was good she had that. It was good some people still lived that way.

It could have been you.

No. It could never have been him.

He saw the sign for the visitors' center and turned in. There were three other cars in the small parking lot, along with a truck with a familiar logo. Ben rolled down the windows, checked on the birds, and got out.

Strolling over to the door, he turned his face to the sun and just breathed.

Life. It was all around him.

"Ben?"

He turned toward her voice, marveling at his own luck.

"Hey! Good to see you." His cousin walked over with her hand extended. "You look a lot better. You feeling okay?"

"Yeah." He shook her hand. "Thanks. My uncle got me patched up, and I'm feeling a lot better. I can't believe you're here. I was going to ask someone in the office, but I didn't expect—"

"I'm usually around unless I'm jumping offices like I was last week."

Had it already been a week? No, it was just the weekend. He hadn't lost as much time as that.

Liza was in the same work uniform she'd had on when they met. In fact, she looked exactly the same. Same hair. Same clothes. Same tiny bit of makeup and simple earrings.

That's what it means to wear a uniform to work, genius.

"So," she said, "did you ever find out what happened with your flaky friend?"

He let out a breath. Then he laughed. "Yeah. Kinda. It's a long story."

Liza gave him a skeptical look. "Long story?"

"So long. So complicated." He waved a hand. "We're okay. With her, I just need to manage expectations a little better, you know?"

She shook her head. "Sounds way more complicated than I want to deal with. So what brings you to El Yunque? Is this your first visit?"

"First, I wanted to find you and say thank you. Again." He put his hand over his heart. "Thank you so much. I don't know what would have happened to me if you hadn't found me."

"Ah, you'd have been fine. It's not like it freezes at night around here."

"Still. Thank you again. And thanks for not giving me a ticket or anything for being in the park."

She lowered her voice. "Just don't tell my boss and we'll be good."

"Done." He took a deep breath. "And the second thing is... I don't suppose you know anyone who loves birds?"

"Birds?" Liza frowned. "Like... I mean, who doesn't like birds? Do you mean birdwatching? I can tell you some good locations if you're into—"

"No, I mean..." He made an arching shape with his hands. "In cages. Birds. Domestic birds. Pet birds."

"Oh! Pet birds? Huh. Like a parakeet or something? Um... I mean, I can think of a few people—"

"My uncle, part of the reason he came down here was to help a friend with... his grandfather's estate. You know, the grandfather passed and—"

"I'm so sorry."

"It happened a while ago." Two nights was a while. Kinda. "Anyway, the grandfather had these two birds, and the friend can't take them in his apartment. And he doesn't want to just send them to a shelter." Ben walked over to the back of his Jeep and Liza followed him. "And I don't know why I thought of you, but I don't know many other people who live here, and I thought with you being a park ranger and liking the outdoors and stuff..."

"Well, I usually prefer my birds out in the wild, no offense to your friend."

Ben lifted the drape over the bird cage and saw Liza's expression go soft.

"Oh! They're lovebirds. My mom had a pair when we lived in New York. I adored them."

I thought you might. It had occurred to Ben that the birds he remembered at his abuela's house hadn't been his abuela's. The apartment and the birds must have belonged to Liza's mother, the aunt he'd never met.

"Do you think you might be able to keep them? Or find someone who would? I trust you, and you know more people around here."

"I'd be happy to." She put her hands on her hips. "The real question is if I should bring them home. If I bring them home, my abuela won't let them go. She had birds when she was younger."

"Well, it sounds like a perfect match. Maybe I should have asked where you live. I could have just told your grandma you sent me over with them as a gift." That would never happen. Ever.

She gave him a sly smile. "Sneaky."

Ben lifted the cage from the back of the Jeep. "So can you take them?"

"I'll help you out. Give me a few days to make sure I can find someone who'll take good care of them, okay? How much longer are you in PR?"

"At least a few days. Probably closer to a week."

"Okay. We'll exchange numbers and I'll call you if I find someone." She raised a finger. "But don't stick me with your friend's birds. If I can't find anyone, you're taking them back."

"Fair enough." He could tell by her expression he wasn't going to have a problem. "Thanks, Liza. Thanks again."

20

He spent the rest of the day driving through the open areas of the park, listening to the birds and the coqui frogs, watching families play in the river, and wondering what life might have been like if he hadn't been so afraid.

The sun was out, the park was busy, and Ben didn't think once about vampires, gold, or immortal politics. He was too busy enjoying the day.

But driving back to San Juan, the Jeep was eerily silent. It was almost a relief to get back to the rental house and find Giovanni and Tenzin arguing.

"You're not going underground with him again. I won't have it," his uncle yelled.

"I'm not going to push myself this time. And we had no cave-ins in the drier tunnel. It was only in the muddy—"

"I can't believe you're even fighting me on this. It's not happening, Tenzin."

"And you think you can stop me?"

Ben entered the living room and tossed his keys on the counter. "Hi."

Tenzin turned to him, squinted. "Where are the birds?"

"My cousin is going to keep them. I mean, she didn't say she definitely was, but I saw her face. I'm pretty sure she's going to keep them."

Was he mistaken, or was there a slight tinge of disappointment on her face? It quickly cleared as indignation returned.

"Gio thinks I can't go down in the tunnel without biting you."

"So many jokes," Ben muttered.

"It's not a joke. Tell him you trust me underground."

Ben forced back the smile that wanted to break through and cleared his throat. "Uhhh, as long as there's not a cave-in, I trust you not to bite me."

Her look of indignation remained.

Ben pointed at her. "You can't fault my logic on this one, Tiny. Bite me once, shame on you. Bite me twice... shame on you again, but stupid me."

She opened her mouth, then closed it.

"I can't fault your logic either," Gio said. "That settles it. Ben and I will explore the third tunnel. Tenzin will wait in the cavern."

She spun and walked to the patio. "I hate you both."

"No, you don't," they said in unison.

Ben ignored her as she flew off into the night. "Have you eaten anything?"

"No."

Giovanni sat at the counter and watched Ben putter around the kitchen. He'd bought enough chicken to grill and produce to make a salad. He set about preparing a simple meal that wouldn't be too complicated. He was trying to cook more, but he only attempted complicated dishes when Tenzin was there to observe and intervene when necessary.

"You're better."

Ben glanced up. "Pardon?"

"You needed a day in the human world. Away from all this."

Ben shrugged. "Probably. I was underground for a while."

"You were."

"How do you live without sun?" Ben glanced up as he was trimming cucumbers. "I was thinking about that today. How do you do it? Human beings get seasonal affective disorder without enough sunlight. Do vampires get anything similar?"

Giovanni took a deep breath and let it out slowly. "It's difficult. I can't lie. The full moon is very bright to our eyes, but it doesn't contain the radiation the sun does. So that's helpful and also not, if that makes sense. Our bodies don't react to a lack of vitamin D. And those of us who are older can stand to look at sunlight as long as it doesn't touch us directly. Once we get to that stage, life is really quite tolerable."

"So only a century or so of utter and complete darkness?"

His uncle smiled. "It doesn't always work that way. Look at Beatrice."

Ben's aunt had been sired from her own father's blood, but that father had been exchanging blood with Tenzin, who was extraordinarily powerful and didn't sleep at all. So much of Beatrice's elemental strength was borrowed from Tenzin, even though Tenzin wasn't her sire.

"Truthfully, the sun can seem quite harsh. I prefer the moon even though I can handle looking at sunlight. You manage, Ben. When there is no other choice, you manage."

"And when there is another choice?"

Giovanni was quiet for a long time. "You make the one that's right for you. You. No one else. It's your eternity. Your life. Not mine. Not your aunt's. Not your human family's. Not anyone else's either."

You're wrong. Ben didn't say it, because Giovanni didn't think the way he did. Not about family. "Don't worry," Ben said blithely. "As Tenzin will inform you, I'm incredibly selfish."

"And she's a model of sacrifice?"

"Don't be absurd, Gio." Ben glanced up with a smile. "She's its patron saint."

TENZIN ARRIVED BACK WITHIN AN HOUR. She was carrying two bright red fish.

Had she bought them? Had she stolen them? Had she caught them with her bare hands while flying over the ocean? Ben had no idea. He didn't ask any questions. He just put them on the grill and said thank you. They were delicious.

Giovanni, Ben, and Tenzin finished their dinner, cleaned up the house, and left for Camuy within an hour. Driving at night made traffic nearly nonexistent once they got out of San Juan, and since Tenzin didn't seem to want to continue their earlier fight, the Jeep was quiet except for the beat of salsa, cumbia, and reggaeton Ben put on the speakers.

He navigated the now-familiar smaller roads when they exited at Arecibo and drove through towns where the walls of dark greenery grew taller and taller as they approached the hills. He turned off before the entrance of the national park and drove deeper into the forest. Lights were nearly nonexistent. He rolled down the windows and let the smell of soil and growing things fill the Jeep.

"We're almost there," Tenzin said. "Let me out."

"No," Ben said. "I want you to help hide the car."

"The ranger cabin should be empty this time of day. Liza is gone. The only ones here are the regular park employees, and they won't be around."

Ben glanced over his shoulder. "You can help."

"Fine." She pouted.

Such a child. She drove him crazy so many times.

Ben pulled onto the dirt road and navigated by memory toward the parking lot where he'd parked before. Instead of pulling into it, he pulled past it and into the trees.

"Out," he said. "Branches and brush."

There was plenty of fallen brush to block the view of the already dark green Jeep. Ben, Giovanni, and Tenzin took their backpacks out of the Jeep and piled brush around it before they walked into the trees.

"Do you remember the drop-off by the sinkhole?" Tenzin asked.

"Yes. I'll show Giovanni how to avoid the slide."

"And I'll see you there." She took off into the night.

Giovanni stood looking up into the darkness. "It's the only vampire gift I've ever actually envied."

"Not tunneling underground like a giant gopher?"

Giovanni shuddered. "Definitely not."

Ben smiled. "I can't blame you. I dream about flying. Probably everyone does that, right?"

"I think it's a fairly common dream, yes."

Ben noticed that Giovanni didn't agree that everyone dreamed about flying. But then again, from what he could tell, most vampires didn't dream much of anything.

"Follow me," he said. "It's not far."

Ben took the path he'd cut the week before, ducking through the brush and occasionally warning his uncle about a branch or a root in the way. Despite it being clearer, the trail seemed longer this time, but when they reached the sinkhole, Ben was ready.

"Okay. Here's where we don't charge straight ahead. Trust me on this one."

Giovanni chuckled. "Learn a hard lesson?"

"Yes. That it's a good thing I have a hard head."

Ben clipped on his headlamp and walked in a circular

pattern until the sinkhole sloped down near enough to the base that he could jump. He could see the sky getting lighter.

"Let's see what's left. We had a full setup down here, but I don't have an extra mattress for you. Tenzin has one though, and she might not want to sleep."

"I'll manage," Giovanni said, ducking under some hanging vines. "This place is primeval."

Ben grinned. "I know. It's pretty amazing during the day."

"The hurricane doesn't even look like it touched it. Nothing uprooted. A few trees along the top maybe."

"And you haven't even seen the best part."

Ben led Giovanni into the cavern where the waterfall dropped. Tenzin was already there, work lamps set up and plugged into the generator she'd placed outside.

"The generator is off at dawn, Tiny."

"I know, I know. Did you want your tent warm or not?"

Seeing as his skin was already prickled from the cold, he couldn't argue with her logic.

"Someone has been here," Tenzin said. "The scent isn't clear, but we've had visitors. I don't think anything was taken, but it's definitely been looked through."

Which means they might have looked through the caves. "Human?"

Giovanni shook his head. "Vampire. And one of them was in August's apartment. It's familiar."

"Is the third cave disturbed?"

"Not that I can see," Tenzin said. "The other two were investigated—at least until they ran into that mudslide in cave two—but the third one didn't have any trace of them."

Ben muttered, "They were looking for our trail."

"Yes. They only went where we did."

Ben recalled the book in Camino's hand. "Gio, do you have that book of folklore handy?"

He nodded and set down his backpack. "I secured most of the files, but I brought this."

Ben looked through the small journal, flipping until he saw a familiar heading around the middle of the book. There was a smudged thumbprint in dark brown near the corner.

Blood.

"El Diablo de Camuy," Ben read. He skimmed the page in Spanish. "A mysterious demon with claws and long hair that snatches children who wander near the caves at night? Their bodies are sometimes found with all the blood gone." Ben looked up. "Definitely could be a vampire."

Giovanni said, "Does it say when the legend originated?"

Ben turned the page and found a note toward the end. "First recorded by a local priest in the summer of 1743." Ben looked up. "Holy shit."

"Enríquez died in late 1743. He'd already hidden the treasure at that point. His letters indicate that it had been hidden sometime in 1732, before the government started confiscating his money."

"He hid the majority of his wealth where no one could find it," Tenzin said, looking around the cavern. "Smart human."

"And the demon of Camuy began hunting during that time," Giovanni said, "further protecting the site where the treasure was hidden."

"Do you think Tomás was the priest who reported it?"

"Possibly," Giovanni said. "Or it was a coincidence."

"You don't believe in coincidence," Ben and Tenzin said together.

"No, I don't." Giovanni wandered toward the third cave. "But it wasn't wholly a fabrication either. There was something hunting down here. I can smell it the same as Tenzin can. That tunnel smells like the dead."

"And tomorrow night, when we've all had some rest, we'll

start digging," Ben said. "But until then, I want to get some sleep." He held up the book. "And I want to read a little more. Good night. Good morning. Whatever. Don't forget to shut off the generator." Ben unzipped his tent and took the opportunity to disappear, but not before he heard Giovanni.

"He's doing original document research."

"You're really proud right now, aren't you?"

"So proud."

"You're a strange man," Tenzin said. "I don't know why we've been friends for so long."

Ben woke after a day of scattered sleep. He wasn't rested, but he was ready to start searching. He left his tent and found Giovanni and Tenzin sitting by the reflecting pool, both entranced by the reflection of the pink sunset dancing on the water.

"A barrel of laughs, both of you," Ben said, starting the stove to warm water for coffee.

"Good evening, Benjamin," Giovanni said. "Did you rest well?"

"Sure. Coffee?"

"No thank you."

"Tea for me," Tenzin said.

"I didn't bring tea."

She pulled her gaze away from the reflecting pool. "How did you not bring tea?"

"Because I felt like bringing coffee."

She stared at him. "You're very selfish."

"I know." He poured ground coffee in the french press. "I try to follow your example. Next time, you pack the kitchen stuff and we won't have this problem."

Giovanni rose. "Before we get into a fight, children, why don't we go over the plan for the evening?"

"I'll be sitting bored in the cave without tea while you have fun exploring the tunnel," Tenzin said. "What is there to clarify?"

Giovanni stared at her. Then he turned to Ben. "Next time just bring tea so she's not so cranky."

"If you think tea is going to solve her attitude problem, you're wildly optimistic."

THEY SUITED up after Ben had eaten and revived with caffeine. He'd brought his clean coveralls from San Juan and found another pair for Giovanni at the local Walmart with a pair of thick rubber boots. With helmets and headlamps, they were ready to explore the third cave. Ben carried the tool belt with the hammer, gear, pitons, and ropes.

"We'll anchor pitons as needed to keep track of what passages we've explored. The ropes are mainly for navigation, not anchoring. The other two caves had relatively even surfaces, so we didn't have to use ropes for climbing. If this one is different, we'll have to leave and get more gear."

Giovanni stared at Ben as he rattled off basic safety precautions. "Where did you learn all this?"

"YouTube!" Tenzin shouted from the mouth of the tunnel. "There are hours and hours of video. You can learn anything on YouTube."

Ben shrugged. "She's mostly right, though I have taken some climbing classes. There are principles that cross over. These caves are pretty even and I'm exploring with vampires, so it's not as risky as most human caving."

"Not as risky except for the cave-in during the last trip?"

"That was my fault. That cave was too muddy to explore. We shouldn't have risked it. I was being stupid."

"Don't get gold fever, Ben. That's all I ask."

He nodded. "You ready?"

"You have enough light?"

Ben patted the flashlight at his waist, his helmet lamp, and the glow sticks in his pocket. "I'm good."

"Let's go."

The tunnel floor was even, with about as much variation as the first tunnel. With Enríquez's map in hand, they marked off the turns, taking their time to set pitons as needed and mark passages with tape. Ben didn't like using it, but it was necessary. He'd remove it before they left, along with as many of the pitons as he could find.

"First turn. Left is clear."

"Marking."

They worked in steady silence broken by directions as Ben called for Giovanni to mark on the notebook he'd started for the other two tunnels.

"Third turn, straight ahead. Clear."

"Marking."

"Fifth turn."

"Marking."

Steadily making his way deeper, his uncle at his back, Ben felt a sense of calm he hadn't felt before.

This was it. This was the tunnel. They were going to find it this time.

"Eighth turn." Ben felt his heartbeat pick up when they reached the last turn on the map. This was it. They'd never gotten this far in any of the other tunnels. "Right." He shined the light ahead of him, searching the darkness of the passage for the final left turn.

Nothing.

Dead end.

"No."

"What is it?"

"Nothing."

"What do you mean?"

Ben turned and angled his headlamp down. "I mean it's a dead end. We messed up somewhere."

"Are you sure?"

"It's limestone," Ben said. "No sign of a cave-in. We've just got the wrong tunnel. Or we made a wrong turn somewhere." He sighed. "It's fine. We go back. We work it again."

Giovanni was looking at the map in his hand. Not the neatly marked notebook, the map. It wasn't the real map, of course. It was a copy.

"Come on." He started to back out of the tunnel. "I have an idea."

"THE MAP WAS DRAWN by Enríquez and intended for him alone." Giovanni was sitting near the stove while Ben heated water for coffee. "But he had to know it could be stolen if his papers were confiscated."

"So you're saying he wouldn't draw an accurate map?" Ben said. "That kind of defeats the purpose of a treasure map."

"I'm not saying that. I'm saying on the original map—" Giovanni pulled out his heavily insulated tablet and handed it to Tenzin. "You know my password. Pull up the pictures. On the original map, there was a marking on the back that I couldn't quite make sense of."

Tenzin scrolled through countless shots of Giovanni's newly adopted daughter and Beatrice, Giovanni looking over her shoulder.

"There." Even pointing his finger at the screen caused it to flicker. "I hate this thing."

"Fire vampires really can't use electronics, can they?"

"It's a recipe for disaster," Giovanni muttered. "Not that shot, scroll right."

Tenzin scrolled right.

"There," Giovanni said. "Look at that marking."

Tenzin held up the tablet. "What does that look like to you?"

Ben glanced over. "A chicken scratch. I saw it before. I assumed it was a crease in the document."

Giovanni shook his head. "It's not. It's very obviously not when you see the original."

Ben squinted in the low light. "Then I guess... the letter *T*?"

"Yes," Giovanni said. "Doesn't that make sense?"

"Doesn't what make sense?" Ben lifted the boiling water from the stove, poured it over the coffee grounds, and inhaled deeply. *Heaven.*

"The *T* on the back of the map."

"Ohhhh," Tenzin said. "Brilliant. A simple trick only he would know. But then he left the map for Tomás. He had to give him a sign."

"I think so."

"What the hell are you talking about?" Ben said. "The map—"

"The original map was written on vellum," Giovanni said. "Very thin, very fine vellum."

"Yeah, so you said—"

"Which means if you put a light up to it, it was nearly translucent."

Ben looked up. "And the *T* was on the back of the map."

"Yes."

Oh, well that was just perfect. "We've been looking at it backward."

"No, you've been looking at it from the front. The only problem was, Enríquez made it to be viewed backward. A very simple trick to fool anyone who might steal the map. Maybe not enough to fool them forever, but enough to discourage them. For them to think it was a fraud."

"But when he left it for Tomás—"

"He had to leave a sign for Tomás to look at it from the right angle." Giovanni closed his eyes. "Now, if we look at it backward—"

"All the turns are reversed. We should be going left, left, straight, right, not the other way round."

"Exactly."

Ben left his coffee where he'd poured it. "Come on."

"Right back in?"

"Are you kidding?" he said. "This is the first encouraging thing I've heard in weeks. Let's go."

Ben and Giovanni zipped up their coveralls and put on their helmets, quickly tying a new anchor at the mouth of the tunnel.

"You have the notebook?" Ben asked.

"Yes. And the map. We'll just be going the opposite way this trip."

"Marking the first turn... left."

"Left."

They walked forward slowly; the ground was a little more uneven on this side of the cavern.

"Left."

"Marking."

The passage opened up into a larger room, and Ben could see the tunnel directly opposite the one they'd just exited. That must be the tunnel where they needed to go straight. Excitement humming in his veins, he stepped forward, nearly tripping over a rock that blocked his path.

"Benjamin."

"Shit." He shined his flashlight down and gasped at the gaping mouth of the skeleton crumbled against the rock. Which wasn't a rock. It was the remains of a small wooden chest with the lid flung open. Ben carefully stepped away.

"It smells like death," Giovanni said quietly. He shined his flashlight around the cavern, and Ben saw what Giovanni and Tenzin had both sensed.

Human remains lined the walls of the limestone room, tumbled carelessly in piles. Dozens of skulls were visible.

"Vampire?"

"There is nothing left but bones," Giovanni said quietly, "so there's no way of knowing for sure, but it's certainly more likely than a demon."

"It is a demon. The demon of Camuy." Ben shined his flashlight on the chest. "Did you see this?"

"Yes." Giovanni bent down, picking through the remains.

There were scraps of cloth and an old pair of muskets. A scattering of dull black coins spilled from under the bones.

"What are you looking for?"

"Time period," he said. "I'm guessing these are several hundred years old, which would match with the era we're looking at."

"Which means this chest..." Ben couldn't take his eyes off it.

"Yes. It could be Miquel Enríquez's treasure."

The simple wooden chest was covered in dirt and mold. The bones draped over it had tumbled to the side, revealing a brass plate too dirty to read. An old chest, a few coins, and weapons too corroded to use.

"If this is the whole treasure—"

Distant sounds of shouting caused both Ben and Giovanni to stand up straight.

"Tenzin?" Ben shouted.

Nothing.

He and his uncle exchanged a look before they quickly left the bones and the chest where they were lying and retraced their steps. Ben slid the notebook and map in his coveralls to keep them safe. When they entered the cavern, Ben saw Tenzin sitting with a cup of his coffee.

Vasco, Inés, and half a dozen other vampires were standing over her.

"You might need to make more coffee," she said.

21

"Inés," Ben said cautiously. "It's nice to see you. Can I ask why you're here?"

Inés didn't speak. Her eyes moved between Ben and Giovanni, narrowed with suspicion.

Tenzin piped up again. "I believe she said something about arresting me."

Ben's eyebrows rose of their own accord. He looked at Vasco. "I really don't suggest that. It won't end well for you."

"That's what I told them," Tenzin said.

"Tenzin, you should probably be quiet," Giovanni said calmly. He stepped forward. "Are you here about me?"

Vasco spoke. "All of you will be taken to the cacique."

"May I ask why?" Giovanni said. "I am Giovanni Vecchio. I have been on the island a matter of days, assisting my nephew and business partner. I had fully intended to introduce myself to the court of Los Tres, but I did not expect this unfriendly welcome."

"You call us unfriendly?" Inés finally spoke. "A respected human scholar known to be an associate of yours was found dead two nights ago, just hours after you visited him, and yet you object to *our* greeting?"

The silence of the cavern was broken only by the sound of the flowing waterfall. Ben didn't turn to look at his uncle, but he could feel the heat from Giovanni's skin. Hear the barely controlled rage when he finally spoke.

"This has nothing to do with August," Giovanni said. "Take me to your cacique." He stepped forward. "I believe a meeting could be most... illuminating." He looked at Ben and spoke in Chinese. "I smell someone familiar."

Tenzin began to laugh, and the sound was enough to chill Ben's skin.

Familiar? Like one of the vampires in Camino's apartment? The male or the female? Ben was dying to ask, but he didn't say a word.

Vasco jerked his head toward the vampires waiting near the entrance to the cavern. They surrounded Giovanni and Tenzin.

Six against those two? You really have no idea, do you?

Vasco and Inés walked over to Benjamin. "You will take us to the treasure," Inés said.

"What treasure?"

"The treasure of Miguel Enríquez," Vasco said. "The treasure that belongs to the people of this island."

"We haven't found any treasure," Ben said.

"I don't believe you." Inés shoved him toward the tunnel. "Show us."

"Ben," Giovanni called across the cavern. "It's okay." His eyes met Ben's in the dim light. "Show them the chest."

What are you doing? Ben's eyes screamed.

Giovanni's gaze was calm. *Trust me.*

Ben put his helmet back on. "You're going to want to watch your head."

Vasco and Inés followed Ben back into the tunnel. Since the

paracord had remained threaded through the pitons, it was easy to find their way back.

Inés and Vasco entered the bone-filled chamber, their noses twitching.

"What is this place?" Inés said.

"The lair of the demon of Camuy," Ben said. "And the place where Enríquez hid his treasure."

Vasco wrinkled his nose when he saw the piles of bones. "Savage," he muttered under his breath.

"It's here." Ben swung his flashlight toward the wooden box.

It was a plain sea chest, the kind a sailor might take with him to carry his personal possessions, which meant it was far from fancy. No iron bars or fancy scrollwork around the lock. The metal was black with corrosion. The wood was dirty but intact. Only the lid had fallen apart.

Vasco used his boot to scatter the bones surrounding the chest. In the low light, it was nearly impossible to see what the broken chest revealed. Inés walked over and bent down to the ground. She picked up a small piece of metal and lifted it to the light from Ben's headlamp. It looked like a coin at first, but Ben realized it was a blackened silver medal, like a saint medal a Christian would wear around his neck.

"Is this all?" she asked, glancing at Ben. "You've been searching for weeks."

Ben hadn't even looked inside the chest yet, but it gave him a perverse satisfaction that she was disappointed. "Do you realize how many tunnels and passageways there are down here?" he asked. "This place is a maze. We were lucky to find this." He glanced at the dozens of skeletons. "And honestly, anything else more valuable was probably taken years ago by whoever killed all these people."

Inés gave a short dismissive grunt and waved at Vasco. "Bring it," she said. "It might be useful."

"You." Vasco pointed at Ben. "Carry it."

Ben tried not to groan.

Vampires.

THERE WERE two pickup trucks waiting at the top of the trail to take them back to the mountain outside Lares. Ben, Tenzin, and Giovanni were loaded in the back of one while Vasco, Inés, and the sea chest were loaded in the other.

Ben and Giovanni were exchanging glances with each other while Tenzin was glaring at the pickup truck behind them containing the sea chest.

"You gave them the treasure," she muttered in Chinese.

Ben answered in the same language. "Did I really have a choice not to?"

"Both of you, shut up." Giovanni joined them. "Don't bicker."

"If he hadn't—"

"She never thinks about the fact that—"

"Shut up!" Giovanni snapped. "You're both being short-sighted idiots at the moment. I'm thinking."

Ben was thinking too. About how Inés and Vasco had found them. About why they'd stopped them. About why Giovanni was calling him shortsighted. They'd spent weeks searching for the treasure of Miguel Enríquez, only to find a single chest nowhere near the location their map—

"Oh!" Ben's eyes went wide when he realized why Giovanni was calling him shortsighted. He glanced at his uncle, only to see his uncle giving him a "shut up" expression.

Tenzin was still glaring at him.

He settled in for the ride, taking mental notes about their

captors and wishing he could have hidden the notes and map better.

The vampires guarding them had to know they were risking their lives, because all four in the back of the truck looked terrified.

Vasco, Inés, and their driver were all in the rear truck. Four vampires and a driver were with Giovanni, Tenzin, and Ben. They hadn't tried to tie them up or pull any weapons on them, which was smart. Tenzin usually had a negative reaction to anyone pulling a weapon on her.

She looked sullen. Giovanni looked stoic.

Vasco and Inés knew about Camino. Did that mean they'd killed him? Were they trying to frame Giovanni?

Giovanni had smelled someone familiar. Was it Vasco or Inés? One of the other vampires?

Who was the demon of Camuy? Did it matter? And if there was treasure in the demon's lair the whole time, did that mean the demon of Camuy had already taken anything worthwhile?

Ben typically didn't get carsick, but sliding back and forth in the back of a truck while facing backward going up twisted dirt roads left him feeling more than a little queasy by the time they stopped.

He followed the parade of immortals from the back of the truck, through the house, and down the sloping avenue toward the mountain court of Macuya, the cacique of Puerto Rico. Tenzin walked in front of him, floating over the ground every now and then just to make their captors look a little panicky. Giovanni walked beside him, his head held high, looking down his nose at all the vampires surrounding them.

Ben had to admit his uncle had been trained to be superior, and when he wanted to, Giovanni pulled it off better than any aristocrat Ben had ever met.

Vasco and Inés walked at the head of the party, the two vampires carrying the broken chest directly behind them.

The atmosphere in the throne room was oddly unchanged. Music was playing. A dance was going on. Female wind vampires twisted and rolled overhead while more women danced in circles before the throne. Macuya sat watching them with Jadzia and Valeria on either side of him, looking bored.

For the first time, Ben noticed the startling gender disparity. Most vampire courts were comprised of a roughly equal number of male and female vampires, but this court...

Female dancers. Women serving blood-wine and fruit. A few male drummers around the room and a notable number of males serving as guards. But the vast majority of those dancing or gossiping in the corners of the room were women. Beautiful, immortal women with flowers and feathers decorating their hair. Women on display for the proud man in the center of the room.

A scene that had amused Ben only weeks before suddenly made his skin crawl. There was something very wrong with this picture. Something was happening in the court of Los Tres.

"...that old man has been running Puerto Rico long before anyone from Europe arrived. He's just pissed Columbus spoiled his food supply."

"Three rulers. Three elements. Three peoples."

"My brother shares his power from a sense of goodness and fairness... But make no mistake: we were here first."

Who was really running Puerto Rico? Was it the man on the throne? The women beside him? Ben glanced at Inés and Vasco. Or was it someone else entirely?

The music fell silent as Inés stepped forward. "My brother, Macuya, I have brought the European, Giovanni Vecchio, to you, along with the treasure of our brother Miguel Enríquez."

The crowd of vampires began to murmur.

Macuya turned his attention to Inés. "My sister, why do you trouble me with this European?"

The irritation was evident on Inés's face. "Cacique, this is the man I told you of after we had news of the old scholar's death."

A dawning realization on the king's face. "He killed the old human? Why?"

Giovanni spoke up. "I killed no one, honored cacique. But I believe I know who did."

The murmurs grew louder. The two queens came to attention on their thrones. Jadzia's eyes narrowed. Valeria's eyes went wide.

Macuya turned his attention to Giovanni. "Señor Vecchio, why did you not present yourself to this court when you arrived on my island?"

Ben saw Jadzia bristle. Interesting.

Giovanni spoke to the cacique in a familiar way, one peer addressing another. "I do apologize. I was assisting my nephew with a business matter he could not handle on his own. You understand, of course."

Ben revealed nothing with his expression, playing the part of the dutiful apprentice to the older, wiser immortal.

"I'm sure you've had the same experience with those in your court. Young ones who take on more than they are capable of." Giovanni stepped next to Inés and continued to address Macuya directly. "I had every intention of introducing myself and enjoying the many pleasures of your court once the fire"— Giovanni snapped his fingers, rolling a ball of fire around his hand before he grabbed it and snuffed it out—"was put out. If you understand my meaning."

It was a very clever play. In one short speech, Giovanni had asked forgiveness, demonstrated his power, played with it like a figure of speech, and excused himself from blame, all the while flattering the cacique and his court.

I want to be him when I grow up.

It was a thought Ben had entertained more than once.

Macuya was similarly impressed. He liked this powerful immortal wanting to spend time in his court. "I do understand. Many times my wives or my sister take on a task they are unprepared for. I often have to intervene on their behalf."

Ben watched the reaction of Jadzia, Valeria, and Inés. All three quickly schooled their expressions, but not before Ben caught the bristle at the old man's insult.

"I do appreciate the intricacies and riches of your court," Giovanni said. "And I wish I could linger and enjoy its pleasures. But I am grateful that your sister interrupted our work, because the matter of August Camino is a very grave one."

"Oh yes." Macuya frowned as if he'd suddenly heard something discordant. "The old man."

"Señor August Camino was a friend of mine, a respected international scholar who had consulted with many immortals and remained under the continuing aegis of the O'Briens of New York City."

"He was on my island," Macuya said.

"As a guest, was he not? He had proper introductions and protections?"

Inés said, "He did."

"So what can be said of the court of Macuya?" Giovanni said. "What do I tell my friend Cormac O'Brien when I inform him of August Camino's death?"

The court once again grew utterly silent.

What are you doing, Gio? Ben began to look for exits. There was still one way in and one way out. Tenzin had moved to his side and was hovering off the ground. No one was paying attention to them. All eyes were on Giovanni speaking before the Macuya's throne.

"Are other immortal rulers to understand their aegis cannot be respected on this island?" Giovanni asked. "Will murderers be welcomed in your court as I smell the scent of those who killed my friend in yours?"

Dead silence greeted Giovanni's challenge, and the atmosphere in the court went from serious to volatile.

Macuya rose to his feet, his face cold with anger. "You accuse me of murder? You, a *thief* who was trying to steal my people's treasure from them?"

"You call me a thief when my associates and I are here on behalf of a client and we received proper permission from you to search for his property?" Giovanni turned and addressed the crowd. "Does the word of the court of Puerto Rico mean nothing?"

"Who is your client?" Macuya roared.

Giovanni was silent for a long time. "My client is Roberto Cofresí."

The whispers of the court grew louder.

"Are you kidding me?" Ben turned to Tenzin. "How many damn pirates became vampires? Seriously, was this a trend during the seventeenth century or something?"

Tenzin shrugged. "Cofresí was eighteenth, I think. And I don't know what to tell you. We tend to run in the same circles."

"Did you know he was Giovanni's client?"

"No. I did have my suspicions when Gio told me he wasn't welcome on the island. Cofresí annoyed a lot of vampires here."

Macuya was livid. "*Cofresí?* The thief! The pretender! Does he have more right than *me?* I, who am king of this island? I, who am the heart and soul of this place?" He pounded his chest. "I, who am the oldest vampire in Puerto Rico, the most power-ful, the beloved of my people?" His arms spread, as if to embrace the court, but the walls of the mountain began to shake.

Sounds of panic from the air as flying vampires rushed to the ground, searching for escape from the shaking walls and falling rocks.

"Be ready," Tenzin said.

"For what?" Ben hissed. "We need to go *now*. Forget the treasure!"

"Not yet." She grabbed his arm. "Giovanni is poking the hornet's nest, but he won't be the one who gets stung."

The shaking continued as Macuya's face grew red with rage and indignation. Larger rocks began to tumble down the walls. The earth beneath their feet began to move.

Jadzia and Valeria both rose to their feet. Valeria frantically searched the crowd while Jadzia shouted, "Inés, what are you waiting for?"

Macuya's sister stepped forward to the foot of his throne. She raised one hand, stomped a bare foot, and the walls of the mountain grew still.

"Enough."

22

B en watched in wonder as Inés stood in defiance before the cacique's throne.

"What are you doing?" Macuya shouted.

"What are *you* doing, brother?" Inés kept her hand up. Her expression was as immovable as her power.

Ben could smell the amnis in the air. There was a scent of churning earth and the snap of ozone, like the air after a lightning strike. Though it wasn't visible, he knew there was a terrible battle going on between the elemental powers of Macuya and Inés. The earth rolled, but the walls remained stable. Wind vampires along the edges of the room began to flee toward the exit, but Tenzin held on to Ben's arm.

"Wait."

Giovanni had stepped back, melting into the crowd that had pushed forward toward the throne. Ben was guessing they were earth vampires who didn't worry for their safety and were more curious to watch what would happen.

"For too long you have believed your own lie, Macuya." Inés spoke in a loud voice. "For too long I have been content to allow you. But you go too far. You threaten our people. You ignore our alliances. This cannot continue."

"I am the cacique," Macuya said. "Oldest of immortals—"

"You lie!" Jadzia yelled. "She is your elder! Look." She stepped forward and addressed the crowd. "She is more powerful than he is! Look who protects us from the mountain coming down! It is not Macuya. It is *Inés.*"

The guards advanced on the thrones, their swords and spears raised, but Ben could tell they were confused. They looked to Vasco, who was standing at Valeria's side.

"Do nothing!" Vasco said.

"Kill her!" Macuya shouted. "Kill anyone who threatens the cacique. *Kill Inés!*"

"Do not call me Inés." The ground beneath the earth vampire rose until she was face-to-face with her brother. "I am *Yahíma,* eldest born in mortal blood of our mother and eldest born in immortal blood of our sire. I am *Yahíma,* caretaker of my people. I am *Yahíma,* rightful cacica of this island." She lowered her voice, but the room was dead quiet. "Step aside. Or I shall remove you."

Macuya sneered. "You are nothing."

With a single stomp, Yahíma ripped the earth in two, opening a gash beneath Macuya's feet. He fell into the earth and it swallowed him to the neck.

The scent of blood was in the air, and the vampires around Ben were in thrall to it. Those who had fled poured back into the mountain, drawn to the fight. Some of the guards charged the throne while others hung back, confused by the conflicting orders of their king and their general.

Vasco pulled out his sword and shouted, "For Yahíma!"

"Time to go." Giovanni appeared at Ben's side as all hell broke loose.

"You think?" Ben turned and tried to remain as inconspicuous as possible as he, Giovanni, and Tenzin walked up the ramp and toward the exit. When they reached the outside, Tenzin took to the air and Giovanni and Ben began to run.

"Were you planning on provoking a coup while you were here?" Ben shouted as he ran. "Was that on your to-do list? Find treasure, hand out relationship advice, provoke Puerto Rican vampire coup?"

"Sometimes an opportunity presents itself." Giovanni didn't pant when he ran. "I may have had a heads-up that political changes were happening. I just decided to use them to our advantage when the opportunity presented itself."

Ben glanced at the starry night sky. "Any idea where Tenzin went?"

"Probably back to the caves. Any idea how we're going to join her?"

Ben jogged down the front steps and toward the garages, pulling something from his pocket. "You're kidding, right?" He held out the keys he'd pocketed from their driver.

Giovanni grinned. "I knew I adopted a pickpocket for a reason."

Ben spotted the truck they'd come in and ran toward it. No one was guarding the vehicles. No one was near the garages or wandering around the front of the house.

"Vampires do love a fight, don't they?" Ben opened the doors, and he and Giovanni jumped in the cab.

"There has been dissatisfaction with the leadership on the island for years now," Giovanni said. "Cormac and Novia have been monitoring it. The response to the hurricane was the final straw."

Ben started the truck and put it in gear. "Vampires don't get involved in human disasters."

"Do you really think that's true?" Giovanni asked. "Do you think Ernesto does nothing to help when there are wildfires in

Southern California? Do you think Cormac sat back and did nothing during hurricane relief in New York City? If nothing else, it is in their financial interest to have their communities operating smoothly again. Not to mention it fosters goodwill with their human associates."

"I'd honestly never thought about it," Ben said. "Immortals just seem so... removed from human suffering."

"Suffering on a grand scale affects everyone, Benjamin, human and immortal alike. Macuya did nothing to alleviate the disaster after the hurricane hit the island. From reports that Cormac and Novia received, he welcomed a return to what he called the original state of the island."

"What does that mean?" Ben gaped at him. "You mean he didn't like electricity, so isn't it better if no one has it? People died because they couldn't get medical care. People ran out of food and water."

Giovanni nodded. "He was shortsighted and cruel. He didn't even pressure his contacts in the human government, which is the minimum most vampire leaders would do. Inés has long been his equal in power, and she's far more in tune with the modern world. Novia says she has been waiting to take his place for years."

Ben smiled. "Don't call her Inés."

"I don't plan on it." Giovanni shook his head. "Macuya was an idiot. He would have had three powerful women on his side if he'd been willing to share his authority. Now he will have nothing."

"You think he's dead yet?"

"If he's not, I think he's wishing he was."

"Who killed Camino?" Ben asked him. "I know you know."

Giovanni's face went blank. "I know."

"And?"

"It's going to be complicated."

Ben sighed. "Shit."

"So let's find the rest of the treasure first," Giovanni said. "Let's get you and it away from that mountain. Then let me and Tenzin take care of the rest."

"And what about your client?"

Giovanni frowned. "Cofresí? He got his map. That's what I was hired for."

"You mean he's not still a client?"

"No. But he *is* the reason your taking the gold off the island in a boat is a very bad idea. He wants Enríquez's treasure. He's not going to give up easily."

"Great. Just... great."

THEY MADE it back to the caves while the moon was still high. Glancing at his watch, Ben noted that it was only two a.m. They still had a good amount of nighttime left, and once the sun rose, every vampire in Macuya's mountain—or was it Yahíma's mountain now?—would be locked inside while humans had the run of the island.

This could work.

"Okay." Ben pulled out the notebook and map from the coveralls he was still wearing. "Luckily, they didn't search us."

"We're going right back the way we came." Giovanni walked into the cavern ahead of Ben. "We need to find it and get you somewhere safe by sunset today."

"Got it."

Tenzin was pacing in the cavern. "About time," she said. "What took you so long?"

"Oh, you know, we can't fly."

She rolled her eyes. "So annoying."

"Stop complaining," Giovanni said. "We're going in. Your job is next."

Ben and Giovanni put their helmets back on and grabbed flashlights, along with Ben's metal-detecting gear.

"Don't touch," he told his uncle.

"Would not dream of it."

They walked back into the tunnel, following the cord to the chamber with the bones. Giovanni bent down to examine the bones that had been draped over the chest. He stood up with a frown. "Where's the medal?"

"What?"

"There was a saint's medal around this skeleton's neck."

"I think Inés—Yahíma took it."

Giovanni nodded. "There's no way of knowing, but I think this skeleton was Tomás. I don't think he ever left this cave. The clothing scraps match the time period. And from the glance I caught of that medal, I think it was Thomas Aquinas, which would have fit with a Dominican. How many other Dominicans are likely to be poking around caves in Camuy?"

"Okay, so..." Ben evaluated the scene. "Tomás follows the map, finds the treasure, and he's bringing it out when he runs into a vampire?"

"The treasure would have been hidden here for years at that point. It's very possible he surprised one when he was searching. Or maybe he was able to sneak by the creature on the way in because it was sleeping, but the noise and exertion of a human carrying a heavy chest woke it."

"So why didn't the vampire take the treasure?"

"That old box?" Giovanni smiled. "How heavy was it, Benjamin?"

"I mean, pretty heavy, but I was able to carry it."

"Gold heavy?"

Ben thought about the crates of gold he and Tenzin had

moved through China one summer. "No. Definitely not gold heavy."

"I don't know all of what was in that chest, but it looked like mostly weapons and some silver coins. Maybe some journals or other goods. But it wasn't gold. It wasn't something that would tempt a vampire."

Ben nodded toward the far tunnel on the other side of the chamber. "So you think there's more still back there?"

"Don't you want to find out?"

"Hell yeah."

"Eighth turn, left."

"Marking."

It had taken them another two hours to carefully work their way through the honeycomb of the limestone caverns beneath the surface. They had gone up and down, though nothing was uneven enough to use ropes. They were careful and still nearly marked wrong turns twice. No other signs of treasure or exploration had been found. Nothing that gave them a clue that they were on the right track.

"Ninth turn." Ben swallowed hard. This was it. "Right."

He turned right and shined his headlamp into the darkness. The musty smell of earth was the only thing that greeted him. He grabbed his flashlight and traced it along the limestone walls of the cavern. In his enthusiasm, he nearly missed it.

"There." Giovanni grabbed Ben's hand and pulled it back to the right. "Up."

He'd been looking along the floor and almost missed the natural shelf formed by the rocks. The canvas was covered in dust and mold, but it was definitely man-made. Ben and

Giovanni walked forward, and Ben reached for the edge of the tarp.

He pulled it off and it fell apart in his hands.

"It's molded," Giovanni said. "The air is damp."

They peeled the molded cotton back in pieces, revealing three smooth wooden chests. Two were sturdy, made of teak with iron banding. They were a little over two feet long, nearly two feet in width, and maybe a foot and a half tall. The other was smaller, more of a document box than a chest. They were in near-perfect condition, though the metal locks and seals were corroded.

"Boom." Ben stared. "That's what I call a treasure chest."

"Let's see if we can't find out what the fuss is about." Giovanni bent over one of the larger chests and rubbed his hands together. "I think I can soften this metal a bit."

He heated his hands up and pressed them to the first lock. In seconds it fell apart, as did the plate holding the lock in place.

"Score." Ben let out a slow breath. "Tenzin is going to be so pissed we're doing this without her."

Giovanni chuckled. "They're quite heavy. We don't want to move them without checking that it's worth it."

"Exactly."

Giovanni lifted the wooden lid and the hinges in back cracked, but Ben wasn't thinking about hinges. He was thinking—

"Silver." Though it was black with age, he could see the definition of the coins, and a few fine pieces had escaped corrosion. "Definitely silver."

The chest was filled with silver of all kinds. Coins filled half of it, but the rest was cups and teapots. Spoons and plates. Small pitchers and lots and lots of flatware. Miscellaneous parts gathered from ships across the Atlantic if Ben had to guess. None of it matched, except in tarnish. Ben picked up an intricately wrought cup shaped in the form of a nautilus shell and tried to brush some of the black away.

"How much do you think this is worth?"

Giovanni looked at it. "You could probably estimate better than me, but depending on the mark... one hundred to one hundred fifty thousand?"

Ben smiled. "Pounds, not dollars."

Giovanni gave a slow whistle. "And it's beautiful."

"Yes, it is."

The silver mostly appeared to be English, which fit with Enríquez's pattern of attacking English ships. Ben couldn't have been more pleased. English silver was highly collectible.

"Okay." He rubbed his hand together. "Next chest."

It was gold. Lots of it.

Ben felt his heart pounding. "Oh my God."

Giovanni just stared at it, shaking his head.

Though there were silver coins mixed in, the chest was over half full of gold coins. It was a fortune. A single gold guinea could reach five thousand dollars at auction, and there were hundreds of them. Hundreds. Other coins were mixed in. Spanish gold. Gold bars.

"It was reported that he was the richest man of his time in the Caribbean," Giovanni said. "Powerful. Influential. Ruthless in business and skilled on the water."

"It didn't make sense that he died a pauper."

"He was too smart not to have some insurance."

"This is... some insurance plan." Ben glanced over his shoulder. "She's going crazy out there."

"Oh, she definitely is." He closed the chest of gold. "Should we wait on the last one?"

Ben shrugged. "We gotta leave her something. And this is gonna take at least two trips, even with you helping me."

They tried lifting the chests from the shelf with the metal

handles, but the iron hoops were too corroded. They quickly fell apart. Instead, Ben looped the paracord around the chests with Giovanni's help, creating handles that secured the bottom of the chest while fitting over their shoulders. They would dig in, but it would be the easiest way to move each chest through the narrow passageway.

Ben and Giovanni lifted the gold chest first and started through the tunnel, following the line they'd set to guide them back to the main cavern.

"How do you think Enríquez moved all these back here?" Ben asked. "He couldn't have by himself. They're too heavy. Who would he have trusted to know the location of the treasure?"

"I have a feeling if we checked all those skeletons in the first room," Giovanni said, "more than one would have a bullet hole. Miguel Enríquez wasn't known for his charity to anyone other than the church."

It was a grim thought, but probably an accurate one.

It took over an hour for them to make their way back to the main cavern. Ben had to stop for a few breaks. By the time they reached it, Tenzin was nearly out of her mind.

"I knew it!" she crowed. "I knew it!"

Ben couldn't help but grin. He set down the chest, walked over to her, and grabbed both her cheeks. With a giant smile, he kissed her. Full on her shocked mouth.

"Worth it." He lifted her up by the waist and spun her around. "You brilliant pain in the ass!" Ben set her down by the chest and pointed at it. "Look. Go ahead and look."

Tenzin didn't waste a second. She flipped open the lid and knelt before the glowing gold, digging her hands into the coins. "So beautiful."

Giovanni laughed. "Why don't Ben and I leave you two alone while we go get the last two chests."

Her eyes went wide. "There's more?"

"A chest of miscellaneous silver and another one we haven't opened yet," Ben said. "We decided to wait for you."

She looked like she was going to cry. "You do love me. Both of you."

Ben and Giovanni laughed and checked their lights before they walked back toward the tunnel. This time Ben grabbed straps.

"Guard it with your life, Tiny."

"You know I will."

The lethal tone of her voice made a shiver run down Ben's spine.

"That woman really loves gold."

A LITTLE OVER AN HOUR LATER, they were sitting in front of the two chests with the document box sitting on top. It was designed for scrolls and maps, but that wasn't what was in it. It was far too heavy to be carrying papers.

With a slow breath, Tenzin lifted the lid.

"Jewelry." She sighed in contentment. "It's very modern, but it's beautiful."

Only Tenzin would declare three-hundred-year-old jewelry to be "very modern."

"Lots of gold chain." Ben picked through it. "Some silver signets." He handed one to Tenzin. "This is cool. Oh. Ruby." He spotted it near the bottom and dug though some enameled brooches that would have been fashionable in the sixteenth and seventeenth centuries. "Nice color."

"We'll have to take our time with these," Tenzin said. "Some of it we'll want to keep, but the majority of it would be better to sell."

"This sea monster is cool." Ben picked up a gold necklace with a bright green enameled sea creature hanging from the base. It was decorated with pearls and small diamonds. A siren was riding its back.

Giovanni held out his hand. "That's beautiful."

"It might be the nicest piece in the box," Tenzin said. "Though there are a few pearl pieces that aren't bad."

Ben glanced at the waterfall and a night sky that was growing lighter every moment. "If we don't move this to the Jeep soon, we'll be stuck in here all day."

Tenzin's eyes went wide. "You're not transporting all this by yourself."

"If I don't, then I'm transporting it when the vampires are awake."

"The vampires aren't the only risk here," Tenzin said. "There's no telling what could happen between here and San Juan."

Ben rose to his feet. "Are you saying you don't trust me to drive these three chests a couple of hours from here?"

Tenzin stood too. "I'm saying that you're human and you're vulnerable."

"I'm not vulnerable to sunlight. That's your problem, not mine."

Giovanni said, "I think you should both calm down."

"I can't believe you don't trust me," Ben said. "After all this?"

"I trust *you*," Tenzin said. "I don't trust other humans."

"Once the sun goes down, the vampires come out. Did you forget that part?"

"We're the only ones who know what is here!" Tenzin said. "We're the only ones who know the extent of Enríquez's treasure."

"Do you really think Los Tres is going to forget about us?"

Ben replied. "Listen, Inés—Yahíma—has probably killed all her rivals by now, but she's not going to forget us or this cave. We need to get this stuff out of here before she has a chance to regroup."

"I agree with Ben," Giovanni said quietly. "We need to move the treasure out of here tonight before dawn."

"You *would* agree with him," Tenzin hissed. "You've spent half his life putting him at risk."

Giovanni narrowed his eyes. "Are you really pointing fingers in that regard?"

"Will you both stop talking about me like I'm not here?" Ben asked. "Tenzin, this is not as big a deal as you're making it. I can move this gold safely to San Juan. I'll start driving at the crack of dawn, and the biggest threat I'm going to face is rush hour traffic. I'll keep everything at the house until tomorrow night. Then we can move it to Gio's plane and we're out of here."

"No good," Giovanni said. "They know where the rental house is. They have people in San Juan, and if they're smart, they'll be there at dusk, before even Tenzin could fly back."

"They know where the Quebradillas house is too," Tenzin said. "You can bet on that. They're going to be suspicious we took off the way we did. They're going to suspect there's more. And let's not even talk about the pirate Giovanni is working for."

"Worked! Past tense."

"Are you saying Cofresí isn't going to try for the gold?" Tenzin asked. "Or are you saying I can kill him? Because I'm more than willing to do that, but you and Ben keep telling me not to be a sociopath, which I think is unfair. I looked that up and I do not fit all the criteria."

"We're not killing my client."

"You said he's not a client anymore. He's a *former* client."

Giovanni wiped a hand across his face. "Do you even realize how bad for business that is?"

"I don't care."

"No, you don't, do you?" He rose to his feet. "You take what you want and damned with the rest of us. Isn't that your way?" Giovanni said. "Damn what others want. Damn what others plan. Damn their desires and their lives and their future!"

"This isn't about this treasure," Tenzin said in a low voice.

"You're absolutely right." Giovanni stared at her. "It's about something much more important. You spend every waking moment walking on the edge of disaster, Tenzin, and you won't be the only one who falls."

"Stop." Ben swallowed the lump in his throat. "Just stop."

Silence fell across the cavern, and the echo of the waterfall filled the space between them.

"We have one problem right now. Can we focus on that, please?" They were arguing about him, and he hated it on so many levels.

Giovanni let out a slow breath. "Actually, we have four problems."

"Which are?"

"Los Tres. August's murder. Cofresí. And getting the gold off the island."

Tenzin said, "And keeping all of it."

Giovanni looked at Ben. "Tell the truth: Do you want to come back here? If you don't, then we pack everything into my plane, we take off, and you never set foot in Puerto Rico again."

"That doesn't get justice for Señor Camino," Ben said.

Giovanni said, "No, it doesn't. But that's not what I'm asking."

"It's not all about me." Ben racked his brain. Everyone wanted this treasure. Everyone was going to try for it. "We're safe from Cofresí as long as we're in Puerto Rico. But if we leave this island like thieves, we're safe from no one. Everyone will assume we've stolen something. Some might assume Giovanni killed Señor Camino, which would hurt his reputation in the book world."

Giovanni asked, "So what do you suggest? We surrender the treasure to Los Tres?"

"Absolutely not." Ben wasn't that generous. "But the only way we're going to get what we want is to give them what they want."

Tenzin said, "That makes literally zero sense."

Giovanni frowned. "I'm listening."

"Tenzin is right."

She blinked and walked to the camp table, grabbed her tablet, and walked back to them. "Cara, activate voice recorder. Ben, could you repeat that?"

"You didn't say please." He smiled. "You said we're the only ones who know what is in these chests. You were right. But I'm also right. The only way we get what we want is to give them what they want."

A smile slowly grew on Giovanni's face. "I like the way you think."

23

Giovanni and Tenzin loaded the two chests in the back of Ben's Jeep before they hid in the cavern before dawn.

"Do you think this is going to work?" she asked.

"Yes. It's a good plan. He's very bright."

"You trained him well."

Giovanni looked at her. "Some of it is me. A little of it is you. A lot of it is just him."

"He also learned things from his horrible mother, but he'll never admit it."

Giovanni shook his head. "To this day, she is a very convincing con artist. But she has no conscience whatsoever. That is all his own."

"And his grandmother here, I think."

"Perhaps."

Tenzin heard the Jeep's engine start in the distance. "You keep track of the mother?"

"Always."

"Where is she?"

"Currently she's in Texas. Married to a very old man and planning to slowly poison him."

ELIZABETH HUNTER

"Have you ever considered killing her?"

"Many times." He looked at the waterfall. "But I am not her. And I've already taken her most precious possession. One day the human authorities will catch on to her. Hopefully."

Tenzin watched the play of emotion over her friend's face. "You saved him."

"He has saved himself," Giovanni said. "Many times over." He rose and walked to Ben's tent. "I'm going to sleep in here today."

"I'll keep watch and start cleaning up."

"Don't forget the bags."

"I won't."

"Are you sure you'll be stable in the tunnel?"

"It's dry?"

"Completely."

She nodded. "I'll be fine."

While the sun rose and Giovanni took shelter in Ben's tent, Tenzin went to work. Not many people knew she didn't sleep. It was one of her greatest weapons. Vampires assumed that time stopped when the sun came up and they didn't often question what happened during the day. Insignificant human life pattered on. The important work went on at night.

Vampires could be really stupid sometimes.

She quieted her nerves and followed the cord through the tunnel. She kept her eyes focused on the cord slipping between her fingers and the scent of Ben and Giovanni heavy along the path. Ben had been perspiring when they moved the treasure, and the familiar scent of him steadied her.

Of course, the same markers that steadied her could also lead others to find their trail, so Tenzin gathered the dirty laundry and scraps of coveralls that she'd torn from Ben's clothing and randomly tossed them down paths they didn't take. If she did her job right, the whole maze of passages would smell like Ben, causing nothing but confusion should any vampire try to follow his scent.

She reached the end of the cord and entered the chamber where the remains of the canvas tarp lay in a heap. She blocked out the musty smell and bundled up the fabric. Giovanni would burn it at nightfall.

Then she slowly made her way back out of the tunnels, dragging the canvas behind her to obscure her footprints, tossing bits of molded canvas along different corridors as she walked. She pulled out Ben's carefully set pitons and wound up the cord. If someone was looking very, very carefully, they might notice the piton scars, but Tenzin was betting that any vampire trying to find their path would depend on vampire senses and not human tracking.

She stopped in the cavern where the first chest was found and tossed the rope on the ground. Then she dragged the canvas out to the main cavern.

Inés and Vasco already knew about the first cavern. It was pointless to try to hide it. What Tenzin wanted to do was make them believe there was something else there. Some other treasure they'd missed the first time through. That would be believable. Or at least believable enough to give them time to get away.

She walked back to the cavern with Ben's shovel and found a spot where the earth was malleable. She dug a hole big enough for the document box they'd found, then she took the mostly empty box, rolled it around in the dirt, and pulled it back out.

Again, it wouldn't hold up to serious scrutiny, but she was counting on the natural excitement about treasure clouding more suspicious natures.

Tenzin refilled the hole and patted the earth down. Then she went searching among the skeletons.

Most of the fabric was too molded to use, but there were two cloaks belonging to wealthier victims that would work. She bundled the two cloaks out of the cave, grabbed the shovel and the box, and headed to the main cavern.

And when she was out, she made a silent vow not to go after treasure hidden in caves again.

At least... not unless it was really worth it.

She sat down near the reflecting pool with two ruined pieces of fabric and a sewing kit she'd taken from Ben's camping supplies. Her goal was to create two passable coin purses that a gullible vampire would believe came from the middle of the eighteenth century. One large and one fairly small.

She closed her eyes and tried to remember what she was doing during the mid-eighteenth century. Early in that century she'd done a job in Russia with Giovanni. She'd bought the Venice house a bit earlier than that.

India.

North Africa.

Damn. She didn't remember being anywhere near Europe in the mid-1700s.

But by the late eighteenth she'd been in Vienna. She shrugged and started picking at the cloaks to get a decent thread. It would have to do. She didn't imagine cloth coin purses had changed all that much in forty years.

Tenzin used a knife to cut the fabric into reasonable pieces, then she began to sew. She remembered the first time Ben had seen her embroidering in the loft.

"You sew?"

"You don't?"

He'd looked confused. "Uh... no."

Tenzin shrugged. "Well, up until the modern age, if I wanted clothes for myself, I usually had to make them unless I could steal them."

"Or you could, you know, buy them."

"*I did that sometimes too.*" *She'd been working on a particularly tricky stitch and she poked herself.* "*Of course, if they tore, I had to fix them. If I wanted an extra pocket for a dagger, I had to make it.*"

"*Huh.*"

"*Giovanni sews too. I taught him.*"

"*Just when you think you know a vampire...*"

She smiled at the memory. Modern humans were so helpless. Ben could cook, but he had no idea how to hunt. He could dress himself, but if no tailors or stores were available, he'd be wearing fig leaves or togas.

It was truly amazing humanity had gotten to where it was.

Of course, ancient humans didn't have YouTube or the ability to learn caving techniques from strangers on the internet, so every age had its trade-offs.

BEN DROVE NORTH THEN EAST, driving directly into the sun as it began to rise. As the morning grew warmer, he stripped off his shirt and put on his sunglasses, hungry for warmth. He'd decided if he only had a few days left on the island, he was soaking up as much sun as he could before he headed back to New York. Spending his life with vampires had led him to a serious vitamin D deficiency.

He turned east and drove through Camuy, Hatillo, and Carrizales. He dipped south and around the main part of Arecibo to avoid any morning traffic. Then he turned north again and drove for the beach. He followed the coastal road past the lighthouse and the scattered neighborhoods east of town, going with the flow of traffic as people headed into the city to work. He passed small local beach clubs and houses. A few cars and familiar sights. He drove until he spotted the small house he'd rented with cash, sitting on an isolated curve of beach not far from a local beach club.

There was a reason Ben had rented this house, and it wasn't only the lack of tourists and access to a passable harbor. He opened the house and searched it, checking the silent alarms he'd set the last time he'd left.

Nothing.

The cameras were on motion sensors and so far had only alerted him to a few birds fighting in the palm trees near the front door.

Ben walked to the bedroom, pulled back the rug, and opened the hidden doors set into the concrete foundation of the house.

Yes, there was a reason he'd rented this place.

The concrete chamber was roughly six by four feet and nearly three feet deep. Ben didn't know why it had originally been built, though he had a few guesses. The heavy doors closed flush with the floor and were secured with two padlocks.

He wrested the first chest from the back of the Jeep and onto the dolly he'd bought days ago at a local hardware store, grateful that some enterprising owner had added a ramp onto the back of the house even if the ramp was cracked and leaning. He checked the surrounding area to see if he had any watchers, but there was no one around.

He rolled the gold chest into the house and managed to lower it into the safe without crushing his toes, then he did the same with the silver chest.

The document case he'd left with Giovanni and Tenzin. It would be their problem to sort out. This one was his.

He closed the heavy doors, locked the padlocks, and rolled the rug back out. Then he went to the kitchen, drank a tall glass of water, and walked outside to lock up the Jeep and grab his duffel bag. He reset the cameras and the alarms, then he walked out to the beach.

Dragging an old plastic lounger from beneath a wind-battered palm, Ben stripped down to his boxers and lay fully in the sun, basking in the morning heat. He could feel his skin turning browner by the minute.

In minutes, he was asleep.

~

"DO THEY HAVE NAMES?" Ben tapped on the cage, only to have his abuela tug his hand away a second before the orange-faced bird pecked at his finger.

"They do. Papa and Ruby. But they don't like it when you tap their cage like that."

"Why not?"

The old woman smiled at him. "Would you like it if someone came to your door and, instead of knocking politely, they pounded with a fist?"

That was usually the way his father knocked on his mother's door, but Ben didn't say anything.

Joe had picked him up that morning with a bang on the door. It was a Saturday, and he'd said Ben's grandmother wanted to spend the day with him. Ben had answered the loud knock because his mom was passed out in the bedroom.

"You want to go hang out with my mom?" Joe asked. "She's in town for the week."

Ben shrugged. "Sure." He grabbed his coat and got in Joe's cab.

"Don't worry about your ma. I'll call her later."

"Okay." Ben wasn't worried. He was nine. As long as he was home at night, his mom didn't even ask where he'd been.

Joe had taken off; Ben's abuela was making pancakes. After breakfast, she would take him into the city to visit the Met.

Ben was familiar with the Met. More than familiar, in fact. It was one of the few places a kid in New York could go for free. A street kid had told him about it one time. The price at the counter was only a "suggested donation."

That was especially useful information in winter when it wasn't good to be outside and Ben didn't want to be at home. Ben could take the train to 77th Street and walk the few blocks to the museum. He'd find a coin on the sidewalk—he always tried to find a quarter if he could—then he'd walk up the counter and slide it across. The person at the counter usually asked him the same question every time.

"Where's your mom or dad?"

And Ben would answer the same way every time. "She's in the bathroom."

There was usually a look, but they slid the little sticker across the counter anyway. Then Ben would grab a map, walk past the ticket counter, and enter the arms and armories hall.

He'd spent hours looking at swords and armor, statues, and Egyptian mummies. He read all the little signs next to the paintings and learned about the different periods of European painting. It was a lot more interesting than the stuff they learned at school. He'd probably spent more time in the art museum than fancy grown-ups did.

But when Joe told him his abuela wanted to take him to the museum, Ben didn't complain. He liked the Met, and his abuela always bought him a big lunch and usually an ice cream too. If it was cold, she'd buy him a cupcake or a soft pretzel.

"Why do you keep birds in a cage?" Ben asked. "Wouldn't it be better to let them outside?"

His abuela smiled. "These aren't wild birds. They're domestic. They were born in a cage. If you let them out in a tree, they'd probably panic and go into shock."

It was a funny picture in his head, but Ben had his suspicions about whether it was true. Birds were made to fly. If you put them in a cage, they couldn't do that. Ben had a hard time imagining a bird that didn't look out the window every day and imagine flying off into a sunny sky. If he could fly, he'd fly around the world.

He'd go to Africa and Peru and Japan. He wondered if anyone in Japan wore armor like he'd seen in the armory exhibit. There was one helmet that had a rabbit on it! Ben would love to see a badass with a sword wearing a rabbit helmet on his head.

If he could fly, it would be the worst thing in the world to be stuck in a cage. Ben looked at the two birds, then at the window looking over his aunt's street. Then he glanced at his abuela. She was still making pancakes at the stove.

Slowly, he opened the birds' cage. They chirped and hopped closer to the little open door.

Come on. Come on.

Ben eyed the window. He didn't want to open it too early. It was cold outside.

Would the birds be okay in the cold?

If they weren't, they could always come back inside. Ben would leave the window open.

The birds hopped close. Closer.

"Come on," he whispered.

"What's that, Benjamin?"

"Nothing. Just... talking to the birds."

"They're sweet, aren't they? Like having sunshine on a cloudy day."

It wasn't cloudy that day. The sun was shining even though the air was cold. Ben willed the birds closer to the little gate.

Closer.

Closer.

How would they get from the cage to the window? Ben stuck his finger out and watched the birds' claws. He hoped they weren't too sharp, but it was a sacrifice he was willing to make for freedom.

"Benjamin! What are you doing?"

Ben slapped the door shut and backed away from the bird-cage, his hands clasped behind him. "Nothing."

His abuela blinked. "Were you letting my birds out of their cage?"

Ben glanced at the window. "No."

"Were you going to let them outside?"

Ben said nothing.

His abuela sighed, and Ben knew he'd disappointed her. She'd probably call his dad to take him home now. So much for the museum. He'd been looking forward to showing his abuela how much he knew about art, but now he wasn't even going to get pancakes.

Her frown eased. "Don't let the birds out. They'll get hurt if you let them out into that big city. They're not smart boys like you. They're just little silly birds who like apples and sunflower seeds." She nodded at the table. "Now sit. Otherwise these pancakes will get cold."

BEN WOKE when he felt his alarm going off against his hip. He'd tucked his phone under his leg and put it on vibrate. The sun was high in the sky, his skin was baking, and something had alerted the front door.

Ben didn't make a sound. He silently opened his phone and the app that controlled the cameras.

It was a bird again, banging against the screen door.

A bird. Just a bird.

He closed his eyes against the glare of the midday sun just as his phone went off again.

Ben sat up, wondering if he could do something to keep that bird away from the screen door, only to see that he'd received a picture message from his cousin.

I think your birds found a new home.

The picture showed an old woman with pure white hair tied back in a braided knot. She was wearing a bright red T-shirt and a pair of jeans that were muddy at the knees. She was sitting in what looked like a sunroom with two peach-faced love-birds perched on her finger. She was laughing, and her eyes wrinkled at the corners.

Abuela.

She wasn't like he remembered her. Of course she wasn't. This woman was older and more worn. The picture wasn't taken by a detective from a distance. It was up close and personal, taken by a beloved granddaughter.

He texted back, *Looks like they're very happy with each other.*

She loves them.

I'm glad.

Should he see her?

Should he let her know he was alive?

What would she think of him?

Hi, Abuela. It's me, Ben. I'm not a criminal, but I do hang out with them. I live with vampires and steal things sometimes, but usually only from bad people. My life is a series of morally ambiguous decisions and I'm not married and I'll probably never have children.

What grandparent was going to be proud of a man like him?

He was like a wild bird that had been caged its whole life, a prisoner to parents who didn't understand him or only wanted

to use him for their own gain. Now he had a measure of freedom, but he was still battling against barriers. Physical limitations. Emotional limitations. A sharply increasing cynicism he
didn't know how to combat and a creeping knowledge that his
fate was out of control.

If only real life were as peaceful as one of the impressionist
paintings he'd studied at the Met or an old woman in a kitchen
playing with birds.

Then again, if real life were peaceful, Ben doubted he'd
have millions of dollars in gold and silver sitting underneath the
foundation of a surf shack in Puerto Rico.

So... there was that.

24

It was near dawn when Giovanni woke. Tenzin was waiting for him with tea, a packet of preserved blood, and two beautifully constructed coin purses. A larger one filled with tarnished silver and a smaller one filled with gold. She'd finished them, then thrown the purses against the wall a few hundred times to wear the stitching.

Giovanni picked them up and examined them. "You're a genius."

"I know."

"Between this and the jewelry—"

"I think it'll be enough."

Giovanni nodded. "Agreed."

"I checked with Ben a few minutes ago. Everything is secured and he'll be waiting for us at the pickup location when we're finished."

"That is, if everything goes according to plan."

"It'll be fine." Tenzin rose and patted Giovanni on the shoulder. "You worry too much."

"And you never worry enough."

"Which is why I have you and Benjamin," she said. "We make the perfect team."

"The real question is, which one of us is going to drive that truck?"

She looked at him with a blank stare. "I don't drive."

"Shorted out electrical system it is."

THEY WERE STOPPED at the base of the driveway before they even reached the garage. The guard recognized them immediately. He also recognized the box lying between them. He yelled over his shoulder, and a wind vampire took off into the night.

"You will come with me," he said in heavily accented English. "The cacicas will want you."

"Very well," Giovanni said. He tried to roll up the window, but it had shorted out when he rolled it down. Most of the instrument panel was dead. The lights were still working, so he followed the man up the driveway and into the garage.

"You'd think they'd thank us for bringing their truck back," Tenzin said.

"It's only a little bit broken." Giovanni glanced out the window. "Of course, I think they're a bit distracted by what we have with us."

The document chest wasn't as big as the treasure chests, but it was sizable enough—and old enough—to be noticed.

Giovanni said, "Tell me again *exactly* what Benjamin said when he first made the agreement with Inés."

"He said you were working for a client who had a claim on the property. And that if there was any dispute arising from our search, he would bring it to Los Tres. And that the origin of the object was not Puerto Rican."

"There's nothing but English coins in that box. English

silver, English gold, and stolen jewelry," Giovanni said. "They can't dispute that."

Tenzin smiled at his moral gymnastics. "No, I think you've covered your bases nicely."

She didn't mind Giovanni's moral gymnastics. They were part of who he was, and they also made people trust him. He could speak with absolute confidence and people believed what he said. With Tenzin, people never believed what she said.

Unless she was threatening them. They believed that.

Of course, Tenzin lied a lot. She didn't consider it a moral failure. Lying was a strategy, and one that had worked well for her for thousands of years. If vampires always expected her to lie, she was never a known quantity. She would never be predictable. Her loyalties were always in question.

Except for Benjamin.

You should eliminate him.

The voice in the back of her mind had said it a thousand times, and yet she didn't. Tenzin told herself she didn't want to, but that wasn't exactly correct. Sometimes she did want to erase him from her world. Sometimes the mirror of his presence became too accurate. Too clear. But when it came down to it, she was afraid of what she would have to admit if she tried to remove him from her life.

It wasn't that she wouldn't. It was that she couldn't.

Giovanni and Tenzin exited the truck and followed the guard up the stairs and toward the house. Giovanni held the document chest in his arms. Tenzin resisted the urge to fly up to the edge of the waterfall falling into the pool. It really was enchanting.

"I love this house," she said to no one in particular.

"Thank you," the guard said. "It was designed by our cacica, Yahíma. She designed every part of this place for her court."

So it wasn't Macuya who had built the mountain. It had been Yahíma all along.

The way the guard spoke of his new regent had an echo of reverence. Tenzin smiled. She'd never desired leadership—she actively avoided it—but she could still admire those who obtained it cleverly.

Inés had spent years cultivating the loyalty of the everyday immortals who surrounded her brother. She'd been the one solving their problems and meeting their needs. She'd likely arranged lodging for newly sired vampires and helped their transitions. She'd probably been the one responsible for dealing with government paperwork and the pesky humans who came with it.

When it was time for her to seize power, it would have been seen as inevitable by the majority of the court.

Who else could lead them? Who else had the right?

The fact that she was extraordinarily powerful only enhanced her claim. She had birthright, she had loyalty, she might have even had love.

"Your ruler is a wise cacica," Tenzin said.

"She is one of three," the guard said.

"Then you are three times blessed," Giovanni said.

The guard offered him an agreeable nod as he led them through the gardens and across the bridge leading under the mountain.

Though the path to the mountain was the same one they'd walked only one night before, the atmosphere was completely different. Gone were the raucous drums and feathered dancers. Gone was the decadence and the party atmosphere.

The scene that greeted Tenzin and Giovanni was entirely different.

There were still three thrones, but no longer was one sitting in front of the others. All three were in a line and the raised dais was gone. Each queen sat as an equal with a small table beside her throne and an adviser at her side.

Gone were the luxurious gowns of the previous nights. Valeria was wearing a smart rose-colored suit, beautifully tailored to show off her slim figure. Yahíma was wearing a simple tan sheath dress with a brightly patterned jacket, though her bare feet touched the ground in a show of elemental power. Jadzia wore a pair of leggings and a richly textured green tunic that floated around her body.

The women were feminine and utterly regal. Tenzin approved.

Valeria was signing a paper. Jadzia and Yahíma were listening to a petition. There were guards, but they stood along the edges of the room while vampires and a few humans bustled back and forth in the background, clearly busy with tasks. Vasco, the general with the solemn presence, was nowhere in sight. The whole atmosphere was one of industry, not intrigue or political tension.

"As I've said," the petitioner was saying, "the property belongs to me. The family that is living there now—"

"When were you turned?" Jadzia asked. She looked up and locked eyes on Tenzin.

Hello there.

Some unspoken current ran between the three women in the front of the room. All of them turned and watched Giovanni and Tenzin as they approached, even though the vampire in front of them was still speaking.

"I was turned in 1896."

Jadzia stared at Tenzin as she asked, "And how long has the human family been living there?"

The vampire shrugged. "Does it matter?"

Yahíma turned her attention back to the man in front of them. "It does, Bertrand. We have a corporation that deals with this sort of thing, but if it is seen as stealing land or strong-arming humans who have been living on the land for many years, we will face questions from the government that are most inconvenient and do not benefit the good of our island or our court."

Jadzia said, "I advise you to find out how much money the humans would want in order to sell the property."

"With respect, cacicas, it is my land."

"And have they built a house on it?" Jadzia said. "Have they improved it and cared for it?"

"I suppose."

"Then think of the contribution they have made as care-takers and consider that," Jadzia said. "We cannot discount the humans living there. They have likely paid money for the land, though it was not to you. They have paid taxes to the human government and cultivated it."

Valeria finished with the papers she'd been signing and handed them to a secretary. "My sister Jadzia is wise. These are reasonable requests, Bertrand. You may yet have a claim if the humans are unreasonable; come back when you have more information and we will see if we can help."

Tenzin could tell the vampire wasn't pleased, but he also was out of arguments. "Thank you, Cacicas."

Before another petitioner could come forward, the guard announced them. "Giovanni Vecchio and Tenzin of Penglai have come to petition Las Tres."

Tenzin tried not to bristle at the word petition. She hadn't petitioned anyone in her life. But she followed Giovanni's lead and nodded respectfully. Bowing wasn't appropriate—Tenzin did not bow—but a respectful nod wasn't out of line.

"Señor Vecchio," Yahíma said. "My sister Tenzin. Welcome back."

Tenzin was both taken aback and curiously charmed by

Yahíma addressing her as a sister. It was a tradition used only by very old vampires who considered themselves royalty, and they only used it addressing those they considered royal peers.

Unexpected and illuminating.

"Cacicas." Giovanni addressed them. "May we offer our congratulations on the formation of your new court?"

No one asked what had become of Macuya. It was as if he had never existed.

"You may offer your good wishes," Valeria said quietly, "since it was your actions that provoked it."

If Giovanni was thrown by the accusation, it didn't show. "Though that was never my intention, I cannot deny that I'm pleased by your wise leadership." He moved his attention, addressed each woman in turn. "I believe this island will benefit from your wisdom and experience."

Tenzin had agreed to stay quiet unless things turned violent, but she spoke up to add, "It is clear your administration is already caring for previously overlooked needs of your court."

"Thank you," Valeria said, glancing nervously at Tenzin before she turned her attention back to Giovanni. "Now that you have offered your congratulations, I wonder why you have returned to us and where your nephew has gone."

"My nephew is dealing with a business matter in San Juan for me." Giovanni's careless wave communicated what he'd intended. Whatever they were there for, it was vampire business, nothing to do with human apprentices.

"But you and your partner have returned to us," Jadzia said, her eyes on the box. "And you bring something with you."

"My queen." A new voice spoke from behind them. Tenzin turned and saw Vasco. He was addressing Valeria, and it was clear he was reluctant to interrupt. "I would beg your attention in your chamber."

"I'm sure you would," Giovanni said quietly.

The whole of the room froze. No one missed the quiet pronouncement.

"Vasco," Yahíma said. "Your services are not needed right now. There are no security matters before the court."

The general was undeterred. He stepped forward, his expression giving nothing away.

"My queen Valeria," he said again, his voice rough, "I beg your ear in the privacy of your chamber."

Valeria's eyes were wide and blank. Whatever thoughts were turning in her head, Tenzin could not read them.

A few silent beats later, Yahíma said, "Will those of the court leave us." She pointed at Giovanni and Tenzin. "Not you." She looked at Vasco. "And not you."

The working vampires and guards along the edges of the room disappeared in seconds.

Giovanni set the wooden box down in front of him. "We have unfinished business."

"That we can agree on," Yahíma said. "It appears you have found your treasure."

"Only part of it. The other part was left here."

"Oh?" She waved a hand. "Weapons of Spanish design. A few good blades. Some coin. Nothing so interesting that they would be worth much money. And, of course, those were arti-facts of the island, so they could not be the items you were looking for as your nephew assured me the object you were seeking was not of Puerto Rican origin."

"Since I haven't been able to examine the chest, I cannot say for certain."

Yahíma smiled. "You will have to take my word for it."

"I am happy to do so, Cacica." Giovanni nodded. "And should you have any desire to value the objects for auction, my company would be more than willing to assist."

Jadzia said, "You're most generous, Señor Vecchio. But I'm more interested in what you have in the box at your feet."

"I'm sure you are." Giovanni said. "I'm also sure you know I have a plane in San Juan. You know that I have connections all over the world. If I wanted to disappear with the contents of this box, then I am very capable of doing that."

Yahíma arched an eyebrow. "So you say."

Tenzin mentally screamed at Giovanni. *Shut up, shut up, shut up!* It wouldn't pay to challenge her over a slight so minor. Yahíma was a new monarch. No matter what Giovanni's reputation was, she had to save face.

"I am here today"—he moved past the minor insult with aplomb, and Tenzin heaved a sigh of relief—"because my nephew made you a promise, and neither he nor I break our word."

Yahíma was interested. "Continue."

Vasco had moved to the side, closer to the thrones. Tenzin watched him, but he made no move to approach either Giovanni or herself. Everyone was too curious about what was in the chest.

"My nephew told you that the treasure we were searching for did not originate on this island," Giovanni said. "The coins in this chest are of English origin. We were correct in our assessment."

Yahíma glanced at Jadzia and Valeria. Both women nodded. "Agreed," she said.

"He told you our client has a claim on this treasure, which he does by the ancient rules of conquest. Miguel Enríquez died a natural human death in 1743. No heirs claimed his estate or his debts. The map leading to this treasure was obtained by Roberto Cofresí, a vampire turned in 1824. He hired us as his agents to find it."

It wasn't strictly true, of course. Cofresí never hired Giovanni to find the treasure—only the map. But making Cofresí the client was a useful fiction that would work for the moment.

Yahíma said, "Some may argue, but I believe in the old laws. You are within your rights. As we were within our rights to take our portion of the treasure by force."

By force, my ass. We gave it to you. Tenzin bit her tongue and reminded herself about new monarchs and saving face.

"I am happy to accede to your claim on the first chest," Giovanni said. "But Benjamin further promised you *personally* that should there be a dispute about the ownership of this item, we would bring it before Las Tres."

Jadzia leaned forward, her eyes gleaming. "Are you saying there is another claim greater than your own?"

Giovanni spoke directly to her. "I believe you know there is."

Vasco had come to stand by Valeria. His hand was on her shoulder, and his face was even paler than usual.

"Cacica Yahíma," Giovanni said. "I have come before you, honoring the promise my nephew made in good faith."

"I appreciate that honor and your good faith, Señor Vecchio."

"With that in mind, I ask that we return to the death of my friend, the human August Camino."

She frowned. "Camino? What does the old man have to do with Enríquez's treasure?"

"Because he owned documents that demonstrated a prior claim. I believe that was why he was killed, even though he had been promised protection by the rulers of this island."

Yahíma's face was frozen. "Do you have proof of this?"

"I have the documents he owned, and I identified two scents on his body after death." Giovanni looked at Vasco. "Both vampires are in this room right now."

The vampire stepped forward, his mouth open, but he didn't speak. His eyes darted between Giovanni, Valeria, Jadzia, and Yahíma.

Busted.

Tenzin couldn't gloat. She and Giovanni had talked it over before they arrived. There could be no real justice for Camino—not unless they wanted to throw the island of Puerto Rico into more chaos that it would likely not survive.

But there had to be accountability.

An eye for an eye.

A life for a life.

Valeria stood. "Sisters—"

"Valeria, don't," Yahíma said. She slowly turned, but it wasn't toward Valeria. She turned left. To Jadzia. "You did this."

Jadzia's face was stone-cold. "Vasco, come to me."

Vasco turned toward Valeria and gave her one pleading look before he walked slowly to Jadzia. "Cacica," he said quietly, "I am your nitayno."

Jadzia looked at Tenzin, then at Giovanni. Her expression was ice-cold. "What do you want?"

"I want the murderer of August Camino held to account."

Jadzia nodded. Then she walked behind her throne and removed a long, curved blade, a *shotel*, Tenzin realized. Double-sided and deadly. She walked over to Vasco and, without a single word, sliced his head from his neck.

25

Ben tapped his fingers on the steering wheel and watched the cameras from the app on his phone. It was after dark, vampires roamed the island, and even cheerful texts from his cousin with more bird pictures weren't cutting the tension.

What if it didn't work?

It wasn't as if Ben was worried about Tenzin and Giovanni. The two had taken on far more powerful opponents than the vampire court of Puerto Rico. But he was starting to love this place. He'd stayed on the beach nearly all day. He'd gone to the market and barbecued fish on the sand. Families at the beach club had waved him over and welcomed him to visit and asked how he was enjoying their home.

It was enough to make Ben damn near fall in love with the place.

Vampire politics infected human politics no matter how much vampires might try to avoid it. The island was just starting to recover. Life still wasn't close to normal. On the beach that day, he'd heard about battles with insurance companies and schools threatening to close. He'd heard about unemployment and neighbor after neighbor moving away. Moving to the States. Empty houses and lost friendships.

It was the lost friendships and broken communities that seemed to bother people the most.

What could he do to help? What could any of them do to help? God knows, he wasn't going to change any vampire minds about how to deal with the challenges, but if he could just keep more chaos from happening, that would be something.

He wanted to do something.

Liza sent through another text. *My grandma wants you to come for dinner before you leave the island.*

Shit.

He texted back. *I'm not sure. I'll have to check with my friend and see what her plans are.*

Is this the flaky friend?

Yeah. My uncle is gone first thing in the morning.

Is this flaky friend really a flaky girlfriend?

Ben shook his head. *No, we're not—* He deleted and started over. *It's complicated.*

Sounds like a girlfriend to me. LOL.

Ha ha.

Ben tapped his fingers on the dashboard and closed his eyes. *Tenzin, where are you? Please don't tell me you've started another fight.*

No one in the throne room moved as Vasco's head fell to the ground and came to rest at Yahíma's feet.

Valeria gave a sharp snarl and covered her mouth, but not before Tenzin spotted the fangs that had fallen.

"Valeria!" Yahíma snapped in warning.

Gone was the atmosphere of courtly manners. The scent of

blood filled the air, and Tenzin felt the instinctual urge of her race. To feed. To fight. To kill. She swallowed her instincts, shoving back the urge just as Valeria had suppressed the instinct to avenge her lover.

Tenzin watched Valeria. Her face assumed a careful mask as she slowly turned and went to stand in front of her throne. She looked away from Vasco's body. She looked at Yahíma, who stared back at her and gave her a solemn nod.

Valeria sat, a queen even in anger.

Tenzin watched as Jadzia lifted the edge of her tunic to clean her blade, making no move to hide the bloodstains. Then she calmly walked behind her throne, stowed her sword, and returned to her seat.

"The murderer of August Camino has been held to account." Jadzia held out her hand. "Give me the documents."

Tenzin could read Giovanni's thoughts.

You are the murderer.

You are responsible.

You killed my friend.

But he could not say it. Killing Jadzia would only throw the newly formed government of the island into chaos, and Giovanni had smelled both Jadzia and Vasco in the library. There was no way of proving who had killed the old man even if they both had their suspicions.

An eye for an eye. A life for a life.

Giovanni opened the box and handed the folded documents to Jadzia. "You are the illegitimate daughter of Miguel Enríquez and a free black woman named Antonia. Born in 1715, immortally sired to wind in 1737, years before your father died. That was why you never made a claim on his estate."

Jadzia opened the documents with a small smile across her face. "You are correct, Señor Vecchio. As you have proven with these papers, I am the only living heir of Miguel Enríquez."

"And to think," Valeria said, her voice tightly controlled, "you were so close to it for so long."

Jadzia glared at her. "You must be confused."

"I don't think she is," Giovanni said. "You were the demon of Camuy, were you not? It's understandable for a young vampire to be so uncontrolled. It wouldn't be the first time. You killed Tomás when he came searching for the treasure, but you never found more than the first chest. You never connected that chest to your father until you heard rumors about a map."

Jadzia leaned back on her throne. "You know nothing."

"I wonder," Tenzin said, "why August Camino reached for the book about the demon of Camuy? Did he know? I wonder how. But then, August knew many things, didn't he? He kept many secrets."

"This is all speculation." Jadzia was annoyed. "Why are you still here? I have avenged your friend. You may leave and send our best wishes to Cormac O'Brien."

Giovanni gestured at the box near his feet. "There is still the matter of Enríquez's treasure. As my nephew promised, since there is a dispute on my client's claim, we have brought the matter before Las Tres." Giovanni spoke to Yahíma again. "For *you* to decide how this treasure will be divided."

Jadzia's head shot up. "What? The treasure is mine."

"No," Valeria said, her voice tightly controlled. "The right of conquest must also be honored."

Jadzia's face twisted. "Says who?"

"Your coregent," Valeria said. "Your *sister*."

Yahíma spoke. "Valeria is correct. You have known about your claim on this treasure for years, Jadzia. What have you done to search for it?"

Jadzia clenched her jaw in anger. Everyone in the room knew exactly what she'd done to stake her claim. She'd killed an old man who had the proof of it, but she couldn't say that, not without incriminating herself after she'd just killed another.

Tenzin could tell both Yahíma and Valeria—Valeria especially—balked at rewarding Jadzia for murder. But she could also see they were unwilling to upset the balance of power.

Yahíma spoke to Giovanni. "You present an interesting dispute to us. You have found the treasure and done the work at some considerable cost to yourself. Your client has paid you for your work, I presume."

"He has."

Well, that was true. Roberto Cofresí had already paid Giovanni a handsome sum to find the treasure map. The old pirate just couldn't go after the treasure himself.

Yahíma nodded. "Therefore Roberto also has a claim. Before we proceed, will you please show me what is in the box you have brought?"

Giovanni lifted the document box, leaving the lid open. "As you can see, there is a sizable purse of various English silver coins—some of them highly collectible—and a smaller purse with a number of gold William and Mary guineas. The box also contains sterling silver flatware, along with various pieces of jewelry, all of considerable value."

"And in your experience, how would you value this treasure?"

"My nephew is more skilled at valuation than I am, so please take this as a very rough estimate that would greatly depend on the sales channel. But if we found the right collectors, I would feel comfortable valuing this box of treasure at roughly three-quarters of a million dollars. The weapons would add value, possibly significant value, depending on how collectible they are. Based on what I know right now, the treasure of Miguel Enríquez would be valued at roughly 800,000 US dollars in today's currency."

Yahíma nodded. "I see."

It was nothing compared to the real value of what they'd found, but as Ben and Tenzin had both said, *No one knew what was in the cave but them.*

Perhaps if Jadzia wasn't a murderer, Tenzin would have had more sympathy.

But she was.

So she didn't.

Tenzin couldn't have been prouder of Giovanni. Her old friend didn't often lie, but when he did, he was excellent at it. She never would have guessed the truth from his face.

"It's mine!" Jadzia said. "I am Enríquez's daughter!"

Valeria's face hadn't changed. "The right of conquest must be honored. After all, by what other right do we sit on our thrones... *sister.*"

Yahíma turned to Jadzia. "You will have half."

"Unacceptable."

Yahíma pressed her bare foot to the ground, and Vasco's head rolled to Jadzia's feet. "You will have half," she said again in a lower voice.

Jadzia said nothing. There was nothing to say. Her throne was worth more than her treasure. "Very well. But I will pick the pieces I keep."

"Agreed," Yahíma said.

"Agreed," Valeria said.

Giovanni nodded at Yahíma. "We will leave you to divide your half. I'm sure one of your guards can meet us outside with the remainder of the treasure. We don't want to take any more of your time."

Yahíma said, "We appreciate your honesty and trust in this matter, Señor Vecchio."

Tenzin spoke up for the first time. "And I look forward to telling the O'Briens that the tragic death of their friend and colleague has been accounted for." Her eyes turned to Jadzia. "Though of course he will never be forgotten."

Jadzia's eyes might have been burning with rage, but Tenzin had no doubt the message had been received.

GIOVANNI LET OUT a long breath as they drove down the mountain in the car loaned to them by Las Tres. They would drive it to the meeting point with Benjamin and leave it there. He had no doubt there were tracking devices and listening equipment in the car.

Tenzin and Giovanni were both silent as they drove northeast, through the dark mountain roads, and down toward the ranger station where Ben was meeting them.

When they finally arrived in Camuy, they got out of the car, grabbed the much lighter document box between them, and wordlessly got in the back seat of Ben's Jeep, dropping the truck keys in the mail slot of the ranger's cabin.

They'd been driving for miles before any of them spoke.

"How did it go?" Ben asked, glancing at the document box.

"Is everything safe?" Tenzin asked.

Ben held up his phone with the camera app open. "Everything is quiet. How did it go?"

"Two problems down," Giovanni said. "Two to go."

THE SURF SHACK was anything but light safe. They could only stay there long enough to exchange treasure chests and lock up again before they drove to San Juan. Ben called Giovanni's pilot on the way there, gave him the airport name near San Juan, and instructed him on what time to arrive.

"You'll stick with your original plan," Giovanni said. "It's possible that Cofresí already has your boat and contacts identified."

"And the house?"

"Possible, but like I said before, he's not going to step on land here. Too dangerous for him." Giovanni glanced behind them at the two heavy chests. "He won't expect me to get involved. He knows I usually let you do your own thing."

Tenzin said, "What are you going to want in return for all this?"

Ben smiled at Giovanni's offended expression. "You expect me to ask for a cut of your pirate treasure?"

Tenzin and Ben said, "Yes."

"You're absolutely correct. Twenty percent."

Tenzin nearly choked. "Twenty? It's our gold!"

"It was my map."

"It was your client's map," Ben said. "You didn't even believe the treasure was real. Five percent."

Tenzin said, "To be fair, Ben, neither did you."

Ben shrugged. "But I went along with it, didn't I?"

"Fifteen percent," Giovanni said. "I'm the only one with a plane."

"Ten percent," Ben said. "Tenzin and I found the treasure. I came up with a plan to make everyone happy. You just helped carry it out."

Tenzin pouted.

"Fine," Giovanni said. "I can't argue with that."

"Settled." Ben reached a hand over the back seat. "Ten percent."

They shook on it.

"Of the whole treasure," Tenzin said. "Not ten percent from each of us."

"Oh, good catch," Ben said.

The wicked laugh Giovanni gave them told Ben he would have absolutely tried to weasel ten percent from both of them. "Fine," he said. "Ten percent of the *total* treasure. You two greedy monsters can split the other ninety."

Ben and Tenzin exchanged a smile before Tenzin turned to shake hands.

"Done." She situated herself back in the front seat. "Now, how are we going to keep Cofresí from taking his share?"

"Dammit, Tenzin, stick to the plan!"

THE PLANE that took off from the private airport in Miramar was a retired Russian cargo plane that had been retrofitted for vampire use. It had a reinforced cargo chamber to protect the plane's electronics from vampires like Giovanni and multiple storage compartments and sleeping quarters for the discriminating vampire guest.

Since the one who had designed it was Giovanni's thankfully dead criminal offspring, there were lots of places to smuggle two small chests.

Tenzin and Ben loaded the gold and silver onto the plane while Giovanni spoke to his pilot and gave him a flight plan. They would go to New York first to pick up Beatrice, then head back to Los Angeles where Tenzin had her warehouse and storage facilities. All three of them had deemed Los Angeles the safest place to keep the gold until they could hide it more thoroughly.

"Besides," Tenzin said, "I like Cormac, but we're guests in his city. We don't have any standing there. At least Ben doesn't."

"And you do?" Ben asked.

Tenzin sat on the low couch in the belly of the cargo plane. "Cormac likes me."

"Cormac is afraid of you."

"Don't they call that splitting hairs?" she muttered.

"I agree with taking it back to Los Angeles," Giovanni said. "Our agreement with Ernesto means even if by some chance rumors about the gold get out, we'll still be safe in his territory. He won't risk his relationship with Beatrice."

The don of Los Angeles was Beatrice's great-grandfather many times removed, and the immortal had a special regard for Ben's aunt even though they often didn't see eye to eye.

"Los Angeles," Ben said. "Which means it'll be a few weeks until you can roll around like Scrooge in your new pile of money, Tiny."

"Weeks?" Her eyes went wide. "How long do you expect me to stay on this boat with you?"

"All the way to the mainland, my friend. All the way."

She fell back into the sofa. "We'll see."

"Don't piss me off, Tenzin."

"Why not?" Giovanni said. "It's pretty much her favorite pastime."

"You know, you encourage her when you get like this." Benjamin rose and walked to the door. "Not helpful. Now get going, Señor Vecchio. Or the night will be over before we get home."

Giovanni stood and embraced Ben. "Be careful," he said quietly. "Cofresí isn't usually violent but—"

"I know."

"And be careful"—Giovanni glanced at Tenzin—"with everything."

Ben looked him right in the eye. "I will."

26

Ben and Tenzin were silent when they pulled into the garage near the house in San Juan. They were silent when they went inside and silent when Ben pulled a pot of stew from the refrigerator.

How long had it been since he cooked it? Three days? Was that all it had been since he'd left the lovebirds with Liza and taken off west to search for the rest of Enríquez's treasure?

Ben put the pot of chicken stew on the stove and turned on the flame. He was hungry. He'd been forgetting to eat too often. He'd eaten a full lunch with the nice family on the beach today and forgotten to eat dinner afterward because he was anticipating the night's activities with Tenzin and Giovanni.

He reached a hand up to feel the bruises on his neck. They were still visible, though they didn't hurt as much, reminders of the last time he and Tenzin had truly been alone.

She walked into the kitchen and peeked at the stew. "That looks good. I think it's been two days since I've had anything in my stomach."

Because you're flush with all my blood in your system.

He didn't say it, but he thought it.

Tell her you remember.

Nope. No, no, no. That would be...

What? What would it be?

What was it that he'd texted Liza?

Complicated.

His phone buzzed. It was that damn bird at the surf shack again. "I'm going to have to go west tomorrow," he said. "Get all our stuff from Quebradillas and close up the house. Then we'll come back here and close this place up before we head to the beach."

"Sounds good." She gave him a searching look. "Are you really not going to see your grandmother before we leave here?"

He stirred the stew. "What am I supposed to do? Catch her up on my life? She'd call me crazy or have a heart attack."

"You don't have to tell her who you are. You didn't tell your cousin."

"She might recognize me," Ben said. "I don't know... probably. I wasn't a baby the last time I saw her. I was ten, and even with a beard, I haven't changed that much. She's not senile; she would probably recognize me."

Tenzin got an odd look on her face. "She wouldn't. Not unless you told her."

"I know you didn't know me when I was that young, but have you seen pictures of me around Gio and B's house? I don't look that—"

"She wouldn't recognize you, Ben. She's legally blind."

Ben turned to stare at Tenzin. "What?"

"She only told me because I asked. I doubt most of her neighbors even realize because she's so functional. But she's nearly blind. That's why she stays in her house even though it's in the country and more room than she really needs. She knows every corner of it. She can work in the garden and walk around

299

and live mostly on her own. Liza knows. That's why she moved back in with her three years ago."

Ben tried to wrap his mind around the idea. The agent he'd sent never mentioned it, but then maybe he didn't know. Maybe he thought Ben already knew.

He pulled out his phone and scrolled through the pictures his cousin had sent him of Abuela with the birds. There was no way of knowing from the expression on her face. She looked at the camera, but then that camera was being held by Liza, and she knew her own granddaughter's voice. She looked at the birds, but the birds were probably chirping.

"She's blind?"

"It's macular degeneration. She has some peripheral vision," Tenzin said. "She can see light and dark. It didn't happen all at once." She bit her lip.

Ben didn't know how to feel. Clearly his grandmother was living a happy, safe life. And Tenzin was right. This disease meant he could probably go see her without endangering her or Liza. She wouldn't have to know who he was.

"But she's okay, right?"

"It's progressive. And can be genetic. Liza is already getting regular eye checks even though her vision is perfect. Just to be safe. But yes, other than that, she's in perfect health. It's not related to any other sickness."

Ben nodded. Was he relieved? Excited? Relieved that his own grandmother was blind? What kind of person was he?

He stirred the chicken stew and reached for the bowls on the shelf above the stove. "I need to think about it."

"Think fast," Tenzin said. "We only have a few more days."

"I know."

He drove to Quebradillas the next morning with his shirt off and his windows down. He blasted cumbias and reggaeton on the speakers. He drove slowly and didn't complain about the traffic. The usual annoyances of the human world—rude drivers, waiting in lines at the lunch counter, burning his tongue because he ate too fast—none of it bothered him. Heat. Flies. Honking trucks. He wanted to feel everything in this place. He wanted to absorb it. Wanted it to become part of his DNA.

It is.

For the first time, Ben allowed himself to think about his history here. His ancestors had come to this place, paddling in on wooden canoes, sailing in on merchant ships, dragged here against their will on slave ships. They had come here, and they had survived. Part of them survived in him.

People had gone to war for this place. Nations had fought to control this small island. His father had run away. His grandmother and his cousin were continually drawn back.

"Three elements. Three peoples. We boriqueños are all of them, are we not? Native and Spanish and African. Made of the ocean and the mountains and yes, even the hurricanes that test us."

Camino's words haunted him. Why was this place any more or less special than another? What did blood really matter? Why did it matter where your people came from?

Ben didn't have a home. Not here. Not anywhere.

But something in his blood tugged on him in this place. Some instinct told him to dig down to find more.

Impossible.

The little voice at the back of his mind spoke up again. *The human things of this life are not for you. You made your choice when you lied to the vampire. When you chose the monsters.*

Enough.

He *had* made his choice. Maybe it was time to say goodbye.

Ben pulled out his phone and texted Liza.

Dinner tomorrow night? I have to leave the next day.

A few minutes later, she texted back. *Let me check if I can switch at work.*

Part of him hoped she wouldn't be able to manage it. It would give him an easy out. He could always promise to text her the next time he was on the island and just never come—

My friend can switch with me. Liza added a thumbs-up emoji. *Grandma = excited. She wants to know all about the adventurer from New York who gave her birds. Is the girlfriend coming?*

Ben squeezed his eyes shut. *Complicated =/= girlfriend.*

Yes, absolutely. I totally believe you.

Ben checked the sunset time for the next day. *She's not free until 6:30. It's okay. We don't have to wait for her.*

He whispered, "Please don't want to meet her. Please."

6:30 is perfect. See you then.

"Shit."

Now he had to call Tenzin.

BEN LEFT San Juan well before sunset the next night, giving himself enough time to drive most of the way to Río Grande from Old San Juan. Evening traffic was in full force, and it took him an hour and a half to get there, even using the shortcuts Liza recommended. He drove from the city into the country, using mostly back roads, until he came to the place he'd agreed to meet Tenzin.

Sadly, she'd been more than enthusiastic about going to his grandmother's for dinner.

"She's an amazing cook. I smelled it."

"How much time did you spend at her house?"

"It didn't take long to smell what she was cooking. It was delicious."

"That did not answer my question, Tenzin."

Ben pulled over at the service station and waited for her; she was flying in from the rental house. Would she actually meet him? No telling. Luckily, he'd already told Liza his friend was flaky, so should she not show up—

Tenzin banged on the roof of the Jeep a second before she opened the door and slid inside. "It was raining up there!" She didn't look annoyed. She looked thrilled.

"Well, it's a rain forest."

"I'm so curious to see your grandmother's garden. I bet she can grow everything here." Tenzin was constantly frustrated by the limitations of growing vegetables on their roof garden in New York. "I'm quite envious."

"Please remember that you're just now meeting her for the first time ever and know nothing about her at all, especially anything personal."

Tenzin frowned. "Right. We'll see how that goes."

"This is going to be a disaster."

"Disaster seems a bit dramatic."

They drove the last five miles to the Rios family home with a light mist falling around them. The night was warm but damp. Ben wore a pair of tan linen trousers and a light blue guayabera shirt he'd picked out in Quebradillas the day before when he realized he didn't have any dress clothes that hadn't been left behind or destroyed.

He glanced over at Tenzin. "You're wearing a dress."

"You said it was a party."

"Probably it's a party." Why did she have to look so damn beautiful? She'd washed her hair and it smelled like coconut. The dress fell to her knees, leaving her arms and shoulders bare. It was bright green and yellow.

"You look great," he muttered.

"You look nice too. Did you shave?"

He rubbed a hand over his neck. "Just trimmed a little."

"That's good. Neck beard isn't a good look for you."

"Thanks."

"You were looking like a cave creature a few days ago. Your skin is very nice and brown now."

"I tan quickly."

"I don't."

Ben couldn't help the laugh. "Yeah, tanning's not really a good idea for you, is it?"

"Definitely not." She was staring at him.

"What?"

"Does it feel strange to have family you share blood with?"

Ben tried to imagine how long it had been since anyone blood-related to Tenzin had been alive. "I don't know. They've always been this distant... thing. This memory in the back of my mind. Ideas more than real people. Meeting Liza—and meeting my grandmother—it makes them real."

"But not according to them, because you're not going to tell them you're Benjamin Rios. You're Ben Vecchio."

"Exactly."

"And who am I?"

"You erased Abuela's memory?"

"Yes."

He smiled. "Then you're Tenzin. You're you."

"And how do we know each other?"

"Uh... we're friends. From New York."

"Do they know we're business partners?"

Shit. This was going to get interesting. "No. They think I'm here as a tourist, so I didn't tell them we're partners. I just called you my friend."

"Okay. We're friends." She nodded. "Being tourists together."

"Yes." Shit shit shit. "And... Liza maybe thinks you're my girlfriend. I didn't tell her that, she just thinks it for some reason."

Tenzin frowned. "Why would she think that?"

Because I stupidly didn't know what to call you right after you'd bitten me and dry-humped me in the caves.

"No idea." He cleared his throat. "Yeah, it's weird. She probably has an active imagination. Maybe she thinks anyone traveling together has to be *together*, you know?"

"Okay, so she thinks I'm your girlfriend."

"I didn't tell her that, so—"

"Do you want me to kiss you while we're there? Otherwise show you physical affection?"

GOD YES.

"Nope." He shook his head. "Not... not necessary, Tiny. Just be normal." What did that even mean with her?

She shrugged. "It's not a problem. From what I can tell, Puerto Ricans are a culturally affectionate people. Public displays of affection would be very normal."

Ben made the last turn and nearly considered driving right past the house.

Sadly, it was a dead-end road.

"Kill me now."

THE RIOS HOUSE was set back on a hill, two stories of soft-pink stucco with a carport underneath a wide balcony above. Colorful lights were hung across the balcony, music was playing, and half a dozen cars already crowded the front of the house.

He stared at the house. "It looks like they've been planning a party for weeks."

Tenzin said, "It appears they're not social hermits like us."

"I like being social hermits."

"You didn't used to be."

That was true. Before Ben had moved to New York he went out a lot. He had lots of human friends—mostly children of day people—along with vampire friends. He'd lost touch with most of them when he moved.

There was a staircase along the side of the house, lined with bright potted plants and leading up to the second-floor balcony. Ben and Tenzin walked upstairs. The sky had cleared and stars had started to break through the clouds. Ben could see hibiscus, plumeria, and potted ferns spilling over the side of the balcony.

"It's old, but it's very beautiful."

Ben could see damage from the hurricane. Parts of the stucco had broken off in the wind and the rain. Stairs were cracked and some of the trees were still a little bare. But he could also see that the house was spotless and well built.

This is where your father grew up.

He walked onto the balcony and looked around with trepidation.

This is where he played with his sister.

There were at least a dozen people milling around. Old people. Little people. Neighbors.

These are the people he knew.

The music was loud, but the guests were laughing and a couple in the corner danced. Others stood around a barbecue, drinking beer and arguing about football. A few curious glances drifted their way along with a few smiles, but no one approached them. He felt Tenzin slide her hand into his, and he squeezed it for reassurance.

Just then Liza came out of the house carrying a tray of

drinks with limes squeezed on top. "Ben!" She passed the drinks off to a friend and came over to embrace him. "So great to see you." She stuck out a hand. "You must be the mysterious friend."

"Tenzin." She smiled a little, keeping her teeth covered. "I've heard a lot about you. Thank you for inviting us."

"You're very welcome. Nice to finally meet you." Liza was finally out of her uniform. She was dressed in a pair of denim shorts and a bright yellow top. Her hair was pulled up in a wild ponytail instead of bound back in a tight bun.

Her hair is curly like mine.

His cousin turned and waved at the crowd. "I hope you don't mind. When Grandma started talking about what she wanted to cook, it sounded like enough for a small army, so I invited some neighbors."

"It's fine." More people meant less attention on him. "Looks fun."

"Everyone knows you're visiting from New York and most of them speak English, so you'll feel at home. Do you want a drink?"

"Please." He'd been cutting back, but this evening definitely called for liquor. "Anything with rum is good."

Liza laughed. "You sure you're not Puerto Rican?"

Tenzin said, "People ask him that all the time."

"I'm sure they do."

Liza turned to find drinks for them, and Tenzin pulled him down to whisper in his ear. "You look scared to death. Relax. No one is here to judge you, and they have no idea who you are."

"I know." He looked around. "My father grew up here. I could have lived here."

"Yes." Her eyes locked with his. "But you didn't. You chose something different. Are you sorry?"

Ben opened his mouth, but nothing came out.

Tenzin cocked her head.

"Maybe tonight," he whispered, "just a little bit... yes."

Tenzin put her hand on his cheek. "You don't have to apologize for that."

"I love my life." He blinked back unexpected tears. "I do, Tenzin."

"I believe you." Her voice dropped to a whisper. "But maybe some days it would have been easier to be Benjamin Rios and live in this normal house on this beautiful island with this human family."

He nodded. He couldn't speak.

"It's okay to feel regret." Tenzin's eyes took on a distant gaze. "Just don't let it live in your heart."

"If I were Benjamin Rios," he said. "I wouldn't know you. Or Giovanni. Or Beatrice."

"No, you wouldn't."

He stood up straight and wrapped her in his arms. Bending down, he said, "You may drive me crazy sometimes, but I'll never regret knowing you."

"I'll remind you of that when I need to," she said. "For now, your cousin is coming and she has three other people with her. Prepare to socialize."

27

It took nearly an hour for Ben to make his way down to the first floor where his grandmother held court in the kitchen.

"This is her throne room." Liza laughed. "I have to ask permission if I want to light the stove. She's going to be so excited you're here."

Liza led him down around the garage to the back of the house where the sunny kitchen he'd seen in photographs was located.

"*Abuelita, abuelita,*" Liza sang. "*Ben está aquí.*"

The old woman from the pictures turned toward him, and Ben felt his heart seize.

She's going to recognize me. Even blind, she's going to know.

"Ben!" She rose with her arms out like Ben was an old friend. "Finally! Girls, this is the giver of gifts. The one who gave Liza the birds for me."

A chorus of older women responded.

"So sweet!"

"You've been wanting more birds. You mentioned it three weeks ago at church."

"They're perfect for you."

"God sent them. Obviously."

His grandmother's English was clear, but more heavily accented than he remembered. He wanted to hear her speak Spanish—wanted to speak it with her—but he couldn't. Not if he wanted to maintain the illusion he'd created. "It's so nice to meet you, Mrs. Rios." He accepted her hug and tried not to hold on too long. "I'm so glad you like the birds."

"Sit, sit." She waved to the table. "Luz," she said in quick Spanish, "move your big backside and give this boy someplace to sit."

"You're so rude." Luz cackled. "He's a handsome one," she responded in Spanish. "Is that why Liza brought him home?"

"Don't be silly; he's traveling with his girlfriend." Abuela switched back to English. "Ben, you must call me Ana Lisa. And this is Luz and Rocío and Alice. They live on this street with me. We're the old-lady gardeners."

"Don't call me old," Rocío said. "You're the only one here who admits that, Ana."

"He needs some food," Alice said. "Liza, get him a plate. He's much too thin."

Ben watched mostly in silence as they chattered and served him a giant plate of mofongo with chicken and a heaping spoonful of salad on the side. They talked about their gardens and the children upstairs. They asked about Ben's family and what he did in New York.

"I'm in art research," he said. "I work with my uncle. We deal in antiquities." Ben drank it all in. His grandmother bustling around the kitchen. Mashing more mofongo as her friend cut fresh fruit and people darted in and out to grab plates and bites behind his abuela's back.

"That sounds fascinating," Luz said. "How did you get into that business?"

"It's a family business," Ben said, digging into the food. "Following in my uncle's footsteps, I guess." He watched Ana Lisa carefully anytime she went near the stove.

Tenzin was right. If she hadn't told Ben his grandmother was blind, he never would have guessed it. She had a few tells, the way she reached for things and put them back carefully. The way her head would tilt to the side to take advantage of her peripheral vision.

"That's good that you work with your uncle," Abuela said. "Family is so important."

"I agree." His heart hurt looking at her.

You would have taken good care of me. You would have given me a good life.

"You know, I have a grandson in New York," his abuela said. "He loves art too. You won't believe me, but he knew every single placard at the Metropolitan Museum when he was only ten!"

Ben couldn't even speak.

Alice nudged him. "She tells that story all the time. Every single sign." Her eyes twinkled. "Can you imagine?"

"No." Ben managed to speak. "Sounds like someone I should hire."

"His name is Benjamin too." Ana Lisa turned back to the stove. "Like your name. One of these days I'm going to fly up to that city and take his father over my knee until he gets me my grandson's phone number."

Ben could see the lines of sadness around Luz, Alice, and Rocío's eyes. This was something they'd heard before. Ben would bet his life on it.

"Ana, you're not mashing that mofongo enough." Luz rose and shoved Ben's grandmother to the side. "Show the boy where the birds are living now."

"Fine, fine." She waved Ben over, and they walked out to a sunroom off the kitchen where tropical plants flourished in containers and Señor Camino's birds sang and whistled. They hopped around the cage when Ana and Ben entered the sun room.

"There are my lovies," Ana Lisa said. "Look at them. Such sweet babies."

Señor Camino's birds were living in a veritable paradise now. Climbing vines surrounded their cage, and flowers bloomed everywhere.

"This is the part of the house that had the most damage after the storm," Ana Lisa said. "But we're lucky because it was also easy to fix it. I kept lots of extra materials from the men who built it."

"Your house seems like it weathered everything really well."

"Thanks to God." She raised a hand. "The way the land is here, our hill protected us, but it was very terrible. Luckily, this is an old, old house and it was very well built. It's seen many, many storms. Lots of neighbors stayed here too. It's a safe place."

"I can feel that," Ben said. "I'm glad you have it."

He walked over and watched the birds hop around the cage. They sang out as soon as Ana Lisa approached.

"I let them out sometimes. They like flying around all the flowers. They're perfect to keep me company."

"I'm so happy you were able to keep them." Ben glanced at his grandmother, who was looking straight toward the birds, though he knew she couldn't see a thing. "They belonged to the grandfather of a friend. He lived in an apartment in San Juan. He passed away really suddenly, but he loved them."

"Do you know what their names were?"

"I don't. I'm sorry." He nodded toward the cage. "But he kept them right by the window near his balcony. So I'm sure they love the view here."

"They do have a beautiful view up the hill with all the fruit trees and the gardens."

"I wish I'd come by during the day." Torches were lit in the backyard, but he couldn't see much. "I'm sure it's amazing."

"You'll just have to come back another time. Everyone is welcome here. Come anytime you're hungry. You know, I grow almost everything we eat here. Did Liza tell you that?"

"She told me you were a great gardener."

"I'm not *great*. I just know how to grow food. Do you know how to grow food?"

"I don't. But... um, Tenzin. She does. She has a big garden on the roof of our building. She grows a lot. She's pretty amazing."

"That's good. Everyone should know how to feed them-selves." She picked up a handful of seeds. "Here. You can feed them. They're sweet. You know, Rocío, she has a granddaughter who has a *real* farm on the island. She and her husband are teaching classes on how to grow things. It's a good, good thing. More people need to learn."

Ana Lisa chatted about recovery efforts in their neighbor-hood and the area. She sat at the bright red table in the middle of the room and told him all about her life. About Liza's life and work. About their neighborhood and their family. Ben sat across from her and just listened.

He spotted Tenzin in the doorway between the sunroom and the kitchen. He waved her in. "Ana Lisa, this is Tenzin."

Ana Lisa rose and walked over to Tenzin. "I saw you from the corner of my eye. Your dress is so bright and pretty." She embraced her. "Thank you for coming."

To Tenzin's credit, she didn't stiffen up with the embrace. In fact, she looked delighted. "I love your home."

"You're welcome anytime."

"I very much want to see your garden."

Ana Lisa laughed. "Ben mentioned you were a gardener too,

but trying to garden in the city..." She shook her head. "It's one of the reasons I could never live there."

She led Tenzin back to the table and pulled out another chair. Her movements were so effortless Ben was in awe.

"It's not easy." Tenzin turned to Ben. "I'm going to build a glass house like this. It's really the only option."

"That's fine," he said. "Build a glass house if you want. I'm not going to argue."

Ana Lisa asked, "So you two live together?"

"Yes, but—"

"We do." Tenzin scooted closer to Ben and put her hand on his thigh. "I am his girlfriend."

Ana Lisa smiled. "Liza wasn't too sure about that."

"I am. And we live together. And our friend Chloe lives with us too, but neither of us are sexually involved with her. It's not that kind of arrangement."

Kill me now. Please kill me now. Ben closed his eyes and refused to look at his grandmother's face.

"Well...," Ana Lisa said, "you must have a lot of space in your apartment."

Ben cleared his throat. "It's a loft. We have a loft. With lots of rooms. For friends."

"Yes," Tenzin said. "We're extremely wealthy."

"Tenzin—"

"It's good you're not shy about it," Ana Lisa said. "People with money can do a lot of good things in the world as long as they don't think money makes them better than other people."

"No," Tenzin said. "Most of the very rich people I know are horrible."

Ben could do nothing but let it ride. His grandmother was going to think what she thought, and he'd probably never see her again anyway.

"I like you," Ana Lisa said. "You're very honest."

"Yeah, she is." Ben squeezed Tenzin's hand. "Sometimes a little too honest."

"No such thing," Ana Lisa said.

"Can I let the birds out?" Tenzin asked. "They can only fly around in here."

"Yes, they'd love that."

Tenzin and Ana Lisa both walked to the birdcage, and Tenzin opened the little door. She laughed in delight as the birds hopped toward her, cocked their head, and whistled. Then one after the other, they hopped out of the cage and took off to fly around the lush greenery of the glass house.

They flew and sang, chirping at each other and hopping from one branch to the next. They ate at the table where Ana Lisa spread sunflower seeds. One jumped over to her shoulder to bob up and down before he took off flying around the glass house again.

"Look at them." Tenzin had a delighted smile on her face. She looked at Ben. "They're exactly where they need to be."

28

The next morning dawned without a single cloud in the sky. Ben had one day left in Puerto Rico and a lot of things to do. He cleaned the rental house and the car, washed all the clothes he had left, and wandered around Old Town San Juan for hours. He sent a text message to the captain of the boat he'd chartered, then another to the agent on the island who'd arranged for his rentals.

Everything was in order.

Ben did all the touristy things he'd ignored when he first arrived. He went to the museum and walked around the fort. He watched surfers on the water and sailboats along the horizon.

He went to the beach and lay in the sand, soaking up the sun. He planned to soak up as much sun as possible in the week they'd scheduled to get from San Juan to the Florida coast. By the time he got back to New York, he'd be as brown as he could possibly be. Skin cancer be damned.

By the time he got back to the house, he was ready to leave the island. Not that he wasn't going to come back. He was definitely going to do that. Liza and Ana Lisa made him promise to visit again and... he wasn't reluctant. Tenzin had to drag him away the night before.

She was hovering in the living room when he returned. "You were gone all day!"

"I had a lot to do." He tugged on her knee to bring her down to the ground. "What have you been doing?"

"Cleaning. And watching lovebird videos on YouTube."

Ben shook his head when he realized the direction she was going. "No."

"They're very friendly birds!"

"Tenzin, we travel too much."

"We can take them with us."

He grimaced. "Seriously? I'm not going to be one of those people who brings exotic animals on the plane. No. Just no."

Her eyes were wide and shining. "You never let me get a pet."

"This is literally the first time you have ever asked for one. Ever. Are you... are you trying to make yourself cry?"

"Will that garner your sympathy and make you more amenable to giving in to what I want?"

"No." *Probably.* "Don't cry." Ben found the very idea disturbing.

"But I want a pair of lovebirds!"

"We do not have any place to put them."

"We have a whole loft. And I'm going to build a glass house in the garden. They can stay up there."

"When it's snowing?"

"We'll get a heater!"

He wiped a hand over his face. "You have got to be kidding me."

"I feel like having pets would bring our family closer together."

Ben had to bite back the urge to laugh. "You're insane."

"Chloe needs a pet. She's been asking for one."

"She mentioned getting a cat."

"Which she would take care of! So I'm sure she'd be fine taking care of birds too."

"A cat and birds are not even close to the same thing, Tenzin." He raised a hand. "Can we not argue about this? The sun is about to go down. We have to meet the boat at midnight. We have shit to do."

She shook her head sadly. "You never prioritize the things that are important to me."

"Tenzin, we are literally in Puerto Rico because it was all you could talk about, even though I didn't want to go *ever*."

She smiled. "But aren't you glad you did?"

He took a deep breath. "Yes. But that doesn't mean—"

"So don't you think you'd be glad if we got a pair of love-birds too?"

She was impossible.

And they were probably going to end up with birds in the apartment.

THE OUTBOARD MOTOR on the tender dipped in the water and buzzed on low as they made their way away from the beachside bungalow and out toward the yacht waiting for Ben and the captain in the distance.

The captain's name was Marko. His wife's name was Jasna. They were part of a Croatian water vampire's shipping enter-prise and had come recommended by Ben's friend Terrence Ramsay, who also happened to be the VIC in charge of London. Terry recommended them for low-level security and, most of all, discretion.

Terry knew most of the trustworthy smugglers—as much as

that sounded like an oxymoron—in Europe and the Americas. Tenzin had contacts with most of the ones working in Asia and Africa. Between the two of them, Ben and Tenzin could move most things anywhere in the world.

"So you're expecting company on this trip?" Marko asked. "No interference?"

"Don't"—Ben shifted the small chest as they made a turn to move past the cove where the surf shack was fading into the distance—"don't worry about it. I don't even expect you and Jasna to be on deck. Leave me and Tenzin to sort things out."

Marko shook his head. "If you're sure."

"I'm sure."

"Jasna is very accurate with a spear gun," Marko said.

"That's good to know, but for now I'll pass on the offer." He thought for a moment. "Tenzin may want lessons though."

"You're the boss for the next week, my friend."

It was all part of the package. An eighty-eight-foot yacht to take them from Puerto Rico to Florida's west coast, a captain, a chef, and miles and miles of sun and ocean for the duration.

It was certainly promising to be more comfortable than the last ocean cruise Ben had taken, which was an unexpected freighter cruise from Shanghai to Long Beach that Tenzin had tricked him into.

As they pulled up to the gleaming white yacht, Ben saw Tenzin floating overhead and a dark-haired woman waiting with a rope.

Yes. His eyes caressed the wide deck, lounge chairs, and teak furniture. *Much better than last time.*

Tenzin floated down to the deck as soon as he and Marko came aboard. "I still don't know why I have to be here, especially if I have to hide."

"Because I want you here." *And you've stuck me with the boring parts one too many times.* "And you agreed to this when we were going over the plan with Giovanni. Besides, I'm carrying all your stuff." He pointed to the duffel bags in the tender. "Aren't you missing Cara?"

"Yes!" She reached for the bag she'd packed and marked with a red tag. "There's a video about hatching eggs I've been meaning to watch."

"No. Tenzin, we are not—"

"Bye!" She ignored him and walked away from the tender, whistling and cradling her tablet.

Jasna turned to him. "How long have you been together?"

"We're not— It's not..." He sighed. "About five years now."

"Hmm." She nodded. "I can tell."

"I don't know what that means."

"Come," she said. "I'll show you to your stateroom. I've already shown Tenzin the light-safe room we keep for our vampire guests."

"Do you get a lot of immortal charters?"

She smiled. "More than you might expect."

THEY LIFTED anchor and took off into the tropical night, heading northwest to skirt past the coast of the Dominican Republic and Haiti. They avoided Cuba as they headed north toward Turks and Caicos. At night Tenzin flew over the water, dipping down and skimming over the waves, laughing when dolphins jumped up to play with her.

Ben slept during the mornings and spent the afternoons basking in the sun. He reveled in the warmth and the silence on the water, the sound of the waves and the breeze that lifted his hair and settled his soul.

He was lounging on the foredeck as they drifted off the coast of some small Bahamian island. He heard Tenzin take flight overhead, heard her laugh before she floated down next to him. She turned her face into his arm and took a deep breath.

"You smell like sun."

He turned and smelled her hair. "You smell like coconut and saltwater."

"I like this boat. Should we buy one?"

"Why? We can just rent this one whenever we want to."

"I suppose that's true."

They lay in utter silence and peace for another half an hour.

"Do you think he's actually going to come?" she said.

"Yes."

"When?"

"Are you getting impatient?"

"Maybe."

"I think he's going to come... tomorrow."

"No you don't. You're lying. I can tell when you're lying."

"Okay fine. I think he's going to wait until we're fairly close to the Florida coast."

"Why?"

"Because that's where he lives, according to Giovanni." Ben turned to her. "Do a lot of vampires live in Florida?"

"A surprising number, considering how sunny it is."

"Huh." He closed his eyes and turned his face back to the stars. "Well, old people do like Florida."

She elbowed him and Ben laughed.

"He wants to lull us," she said. "Wants us to think we're home free."

"Probably."

"I should stay inside as we get closer. If he's watching, you don't want him to know I'm here."

Ben frowned. "Won't you get bored?"

"I'm sketching out what I want my aviary to look like," Tenzin said. "It's highly distracting. Don't worry, you'll love it."

So they'd gone from a glass house and two birds to an entire aviary?

Ben grimaced. "Goody."

THEY WERE two days out of Cape Coral when Ben got the feeling they were being watched. He was reading a book on the aft deck and watching the wake churn behind them. The moon's reflection rippled on the water as a dark shape cut back and forth behind them.

At first he thought it was a dolphin. They often followed the boat, jumping in the waves the engines made as they pushed the yacht forward.

But no. It wasn't a dolphin.

This shape didn't jump, and it didn't lose interest.

It followed the boat for an hour before it swam away. Ben stayed awake, waiting for something to happen.

Then the sun broke over the horizon, and Ben went down to Tenzin's light-safe room. She was sitting on the center of the bed, meditating.

"He's here."

She opened her eyes. "On the boat?"

"Following us."

She nodded. "He'll come back at dusk."

"Yeah, that's what I'm thinking."

She made a face. "And you're sure I can't—"

"Bad form." He lowered his voice. "We give him the other half. We move on. Everyone gets what they want, remember?"

"Fine."

"I'm going to sleep." He eyed the bed next to her.

Tenzin caught his gaze. "You can sleep here if you want."

"It's easier to sleep in the black room," he explained. "The shades in my stateroom—"

"You don't have to explain." She moved over. "Just sleep."

Ben stripped down to his boxers and didn't miss her eyes following him, but she said nothing when he crawled beneath the linen sheet on the bed.

In minutes, he was asleep.

"Benjamin."

Her voice was in his ear. He turned toward her and threw an arm over her, pulling her closer. "Sleep," he murmured.

"I can't." Her voice was sad. "I wish I could."

"Do you remember what it was like?"

"Only that for a few hours, I forgot everything. And when I woke, I felt new."

Ben took a deep breath, inhaling the scent of coconut and salt. She was a dream. Her voice was a whisper in his ear. Her skin soft against his skin. The frisson of energy along her arm when he ran his fingers up and down the delicate skin.

"You sleep with me," he murmured. "You rest with me."

"I do rest with you."

In the waning moments of his dream, Ben's filter was gone. He didn't think about what came out of his mouth. He just said it.

"I remember."

"Sleeping?" She snuggled closer. "I would hope so."

"Remember the cave."

She froze.

"Remember how you felt." His hand slid from her arm to the small of her back. "Remember your teeth in my neck." His fingers dug in; his voice grew rough as his body reacted to the memory. "Remember how I—"

"Stop." She rolled away from his arms. Got out of bed. Stood over him. "Wake up, Ben."

Ben blinked and rubbed his eyes. What the hell...?

Fuck.

He wasn't dreaming. He was in Tenzin's stateroom and he'd just told her...

"Fuck."

She said nothing. Her face was blank.

"Tenzin—"

"You should go. He'll be coming tonight. The sun is setting."

Ben didn't ask her how she knew. She knew. She could feel it. Ben tugged on the shirt and shorts he'd stripped off at dawn and walked out of the room, not giving her another look. He walked down the hall and up the stairs to the second floor. He opened his stateroom door and shut it, leaning against it for a second until his heart stopped racing.

He walked to the sink in the bathroom and splashed water on his face. Then he looked at his reflection in the mirror, at the rough stubble that had grown down his neck again, at the hair falling into his eyes.

"What the fuck did you just do, Ben?"

BEN POSITIONED himself on the foredeck, pretending to read a tablet in the moonlight. The yacht had dropped to half speed. Ben had requested they run a bit slower tonight.

He still felt the slight shift when Roberto Cofresí, most famous vampire of Puerto Rico, stepped on board. The boat gave a nearly imperceptible shrug.

Ben set down the tablet and reached for the pistol he'd

tucked under his towel. He turned and aimed at the side of the boat just as Cofresí strolled into view.

"That's not very friendly," the pirate said.

The vampire was not particularly eye-catching. Medium height. Medium build. Dark hair and eyes like most of his countrymen. He wore a full beard, not unlike Ben's.

"My uncle warned me you might come calling." Ben tried to appear shaken. "I didn't believe him."

"You should have." Cofresí smiled and there it was, the glowing immortal charm. The smile transformed his face, making Ben understand why so many stories had been written about the legend of the Puerto Rican Robin Hood. "I've come for my treasure."

"I'm the one who found it. I'm the one who did the work." He allowed his hand to shake a little.

"Didn't anyone tell you how this works?" Cofresí said. "I'm the vampire. The map was mine to begin with. Your uncle should never *ever* have made you a copy."

"I found the treasure. Not you."

"I found the map. And you poached it."

"You were never going to go after it!" Ben rose to his knees, keeping the gun on Cofresí. "My uncle told me about your feud with Macuya. He told me you couldn't go on the island."

"But did he tell you my feud with Macuya was about my relationship with his sister?"

Ben blinked. Okay, that *was* a surprise.

"I see he didn't." Cofresí stepped closer. "And a little bird told me that my Inés is no longer under her brother's thumb. In fact, she's running the whole damn place, just like she always should have been."

"She's one of three."

"She is the power, and she always has been. I'll be joining

her soon." Cofresí pulled out a long machete-like knife. "But not until you give me what Enríquez was hiding."

"I don't have it."

"Liar."

"I don't!" Ben's hand shook. "I don't have it all. Jadzia took half."

Cofresí frowned. "Jadzia?"

"She's Enríquez's daughter. She had documents to prove it. She took half."

A flare of anger made Ben's heart genuinely race for the first time. Cofresí wasn't happy with that news. He waved the knife at Ben. "Put that thing away. Unless you're an expert shot, it will do nothing to me and you know it."

"Maybe I'm an expert shot."

Cofresí lunged toward Ben and Ben played the part. He let his aim go wildly off and shot, the gun's recoil shoving his arm back and knocking him off-balance while Cofresí tackled him. Ben fell hard on his back, and the two men, human and vampire, rolled down the foredeck, hitting the wooden walkway hard and driving the breath from Ben's lungs.

Cofresí knocked the gun overboard and held the knife to Ben's throat. "Give me my treasure."

"Fucking pirate vampire assholes," Ben said through gritted teeth.

Cofresí grinned. "I do like your spirit, my friend." The smile fell. "Now give me the treasure."

He stood and waited for Ben to get to his feet, holding the knife to his neck the whole time. The blade cut his collar, and Ben smelled his own blood.

As did Cofresí. The vampire's fangs fell, and his gaze locked on Ben's neck.

"Hold it." Ben held up his hands. "Just... hold it. I'll get you the treasure."

Cofresí swallowed. "Yes, you will."

"And then you leave. Do you hear me? You leave me alone. I won't even get pissed off, okay? We're good."

The corner of Cofresí's lip curled up.

Uh-oh. This could be a definite kink in the plan. Ben knew Tenzin was listening. He also knew that things would get very ugly very fast if she came abovedeck.

"You know who my uncle is," Ben said. "He's not going to say anything about you stealing from me because he warned me and I ignored him. But anything else... I don't think you want Giovanni Vecchio after you for that."

Ben let the threat hang in the air.

His uncle's name seemed to snap Cofresí out of his blood-lust. "Get the treasure. And do it quickly."

"It's in my stateroom."

He smacked Ben's arm with the flat of his sword. "I'll follow you."

Ben turned and Cofresí followed him around the walkway and to the french doors that led from Ben's room to the deck. Ben opened them and walked in.

They'd been careful not to get any of Tenzin's scent inside Ben's room. A little bit on his clothing or luggage was to be expected—they did work together—but Ben didn't want Cofresí to suspect Tenzin was on the boat. Luckily, the light-safe stateroom had an entirely separate entrance and stairway.

Ben knelt down to the cupboard beneath his bed and opened the door before he pulled out the storage tub there. He popped off the plastic lid and lifted the document box out before he put it on the edge of the bed.

"What is that?" Cofresí asked.

Ben stood and turned. Now it was acting time. "The treasure."

The pirate's eyes went wide. "What?"

"This is all that was there."

"Impossible!"

"Okay, not *all* that was there."

He shoved the knife under Ben's chin again. "Show me the rest."

Ben raised his hands and let his voice go higher. "I told you, I don't have it!"

"Where is it?"

"Jadzia has the rest!" He stammered, "There was a bigger chest. It had weapons. Inés and Vasco took it, and I didn't see anything that was in there! A couple of pistols, I think. I don't know about anything else. You can ask Inés! She was there. There was that weapons chest and then we found this later. There's treasure in there. I promise!"

Keeping the knife on Ben's throat, Cofresí unlatched the box. He flipped open the lid and lifted out the enameled siren necklace. "This? This is the famous treasure of Miguel Enríquez?"

"There's some gold. Really collectible stuff. And silver coins. I haven't priced them all. Just this half is worth roughly four hundred grand, okay? It's not nothing."

"Four hundred grand." Cofresí's voice was flat. "Four hundred... total? A total of four hundred?"

"No, a total of eight, but I told you that Jadzia took half, right?" Ben huffed out a breath. "Well, probably a little more than half because she got to pick—I mean, that wasn't my choice, but what are you going to do? My uncle made the deal, and I think she kind of screwed—"

"Jadzia has the rest of the treasure?" Cofresí lowered the knife.

Ben shrugged. "Yeah. I mean, she is his daughter and everything."

Cofresí began to curse under his breath. "Then I have to return."

"Is there something specific you're looking for? I mean—" Ben shut up when the knife went to his throat again. "Okay. Okay."

"You have no more part to play in this, young Vecchio. Tell your uncle you're alive." Cofresí glanced at the necklace in his hand. He tossed it at Ben, who caught it. "And you've been rewarded. This should be enough to limit your losses for this hunt. Next time listen to your uncle."

Ben's mouth screwed up in a bitter smile. "If he even lets me work for him after this."

The charming pirate smile was back. "That sounds like a personal problem to me." He flipped the document box closed, latched it, then tucked it under his arm. "I'll be seeing you, Benjamin Vecchio. Be smarter next time."

And with a blur and a splash, the pirate disappeared.

29

Ben walked down the stairs to let Tenzin know that everything had gone mostly according to plan. He held a towel to his neck and wiped at the blood Cofresí had left, but he couldn't wipe away the smile on his face.

"Tenzin?" He knocked and waited for her to answer.

Her voice was muffled. "Come in."

Ben opened his mouth to speak but stopped when he saw her bag was packed and placed in the middle of the bed.

"What are you doing?"

"I heard everything," she said. "Well done."

"What are you doing?" His heart was in his throat.

Her face was a total blank. "It's finished. I'm going to fly back to the mainland, and then I'll be going to Tibet for a while. I need some time in the mountains. If you could bring my things back to New York and store them, I'd appreciate it. I'll probably be gone by the time you get back to the city."

Ben felt like she'd clobbered him upside the head, knocked him over, and then kicked him to really drive it home. He had to replay her words a few times for them to make sense.

...going to Tibet...

...time in the mountains...

...gone by the time you get back...

"What...?" He blinked. "I mean, what about the glass house? And the birds?"

"They can wait. Obviously. I'm not committed to the idea."

He shook his head. "Why are you doing this?"

"I told you, I need some time in the mountains."

"How long?"

"I don't know." Her face was still unreadable.

Ben started to get angry. "Is this because I told you I remembered what happened in the cave?"

"This has nothing to do with that."

"Bullshit."

"I'm not lying."

"You're lying your ass off."

Her eyes narrowed. "I've been thinking about this for months. This has nothing to do with you."

"Let me guess," he said bitterly, "you'll be making a stop in Shanghai on the way."

"I have business with Cheng that has nothing to do—"

He threw the bloody towel across the room. "Fuck yes, it has something to do with me!"

Ben slammed the door and stormed over to her. The cabin was small, but she still managed to be completely alone in the middle of it. Completely alone. Completely cold. Shutting him out like she always did.

"Tell me this has nothing to do with me." He bent down and forced her eyes to his. "Look me in the eye and tell me this has nothing to do with you and me and what happened in that cave and what's been happening for months—for *years*—now between us."

Her grey eyes were beautiful and unfathomable and they broke his heart.

"This has nothing to do with you," she whispered.

"You fucking liar." He blinked back tears. "Don't do this, Tiny."

"I'm taking a break from work."

"You're running away."

"I don't run away."

"You're doing it right now." He put both hands on her cheeks. "Don't do this."

She said nothing.

"Don't do this." He moved closer and pressed his lips to hers in the softest kiss he could manage. "Please."

He'd kissed her full on the mouth in wild celebration. She'd sucked his tongue down her throat and drank his blood while he lay writhing under her, aching with desire.

This was not the first their lips had met.

But the soft feel of her breath against his mouth nearly broke him.

Tenzin didn't kiss him back. She took his chin in her hand and slowly turned his head to the side. She put her mouth on his neck where the pirate's knife had sliced him. She licked the wound clean, paused, and licked it again.

Ben closed his eyes and felt his skin heal under her mouth, savored the warmth of her tongue.

And then... nothing.

When he opened his eyes, he was alone in the stateroom. Her bag was on the bed, and the door swung with the rocking of the boat.

She was gone.

THE ENTRY DOOR to the loft was locked when he finally arrived home a week later. The final stop in Cape Coral had been far easier than he'd anticipated, mainly because he wasn't smuggling anything into the country except a single necklace he was going to give to Novia O'Brien because he'd promised her something shiny.

The luggage was waiting with the doorman downstairs. The only thing Ben was carrying was his backpack and a bag of corned beef on rye from the deli a block away from the loft. New York was cold and dreary and everything Puerto Rico wasn't.

It was good to be home.

Though the sun was still up, Ben wasn't expecting Tenzin to be in the apartment when he arrived. He knew she was gone and would likely be gone for a while. Months, at least. It could be years. He'd called Giovanni and told him Tenzin had taken off "to the mountains" and asked how long he thought it would be until she came home.

His uncle didn't answer him.

Though he wasn't expecting Tenzin, he was expecting Chloe. He'd called her on the way back and left a message telling her when he'd be home.

"I'll pick up sandwiches," he'd told her voice mail. "I'm too tired to cook."

But Chloe wasn't there. Tenzin wasn't there.

There was, however, a cat.

It was black and slim, short-haired with golden-green eyes, and sitting on the edge of the counter, staring at him.

"Chloe!"

The cat gave a slight *hrrrrmph* and jumped down, winding its body around Ben's ankles.

"Chloe?"

He heard the key in the lock moments later.

"Hi!" Chloe tumbled into the entryway with two brown paper bags in her hand, her hair flying around her head, and a raincoat dragging on the floor. "Hi, hi, hi. Oh my gosh, this weather!"

Ben set the bag on the counter and caught her in a tight hug. "Hey."

Chloe paused and hugged him back. "I missed you. I'm glad you're home and everything went well. Beatrice kind of filled me in, but she didn't tell me everything, of course." She pulled away, set her bags on the counter, and hung her coat on the rack by the door. "Where's Tenzin? Is that corned beef? It smells amazing."

His heart sank. "Tenzin didn't come by?"

"I don't think so? I've been..." Her cheeks went rosy. "I've been staying with Gavin mostly, but I've been over every day to check on things, and there was one day earlier this week when I thought she'd maybe been here because there were some things moved and the light in her loft was on, but then she didn't show up again, so I didn't know what was going on."

Ben didn't know what to tell her.

"Benny, what's going on?"

"Tenzin went to China for a while." Ben was more confused than ever. "Or Tibet. I don't know."

Chloe must have seen something on his face. "What happened?"

"Nothing." He cleared his throat. "I... don't know."

Liar.

"You're not telling me something."

"I can't..." He shook his head and looked down as the cat rubbed its cheek against his shoe. "We have a cat."

"We don't. I mean— He's just over here today because I knew you were coming back and I wanted to be here, but I didn't know how long it would take, so I brought him with me. *You* don't have a cat. I wouldn't do that without asking you and Tenzin. *I* have a cat."

"And you live here. So we have a cat. That's fine. It's not a big deal." He almost told her about Tenzin's birds.

Only Tenzin wasn't here. She wasn't going to get any birds that Ben could complain about. She wasn't going to build a greenhouse or plant her garden in the spring.

"No," Chloe said. "I don't want you to misunderstand. I have a cat. With Gavin. I mean Gavin and I have a cat. At his house. His name is Pete. Only Pete is here now. But he's just visiting."

Ben was growing more confused by the minute, so he grabbed the only thing in the previous sentence that made sense. "The cat's name is Pete."

Her cheeks were near flaming. "Yes. And he lives at Gavin's. With me. Because... I kind of live at Gavin's now. Sometimes. But not all the time. If I need a break, I'll be here."

Ben let out a long breath and looked at his phone. "How long was I in Puerto Rico?"

"Three weeks."

"I feel like I missed a lot in three weeks."

"It's kind of a long story."

Ben reached for the corned-beef sandwich bag. "Sit down. Eat. Tell me everything. Does this have to do with the thing you wanted to tell me weeks ago, but you didn't because it was Gavin's business?"

"Yes. I'll tell you as much as I can. Some of it is—"

"His business." Ben dug out half a sandwich and handed it to her. "I get it."

"But I'll tell you what I can. Beatrice can probably tell you more—I love her so much, by the way—but I can't tell you everything. After that, you can tell me what's going on with you and Tenzin, because I know you're lying and something is going on."

He should probably tell someone, just so it didn't eat him

alive. And he didn't trust many people more than he trusted Chloe. "Deal."

"So it all started this one night when I was hanging out at Gavin's. He got this phone call and he ended up talking for ages, and when he finally came back, things got... a little weird."

"Why do we do this to ourselves, Chloe?" He shook his head and took a bite of his sandwiches. "Why?"

"Uh..." She shrugged. "Vampires?"

"Yeah." He sighed. "Vampires."

EPILOGUE

One week later...

J onathan opened the door to Cheng's study a second before
he heard her familiar steps marching toward him.

"Sir..."

Cheng smiled. "I hear her."

"It's Tenzin."

"I thought it might be."

She stormed into the room like a miniature typhoon and
immediately made for the training area he kept in his spacious
private quarters on the converted barge.

"Hello, Cricket."

She didn't say a word. She picked up a dao and spun toward
the training dummy, hacking at the torso with more anger
than skill.

Interesting.

Cheng stretched his legs on the ottoman and crossed his
arms behind his head. "How was your trip?"

She spun and stabbed the training dummy directly through

the heart. Then she left the sword in the dummy and went for another sword.

"Oh no you don't." Cheng sprang to his feet. "You're not going to ruin my weapons because you're in a mood."

He rushed toward her and grabbed the dao from the dummy, blocking her before she could stab him with a brand-new *jian*.

"If you want to do this"—Cheng grunted and pushed her away—"then we'll do this."

She fought furiously, but not with her usual skill. If Tenzin was concentrating, she could always best him at blades. But she was angry and clumsy and not fighting with her head.

Cheng drew blood three times. Tenzin drew blood twice, but the cuts were deep. She was out of control, furious, and wild. He'd only seen her like this two times before in all the years he'd known her.

He was perversely glad she'd come to him, because if she'd gotten into a fight with a vampire who didn't care about her, she could have lost her head.

Tenzin managed to knock the sword from Cheng's hand, but before he could grab for it, she threw her own across the room and came at him with fists.

She normally fought in a very old form of wushu she'd once taken the time to teach him. The problem was, Tenzin was constantly innovating. She'd incorporate anything and everything into her fighting technique. She played by no rules but her own. Within minutes, she had him on the floor with her legs wrapped around his neck. If he'd needed to breathe, he would have been out of luck.

He finally managed to wrench himself out of her grip. He stopped using any kind of technique and simply tackled her to the ground, using his greater weight to pin her.

He yelled, "I said, *Hello, Cricket.*"

She stared at the ceiling as if she didn't even see him.

"Tell me what's going on," Cheng said.

She said nothing.

"If you came here because of a job, you wouldn't have shown up pissing mad and without Benjamin."

Benjamin's name made her flinch.

A horrid dread speared Cheng's stomach. "Did something happen to Benjamin?" He wasn't particularly attached to the young man, but what it would do to Tenzin... "Cricket, is he alive?"

She forced the word past tightly pressed lips. "Yes."

"Did something happen to him?"

"He's fine. He's in New York. I called Giovanni to check this morning."

She shoved him off her chest and rolled up to sitting.

What was going on?

Tenzin looked small. Tiny, in fact. He couldn't call her vulnerable. She was too lethal for that. But something about her mental state seemed... fragile.

Be wary. A fragile Tenzin is as harmless as a spitting cobra.

Keeping his own warning in mind, Cheng rose and offered her a hand. "You need blood and you need rest."

"I'm fine."

He didn't want to argue with her. "How was your trip?"

"Uneventful. I'm just stopping by here for a few days, then I'm going to Tibet."

Cheng frowned. "I thought you were here about the job Jonathan emailed to Chloe."

"To be completely honest, I forgot about that." She was silent for a long time. "What's the job?"

"A sword. A very old sword. And I wouldn't be the one hiring you. That's why I told Jonathan I wanted a phone call. I wasn't expecting you to fly all the way out here to—"

339

"Who's the client?"

Cheng paused. He wasn't sure how she was going to take this part. Of course, he didn't know why the old man had asked him in the first place.

Tenzin looked up. "Who's the client, Cheng?"

"Your father."

She looked as confused as he was.

"I know," he said. "For the life of me, I don't know why he wouldn't ask you directly. But he sent a messenger with the request, and after I read it my only thought was—"

"Whatever he wants to find is at the bottom of the ocean and in your territory," she said. "That's why he asked you."

"Yes."

Tenzin no longer looked fragile. She lifted her head, and instead of anger or blind aggression, he saw cunning.

"Send a messenger to my father," she said. "Tell him we're coming to Penglai."

"You are certainly welcome to visit that island of vipers, but I don't want to go to Penglai."

Tenzin ignored him. "And get Jonathan. I need a tablet equipped with Nocht." She put her head in her hands. "I'm going to have to call Ben... eventually."

THE END

Continue reading for a preview of
The Devil and the Dancer: A Gavin and Chloe Novella
Available for preorder today.
For release March 12, 2019

PREVIEW: THE DEVIL AND THE DANCER

The letter was like a dozen others on the surface. It committed to nothing. It was a test.

Of what, Gavin Wallace wasn't certain.

The writer of the letter corresponded with him regularly. They weren't friends. They never would be. But their connection couldn't be denied. It definitely could not be ignored.

I am thinking about coming to New York City. Your introduction to the O'Brien would be most welcome. This is regarding a business matter, not a personal one.

Vivian

Gavin didn't need to breathe. No physical compulsion demanded it. He was a wind vampire who didn't need to breathe except to smell the air and to speak. He could hold his breath for as long as necessary and not feel the effects.

So the sigh that left his lungs was entirely one of habit.

Vivian.

Was it truly a business matter or did she have an ulterior motive? It would be impossible to tell until he talked to her, but he suspected the latter, simply because Vivian always had an ulterior motive.

A laugh made him look up and across the bar. The smile that touched his lips was as much a habit as the sigh that had come before. The smile, however, was far more recent.

Watching Chloe Reardon talk to the bar patrons was one of his favorite pastimes. He pretended to do paperwork, sort through letters, or read a magazine while he surreptitiously observed her chatting with a regular, polishing glasses, or advising one of the younger servers.

She was a woman who could enjoy talking to anyone. It was a skill Gavin had never developed, even at over a century of life. He was more likely to sit in a corner and look aloof, hoping his demeanor would frighten off anyone who didn't already know him.

It wasn't the most advantageous attitude for a publican. And even after many years, dozens of properties, and millions in hidden accounts, it was still what Gavin considered himself. He was a barman, and he was a good one. Of course, part of the reason he was good was that he excelled at the one skill every publican needed.

Gavin Wallace was a genius at reading people. He under-stood what they wanted, and he knew what to give them to get what he desired.

Sometimes, all a human or an immortal needed was the right drink and the right ear. Blood or wine or whiskey. Gavin didn't need to be Captain Sunshine to supply those. Other times, it was an introduction or an invitation. For vampires, it was often a safe place to meet a dangerous person.

Gavin provided any or all of those things, and in exchange he received wealth, safety, and influence he wielded very, very judiciously.

"Boss, you want another?" A server was standing at the edge of the table with a golden glass of whiskey on a tray.

Gavin glanced up. "Thank you, Priscilla."

"No problem." She set down the drink. "Let me know if you want something to eat. Raf is just about to shut down the kitchen." Gavin looked over to the bar as he raised his glass and sipped the unlabeled scotch he kept in a small cupboard. It was from his own distillery, but it wasn't in his nature to advertise he owned it.

Chloe caught his gaze and offered him a quick wink before she returned her attention to the human across the counter.

And what do you need, Chloe Reardon?

Space.

And time.

Damn my luck.

She laughed at something the customer said. It was an older man, a stage manager for one of the larger off-Broadway theaters, if Gavin's memory served him correctly. Gavin didn't know how the man knew Chloe, but familiarly radiated between the two. She reached for the bottle of Jim Beam without the customer asking, filled his glass before she read another order and shook two gin cocktails, all the while nodding while the older man told a story.

She'd been working for him over a year. She was a gold star employee, the kind immortals valued above the common swarm of humanity. She was trustworthy and discreet. She was independent and considerate. Smart, quick, and flexible. Aware of the dangers of the vampire world without being paralyzed by fear.

Chloe was also a brilliant and bright young woman. A gifted artist and a good friend. She was wise and funny, empathetic and loyal.

Chloe Reardon was everything that made Gavin feel like living again, but for the first time in one hundred twenty years, he found something he couldn't win in trade.

He couldn't buy her.

He couldn't trade for her.

He wanted to seduce her—fucking hell, he wanted to seduce her.

But more, he wanted her to be *his*. Of her own choice. He wanted her to come to him, surrender, and throw her lot into the darkness with Gavin.

In the year since they'd met, her surrender had become his singular desire.

But it had to be her own.

So he played the patient suitor. He took her to shows and dinners and parties. He gave her a safe room in his home. Ever the gentleman, he demanded nothing, but made it clear she could take anything she wanted.

Gavin was starting to believe they would never move past the strange neutral zone they existed in. The thought made him edgy. He was a patient predator, but he needed an end in sight. He needed to make her... just a little uncomfortable.

It was a risk, but one that he was comfortable taking. After all, Gavin Wallace was a genius at knowing what people needed. And though he knew Chloe needed time and space, he fervently believed she also needed something else.

She needed him.

SHE FELT Gavin's eyes on her back as they walked from the pub to the corner where Gavin had a car waiting, and Chloe would be lying if the idea didn't put just a little more sway in her hips. In the year since they'd met, the idea of his eyes on her had become welcome. Enticing instead of intimidating.

"Your rehearsal is at what time tomorrow?" Gavin's right hand came to the small of her back. His left reached for the messenger bag she carried, which he slipped off her shoulder and slung over his.

"Eleven. I can carry that, you know."

"But why not let me?" He brushed a kiss across her temple as he walked beside her. "Good. You can get six hours in tonight and take a nap in the afternoon."

"Is Veronica working tomorrow?"

"I believe so, but you know she won't bother you unless you need something."

Veronica was Gavin's house manager, his day person, and an utter and complete professional. Chloe found her competence a tad intimidating, even if Veronica was polite at all times.

All of Gavin's people were professionals, from Veronica to the security crew she'd met, his business manager to his sommelier. They were all professionals. Gavin surrounded himself with professionals.

If it wasn't for her, Ben, and Tenzin, Chloe wondered if he'd interact with anyone he didn't employ.

"Did you see the invitation from Cormac?" Chloe asked.

"I did."

She watched him from the corner of her eye. "Did anything seem strange about it to you?"

The corner of his mouth turned up. "No."

"It was addressed to both of us."

His fingers curled into her back. "Because I believe he wants both of us to attend the reception."

"It was addressed to both of us at your address."

He paused and nudged her to stand in front of him, pressing her closer. "Is that a problem?"

"I..." Was it? It seemed like everyone knew she stayed with Gavin regularly, and as far as Chloe knew, she was his only regular social companion. She was his plus one. And if she couldn't attend something with him, he went alone. "It's fine," she whispered.

He angled his head and bent down. "Good." His lips moved softly over the arch of her cheek. "You smell lovely tonight."

"I spilled Knob Creek on my shirt."

"Aye, I know." His mouth moved to the side and she felt his breath tickle the sensitive skin under her ear. "I don't mind a little southern flavor, Miss Reardon."

Chloe had learned that Gavin's Scottish came out when he was angry—which happened rarely—or turned on, which happened regularly. Much of the time, Americans mistook him for British.

He wasn't. He'd made that very clear.

"Shall I see if you've spilled any other spirits, lass?" His mouth moved to the other side of her neck. "Do I detect a bit of Cointreau here?" His tongue licked her skin and she gripped his shoulders. "So sweet."

She was going to melt into a puddle. "The car is waiting."

"Aye, I pay it to do that."

Her head spun at the low timbre of his voice.

One day soon, Chloe Reardon.

The memory of his furious kiss a year ago hadn't become any less potent with time.

Gavin took one more long breath at her neck before he pulled away, put his arm around her, and kept walking. "The reception on Friday sounds like a complete bore. If you don't want to go, I'll make our excuses to Cormac."

"It's fine." She cleared her throat and tried to focus on walking toward the waiting car without her knees buckling. "The artist sounds interesting."

"If you want to go, we'll go. You won't be the only human there." He opened the door and ushered her inside.

"Oh. That'll be nice." She settled in and buckled her car

seat just as the driver pulled into the sparse middle of the night traffic. Chloe felt the day catch up with her. She leaned into the plush sedan seat and closed her eyes. She felt Gavin shift beside her, his electric presence filling her senses, even as she drifted with exhaustion.

When she'd first left her abusive ex and moved in with her friend Ben and his vampire partner, Tenzin, she'd had no idea that vampires existed. She'd always known Ben's family was a little strange, but in the past year, she'd become ever more immersed in the immortal world. She knew Ben had mixed feelings about it, but Chloe walked in with her eyes open.

After all, while vampires could be horrible, so could human beings. She knew that first hand. On balance, she'd had more compassion and patience from the vampires in her life than most of the humans. Ben's aunt and uncle made her feel like part of their family. Tenzin was one of the oddest friends she'd ever made. She was also one of the most loyal.

And Gavin?

She didn't know what she was to Gavin, but it was something. She'd worked for him over a year, following him from his first New York pub, The Bat and Barrel, to his newest venture in Hell's Kitchen, the Dancing Bear. It was an easy job made easier by the fact that everyone at the bar assumed that she was in a relationship with the boss, so no one messed with her.

Which she was. They had a relationship. She wasn't sure exactly what that relationship was, but it was a relationship.

Chloe didn't care that everyone assumed she was sleeping with Gavin. They had every reason to assume it, even though she had her own room at his house. She stayed at his place on nights when she had early rehearsal the next day or just needed a break from the blistering chemistry growing between Ben and Tenzin at their loft.

He was a picture of patience, but he had his limits. She didn't push him and he didn't push her.

Someone needs to push someone soon, her libido shouted. *This is getting ridiculous.*

Ridiculous maybe. But also safe.

Chloe liked safety. She liked knowing what to expect. She'd spent years with Tom never knowing when the next blow would come or what could precipitate the next argument. She'd fallen in love with Tom partly because he was "edgy," which to an overprotected girl from Southern California felt exciting and forbidden.

She'd learned her lesson. Edgy wasn't exciting. Edgy was painful. Edgy was dangerous. Edgy could get your bones broken, your body bruised, and your dreams crushed.

What boggled her mind—what she still couldn't make sense of—was why Gavin, who was exponentially more dangerous than her human ex could ever dream of being, had become her anchor of safety in the strange new immortal world she'd entered.

She knew Gavin wasn't safe, and there was no way he wasn't dangerous.

"A good man would stop pursuing you. A deserving one would wait. He'd be patient. I'm not a good man."

His words said one thing. His actions another.

Which one was she supposed to believe when her heart was pulling her in one direction, and her head was pulling in the other?

SHE WAS NEARLY SLEEPING when they reached his apartment. Gavin was tempted to lift her in his arms, but he knew she didn't like it. She didn't like being carted around, unless it was with a dance partner.

You should learn to dance with her.

He should do lots of things. He should be more empathetic to homeless people. He should donate more to the environment. And he should take the dance classes Chloe teased him about. But what vampire took ballroom dance classes? Gavin wasn't the dancing type, even if he had a keen appreciation for the art form. He always went to Chloe's shows and he'd bought season tickets to the ballet. He even watched the horrid reality show dancing she was addicted to on the television. Mostly, he appreciated watching Chloe dance around the room he'd had quietly retrofitted for her.

"Wow! I can't believe your apartment came with a gym like this."

"I know. I was shocked myself. Not sure what I'll do with the space, but you're welcome to use it while you're here."

He'd had the gym renovated with mirrors, a wooden floor, and a practice barre two months after they'd met. It had taken less than a week when the right money was thrown at the project.

It had been an impulse decision. Gavin didn't usually get impulsive about humans. So when he felt the urge, he indulged it. Luckily, it had garnered many hours of pleasure for both Chloe and himself. Chloe because she liked to dance. Gavin because he liked to watch her.

He leaned across the back seat and touched her cheek. "Home, dove."

She sighed and leaned toward him. "Huh?"

"We're home." He ran a finger down her cheek and slung her messenger bag over his shoulder. "Good lord, woman, what do you keep in this thing?"

Her eyes were still closed. "Contact lens stuff. Glasses. Change of clothes. Leggings. Shoes."

"When are you going to start leaving things here? You have a closet bigger than most East Village apartments."

She sighed and opened her eyes. "Pushy."

Gavin shook his head and opened his car door, waiting outside for her to wake up and join him. The driver sat idling and silent while Gavin waited with a clenched jaw.

Pushy? For fuck's sake, he was anything but pushy. If he was pushy, she'd have been in his bed months ago. If he was pushy, Chloe Reardon would be in his thrall.

You don't want that.

Chloe got out of the car and walked around to him. "I'm sorry."

"It's fine."

"So you're saying that"—she stood in front of him as the car pulled away—"but your tone says you're pissed off at me."

Gavin walked toward the elevator. "You're tired. I don't want to talk about this right now."

Chloe followed him. "I shouldn't have called you pushy. You're not pushy. You're like... the opposite of pushy."

He pressed the button to call the elevator and felt the air stir across his skin. He needed a nice long flight tonight. Needed the wind across his skin. Needed—

Chloe nudged his arm out of the way, slid her hand across his back and into the rear pocket of his trousers.

Gavin looked down in surprise. "Miss Reardon, you have your hand on my arse."

The corner of her mouth quirked up. "Are you complaining?"

"I don't know," he muttered. "You're being a bit pushy."

Her laugh was punctuated by a small snort and Gavin broke

into a smile. She started to slide her hand out of his pocket, but he grabbed it and kept it exactly where she'd put it.

"Are you planning to keep that there all the way up to the penthouse?"

"Are you worried someone has seen you stake your claim? It's three in the morning; I think we have the elevator to ourselves."

Her cheeks flushed a little. "Stake my claim?"

"It's about fecking time, I'll add. I like it when you get territorial."

She pressed her face into his shoulder. "I'm never going to hear the end of this."

"Aye, no." He chuckled. "If I could get the angle right, I'd take a picture."

He watched her laughing against his shoulder, ridiculously pleased that she was sleepy and silly and walking home with him. That she trusted him. That she looked at him and didn't see a monster, but a man.

Oh, fuck me. Gavin felt his heart thump twice.

He didn't just want Chloe Reardon. He was in love with her.

The Devil and the Dancer will be available
at all major retailers on March 12, 2019.

AFTERWORD

Dear Readers,

Thanks for diving back into the Elemental Legacy series again. I hope you enjoyed reading *Blood Apprentice* as much as I enjoyed writing it.

The next book in the series will be Gavin and Chloe's novella, *The Devil and the Dancer*, which will be out in March 2019.

After *The Devil and the Dancer* I'll be returning to my contemporary romance series, Love Stories on 7th and Main for two books. Then I'll be back with Ben and Tenzin for the third and fourth Elemental Legacy novels, which have not been titled yet.

I hope you take the time to sign up for my newsletter or my blog at ElizabethHunterWrites.com to keep up with all the latest news, teasers, and contests happening for my books.

And of course, honest reviews at your favorite retailer are always very welcome and help a writer out!

Thanks for reading,
Elizabeth Hunter

ACKNOWLEDGMENTS

Readers who follow my writing know this book has quite a history. I had planned to set the second Elemental Legacy book in Puerto Rico—where Ben still had human family—when I planned the series five years ago. I had outlined the story, planned a research trip, and half-fallen in love with the island without having set eyes on it.

And then, Maria made landfall.

I watched in horror, along with the rest of the world, as Hurricane Maria battered the island of Puerto Rico, destroying homes and businesses, demolishing infrastructure, and ultimately killing thousands of people who died during the storm and its aftermath.

I was devastated to watch a place I had already grown to love suffer such horrible tragedy.

After the winds had stopped, a research trip to the island for a fantasy novel seemed like the last thing I should be thinking about. I put *Blood Apprentice* on hold and joined many of my readers in donating to organizations on the ground like World Central Kitchen and the Hispanic Federation who were working to help Puerto Ricans recover.

Though I still want to visit the island, because of the hurricane and then life complications over the past year, I was not able to visit before I wrote this book, which is why I am so very grateful for all the many bloggers and vloggers who documented their experiences of life before and after Maria, the excellent resources I found online, and most of all, my extremely generous and detail-oriented readers from Puerto Rico who volunteered to beta read this book to make sure I didn't make any egregious errors.

~

Special thanks to **Arlin Feliciano**, **Melanie Miro**, and **Danielle Calleja** for their notes, feedback, and insight to Puerto Rican culture, geography, ecology, and FOOD! (Food is very important.) Any missteps or mistakes left in the book are my own and completely unintentional.

~

Thanks also to my editing team, Amy Cissell, Anne Victory, and Linda at Victory Editing for their excellent work on this book. And additional thanks to Damonza for the beautiful cover for *Blood Apprentice*.

Thanks to my assistants, Jenn Beach and Gen Johnson. Special, socially-awkward thanks to Emily Smith-Kidman, Jenn Watson, and the entire Social Butterfly PR team for making me look cooler than I am.

~

Finally, I want to thank all the many readers who waited so

patiently for Ben and Tenzin's next adventure. I hope it was worth it! You won't have to wait very long to read more about Chloe and Gavin. *The Devil and the Dancer* comes out in March 2019.

~

To my family, who have been my rock through the last year, I love you to infinity.

"I will turn their mourning into joy;
I will comfort them,
And give them gladness for sorrow."
Jeremiah 31:13

ABOUT THE AUTHOR

ELIZABETH HUNTER is a *USA Today* and international best-selling author of romance, contemporary fantasy, and paranormal mystery. Based in Central California, she travels extensively to write fantasy fiction exploring world mythologies, history, and the universal bonds of love, friendship, and family. She has published over thirty works of fiction and sold over a million books worldwide. She is the author of Love Stories on 7th and Main, the Elemental Legacy series, the Irin Chronicles, the Cambio Springs Mysteries, and other works of fiction.

ElizabethHunterWrites.com

ALSO BY ELIZABETH HUNTER

The Elemental Legacy

Shadows and Gold

Imitation and Alchemy

Omens and Artifacts

Midnight Labyrinth

Blood Apprentice

The Devil and the Dancer

(March 2019)

The Elemental Mysteries

A Hidden Fire

This Same Earth

The Force of Wind

A Fall of Water

The Stars Afire

The Elemental World

Building From Ashes

Waterlocked

Blood and Sand

The Bronze Blade

The Scarlet Deep

A Very Proper Monster

A Stone-Kissed Sea

The Irin Chronicles

The Scribe

The Singer

The Secret

The Staff and the Blade

The Silent

The Storm

The Seeker

The Cambio Springs Series

Long Ride Home

Shifting Dreams

Five Mornings

Desert Bound

Waking Hearts

Contemporary Romance

The Genius and the Muse

7th and Main

INK

HOOKED (Winter 2019)

Made in the USA
Las Vegas, NV
10 July 2021

26240654R00215